Hard Dog's Night

Hard Dog's Night

REBECCA HENDRICKS

Sign up for Rebecca Hendricks' Newsletter
And receive and exclusive short origin story
Hound Dogged Beginnings for FREE

at

rebeccahendricksauthor.com

For those of us who
dream,
For those of us who hope,
For those of us who never
give up,
Believe in yourself no
matter what.

Contents

MADISON A WHOLESOME AMERICAN TOWN

MADISON IS A SMALL TOWN located in the Midwestern United States. Prominent businessman Elroy Madison founded Madison on a lovely summer day in 1910. Anxious to get away from the big city, he was scouting for a location to have a picnic with his family. The family had only ventured twenty miles when the Ford Model T overheated. Forced to spend six hours at the location, the family explored the area and stumbled on what is known today as Carter Lake. Madison fell in love with the area and realized it was the perfect location to build low-cost housing for steelworkers. With the new housing project, workers could live quiet, peaceful lives away from the chaos and corruption of the big city.

With a population of 5,000, Madison is the ideal location to make a home and raise a family. The main street is lined with family-owned businesses, such as a general store, a bakery, and a movie theater. The town also has a newspaper, a radio station, and a telephone company, which keeps the residents informed and connected.

Madison's crime rate is low, and the town does not tolerate juvenile delinquency, loud rock 'n' roll music, hot rods, or other shenanigans that many big cities grapple with daily.

Life in Madison is not perfect, but it's a town full of hope and optimism. The people work hard, play hard, and care for their neighbors. They enjoy life's simple pleasures, such as picnics, parades, and dances. They are proud of their town, their state, and their country.

Madison is the ideal town to live the American dream.

1

STATELY ELM TREE BRANCHES SHADED James while he strolled down the tranquil street of Granger. A group of unruly children scampered past him on their way to the park. Their laughter and high-pitched squeals caused a few dogs to bark and a few residents to lift their heads like curious ostriches. Crossing the street, James continued his path toward the Coffee Grounds. He'd spent the entire week at home studying for finals, and he was anxious to see his girlfriend. James had tried to study at the Coffee Grounds once, but it was a disaster because he couldn't keep his eyes or mind off Marcy. It's not like he didn't think about her constantly, but at least she wasn't close enough to talk to or steal a kiss.

A popular college hangout, the Coffee Grounds was generally packed with students. Still, Saturdays tended to be quieter, and the atmosphere was more casual. The large ceiling fan lazily circulated the air through the establishment. Marcy took advantage of the quiet afternoon by cleaning and filling sugar dispensers. James's arrival sparked delight in her grin as he sat at the counter.

Wiping her hands on her apron, Marcy walked over to him. "You're here early."

"Disappointed?" James asked, perching his elbows on the counter.

"Of course not."

"It's been a long week."

"It has," Marcy said, straightening the napkin dispenser. "Would you like a cup of coffee?"

James slid his hand under his chin. "Well, I'd rather have a kiss, but I'll settle for coffee."

Marcy smiled, took a cup from the shelf, and filled his cup. From her shiny auburn hair to her pert little nose, everything about her enchanted James. He would never tire of gazing at her.

Marcy brought James his coffee and sat it on the counter. "I guess you know you're making me nervous."

James picked up a spoon. "And why is that?"

"Because you're ogling me."

"So?" he said, clinking the spoon in the coffee cup.

"So, I know what you're thinking."

James's grin spread, and Marcy nudged him. "I guess you know there is no sugar in your coffee."

"Oh, yeah," James said, taking the spoon out of the cup.

Marcy laughed.

"You'll never guess what I bought the other day," James said, adding sugar.

Marcy leaned across the counter. "What?"

"You need to guess," James teased.

"Can't you give me a hint?"

"It's a book."

"A book?"

"Yep."

Marcy pressed her index finger to her lips. "Hmmm, let me guess. *The Joys of Accounting*?"

"Very funny."

"What then?"

James grinned. "*Kiss Me Deadly*."

"No kidding?"

"No kidding."

Marcy ran her finger over James's hand. "Are you going to lend it to me?"

"Maybe."

She wrinkled her nose. "You better be nice to me, James, or you won't get a kiss."

He smirked. "We'll see about that."

A faint pink hue brushed her cheeks.

"Say, do you think it would be all right if I posted a couple of flyers?" James asked.

"Is it for the drummer auditions?"

"Yep," James said, setting one on the counter before Marcy.

"Sure. You can put it on the bulletin board by the front door and one on the back wall."

"Okay, thanks."

Marcy returned to work, and James walked over to the bulletin board. Advertisements and business cards covered the board like wallpaper. Pulling a tack out of an old advertisement, James covered it with the flyer and secured the tack. Smiling, he pulled out another spare tack and headed toward the back wall.

A young man was sitting at the back table by himself, reading a book. James probably wouldn't have noticed him if his right leg wasn't resting on a chair. At first glance, James thought he was lazy, but when he noticed the leg was encased in a metal leg brace with a thick platform shoe, he knew he was mistaken. James didn't mean to stare and didn't want to feel pity, but he couldn't help himself. Securing the flyer to the wall, his eyes drifted back to the young man. He was wearing a checkered shirt with a worn wool jacket. Tufts of blond hair stuck out from underneath his faded grey porkpie hat with what looked like a turkey feather tucked under the band. Was he homeless? James's heart sunk as his mind fired off several other sad scenarios. The young man sensed James's presence, and he turned around to look at him.

"Hello," James said with a sheepish grin.

The young man didn't say anything. Was he mute too?

"Nice day, huh?" James said.

The young man didn't answer.

James noticed he had a *Life* magazine on the table with a picture of Marilyn Monroe on the front cover.

"You like Marilyn?" James asked.

"She's my girlfriend."

"Ha, ha," James chuckled.

The young man tilted his head with a raised eyebrow.

James walked back to his stool, wondering if the young man was crazy too.

Marcy walked over to the young man's table and refilled his cup. James watched Marcy chat with him for a few moments before she returned to the counter.

"So, you know that guy over there?" James asked.

"What guy?"

"You know, the one over there," James said, pointing into his hand.

"You mean Ronnie?"

"I guess so."

Marcy sat the coffeepot down. "Yes, he comes in here every once in a while."

"He seems to be a little . . . nutty."

"Why do you think that?"

"Because he said his girlfriend was Marilyn Monroe."

Marcy smiled. "He tells everybody that."

"Do you think he believes it?"

"I don't know. I haven't talked to him that much."

James fingered the handle on his coffee cup. "I feel bad for him."

"You shouldn't. He's always in a good mood, even though some people say mean things to him."

"That's horrible."

"If someone is mean to him, we kick them out."

"That's good."

Marcy untied her apron. "I'm going to hang my apron up, and we can go."

"Okay."

Marcy walked away, and James glanced over at Ronnie. He was bobbing his head and tapping his thumbs on the table while he read. Maybe Marcy was right. Maybe he was perfectly happy despite his circumstance. With all his heart, James wanted to believe it. He wanted to believe that the cruel world did not affect Ronnie. With that thought in mind, James gathered his books and pushed his sorrowful thoughts aside and joined the beautiful young woman who waited at the door for him.

2

H E STEPPED ONTO THE SECOND floor with an aura of complete confidence. Dressed tastefully in a tweed jacket, black felt pants, and a dark burgundy tie, he straightened his shirt sleeves before opening the door to Carlton Gates's office.

Carlton's secretary was sitting at the front desk, writing notes, when he approached. Setting his hand on the counter, he waited for her to notice him.

Lifting her eyes, she noticed the attractive young man with a thin smile. "Good afternoon. Can I help you?"

"Good afternoon. I am here for my appointment with Mr. Gates."

"Are you Patrick McNeil?"

Patrick rested his arms on the counter. "I am, and you must be Claire."

"I am," Claire said, adjusting her glasses.

"It's a pleasure to meet you," Patrick said.

"It's a pleasure to meet you as well. Mr. Gates isn't in yet."

"I know I'm early. I have no problem waiting."

Claire stood up from her desk and straightened her skirt. "Can I offer you a cup of coffee?"

"That would be wonderful, thank you."

Patrick sat down in one of the chairs in the lobby. Absently, he gazed at the out-of-date magazines on the low coffee table.

Claire brought him a cup of coffee.

Patrick took the cup from her. "Thank you."

Claire nodded and went back to her desk.

Patrick opened a copy of *LIFE* and read quietly while sipping his coffee.

A short while later, the door opened, and Joe Delaney entered the office. His presence chilled the room like an icebox. His sandy brown hair was slicked back, and sunglasses hid his steel-grey eyes.

"Good morning, Mr. Delaney," Claire said.

"Is he in?" Joe asked.

"Not yet."

Joe glanced over at Patrick. "Is there coffee?"

"Yes."

Joe turned and went into Carlton's office, shutting the door.

"You're welcome," Claire muttered under her breath. Rising, she stepped over to the coffee maker, filled a cup, and took it into Carlton's office. The phone started to ring, and Claire rushed back to her desk. She picked up the receiver. "Mr. Gates's office. How may I help you?"

The door opened, and Carlton Gates came in, looking like he had been in a tornado. His suit was wrinkled, his thinning hair rebelled, and several documents poked out of his overstuffed briefcase. Plopping the burden on the counter, he groaned as he took his coat off.

"Yes, yes, can you hold on one moment? I understand," Claire said, tucking the receiver under her chin.

Carlton motioned for Claire to put down the phone, and she waved her hand.

"Yes, please just hold for a moment," Claire pressed the red button on the phone. "Good Lord, but some people don't get a clue!"

"Is he here?" Carlton said in a hushed tone.

"Yes."

"Damn it," Carlton said, looking at his watch.

"Did you have to take the bus again today?" Claire asked.

Carlton mumbled his answer.

"You know, you need to buy a second car," Claire said, placing a stack of mail in Carlton's hand.

"I'm not made of money. Even if my wife thinks I am." Being too lazy to put on his reading glasses, Carlton squinted at the mail. "Would you mind bringing me and Joe a cup of coffee?"

"Joe already has a cup of coffee and is wearing black today."

Carlton sighed. "Great. Can you let me know when Mr. McNeil arrives?"

"He's already here."

Carlton looked over at Patrick, who smiled. "Oh, hello."

"Hello," Patrick said.

"Sorry to keep you waiting. I'll be but a moment."

"No problem."

"Hold my calls," Carlton said to Claire. Picking up his briefcase, he entered his office and closed the door. Wheezing, Carlton placed his burden on his desk. Joe peered at him from over the top of his coffee cup.

"Morning, Joe," Carlton said.

"Carlton."

Carlton plopped onto the chair behind his desk. "Sorry, I'm late. I had to take the bus in today."

"The bus?"

Carlton nodded. "We only have one car."

"Hmmm," Joe hummed while swaying his foot.

"I know, I know, you hate to wait."

"If you know this, why do you continue disappointing me?"

Carlton opened his mouth like a walrus, but no words came out.

"We can discuss this later. Right now, we have an interview to conduct, and I don't have any more time to waste."

"Agreed," Carlton said. "But before you go, we need to discuss the details about the upcoming show."

Joe knitted his brow. "What upcoming show?"

"The one at the community center."

"Oh, that," Joe snorted. "Can't you take care of that yourself?"

Carlton sighed. "I could, but I'm still wondering how to handle the publicity."

"There is to be no publicity."

Carlton scratched his head. "How does that work?"

"It was one of the stipulations, remember? No one can know The Dice are playing the community center. We are playing under an assumed name."

"So, we keep the show a complete secret?" Carlton asked.

Joe shifted in his chair. "Circulate a flyer. You know, something generic. Nothing fancy. Drop it off at the local hang outs—that should be sufficient."

Carlton wrote down some notes on a piece of crumpled paper. "I will take care of it."

"Wonderful."

The door then opened, and Claire brought Carlton's coffee.

"You may show Mr. McNeil in now," Joe said to Claire.

Claire ignored Joe and acknowledged Carlton. "Right away."

"Your secretary doesn't like me," Joe said.

"What do you mean? Everyone loves you, Joe," Carlton said with a reassuring smile.

Joe snickered.

Patrick entered Carlton's office, and Claire shut the door.

"Patrick, come in," Carlton said, waving Patrick to come forward. "We are thrilled you could come down and meet with us on such short notice."

"Not at all. I was thrilled to get your call," Patrick said.

"You remember Mr. Delaney?"

"Of course. How are you, Mr. Delaney?" Patrick said, extending his hand.

Joe shook Patrick's hand. "I am well."

"Take a seat," Carlton said, waving his hand toward the empty chair.

Patrick sat down and crossed his legs.

"We called you down here today, Patrick, because we have a new opening in the group," Carlton said.

"Oh?"

"Unfortunately, the candidate we picked to join ended up not working out."

Patrick tilted his head. "I'm sorry to hear that."

"I want you to know I was impressed with your audition," Joe said.

"Thank you, sir."

"Would you still be interested in joining my group?"

"Are you kidding?" Patrick said, splaying his hands. "It would be an honor. I've been a fan of yours for a long time."

"You have?" Joe said.

"Oh yes, I've seen your show many times. Twice at the Middleton."

Joe swung his foot. "My, that was a while back."

"You opened the show with 'Great Balls of Fire,' I believe."

Joe chuckled. "Wow, even I didn't remember that."

"I'll never forget it. How you impressed the crowd with your lightning-fast hands. You didn't even break a sweat."

Joe grinned. "You flatter me."

"It's the truth. You are a remarkable talent."

Joe sat forward in his chair. "If I made you an offer, I want to ensure you understand my expectations."

"If I am chosen as your next member, I will do whatever it takes to be the best. I am committed to helping this group achieve the level of excellence it deserves."

Joe ran his thumb over his fingertips as he studied Patrick. Patrick didn't flinch or advert his eyes. His chin was set, and his posture was straight.

"I would need you to start right away. Is that possible?" Joe asked.

"Yes, sir."

"Please, call me Joe."

Patrick nodded. "Joe."

Joe clicked his tongue. "I can tell we will get along just fine, just fine indeed."

3

OUTSIDE UNDER THE LARGE TREES that shaded the South side of the student break area, Anne doodled on her notebook while her girlfriends chattered around her about the upcoming summer vacation. Most girls had fun, exciting plans, from traveling with their families to planning their next year at a major university. But all Anne could think about was her opportunities to see John were limited.

Other than exchanging a few glances in class, there had been no interaction between them. Several times, Anne thought about approaching John, but he seemed preoccupied with his thoughts and life. She was beginning to feel their attraction had been an illusion. Not seeing him anymore was probably for the best. She needed to put thoughts of him behind her and concentrate on her everyday conventional life.

Despite her decision not to look for John, her eyes betrayed her, and she glanced at his table. He was sitting with his friends, laughing, and goofing around. A girl with dark hair sat close to him, hanging on his every word. Anne's eyes narrowed as she chewed on the end of her pencil.

"So, what are your plans for the summer?" Ruth asked Anne.

Anne didn't look up.

"She must be busy thinking about Steve," Lucy said.

The sound of the giggling girls brought Anne's attention back to the conversation. "Huh?"

Her blank stare made the girls giggle louder.

"We want to know what you're doing for the summer, silly," Ruth asked.

Ruth was a lovely young woman with smooth, light brown curls and a body that curved in all the right places. Naturally, everyone wanted to be her friend, but only a few select girls were allowed to be a part of her elite group. Anne knew the only reason Ruth invited her to join the group was because her mother and Ruth's mother were friends who worked on several committees and community projects together.

"I don't have any special plans," Anne answered with a small smile.

"Oh, come now, sure there is *something* you're looking forward to," Ruth pried.

Anne looked into her twinkling green cat eyes. Ruth loved to gossip, and Anne knew to choose her words carefully. "I might work on my sewing skills."

"She's just being modest," Lucy said. "There is no doubt that you will be engaged soon."

A brash blond with playful features, Lucy, was Ruth's best friend. She wasn't as catty as Ruth, but she was just as dangerous.

"Oh yeah, you're dating Steve," Ruth said, as if she didn't know.

"Isn't he going to be a doctor?" Wanda asked innocently.

They all laughed.

"An engineer, sweetheart," Ruth answered.

"Who cares what his profession is as long as he's rich," Lucy said lazily, running an emery board across her painted nails.

"Are you really getting engaged soon?" Wanda, a hopeless romantic, asked.

"Well, I don't know."

"You two have been dating for a long time," Ruth said.

"Can we talk about something else?" Anne asked.

"If I was going to be engaged, I wouldn't want to talk about anything else," Wanda said, gazing dreamily at the sky.

"You need to catch a man first," Lucy said.

'You know I'm not very good at that," Wanda said.

"Show some cleavage, and you will have plenty of dates," Lucy said.

The girls were laughing, but Anne could tell that Ruth was watching her.

After the break, the girls all headed back inside for the last two classes of the day. Anne hung back so she could watch John walk into the building. He hadn't made any physical contact with the brunette, but she was walking very close.

Anne spent her next class thinking about John. She had to come up with some excuse to talk to him. Maybe if she waited for him after his class, she could accidentally run into him. With a plan in mind, Anne turned to her assignment and went to work.

4

TWINKLING PRISMS OF LIGHT BOUNCED off Joe's diamond ring. An old listless tune played on the radio, offering him no comfort as he drove home. He had stopped by the Cornby Club for a drink to calm his mind, but three drinks later, the problems were still there, and so was the confrontation he had tried to avoid for three days.

Monica's performances with The Dice had added extra spice and allure to the dark suits around her. Her mesmerizing persona enchanted the crowd, and they embraced her immediately, but standing in the background, Will's animosity grew with every passing moment. If Will would accept the reality of his failed relationship with Monica, she might be able to join the group. But Will refused to let it rest, and despite all the grief he caused Joe, Joe couldn't afford to lose him.

Joe pulled into the driveway. Only a few dim lights lit the front windows, giving the house the appearance of abandonment. Joe parked the car in the garage and entered the deserted house.

"Monica?" Joe called out, his voice echoing from the cavernous ceiling.

Maybe she had gone out with friends, but that was highly unlikely. She had lost most of her friends when she decided to stay with him after the accident.

Discarding his topcoat over the back of a straight-back chair, Joe flipped on the floodlights in the lounge area on the lower floor. Joe stepped behind the bar and made himself a drink. The ice cubes cracked as the scotch poured over them. The cool glass felt good in his hand as he stepped over to the stereo. The intense intro of "Don Giovanni" threatened to crack the mirror as its dark connotations filled Joe's essence. His heavy feet trudged the staircase to the second floor, then traveling a few steps, he continued to ascend to the third. The dimly lit wall sconces cast shadows along the desolate hallway that led to the master bedroom. Out of the corner of his hazy eye, Joe spotted the golden doorknob. His fingers ached to turn the knob, to invade the fortress she had locked him out of. Placing his forehead against the large oak barrier, he absorbed the pain of knowing the tragedy they harbored inside.

Continuing down the hall, Joe entered the master bedroom and flipped on the light. The large room was decorated with exquisite mid-century modern furniture. The bed was round with a luxurious white satin spread and white tufted headboard. Three sizeable black velvet pillows with silver boarders sat on the bed, and the small white envelope leaning against them looked like a bleached spot on a coalbed's floor.

Joe quietly placed his drink on the nightstand. He recognized Monica's handwriting on the envelope, and his stomach tightened. Sitting on the bed, he opened the envelope and read.

> Dear Joe,
> I am sure the hour will be late when you read this. You haven't bothered to come home at a decent hour since Sunday night because you know I needed to talk to you. I know I can't join the group because of my past with Will, but part of me foolishly believed that after the weekend's success, you might choose me over him. I thought if we had a chance to play together, maybe we

could rekindle what the accident stole from us, but I know now that is a fairytale.

I have tried desperately to make it work between us, but I can't do it alone. You haven't wanted me to be a part of your life for a long time, and I can't ignore what is happening between us. I have decided it's time to move on with my life. I know you're thinking me a fool for leaving you and your money, but I can't live a lie anymore. Believe it or not, I will always love you.

Monica

Joe stared at the paper, the emptiness of the house, and his heart caving in around him. Putting the letter back in the envelope, he threw it on the nightstand. He wanted to block every thought and every memory out of his mind.

Crossing to the dresser, he opened a drawer and pulled out a small wooden box. It had been a long time since he had spent the night with it, but tonight could not pass without it. Wiping a tear away, Joe entered the bathroom and closed the door.

5

CARLTON WAS BEGINNING TO SERIOUSLY question his life choices as he commuted to his office in the city. At fifty-five, he was overweight, overstressed, overworked, and in debt. Another trip to the doctor confirmed that the hole in his stomach and his rising blood pressure were not improving. In fact, his condition was getting worse. It would have been easy to blame his job for all his problems, but sadly, he knew his wife was at the center of the endless turmoil.

When he first met Gina, she had been a sweet, innocent young woman with big almond brown eyes and curly black hair. Carlton was immediately smitten with her and never believed he would ever have a chance with her. She was among the popular and elite at the school, and if he had been smart in the beginning, he would have realized that she was spoiled and self-centered. Gina's father was a wealthy businessman who gave her everything her heart desired. This expectation was passed down to Carlton when they wed, even though she knew he would never be as rich or powerful as her father. She pushed him—constantly pushed him. Now, thirty-five years and two children later, Carlton still pushed himself to please her and his children. He was losing the battle.

Stopped at a traffic light, Carlton's doctor's voice echoed in his head. *You will be in your grave before you're sixty-five, Carlton.* The urge to turn left, head out to the interstate, and never look back tempted

Carlton. Who would genuinely miss him? His wife, whom he could never satisfy? His children, who only saw money signs when they looked at him? His business that was barely hanging on? No one would miss Carlton Gates.

Climbing the stairs to his office, Carlton clutched the railing and panted. He would have been up the stairs in under a minute when he was younger. Now, feeling like he had climbed to the top of the Empire State Building, Carlton might pass out. He had only climbed two flights.

Rubbing the sweat from his brow, Carlton entered his office. Claire didn't have to say anything to him. Her pale complexion and wide eyes told him everything.

He stepped up to her desk to get his mail.

"Joe's here," Claire said.

Carlton picked up his mail and messages. "I know it."

"You do?"

"You get a certain look when he's here."

"I made some coffee, and I have an antacid."

"You can hang on to it until he leaves. Did he say what he wants?"

"No."

Carlton gave Claire a half smile.

"Good luck," she said as Carlton entered his office and shut the door.

◻◼◻◼◻◼◻◼◻◼◻◼◻◼◻◼◻◼◻

Joe was standing by the window, watching the mindless traffic below. His hands were behind his back, and his feet were parted.

Carlton set his briefcase down and unbuttoned his coat. "So, what brings you by this morning?"

Joe was silent.

"Would you like some coffee?"

"She left me, Carlton," Joe said, unmoving.

"Monica? What happened?"

"She was mad that I didn't make her a permanent member of the group."

"I thought you made that clear to her."

"So did I."

Carlton sat down behind his desk. "Do you know where she went?"

"No. I have an idea, though."

"Do you want me to fix you a drink?"

Joe turned to Carlton. Joe's face was always stoic and rarely held an expression, but Carlton noticed the bags under his eyes, and his jaw was grinding. "It may steady your nerves."

Joe nodded, then reclined in the chair in front of the desk. "I know she's been unhappy for some time. We've drifted apart since the accident. At first, I thought we could get past it, but it never seems to go away."

Carlton handed Joe his drink. "I don't think something like that will ever go away. You just learn how to live with it."

"Living with it is killing us," Joe said, taking a long drink from the glass.

"Is there anything you need me to do?"

"I want Lou to confirm that she is at her sister's and to keep an eye on her for a while. I want to know what she is up to," Joe said, tapping the side of his glass with his finger.

"Of course," Carlton said, sitting behind his desk.

"I have a feeling she might see Danny."

"Bruer?"

Joe paused. "Yes."

Carlton sat back in his chair and quietly reflected with Joe.

"She doesn't think I care about her, you know, but I do."

"I know it."

Joe sat his glass on Carlton's desk.

"You want another one?"

"No. I am introducing Patrick to the group this morning and informing them of our situation."

"You need me to be there?"

"No, I can handle it," Joe said, buttoning his jacket.

"I was going to call you later this morning," Carlton said.

"Oh?"

"I heard from Mr. Pierce. He was wondering if you had any updates for him. They're ready to book the studio time for next month."

Joe stood up. "Have them book the time. By then, we will have a song come hell or high water."

Carlton nodded.

"You will call me later with an update?"

"Of course."

Joe headed toward the door and then paused before opening it. "Thank you, Carlton."

"Sure."

Joe opened the door and left. Carlton blinked at the closed door. Joe Delaney had never thanked him for anything. Picking up the phone, he dialed Lou's number.

6

NXIOUS TO MAKE A GOOD impression, Patrick arrived at Joe's
studio early. Dressed in a grey flannel suit and polished black
shoes, Patrick leaned casually against the brick wall and admired
his freshly manicured fingers. At first, it seemed like a vanity move,
but working as a farm laborer wreaked havoc on his hands and back.
He wouldn't miss the long, thankless days of doing manual labor for
dismal pay. Performing with a prestigious band like the Dice was a
dream come true. All his hard work and planning was beginning to
pay off, and with any luck, he would achieve his ultimate goal in less
than a year. Patrick whistled a listless tune and buried his hands in his
pockets to wait.

Thankfully, he didn't have to wait too long before two men
arrived. He recognized them, but they had no idea who he was.

"Good morning, Will and Boyd," Patrick said with a broad smile.

Boyd was reserved, while Will measured Patrick up carefully. "Do
I know you?"

"Not yet. I'm Patrick McNeil, your new bandmate," Patrick said,
pushing himself off the wall. "It's a thrill to meet the both of you. I
have been a fan for a long time."

"Really?" Will said.

"Oh yeah, I have been to several of your shows. I even went as far as Briggsville once."

Will smiled. "That was a few years ago. Boyd wasn't with us yet."

"Yes, sir."

"Please, call me Will," Will said, offering his hand.

Holding eye contact, Patrick shook his hand.

"I'm Boyd. It's nice to meet you, Patrick," Boyd said, holding his hand out.

Patrick shook Boyd's strong hand.

Will put his key in the lock. "Come on in, and we'll show you around."

"Great."

Patrick followed them around the studio, asking relevant questions and hanging on Will's every word. Will's ego swelled with each compliment Patrick fed him. By the time Joe showed up at the studio, Will was laughing and joking like Patrick was an old friend.

"Good morning, gentlemen," Joe said, removing his sunglasses.

"Don't you mean afternoon?" Will said.

Joe dismissed the comment and laid his things on the piano bench. "I see you met Patrick."

"Yes, we did," Will said.

"I trust they made you feel welcome?" Joe asked Patrick.

"Yes, sir, they did."

"Did they show you the guitar I want you to use?"

"Yes, it's a beaut, thank you," Patrick answered, rocking back on his heels.

"Before we get started, I have a bit of news I need to share with you. Why don't you all have a seat?"

Pulling chairs around in a half circle, the group sat down.

Joe leaned back against the piano and crossed his legs. "It's in regards to the song."

"The song?" Patrick asked.

Joe paused. "It's a long story, but I will do my best to make it brief. The Dice have been signed to a recording contract."

"Yes, I know."

"Our plan was to record an original song that our previous member played at his audition."

"Previous member meaning Daniel Bruer?" Patrick asked.

"Yes."

"Okay."

Joe crossed his arms. "I figured it was some random song he picked up somewhere, but it turns out this song was written by a friend of Daniel's, and he assumed I was trying to steal it. Of course, I tried explaining things to him, but he wouldn't listen, and he quit."

"May I ask what the name of the song is?" Patrick asked.

"It has a ridiculous name. As a matter-of-fact, we were going to improve it, but Daniel was convinced his friend would recognize it anyway."

"The name of the song was 'Crawlin' Hogs,'" Will scoffed.

"Dog," Boyd said.

Will snorted. "Dog, hog, it's all the same."

"As I was saying," Joe continued. "Carlton pointed out that meeting with this so-called songwriter friend would be in my best interest. For all I knew, this John Chandler character didn't even exist."

"Don't you mean you were hoping he didn't exist?' Will said.

Joe glared at Will.

"Look, Patrick, Joe found the mystery man and met with him and Daniel. Now you know as much as we do. Can you please tell us what happened at the meeting?" Will asked.

Joe tapped his foot. "I would like to say that I was able to convince Chandler to sell his song, but being the obstinate degenerate he is, he refused."

Will closed his eyes.

"So, we're back to square one?" Boyd said.

"Well, after I reminded Daniel that he had signed a contract and couldn't just walk away, Chandler told me I could have the song if I let Daniel out of his contract."

Will snickered. "Don't tell me you agreed to that? That song isn't worth letting that little weasel out of anything."

Joe shifted his weight.

Will's face fell. "Oh my Lord, you did agree to it?"

"Not exactly."

"Then what, *exactly*?"

Joe stuck his chin out. "Chandler challenged me."

"To a duel?" Boyd asked.

"That would fix things," Will scoffed.

"He challenged me to a kind of talent show."

Will laughed. "Talent shows are something you do in high school."

"Nevertheless, I agreed to it," Joe said.

Will sat up straight in his chair. "Are you out of your mind? Why would you ever agree to such foolishness?"

Joe's face contorted in an evil grimace. "Because I know we are the better group, and once we crush them, we can take the song, and Danny will pay for his indiscretions."

"How does that work? The kid has no money," Will said.

"Who said anything about money?" Joe said, swinging his foot.

"So, when is this fiasco happening?" Boyd inquired.

"Two weeks from Saturday at the community center."

Will's face fell, and his eyes darted.

"The what center?" Boyd asked.

"The community center."

"You mean that small brick building that hosts bingo monthly for old people and bored housewives?" Will said.

Joe straightened his pant leg. "Well, if you want to put it that way, yes."

Boyd sat back in his chair, covered his mouth, and placed his elbow on the chair arm.

"I know what you're thinking," Joe said.

"No, I don't think you do," Will said.

"It's just for one night. We go in, play a couple of songs, and we're done."

"Have you even considered what this might do to our reputation?"

"It won't hurt our reputation because we're not using our name."

Will threw his hands in the air and stood up. "I can't believe my own ears! You have gone completely insane!"

"It makes sense when you think about it."

Will whirled around. "I don't want to think about it."

"Look, it's not about our name or where we play, it's about the simple fact that we can beat them with both hands tied behind our backs."

Will ran his hand over his hair.

"It will be amusing, and it will prove a point."

"What point is that? We agree to stoop to their level?"

"Are you afraid, Will?" Joe asked.

Will scoffed. "Absolutely not."

Joe lifted his hands up. "Then there is no problem."

"What do you think, Boyd?" Joe said, turning to Boyd.

Boyd shrugged. "I think it's a lot of foolishness for one ridiculous song."

"You didn't seem to think the song was so ridiculous the day we talked about recording it," Joe snapped.

"We were trying to make you happy," Will said.

Joe laughed. "Oh, come now, Will. You have never done anything to make someone else happy."

"And you have?"

"This isn't getting us anywhere," Boyd said.

Patrick cleared his throat. "Uh, I know I'm new here, but do you really believe that is the song to put you at the top of the charts?"

Joe pursed his lips.

"I mean, a song about a lame dog doesn't sound like a chart-topper. You need something that the teenagers can relate to. You know? Like, love, moonlight, and romance."

"He's got a point," Boyd said.

"This is your one chance to define your career," Patrick said.

Will sat his hands on the back of a chair and leaned forward. "Do you know of such a song?"

"Well, I wrote the song that I performed at my audition. It does need some work, but it might be more along the lines of what you're looking for."

Joe drummed his fingers on his arm.

"I could play it for you if you like," Patrick said.

"It wouldn't hurt to at least hear it," Boyd said.

"I would like to hear it," Will said.

"Joe?" Patrick said.

Joe reclined in an empty chair. "Sure, why not?"

Patrick strapped on his guitar and played the song for them. Boyd tapped his foot, and Will listened intently, but Joe sat disinterested and didn't offer an opinion. He obviously had his mind made up that he wanted "Crawlin' Dog." The song Patrick had co-written. The song he hated. The song that continued to be a thorn in his side.

7

SQUEEZING THROUGH THE CROWDED HALLS, Anne raced to catch John coming out of his last class. Not one to dawdle when the final bell rang, John made no unnecessary stops as he strolled toward the main doors. Anne thought she had missed him, but his worn green jacket was hard to miss. Anne took a moment to gain her composure before approaching him, but he had already reached the stair's railing and slid down with ease. How would she ever catch up to him now? Sliding down the railing in a skirt wasn't very ladylike, but she didn't have a moment to lose. Throwing caution to the wind, Anne sat on the railing and slid down faster than expected. Falling off the railing, her bottom plopped on the floor with a teeth-jarring thump. The hallway broke out into a boisterous laugh, drawing attention to a humiliated Anne.

"Having problems?"

Looking up, she saw John standing above her with his hands in his pockets and an annoying smirk.

Dismayed, Anne looked around for a dignified way to stand. "I can't figure out how to get up exactly."

"Oh?"

Her cheeks blazed hot. "I don't want to flash everyone."

"That is a problem."

Glaring at his amused face, she snapped. "You know, if you were a gentleman, you would try and help me get back on my feet."

"You're right. If I was a gentleman, I would do that, but since I'm not, I will enjoy the show."

Infuriated, Anne couldn't remember why she thought catching up to him was a good idea.

"You could ask for my hand," John said.

"*You* could offer your hand."

Deciding she had floundered enough, John bent down and helped Anne to her feet. Her face was flushed with embarrassment.

"You may want to brush the dirt off your backside," John said.

Anne's flush turned red as she tried to brush the dirt off her skirt.

John grinned and retrieved her scattered belongings. "So, how did you fall?"

"Oh, I don't know. I tripped, I guess."

"And how many times have you come down those stairs?"

Anne smoothed her skirt. "Oh well, I wasn't paying attention."

John handed Anne her books. "You know what I think?"

"That I'm a fool?"

John's smirk softened. "I think you were in a hurry because you were trying to catch up to me."

Anne lifted her chin. "No, I was too busy thinking about studying for exams and missed the last step."

"Uh-huh," John said, turning toward the door.

"So, where are you headed?" Anne asked, falling in step with him.

"I haven't decided yet."

"Do you mind if I walk with you?"

John looked sideways at her. "I wasn't headed toward the bus."

"Well, I wasn't heading home, at least not yet."

John opened the door for her.

"You got a hot date?"

Anne dismissed the question. "I was thinking about going to the library to study."

"I've been banned from the library."

"You have?"

John walked forward. "Yeah."

"Why?" Anne asked as she scurried to keep up.

"I don't know, something about silence."

"How about the public library? I assume you haven't been banned from that library," Anne teased.

"Not yet."

"Then you'll come with me? I know you need to study."

John frowned. "Why would you think that?"

"Well, I've never seen you study before."

"That doesn't mean I don't."

"Well then, maybe I could quiz you."

John laughed.

"What?"

"Not going to happen."

"Why? Because you don't know the answers?"

"No, I just don't trust the question."

Anne stitched her brow as she tried to figure out what he meant. Turning the corner, they continued strolling down the shaded sidewalk toward the library.

"Did you grow up in this area?" Anne asked.

"No, we moved here when I was sixteen."

"Where did you live before then?

John rubbed the back of his neck. "Ohio."

"Really? What made your parents move here?"

"What about you? You grow up here?" John said, moving away from the subject.

"In Midtown, yes."

"That's a nice area. Not many middle-class people up that way."

Anne avoided the subject of her family's social status as they crossed the street in front of the library. There was nothing remarkable about the medium-sized brick building that occupied a half of the block. One of the oldest buildings in Madison, its stately columns stood like two sentries protecting the door.

Large pine bushes decorated the front of the building, and a small flower garden was planted at the flagpole's base.

Climbing the stairs, they entered through the large, heavy doors. Two librarians were busy helping patrons at the substantial main circulation desk. Anne followed John to a secluded table toward the back of the non-fiction section.

Anne sat on one of the small chairs, and John sat beside her.

"So, now what do we do?" John asked.

"You have your book, right?"

"Do I look like I'm carrying my book?"

Anne sighed. "How do you study?

"At home."

"Is that where your book is?"

John placed his arm on the table. "And my pencil."

Anne hid a smile and opened her book. "Mr. Miller said the test would mainly focus on chapters six through thirteen. You have read them, right?"

"Sure," John said, casually taking her pencil.

"You don't take school very seriously, do you?"

"I do."

Anne shook her head. "Do you have a major?"

"Not yet."

"What are you interested in?"

John absently twirled the pencil. "Music."

"Do you play an instrument?"

"I do."

"What?"

John grinned. "Guess."

Anne tapped her finger on her chin. "Let me see. The tuba?"

"Nope."

She clasped her hands in her lap. "The triangle?"

"Nope. You get one more guess," John said, holding up his index finger.

"And if I guess wrong?"

"You suffer the consequences."

"What are the consequences?"

He flipped the pencil. "I guess you'll find out."

She rolled her eyes with a mischievous smile. "The kazoo?"

Underestimating John's actions was the folly of many. Without warning, he grabbed her, making her gasp in surprise as he began to tickle her. She laughed uncontrollably as he pulled her closer, making her laugh harder,

The enraged librarian came back to their table. Her narrow eyes looked over her square reading glasses. "What's going on back here?"

John folded his hands innocently in front of him on the table. "Nothing."

Anne straightened her shirt and smoothed her hair as she forced down the butterflies in her throat.

The librarian put her hand on her hips. "We don't tolerate any tomfoolery in this library!"

John had a crooked smile, and Anne was pursing her lips so tightly together she looked like a fish.

"If I hear any further outbursts, you will have to leave. Am I clear?"

Both Anne and John nodded their heads. Flashing one more disgusted look, the librarian stalked off.

John looked at Anne, and she laughed.

"Shhh," John warned. "Are you trying to get us thrown out?"

"No," Anne squeaked.

John pulled Anne's book over in front of him. "Now, what chapter are we pretending to study?"

"Six through thirteen," Anne said, pulling out her notebook and another pencil.

"Are you going to let me copy your notes?"

Anne set a protective hand on her notebook. "No."

"Well, at least lend me a piece of paper."

"I saw your notebook in your pocket."

"I won't defile my notebook with schoolwork."

Anne relented and handed him a piece of paper from her notebook.

"Now," John said, setting his hand on the back of her chair. "You read, and I copy your notes."

"No, that's not how this works."

John leaned in closer. "Then refresh my memory."

His closeness was unsettling, and Anne's focus was lost.

"I'm listening."

"Do you have to be so close?" Anne whispered.

John held her eyes. "Does it bother you?"

"No."

"Well, I guess I will read, and you will take my notes," John said, pulling away.

For the next hour, Anne listened to John and made notes. Of course, John never could take anything too seriously, so she listened to his fabricated words and quips that made her laugh. It made the boring subject fun, and sadly, the time to leave to catch her bus had arrived too soon.

Her wish to spend time with him had been granted, but now the heaviness of separation had once more returned. She stopped walking far enough away from the bus stop so that she could have a few private moments with him.

"I enjoyed spending the afternoon with you," Anne said.

"Me too."

Anne looked toward the bus stop and then turned her gaze back to John. "You know the end of the term is almost here."

"Yeah."

She took a step forward and looked up at him. Every part of her being was hoping he would do or say something, but he wasn't making any forward movement or smile. The bus's impending arrival pressed Anne to say something before the moment was gone. "I was wondering if maybe we could see each other over the break."

John tilted his head. "And do what? Study?"

His brusque voice made her take a step back. "Or maybe we could draw."

"Aren't you forgetting something?"

Anne blinked.

"You have a boyfriend, remember?"

Anne's shoulders slumped, and her eyes fell to her feet. John took a step forward and lifted her chin.

"Look, I like you too. A lot, actually, but I can't be with you if you belong to someone else. I've never been one to share, and I'm not going to start now. Do you understand?"

Anne nodded.

"I think you have a lot of thinkin' to do and some decisions to make."

"I know. It's just that I'll be sick if I can't see you again."

John gently touched her face. "I seriously doubt that. I'll be around. It's not like I'm going anywhere."

"But there are other girls."

John smiled and turned her toward the bus that had pulled in. "I will see you tomorrow. Now hurry before it takes off."

Giving him a brave smile, Anne hurried to board the bus that was preparing to pull away from the curb. Once in her seat, Anne looked out the window, but he was gone, leaving her hopeless. She could understand that John didn't want her seeing anyone else, but breaking it off with Steve wouldn't be easy. Her parents loved Steve, and they expected her to marry him.

Maybe she didn't have to get married right away. Surely Steve would understand that she wanted to finish college and become a teacher. He knew how much it meant to her to help children. With his support, her parents would give theirs, and in time, they would realize she was an adult and could make her own decisions. Leaning back in her seat, Anne relaxed. Hope no longer felt lost, and with time, she would figure out a way to make her dreams come true.

8

ANNE SAT AT THE DINNER table, absently picking at her mashed potatoes. Her parents were talking about the boring events of their day, but she didn't hear them. She was daydreaming about being alone on the hill with John.

Leaning close to him, she watches his long fingers sketch a nondescript picture. A tranquil breeze floats over them as he turns to gaze into her mesmerized eyes. His fingers gently brush across her knee as his lips find the small space below her ear. Her eyes flutter as his persistent hand slowly drifts under the hemline of her skirt. . . .

"Anne?" a faint voice calls out to her. "Anne!"

The deep, annoyed voice of her mother caused Anne's head to snap up. "Huh?"

"Huh?" her mother said with a scornful scowl. "Have you not heard a word I've said?"

"I'm sorry, Mother, I was distracted."

With a raised eyebrow, Florence glanced at her husband across the table.

"It's disrespectful not to listen to your mother when she is talking to you," Anne's father scolded.

"I know, Daddy, I was just—"

"I don't want to hear an excuse. You can daydream on your own time, but when you are at the dinner table, I expect you to be paying attention. Your mother should not have to repeat herself. Understood?"

"Yes, sir. I am sorry, Mother, for being inattentive."

Arthur nodded at his wife and returned to his meal without missing a bite.

"Honestly, Anne, I don't know where your mind has been lately," Florence said, shifting in her seat.

"She's dreaming about marrying Steve," Anne's little sister said, fluttering her eyes.

Arthur raised his eyebrow at Tracy, who smiled at him and choked down another bite of Jell-O salad.

Florence adjusted the napkin on her lap. "As I was saying, I talked to Mrs. Dunn at the church committee meeting this afternoon. She needs someone to stay and look after her mother while she's out of town for a few weeks. Naturally, I thought of you, Anne."

"But I already promised Pastor Rollins that I would help teach children's bible school."

Florence salted her potatoes. "I know, darling, but you understand how important this is. It will only be for a few weeks, and Mrs. Dunn is a dear friend."

And she is the head of the board, Anne thought.

"It is the Christian thing to do, after all."

Anne twisted the napkin in her lap. "Of course it is, Mother." *And it will only improve your status and make you feel more important.*

"I am glad we agree on that point," Florence said, picking up her fork.

Anne smiled demurely.

"We will have lunch with her on Saturday to go over the details."

"Yes, Mother. May I ask where Mrs. Dunn's mother lives?"

"In Madison, actually."

Any negative thoughts Anne had evaporated, and a smooth smile raised her cheeks.

Arthur wiped his mouth and set his napkin on the table.

"Would you like some coffee, dear?" Florence asked.

"Yes, I will take it in my study, if you don't mind. I need to review the Barlowe contract before tomorrow."

"Yes, dear."

Arthur rose from his chair and left the dining room.

"I can take Daddy his coffee, Mother, so you can finish your meal," Anne said.

"Thank you, dear."

Anne hummed as she walked to the kitchen, a renewed hope in her heart.

9

T HE SQUIRREL STORED THE GREASY small nugget in his cheek before turning and disappearing into a thick cluster of juniper bushes. John was upset that the tossed peanut hadn't landed in his mouth, but he was happy that he helped to fill the small creature's stomach. The next tossed peanut hit its target, and John smiled widely as he munched his favorite snack. Seeing a young woman bent over a flower bed almost caused him to run smack into a light post. A group of small boys laughed and pointed at him, and John thought about chasing them down the block, but today he was in a good mood because he would be auditioning drummers with Danny. The last few days had been challenging for him because he had been studying and spending more time at home. John's relationship with his stepmother was difficult and strained due to years of dealing with the grief of losing his father.

Evan Chandler was an honorable, hardworking man who made his living as a fireman. He was a good husband and father, but John's mother was a beautiful young woman who couldn't handle the boredom regularly associated with domestic life. Often, while Evan worked late, she would drink and run around with other men. One day, Evan came home to find three-year-old John alone and crying. She had left a note saying she was running away with one of her lovers. It was the last time they ever saw her. The years of being a single father were tough on Evan, but he never let it ruin his positive disposition or his zest for life.

Evan met John's stepmother, Caroline, at the hospital where she worked as a nurse. Caroline was a plain serious woman, but Evan was attracted to her strong personality and astute intellect. He knew it was asking a lot of her to be a mother to a six-year-old boy, but she graciously accepted the challenge.

Caroline had never been warm and nurturing, but she was steadfast and attentive to John's needs.

As long as John and Caroline had Evan, the newly formed family was fulfilled and happy, but

everything changed when Evan was killed while rescuing a child from a burning building.

John didn't take the sudden passing of his father well. He felt abandoned and alone. Caroline, dealing with her grief, had no idea how to support his emotional needs. So, John withdrew into a cold hard shell, and within a couple of years, he wasn't the same boy he had once been.

Maybe if Caroline had tried to reach him. Maybe if Caroline hadn't tried to send him away. Maybe he wouldn't have been so angry if she had told him she had his best interest at heart. Maybe he wouldn't have caused so much trouble. Maybe they could have helped each other through the grief and pain instead of aggravating scars that would never heal.

John turned at the corner and saw Danny reclining on the trunk of an old beat-up 1950 Chevy Sedan. Even from a distance, John could tell the car was in poor condition. The back bumper was crooked and held in place by crude wires. The pea-green paint was faded, and rusted spots peppered the finish like polka dots. John tried to ignore his suspicions, but judging by Danny's wide, goofy grin, he figured the car belonged to him.

"Hey, Dan-O, what's with the grin?" John asked.

"You mean you can't tell?"

John peered at him through squinted eyes. "No. Did you cut your hair?"

Disgusted, Danny's forehead wrinkled. "No. See this car I'm sitting on?"

"I see the old jalopy you're sitting on."

Danny slid off the trunk of the car. "I know she needs a little work."

"A little?" John said, stepping in front of the car.

"But it has potential, and it runs . . . sort of."

John glanced at the cracked windshield. "Sort of?"

Danny rubbed the back of his neck. "Well, it's a little rough. I just need to get a few more parts for it. Then it won't make that funny noise anymore."

"Funny noise?"

"Yeah, kind of like a whirling, thumping noise."

John widened his eyes.

"But the radio works," Danny said with a smile. "Want to go for a spin?"

"Maybe later. I think we should prepare for our busy afternoon."

"That's not a bad idea."

"Do you know how many people are auditioning?" John asked.

"I think Eddie said five."

"Great, we should be able to find someone, right?"

"I hope so," Danny said as he followed John inside the record store.

10

ANNE HELD THE FADED YELLOW gingham dress up to her shoulders. Swaying back and forth, the stiff crinoline slip rustled as she studied her reflection in the mirror. Maybe a white belt or a vibrant scarf would complement the dress, but sadly, nothing would improve the dress or her mood.

Disgusted, Anne tossed the dress onto the bed with all the other rejected garments. Plopping down on the window seat, she gazed at the perfectly landscaped yard. It was the perfect spring day for a picnic. The sun was out, the temperature was ideal, and her escort was a handsome young man. If only the young man was John and not Steve. John would undoubtedly make it fun and exciting. Maybe he would take her to the lake and climb the hill again, or maybe this time, they would go over the hill and explore the other side. And maybe this time, he would kiss her. Closing her eyes, the memory of the night at the movies replayed in her mind. The rapid flutter of her heart, the firmness of his lips pressing against hers, summoned a phantom sensation that teased Anne's reason. Her hands slowly traveled down her legs to her feet, then slowly rising up her calves, her hands paused at the knees and the phantom urged her to quench a distant fire, but Anne pinched her thigh, forcing the phantom into shadow.

A rapid knock on the bedroom door startled Anne. Quickly rising to her feet, Anne patted the embarrassment from her cheeks.

Florence opened the door, her critical eyes summarizing Anne. "You're not dressed yet?"

Anne shrugged. "No, I can't decide which dress to wear."

Florence regarded the pile of dresses on the bed. "You should wear the one with the rosebuds."

"It has a stain on the skirt," Anne answered, twirling a strand of hair around her finger.

"Why didn't you tell me when it happened? It may be impossible to get out now."

"I'm sorry. I guess I forgot about it."

"The yellow gingham is lovely," Florence said, pulling the dress from the bottom of the pile.

"It's too small."

"What do you mean, it's too small?"

"You know," Anne said, waving her hand across her chest.

Florence raised her eyebrow. "I cannot read sign language, be specific."

Anne shut her eyes. "It's tight across my chest, and the buttons pucker."

Florence dropped the dress on the bed. "You neglected to tell me that as well."

"I didn't think it was important," Anne said, her gaze falling to the floor.

Florence turned to Anne and folded her arms. "You're not a little girl anymore, Anne. You need to understand a woman's wardrobe is one of her top priorities. You should always look your best. You never know what the day may bring and must always be prepared."

Anne sighed. "Yes, Mother."

Florence picked up a dress off the bottom of the pile. "How about the green one?"

"I don't like that one."

"Too bad," Florence said, passing the dress to Anne. "Now stop dawdling and put it on. Steve will be here soon, and you need to learn how to pack a picnic basket properly."

"Yes, Mother."

Clicking her tongue, Florence left the room and closed the door with a firm thud.

Anne's shoulders fell. Why did her mother always make her feel inadequate and awkward? She would never meet her mother's impossible standards. Crestfallen, Anne went into the bathroom to dress.

With the picnic basket in hand, Anne waited patiently for Steve to pick her up. She forced a smile when he arrived, and he greeted her with a peck on the cheek. Florence gushed over his impeccable appearance and hung on his every word, making Anne's stomach churn.

Anne relaxed once they were in the car and heading down the road. Steve appeared to be in bright spirits as he drummed his thumbs on the steering wheel. Anne gazed out the window, her mind drifting with a melancholy Everly Brothers tune. Turning the wheel, Steve pulled into the parking lot for the lake.

Anne's heart skipped. "I thought we were going to the park?"

"I know, but I thought a change of scenery might be nice," Steve said, shutting off the car engine.

"Why?"

Steve tilted his head. "I thought you liked the lake?"

"I do, it's just that . . ." Anne's mind scrambled. "There's just so many bugs."

Steve laughed. "Bugs? The bugs have never bothered you before. Now come on." Steve got out of the car and came around to open the door for her.

Anne stepped out of the car. What if John was here? What if he saw them? Her life would be over.

Steve took the picnic basket out of the back seat. "Anne?"

Anne hopped. "What?"

"What is wrong with you? Why are you so jumpy?"

"Am I?" Anne said with a breathless laugh.

"Yes."

"Oh, I'm sorry."

Steve clasped her hand. "Let's sit on the south shore."

"Oh no, let's sit on the north."

"Don't be ridiculous. The sun is shining on the south. Now come on."

Walking to the south shore, Anne's eyes darted, surveying the shoreline.

Steve led Anne up a slight incline, and finally finding a spot that suited him, he spread the blanket a few feet up the hill. Anne calmed her breathing. Sitting further away from the shore was a good idea. It would be harder to spot her this way. Anne set out the plates and Steve lounged beside her, absently twirling a dandelion.

"It's a beautiful day, isn't it?" Steve remarked.

"Yes."

"What more could a man ask for? A beautiful day, a beautiful woman."

Anne almost spilled the glass of iced tea she was handing to him. He sat up abruptly.

"Oh, I'm sorry," she said, smiling sheepishly as she took out the salad.

"Is that potato salad?" Steve asked.

"Yes."

"Did you make it?"

"No, Mother did."

Steve took a drink of tea. "So, did you take any home ec classes in high school?"

Anne put his sandwich on a plate. "A few."

"Was cooking one of them?"

Anne shrugged. "I think so."

"Cooking is an important skill for a woman to learn."

Anne brushed off the comment as she handed him his plate. Fixing her own plate, she took tiny bites and was attentive, listening to Steve talk about subjects that held no interest for her. After he finished eating, he passed her his plate.

"I think we should go for a walk."

"A walk?" Anne croaked.

"Yeah, I wonder what is over that hill over there."

"Nothing," Anne said abruptly, causing Steve to turn to her. "Can't we go for a drive or something? I'm feeling restless."

"Okay, if that would make you happy."

"Oh, it would," Anne said, packing the picnic basket.

"Before we go, I want to talk to you about something."

"Oh?"

Steve set the picnic basket aside and moved closer to her. "You know, my goal has been to work for the Architectural Firm of Cranston and Murdock."

She nodded, her palms moistening.

"Well, your father spoke with them, and they called me this week with a job offer."

"They did?"

"Yes. The pay will be a little less than I hoped for, but Mr. Murdock assured me that if they are pleased with my work, I will get a ten percent raise after six months."

"Oh, that's wonderful. I know it's what you wanted," Anne said with a timid smile.

"They want me to start mid-August."

"Really?"

"I think they wanted me to start earlier, but I knew it would take some time to prepare for the move and find a little house."

Anne stared at the ant crawling across the corner of the blanket.

Steve gently took her hand in his. "I think it's time we move our relationship forward."

Anne's wide eyes met his.

"I want you to know I truly love and value you. You are more than any man could ever hope for, and I want you to share my future with me." Reaching into his pocket, Steve pulled out a small box. "Anne, will you do me the honor of becoming my wife?" Steve opened the box to reveal a lovely diamond solitaire ring. Its brilliance reflected the sun. Anne's thoughts sped past her at a million miles an hour. Words failing her, she rested her hand on her chest.

"Say something, darling," Steve implored.

"I don't know. I mean, I'm so overwhelmed."

"Don't be." He took the ring out of the box and slipped it onto her trembling finger.

The single most important moment in a girl's life had happened to Anne, and the perfect ring had been presented to her, and all she could feel was despair. "It's perfect, Steve."

"Is that a yes, then?"

She met his eyes with a lump in her throat as tears burned her eyes. "I don't know. I mean, it's so sudden."

"We've been dating for two years, Anne."

"I know, but I thought there would be more time," Anne said, her voice failing.

"Time for what?"

"To think things over."

Steve frowned. "What's to think over? Don't you want to marry me?"

"It's just such a huge step right now, and with me almost finishing school . . ."

"The term ends next week, and then you will be done."

Anne pulled her hand away. "For the term, yes, but I want to go back in the fall."

Steve chuckled. "What for?"

"Because I want to become a teacher."

"I know, but now you won't have to worry about that. I will take care of us."

Anne's stomach began to sink. "I know you would, but I want to graduate. I've worked so hard."

Steve reflected. "I understand."

"You do?"

"Sure. If graduating is that important to you, you can finish college in Chicago."

Anne shifted to her knees. "But I don't want to go to one in Chicago. I want to finish here."

"Now you're just being foolish. The colleges in Chicago are ten times better than any colleges around here."

Tears filled the border of Anne's eyes.

Steve felt the side of her face and wiped a tear on the edge of her eye. "I know you're scared to leave home and your parents, but we won't be that far away, and you can come back anytime to visit."

Anne's shoulders fell. "Oh, Steve."

"Come on, now isn't the time to be upset. You should be excited."

Anne ran her hand over her brow. "I just need some time to think."

Steve pulled away and sat his elbows on his knees. Anne knew she was upsetting him, but she couldn't force the words out of her mouth.

Anne set her hand on his forearm. "Please, try and understand."

Steve searched her pleading eyes. "All right, I will give you some time."

Anne's tightly held breath expelled in a hush.

"I think a few days should be sufficient."

Anne opened her mouth to object, but no sound came out.

Steve lifted her chin up. "You know this is the best thing for us. We belong together. I know you will be happy once you have a home to make and a husband to please."

Fighting the tide that pulled her tightly into Steve's arms was useless. Forced to surrender to his inadequate kisses and hands that refused to travel, Anne numbed her senses and slipped into a secret void where her soul was protected and dreams were but a wish away.

11

HE PILE OF DIRT, CANDY wrappers, pop tops, and pieces of paper were swept off the record shop floor and into Eddie's dustpan, while listening to a Buddy Holly record and pretending the broom was his microphone sped up the mundane chore. Eddie recognized almost every customer that came through the doors, but the remarkable young blond woman thumbing through the bin of new releases he had never seen before. She was wearing a wide-brimmed purple hat that hid her features, and he couldn't help but be intrigued. Casually making his way over to her, he leaned on the bin beside her.

"Are you finding everything all right?" Eddie asked.

"Yes," she responded without revealing her face.

Eddie nodded and leaned on the broom. "What kind of music do you like? We have a wide variety, you know. Anything from Bach to the King."

She nodded her response.

"Well, I'll leave you to it. I'll be at the counter if you need me."

"Thank you," she said, moving to another bin.

A young man with a snare drum came down the steps. A large curl hung down his narrow forehead. A huge grin had been on his face when he entered the store, and now a look of disgust replaced it.

"How did it go?" Eddie asked.

The young man didn't look at Eddie; he only mumbled to himself and left the store.

"That one is a no," Eddie said to himself as he emptied his dustpan.

"Hey, Eddie."

Eddie looked up to see Danny jogging down the steps.

"Hey, Dan, how goes it?"

Danny closed his eyes and shook his head. "Not so great."

Eddie set the broom in the corner. "The last one didn't look so happy."

Danny leaned on the counter. "Yeah, he thought he could audition with one drum."

"How does that work?"

"Exactly. Has anyone else come in yet?"

"No, not yet."

Danny nodded. "You got any more sodas back there?"

"Yeah."

"Can you get me a couple, please?"

"Sure," Eddie walked to the back room.

Danny tapped his hand on the counter to the beat of the music. Gazing out across the store, he noticed the blond. Pushing away from the counter, he strolled over to the albums on the aisle across from her.

"Finding anything good?" Danny asked.

"Maybe," she said, not looking up at him.

Danny crossed his arms over the top of the records and leaned forward. "My uncle owns the place, so if you're looking for something specific, I probably could help."

"Thanks, but Eddie offered already," she responded coolly.

"Yeah, he does know a lot about music, but I know more."

"Oh? And why is that?"

"Because I'm a guitar player," Danny said, brushing his hair off his brow and throwing his shoulders back. Usually, that was enough to impress a girl, but this one moved to another bin.

Not one to be discouraged, Danny stepped around to the other side of the counter. "I play lead guitar."

"Is that right?"

"It is."

"Didn't you used to play with The Dice?" she asked.

"I did for a while," Danny said, leaning on the records next to him.

"Didn't work out?"

"Nah, they were holding me back. I need to be the front man because the girls like it when they can see me better."

The young woman laughed. "Is that your best pickup line, Danny?"

Danny chuckled. "Do I know you?"

The girl looked up and smiled.

Danny's mouth dropped. "Monica?"

"Hello, Danny."

"What are you doin' here?" Danny asked, standing up straight.

"I was out doing some shopping when I saw this store and decided to stop in."

"You've never been here before?"

"No, this is my first time."

"You're in for a treat, then."

Monica smiled. "So, this is your uncle's store."

Danny put his hands in his pockets. "Yeah, I joined a new group, and our rehearsal space is upstairs."

"That's convenient."

"Would you like to see it?"

Monica hesitated. "I should probably get going."

"It'll only take a minute."

Monica blinked. "All right, sure."

"Come on, then."

Danny took Monica's elbow and followed her up the stairs. When Danny walked in with Monica, John was sitting on the couch, putting a new string on his guitar.

"It's about time," John said, not looking up. "I could have gone down and gotten my own soda."

"Actually, I ran into a friend," Danny said.

John looked up to see Monica and didn't smile.

"This is my friend Barn . . . I mean John," Danny said to Monica. "John, this is Monica."

"Hi," she said, meeting the unpleasant features in front of her.

"Hi," John said.

"Monica was in the neighborhood and decided to check out the store."

John's smile was strained. "Isn't that nice?"

"Monica plays guitar, you know."

"Danny . . ." Monica said.

"Did you find out how many auditions we have left?" John asked Danny.

"Oh, no. I kinda forgot."

"I bet you did." John set his guitar aside and stood up. Scowling at Danny, he left to go downstairs.

"He's not very personable, is he?" Monica asked.

"Oh, he's just stressed because the auditions aren't going so well."

"What are you auditioning for?" Monica asked.

"We're looking for a drummer."

"Good ones are hard to find."

Danny chuckled. "Yeah, we're learning that."

Monica wandered around the room, looking at the pictures on the wall. Danny delighted in observing her lithe profile.

"It's a nice space, Danny. I love the atmosphere."

"Thanks, we like it."

Monica moved over to the old piano, her fingers trailing over its keys.

"It's out of tune. It belonged to my grandma."

Monica sat down on the bench and began to play. Seeing her sitting on the bench with her gorgeous blond hair spilling down her back made it sound like a symphony to Danny.

He moved closer to the piano and sat down to observe Monica's playing.

Monica could feel his heated gaze, making her hit a few wrong notes, but Danny didn't notice.

"I didn't know you played piano," Danny remarked when the song ended.

"Well, I have to admit, I'm out of practice."

"That's all right. The piano is out of tune."

"Do you have a tuning lever?" Monica asked.

"I don't know, maybe."

"You find one, and I will come back and help you tune it."

"You would?"

"Yeah."

Monica stood up. "Well, I really should be going. I appreciate the tour."

"Sure, let me walk you outside."

They came downstairs. John was leaning against the counter drinking a soda, a look of disapproval on his face.

"I'll be right back," Danny said to him.

"It was nice to meet you, John," Monica said.

The corners of his mouth strained to smile.

Danny walked outside with Monica.

"Who is that?" Eddie said, his tongue almost hanging out.

"Trouble," John said.

"She is smokin' hot."

John took a drink from his soda. "If the next guy comes, send him up."

"Yeah," Eddie said, desperately trying to get another look at Monica.

John shook his head and went upstairs.

Danny stood with Monica on the sidewalk. "So, where you headed?"

"I don't know. I thought I would do some more window shopping."

"Are you meeting up with Joe?" Danny asked.

Monica looked at her feet. "No. Joe and I are separated."

"Oh? I'm sorry."

"No need to be. It was time," Monica said with a small smile.

Danny felt the back of his neck. "Do you need a friend? I mean, would you maybe want to get a drink later?"

Monica held onto her purse strap. "I don't know if that is such a good idea."

"We could go to Be-Bops if you would feel better. Then it's just a causal soda between friends."

She laughed and looked at his boyish grin.

"I would like to hear your thoughts about the show."

"What show?" Monica asked.

"Joe didn't tell you?"

"No, I guess not."

"Well, see, that gives us something to talk about," Danny said.

"I must admit now I'm curious."

"Great. So why don't you come back in, say, an hour?"

Monica nodded. "Okay, I'll see you then."

"Okay. I'll be here."

Monica put on her sunglasses and walked down the block. Danny smiled widely and went inside.

Danny was whistling when he returned to the rehearsal space. John was lying on the couch reading a book.

Danny sat on the floor and stretched his legs. "I guess our one o'clock is a no-show."

"Looks like it," John said.

"We'll see if our one-thirty shows."

"Hmmm."

Danny leaned his arm on the couch. "They weren't all that bad. I mean, the one kid was okay."

"The one with the acne who isn't out of puberty yet?"

"He said he was seventeen."

"My ass."

Danny smiled and opened his soda. "Maybe this last guy will be worth it."

John didn't respond.

"So, what did you think of Monica?" Danny asked.

"I've told you what I think of her."

"I know, but things have changed. She's separated from Joe now."

"Separated doesn't mean over."

Danny gazed out the window. "I am taking her out for a soda tonight."

John turned a page.

"You mad at me, Barnaby?" Danny asked.

"Nope."

"But you think I shouldn't see her."

John closed the book and sat up. "Danny, I'm not gonna tell you how to live your life. You're free to do whatever you want, but as my friend, I have to be honest with you, she may be separated from him, but she is not over him."

"But he's mean to her and . . ."

John held his hand up. "Let me finish."

Danny sighed.

"She is nowhere near ready for another relationship. If anything, she is on the rebound. You know what that means, right?"

Danny refused to meet his eyes.

"I know you like her a lot, and I understand that. I am just sayin' be careful. I don't wanna see you get hurt. That's all."

Danny looked at him. "I appreciate that."

"Howdy, fellas!"

John and Danny turned to see a tall boy with a wide grin crossing his tobacco-stained teeth. A bass drum slung over his back and a snare drum in his hand. His brown hair was combed in a DA, and his jeans were tucked into red cowboy boots.

John started to cough to cover up his desire to laugh.

Danny stood up. "Hi, I'm Danny."

"I'm Hubert, but my friends call me Hubie."

More coughing.

"Is he okay?" Hubert asked.

"Yeah, he's fine," Danny said, fighting his laugh.

"I gotta get some water," John said, leaving the room.

"Where do ya want me to set up?" Hubie asked.

"Right here is fine."

"I have a couple of more pieces in my car."

"You need me to help you?" Danny asked.

"Nah, I got it," Hubie said, going down the stairs.

Danny followed behind him.

"Where's John?" Danny asked Eddie.

"Out back."

Danny went out back to find John leaning on the wall for support and laughing.

"Barnaby! You're not helping anything," Danny scolded.

"Did you see those boots?" John said, laughing louder.

Danny couldn't help but laugh too. "At least he has a kit. Let's give him a chance. Huh?"

"All right, all right," John said.

"You think you can be serious for a few minutes?"

"I'll try."

John managed to pull himself together and returned upstairs with Danny.

Hubie was finishing setting up his drums.

John and Danny sat on the couch and tried to appear attentive.

"So, tell us about yourself," Danny said.

Hubie looked over at them with a toothpick sticking out of his mouth. "Well, I like to play drums and chase girls."

John and Danny nodded.

"Tall ones with big boobies."

John about choked.

Danny coughed. "I can see why you like tall girls."

"Yup, I'm six-foot-one. My mama always told me I was gonna be a big boy 'cause I have a big . . ."

John whimpered and bent over, clutching his stomach.

"Are you sure he's okay?" Hubie asked Danny.

Danny kicked John. "What kind of experience do you have?"

"With what?"

"Playin' in a band?"

Hubie scratched his head. "Hmm, I recently played in my cousin's band."

"Great, what was their name?"

"The Hay Seeds."

That was it. John was on his knees, laughing.

"He's kind of a happy guy, huh?" Hubert said with a smile.

Danny rolled his eyes.

"I'm. . . sorry," John sputtered. He wiped tears from his eyes and sat on the couch.

"Why don't you play somethin' for us?" Danny said.

Hubert sat behind his drums and started. He wasn't half bad, but it was hard for John and Danny to picture him playing rock 'n roll. After he finished, John was able to compose himself.

"So, we're a rock 'n' roll band with some blues thrown in on some of our numbers. Would that work for you?" Danny asked.

"You mean like Presley?"

"Yeah, kind of," Danny acknowledged with a nod.

"How much do I get paid?"

Danny looked at John. "Well, that all depends on when we start to get gigs and stuff. We are kind of new still."

"Oh," Hubert said. "I wanna make money."

"We all do," John said, his humor gone.

"Thanks for comin' in," Danny said, standing and shaking his hand. "We'll be in touch."

Hubert nodded, collected his kit, and left.

Danny flopped on the couch next to John. The two sat in silence, looking at the ceiling.

"You think he has a big dick?" Danny said.

John shrugged before they both broke out laughing.

12

WITH HIS FEET PERCHED ON a stool, Patrick sat strumming his guitar while listening to a Fats Domino record. The calm, quiet rec room was his favorite relaxing space since his brother moved out a few years earlier. A couple of basketball trophies and a faded pennant were the only evidence he had once lived there. Patrick contemplated moving out into his own place soon, but he wasn't in a hurry. He wanted to save money and take his time finding an ideal domesticated girl to complement him.

The door atop the stairs opened, and Patrick's mother yelled to him. "Patrick, you have company."

"Send him down, Mom," Patrick answered.

Stu's jog down the stairs made the old steps groan from his weight. He had just gotten off work, and his cowlick stuck up like rooster feathers. His sloppy work shirt was untucked, and his bland tan pants were rolled over his high tops in an attempt to appear hip.

Stu plopped down into the overstuffed chair across from Patrick and grinned. "Hey, buddy."

Since the night of Patrick's party, Stu had started hanging out with him. Sometimes they would go out for a beer or two and flirt with girls, but mostly they stayed in Patrick's basement and played guitars.

Being separated from John made Patrick more relaxed and patient with Stu's inadequate playing. He tried to coach and mentor Stu, but Stu's lack of commitment to practicing on his own made his progress slow. However, Patrick's extra attention made Stu think he was improving, so his ego expanded without foundation.

Patrick set his guitar aside. "Hey, Stu, how was your shift?"

"Man, I don't know what it is, but some days the housewives that come into the store can be so damn fussy. I swear they live to come in and examine the produce. They hold it up to the light and look for any imperfection on the surface, and then, if that isn't enough, they start to squeeze it! Mrs. Billings squeezed a tomato too hard, and red goo spurt out all over the front of her new dress. Now I ask you, how is that Len's fault? Boy, did she chew him out," Stu said, reclining and setting his dirty shoes on the coffee table.

Patrick frowned. "Hey, remember the rules around here."

Stu removed his feet and sat up. "Oh yeah, sorry."

Patrick pulled himself off the floor. "I brought home some root beer. You want one?"

"Do I!"

Patrick handed him a bottle from the small icebox in the corner.

"So, how was your first day with The Dice?" Stu asked, setting his foot on top of his knee.

Patrick sat on the burgundy couch. "Not too bad, kind of stressful."

"Oh?"

"Yeah, Joe started the day by telling us about the show at the community center," Patrick said, popping the lid off the bottle.

"Oh yeah? What did he say?"

"Pretty much what John told you. Will and Boyd weren't thrilled about it."

"I bet," Stu said, tipping back his bottle.

"I'm not sure, but there is some unrest within the group."

"Really?"

Patrick set his arm on the back of the couch. "Believe me, I know what that looks like."

"Yeah, but The Dice? They're getting ready to make a record. They should be over the moon."

"One would think. I will have to get to know them better before I can determine what's going on."

Stu had finished his drink and was flipping the bottle into the air and catching it.

"You realize if you drop and break that, you will have a hell of a mess to clean up," Patrick warned.

Stu smiled sheepishly and sat the bottle down safely on the coffee table.

"So, how goes the search for the new drummer?" Patrick asked.

Stu shrugged. "They posted some flyers around town. I don't know if there was any interest."

"Chances of them finding someone who is any good and wants to play for free is pretty slim," Patrick said.

"There is no contest without a drummer. You guys are gonna cream us."

"It would seem that way."

Stu tucked his hands behind his head. "Personally, I hope you do."

"Oh?"

"Yeah, I would love to see Danny Bruer be humiliated."

Patrick leaned back on the couch. "I personally would love to see John humiliated."

"No doubt."

"I wonder what made him think he stood any chance of beating The Dice?" Patrick contemplated.

Stu's features fell. "Because he thinks Danny has golden fingers and everyone that looks at him admires him as much as he does. Well, he's wrong. Dead wrong."

Patrick smirked. "Well, I think John could be in for a few surprises. I have a few ideas that could make John and Danny's lives a living nightmare."

"Oh yeah?"

"Are you in?"

"All the way, buddy," Stu said with a broad grimace.

13

ONICA RETURNED TO THE RECORD shop later to find Danny leaning against the wall, waiting for her. His thumbs were hitched through his belt loops, and she could admire him unnoticed from a distance. Danny had been attracted to Monica from the first time he saw her, and if the truth was known, she couldn't help but be attracted to him, too. But then again, most girls were. His charisma, windswept appearance, and soft-spoken voice were enough to melt any girl's heart. Even though Monica had separated from Joe, her consciousness was bothering her like sand in a shoe. She didn't want to lead Danny on, but the thought of spending time with him was undeniably exhilarating.

Danny smiled when he saw her.

"Hey," he said.

"Hey," Monica answered.

"You have any luck shopping?"

Monica shook her head. "I just window-shopped."

Danny pushed off the wall. "So, you still all right with going to Be-Bops?"

Monica shrugged. "Sure. Are we walking?"

"No, I have a car now."

"You do?"

"Yeah, but I should warn you, it's nothing like what Joe has. It's rough around the edges, but it runs."

"Well, that's something."

Monica followed Danny over to where his car was parked.

"Well, this is it," Danny said.

Monica nodded slowly.

"Terrible, right?"

Monica shrugged. "It's not that bad."

"You're just being nice."

"No."

"I know it needs work, but given time, it will shine. Here, let me open the door for you."

Danny gave the door handle a few hard yanks before it opened with a loud creak. Monica put her hand over her mouth to suppress a smile. Danny smiled sheepishly as she got into the car.

Reaching out, Monica tapped the head of the little dog on the dashboard. Its tiny brown head began to bob up and down, and Monica smiled at the novelty.

Danny got inside beside her. "I see you met my dog."

"He is very cute."

Danny looked at the dog and put the keys into the ignition. "Yeah, the guy who sold me the car had a grandson who insisted I take the dog. He said it would keep me company."

"That's sweet."

Danny thanked the Lord that the car started with the first turn of the key.

"Sorry for the strong gas smell. I am working on that too."

"You know a lot about cars, huh, Danny?" Monica asked.

"Yeah, I know some," Danny said, pulling into traffic. "I used to work on my grandfather's tractor. Why don't you turn on the radio?"

Monica turned on the radio; "Lucille" was playing. Monica tapped her hand on her knee as the car rolled along.

Danny pulled into Be-Bop's crowded parking lot. Girls on roller skates waited on the cars that were parked out front. Large windows followed the curve of the restaurant's front. Blue and pink neon lights raced around the large record on top of the building, with Be-Bops flashing in different blinking sequences.

"Stick close to me so you don't get trampled," Danny joked as he opened Monica's door.

"Maybe I should hold your hand," she said, slipping her soft hand into his.

He grinned. "Okay."

The smell of hamburgers and French fries met them at the door. Red and white vinyl booths were filled with laughing, chattering teenagers. Several were gathered around the jukebox, waiting for their turn to put their money in. Short-order cooks shouted numbers out to the busy waitresses. Danny found a booth on the left-hand side, and they sat down. Grabbing a menu, he passed one to Monica.

"What are you going to have?" Monica asked.

"Not much, just a Big Bop burger and fries. Maybe a shake."

Monica smiled at him.

"What?"

"I can't remember the last time I had a shake."

"We could split one."

"If I am having a shake, I am enjoying the whole thing," Monica said.

Danny laughed.

The waitress came by to take their order, then Danny told Monica about the upcoming show. By the time he finished, their food had come, and they were dipping greasy French fries in ketchup.

"So, what do you think?" Danny said.

"I can't believe Joe agreed to it."

"It was kind of his idea."

"Really?" Monica said, rolling her straw between her fingers.

"Yeah, I mean, at first, it was just going to be him and me playing a song, but then he decided he wanted it to be more of a show."

"That's Joe—always the showman. I can't imagine Will was happy about it," Monica said.

"Yeah, I can't either. So, what kind of chance do you think we have?"

Monica scooped some ice cream out of her shake and took a bite. "I don't know, Danny. I mean, there is no doubt that you are very talented, but I don't know if it will be enough to beat Joe and Will."

Danny nodded and dipped more fries.

"I'm not trying to bring you down."

"You're just being honest."

"You know, the venue might be an advantage."

"Yeah?"

Monica licked her straw. "Well, think about it. A Dice show is not just about playing music. It's about costumes, bright blinking lights, and choreography. Take that stuff away, and they will be off their game, right?"

Danny's face brightened. "Yes, you are totally right."

"You know they're not about improvising."

Danny leaned back, slapping his hands together. "Oh, Monica, thank you so much. I could kiss you!"

Monica's breath hitched, but the comment's meaning didn't seem to register with Danny.

"So, did you have any more auditions?" Monica said, moving quickly away from the comment.

"Yeah, this one guy came in wearing bright red cowboy boots."

"What?" Monica laughed.

"Yeah, he actually had his own kit, and we were open to working with him, but once he brought up the subject of wanting to get paid, it kind of killed it."

Monica took a few more bites of her hamburger. "You're not going to give up, are you?"

"No, but we don't have a lot of time. We may have to accept the fact that we won't have a drummer."

"That is going to make it harder."

"I know."

"Rock and Roll Is Here to Stay" started playing on the jukebox, and Monica bounced in her seat.

Danny stood up. "Come on, let's dance."

"Here?"

"Those kids are," Danny said, tilting his head toward the teenagers dancing near the jukebox.

"I would feel awkward."

"Nonsense," he said, taking her hand. Monica had no choice but to follow Danny, who only needed a few beats to start moving. Dancing with Danny was easy because his sense of rhythm moved his entire body to the beat of the music. Monica whirled around the space, her doubts and reservations leaving her with a breathless laugh. It had been so long since Monica had any fun, and the years dialed back, and she felt like a teenager again. The songs played, and their feet flew, and when a slow song came on, the transition was flawless as Danny put his hand firmly on her hip and held her hand in his. Looking into his deep dark eyes entranced her; she stepped into him, letting his arm tighten around her waist. They swayed slowly to the music's soft lullaby. Placing both of her arms around his neck, she laid her cheek on his chest and soaked up his warmth. Reality slipped away, and she was mesmerized by the guitar player on stage at the homecoming dance. Sweat from his dark blond hair caused his pompadour to fall in a curl across his forehead. His tenor doo wops filled the gym, and young girls were jumping up and down trying to catch his eye, but his hazel eyes had found Monica, and her heart skipped a beat.

The song ended, and Danny pulled back. She met his eyes, the music a distorted clamor in her ear. He gently felt the side of her face and moved his lips closer to hers, but before she closed her eyes, she knew the desire she felt wasn't for Danny. It was for Joe.

Monica stepped back, the distance resetting reality.

"I think it's time for me to go home." Turning, she returned to the table and grabbed her purse and hat.

"Monica, are you all right?" Danny asked.

"I'm just tired, and I want to go home. I can call a cab if you want."

"Don't be ridiculous," Danny said. "I'll pay the check, and we can go."

Monica nodded.

The cool evening air chased the fog from Monica's mind. The guilt of her actions began to settle in as Danny drove her to her sister's house, where she was staying. He pulled up out front, and Monica sat looking at the home without moving to open the door.

"Here, let me walk you up to the door," Danny said.

"No," Monica said, turning to him. "It's okay, Danny. I would rather you didn't."

"Is everything all right? Did I do something wrong?"

"No, no, Danny, it's me. It's just too soon. My head is a jumble, and I can't think straight."

Danny reached over and took her hand. "It's okay, Monica, I understand. You're going through a lot right now."

"I don't want to hurt you, Danny."

"I'm okay, honestly. I had a wonderful time."

"So did I. I really don't deserve your kindness," Monica said, half her face hidden in shadow.

"You stop that, you hear me? I don't ever want to hear you talk that way."

"You don't know me. You don't know about all my indiscretions."

"You don't know about all mine either, and let's keep it that way for now. Okay?"

Monica nodded and brushed a tear away. "I'm scared, Danny. I don't know how to get along without Joe. I've been with him since I was fifteen."

"I know, but you're strong, and you can get through this."

Monica's eyes flashed. "But I'm not strong. I haven't held down a job in years..."

"Shhh," Danny said, pushing her hair from her shoulder. "You are upsetting yourself. I'm sure you will find a job someplace."

Monica smiled at his optimism. "I wish I would have met you a long time ago."

"Monica . . ."

Monica pressed her finger to his mouth. "Don't say anything more, please? Let me pretend that you are bringing me home from our first date and that we will see each other again soon."

Monica pushed the car door open, but Danny gently touched her forearm before she got out.

"Monica, if you ever need help or want to talk, I will always be your friend."

She smiled. "If I ever need a knight in shining armor, I know where to find you."

Monica exited the car, and Danny watched her enter the tiny house and close the door.

14

SILENT HUSH SPREAD THROUGH THE coffee shop as the rhythmic thumping noise distracted customers from their reading or casual conversations. Turning their heads, they watched Ronnie as he passed them. Ronnie never cowered from people's stares or whispers. He was used to people gawking at him with either pity or disgust. Sometimes people snickered or made other unpleasant noises, but Ronnie ignored them. Keeping his head up and his eyes focused, he made his way to his favorite table.

Picking up a fresh pot of coffee, Marcy walked over to Ronnie. "Hey Ronnie, how are you today?"

"Okay," Ronnie said, placing his overcoat over the back of his chair and pulling out his book.

"What are you reading?" Marcy asked.

Ronnie set the book on the table, and she saw the title *Don Quixote*. "Wow, that is kind of deep, isn't it?"

"It's epic."

Marcy smiled at him and filled his cup. "You're a mystery, Ronnie."

He cocked his head with a confused look.

"Never mind," she said, walking away.

The crowd had thinned out by the time James arrived. Marcy was busy serving other customers, so he didn't bother her. Finding an empty chair, James sat his books on the counter and noticed Ronnie reading. "Hello, Ronnie."

Ronnie looked over to see the lopsided grin on James's face, then returned to his reading.

"Hey, sweetie," Marcy said, setting a cup of coffee on the counter.

"Hey," James said, sitting down.

"I didn't expect to see you today."

James shrugged. "I thought I would surprise you."

"Or you're procrastinating."

James picked up his book. "I brought my book."

"Uh-huh, you always tell me I distract your studying."

"Well, you do, but I wanted coffee."

Marcy put her hand on her hip. "So, you didn't come in to see me. You just came in for the coffee?"

"Now you're twisting my words."

"You know you're going to ace those tests," Marcy said with a smile.

"I'm going to try."

"Then you better put your eyes in the book," she said, picking it up and setting it down in front of him. "I would hate to distract you."

"Too late."

She chuckled and walked away.

James picked up his coffee cup and looked for his pencil. Realizing it rolled off the counter and onto the floor, he got up and mumbled as he bent over to pick it up. Out of the corner of his eyes, James thought he spotted drumsticks sticking out of Ronnie's jacket pocket. Doubting his eyes, James didn't pay attention when he stood upright and hit his head on the counter. Ronnie's gaze turned to James, who was rubbing his head and cursing. James noticed Ronnie's raised eyebrow and his cheeks turned red. Shaking his head, Ronnie turned his attention back to his book.

James set his pencil next to his book and casually approached Ronnie.

"Hey, Ronnie, what's shakin'?" James asked, still rubbing his head.

Ronnie didn't say anything. He just kept reading.

James sat across from Ronnie, hoping he would acknowledge him, but he didn't. Tilting his head, James tried to read the book title. Ronnie looked up with annoyance.

"I was curious about what book you're reading," James said.

"*Don Quixote*," Ronnie said.

"Ah, good choice."

"You've read it?"

"I have."

Ronnie pulled his book closer and went back to his reading.

James twiddled his thumbs. "You know, I'm curious. Are those drumsticks I see in your coat pocket?"

"They ain't chopsticks, daddy-o," Ronnie said.

"You, play the drums, then?"

"I don't play jacks with um."

James put his elbows on the table and leaned forward. "Are you in a group right now?"

Ronnie raised an eyebrow.

"You know, like a rock 'n' roll group?"

"Nope."

"Have you ever played with a group?"

Ronnie tapped his spoon inside the hollow cup. "They let me play the drum with the school band once."

"Oh yeah?"

"Yeah."

"Is that where you learned to play?"

"Nope."

"How did you learn?"

Ronnie shrugged. "I taught myself."

"Would you be interested in joining a group?" James asked.

"Nope."

"Why not?"

"Don't need the hassle," Ronnie answered.

"Why would it be a hassle?"

"I don't get along well with others."

"Because they are mean?"

Ronnie shifted in his seat. "Because they don't give me a chance."

"Listen, I'm in a group, and we desperately need a drummer. Would you consider meeting the leader of our group? You two have a lot in common, actually."

"I doubt that," Ronnie said, turning a page.

"What would it hurt just to meet him? You might be surprised. I could bring him in tomorrow. No pressure—it would just mean a lot to us."

Ronnie sighed and laid down his book. "If I agree, will you stop bothering me so I can finish this chapter?"

"Yes."

"Okay," Ronnie said, resuming his reading.

James decided to study at Ronnie's table. Ronnie didn't mind as long as James left him alone to read. After Ronnie finished reading, he got up and put the book in his pocket.

"I'll see you tomorrow?" James asked.

Ronnie nodded, and James watched him walk away. His labored steps punctuated the compassion in James's heart. James continued studying until Marcy came over and sat across from him.

"I am almost done here. Can you go out tonight?" Marcy asked.

"I don't think so. I have two tests tomorrow, but I can walk you home."

Marcy rested her chin on her hand. "You do realize that once you're on summer break, you will have a lot of lonely nights to make up for."

James grinned with an enticing glint in his eye. "I promise I will make it worth the wait."

Marcy's cheeks warmed. "I should get back to work."

"Okay," James said, switching his books.

"I do have one question. Why were you talking to Ronnie?"

"I noticed his drumsticks."

"Oh," Marcy said, lowering her eyes.

"Wait a second, did you know Ronnie played the drums?"

"I need to go back to work," Marcy said, standing, but James grabbed her hand.

"Marcy?" James said in a low tone.

Marcy looked James in the eye. "Yes, I knew."

"Why didn't you tell me?"

"Isn't it obvious? I didn't want him to get hurt."

"What makes you think we would hurt him?"

Marcy set her fingertips on the table. "He's had a hard life because of his disability, and he is vulnerable. I just don't see how his involvement with the group would go very well."

"Why not?"

Marcy sighed. "Are you going to make me say it?"

James squinted his eyes. "I guess I am."

"I think certain group members might not be sensitive to Ronnie's circumstances."

"You mean John?"

Marcy wiped her hands on her apron. "I'm not going to say anything more, but I am asking you to please consider the situation before you throw Ronnie into the middle. It would break my heart if he got hurt."

"I know John can come across as callous, but it is just his way of protecting himself."

"From what?" Marcy scoffed.

"Being hurt himself."

Marcy crossed her arms. "I can't believe he has ever been hurt."

"You know, people judge Ronnie based on what they see on the outside. Don't you think you're passing the same judgment on John?"

Marcy lowered her eyes.

"If I thought for one minute that John or anyone else would be cruel to Ronnie, I would have never made the suggestion." James rubbed his thumb across Marcy's hand. "You need to trust me."

Marcy bent over, kissed James's cheek, and whispered in his ear. "I trust you more than anyone else I know."

James smiled at her, and Marcy went back to work.

15

AMES'S CONVERSATION WITH MARCY ABOUT Ronnie played through his mind as he walked over to John's house. He could understand Marcy's concern, but she didn't know John like he did. John had been his usual disinterested self when he met Marcy, and the two had maybe shared a handful of words, but John had never said anything negative about Marcy. James suspected that maybe Mae had filled her mind with all kinds of lies, but he wasn't sure. Luckily, Marcy hadn't spent much time with Mae since the night at the Beaumont, which suited James just fine. Mae was obviously a bad influence on anyone she came in contact with.

James stepped up onto the porch of John's house and rang the doorbell. This time, James was prepared to greet the woman who would answer the door. John's stepmother was a humorless, somber woman who hardly smiled, but she did seem to like James, so at least he had that in his favor. James swung his arms while he waited for the door to open. He was sure they felt if they ignored the bell long enough, whoever was standing on the porch would get the clue and leave, but if James was anything, it was patient.

The door finally opened, and the gatekeeper appeared. Her salt and peppered sleek wave framed her sullen face. A grey pressed pencil dress held no curve, and her high cheekbones pronounced her dark bird eyes.

"Hello, Mrs. Chandler. How nice to see you again." James thought he might have seen the start of a smile, but it was probably just an illusion.

"I suppose you are here to see John," Caroline said, crossing her arms.

"Yes, if that's possible."

Her eyes shifted slightly. "You know he is studying for his finals."

"I do, and I hate to bother him, but this is important."

"Important, indeed. All right, you might as well come in, then," Caroline said, opening the door.

"Thank you."

James stepped inside the quiet hallway.

"You can wait in the living room while I tell him you're here."

"Thank you."

Caroline nodded and went up the stairs. James stepped into the living room and took a deep breath. For a moment, he thought he was standing in a Victorian museum. The room was sparsely decorated with antique furnishings. Every piece was made of dark wood, brought to a high shine. The grandfather clock in the corner was the only sound as it quietly ticked away the minutes. Dainty doilies covered the end tables and arms of the sofa. Long lace sheers were complimented by rose-colored drapes. James didn't dare move for fear of getting dirt or dust on something, so he stood as close to the entryway as possible.

Caroline returned a few moments later. "He will be down momentarily."

"Thank you."

Caroline nodded and sat down in the floral wing-backed chair. "Why don't you sit down?"

"Uh, I'm fine standing," James said with a small smile.

Caroline put on her reading glasses and returned to her reading. John finally came down the stairs. He was wearing dungarees and an old sweatshirt. He was quite the contradiction to his surroundings.

"Hey, John," James said.

"Hey, Professor, did you come by to take me out on a date?" John said.

James's face turned red as he looked at Caroline, who peered at him over the top of her book.

"Always the comedian," James chuckled.

John folded his arms. "So, what's on your mind?"

"I have a bit of news."

"Oh?"

James shifted his weight. "I think I might have found the solution to our problem."

"Which one?"

James chuckled and pushed his hair back.

John glanced over at his stepmother. "You want to talk in private?"

"Is that possible?"

"Sure, we can step out onto the porch."

"Okay. It was nice to see you again, Mrs. Chandler," James said.

She nodded her response. James followed John outside.

"I'm sorry to bother you. I know you're busy studying," James said.

John sat on one of the white wicker chairs. "Yeah, but I needed the break. So what problem are you solving for me today?"

James sat in the chair opposite John. "I met someone who might be interested in the drummer position."

"Might be?"

"Well, he may need a little bit of coaxing. He is kind of . . . well . . . a little different."

John rested his elbows on the chair arms. "Most drummers are."

"No, I mean he has a. . . ." Struggling to find the right words, James moved his hand up and down his arm.

"You're scaring me," John said.

James took a deep breath. "He has a leg brace."

John blinked. "So?"

"I think he has had a hard life, and maybe it has made him kind of . . ."

"Circumspect?"

"That, and he thinks Marylin Monroe is his girlfriend."

"I think we've all thought that late at night," John said.

James rubbed his hands together. "Anyway, I asked him if he wanted to join a band, and he said no."

"Did he give a reason?"

"He said it's because most people don't like him."

"Most people are idiots," John said, leaning back in his chair.

"I talked him into meeting you."

"When?"

"Tomorrow at the coffee shop."

"Great. Do you think he'll mind if I have Danny join us?"

"I don't know. He reminds me of you when you meet new people. The only difference is, he doesn't use any aliases."

John crumpled his lip. "I can't imagine having Danny there would be a bad thing. He's better with people than I am."

"True," James agreed.

"So, we will meet you at the bike rack after school tomorrow?"

"Okay. I think if we can convince him to join us, it could solve a lot of problems."

"Agreed. I guess I better get back to the books," John said, standing.

James stood up. "Me too."

"I will see you tomorrow, then."

"Yep." James stepped off the porch.

"Good work, Professor," John said before going into the house.

James smiled and headed for home.

16

Unorganized like his thoughts, John studied the scribbled composition notes in front of him. To anyone else, the notes would look like uncomprehensive nonsense, but John understood them perfectly. The test would be over in an hour, and his mind would be released from the mindless torture.

He heard the familiar clack of her shoes as she stopped beside his desk. Gazing up, he saw Anne with puffed cheeks that looked like they might explode with excitement.

"Hi," she said.

"Hi," John answered through a strained smile.

Anne was twisting her hips and running the tip of her finger along the edge of his desk. "How are you?"

"Fine," he said, wishing she would get to the point of her disruption.

"I was wondering if you were busy after class."

John reclined in his seat. "Actually, I am."

"Oh," she said, her cheeks deflated.

"Did you need something?"

"I wanted to talk to you."

"About?"

She averted her eyes and pulled on her ear. "Something important."

"That could be anything."

"I don't want to talk about it here. I promise it will only take a moment."

John gave her a blank look, and she tugged on her sore ear. "Please."

"All right, I guess I can spare a moment."

"Thank you," she said, reaching her seat as the bell rang.

John rubbed his temples. Women.

The next hour ticked by painfully slow, and John had a horrible headache by the time he stepped out into the bustling hallway. Leaning against the wall, he waited for Anne to exit the classroom.

"All right, make this quick," John said.

"Do we have to talk right here? In the middle of the hallway?" Anne whined.

"Yep, you spill it here, or you wait."

Anne sighed. "I have good news."

"Oh?"

"Yeah, I will be staying with an older lady that lives here in town for a couple of weeks."

"So?"

Anne took a small step forward. "It means I won't be that far away, and we can see each other."

John folded his arms. "I thought I made it clear that I wasn't interested in a shared relationship."

Anne pressed her books to her chest. "I know, and I broke it off with Steve this weekend."

John glanced suspiciously into the snapping blue eyes in front of him. "Really?"

Anne tightened the grip on her books. "Yes. It means we can spend time together now, right?"

"My, aren't you the anxious one."

"I really enjoy being with you," Anne said, touching the sleeve of his jacket.

"I can see that."

A shy blush colored her cheeks.

John lifted her chin with a firm grip, leaving her with no choice but to look him straight in the eye. "You truly broke it off with him?"

"I did," Anne said, her eyes unwavering under his probing gaze.

John tried to spot a lie, but all he could see was desire. Loosening his grip, he trailed his index finger down her jawline. "I guess I will see you soon, then."

"When?" Anne said, almost breathless.

"Patience is a virtue, Miss Prim."

Anne bit her lip as John disappeared down the stairs, then spinning around, she almost knocked over two other students before bouncing victoriously down the hall.

17

IF JAMES WAS INCLUDED IN Danny and John's conversation, he didn't know it. He sat in the backseat of the car, staring out the window and biting his nails. He couldn't make up his mind if Ronnie would be upset about having to meet another person besides John. What if Danny's presence ruined the whole deal? Then what would they do? Something thumped James on the head, and he turned to see John and Danny staring at him.

"Hey, what frequency are you tuned into?" John said.

James rubbed his head. "What?"

Danny laughed. "You look like you're a hundred miles away."

James pulled his brows together and glared at John. "What did you hit me on the head with?"

"Me? Nothing. It was Danny," John said with a straight face, but James knew better.

"You're so juvenile," James said.

"So, what you thinkin' about, Professor?" Danny said.

"The best way to introduce the two of you to Ronnie."

"Are you afraid we will embarrass you?" John said.

"No, but you may want to dial back the antics for a while."

"He wants you to behave," Danny said to John.

"Me?" John said, setting his hand on his chest. "Why, I am totally offended! I'll have you know that my social etiquette is refined and properly pompous."

James rolled his eyes and got out of the car.

"I don't think he believes me," John said to Danny.

Danny smirked at John and opened his car door.

"Now, remember the plan," James said, stopping Danny and John at the door to the Coffee Grounds.

"You two will wait patiently at the door while I talk to Ronnie. Then, once I know that he is cool with everything, I will signal you to join us. Okay?"

"Okay," Danny said.

"John?" James said.

"What?" John answered.

"You understand the plan?"

John leaned on Danny. "Of course I do."

"Don't worry, James, I will keep him in check," Danny said with a nod.

John batted his eyes. "We will be perfect gentlemen."

James shook his head and went into the shop, John and Danny close behind.

"Wait here," James said.

"Yes, Dad," John said.

Ignoring John, James walked down the aisle, leaving Danny and John watching.

"Do you see anything?" John asked Danny.

"No, you?"

"No."

They bobbed their heads, trying to see around the customers at the counter.

"Wait, I think I see him talking to somebody," Danny said, raising himself on the balls of his feet.

"Yeah? What's he look like?" John asked.

"I can't tell. He's back pretty far."

"This is ridiculous," John said, walking forward.

"Barnaby," Danny protested, following him.

James was in midsentence when John came up behind him. Ronnie was listening to James, but now his attention was drawn to John, who was making faces behind James's back. Ronnie smiled.

"So, you see, we thought it would be a good idea for you to meet Danny too."

Danny came up to stand beside John. Grabbing John by the throat, Danny pretended to choke him. John opened his mouth wide, held onto Danny's hands, and gasped for breath. Ronnie's grin grew, and now James knew something was wrong. He turned around to see the theatrics going on behind him.

"I should have known you wouldn't listen to me," James snapped.

"Ah, come on, Professor, we're only excited to meet him," Danny said.

James turned back to Ronnie. "Ronnie, these are the two *boys* I have told you about. Danny Bruer and Dennis the Menace."

John's face fell, and Danny laughed. James grinned at John, who narrowed his eyes at him.

"Hello, gentlemen," Marcy said, coming over to the table.

"Hey, Marcy, how are you?" Danny said.

"Good, how are you, Danny?"

"Can't complain."

"Can I get you three a cup of coffee?" Marcy asked.

"Not for me," Danny said.

"No thanks," John said.

"I know you do," Marcy said, winking at James before walking away.

John sat down next to James, and Danny took a seat beside Ronnie.

"It's good to meet you, Ronnie," Danny said.

Ronnie nodded at Danny. Ronnie looked at John across the table. Neither one said anything as they sized each other up for a moment. An unspoken respect seemed to pass between them before they nodded in acknowledgment.

"So, the Professor tells us you play the drums," Danny said.

"What professor?" Ronnie asked.

"That's my nickname," James said.

Ronnie still looked confused but didn't say anything else.

"So, you play, then?" Danny asked Ronnie.

"Yep."

"Great! We are lookin' for someone to join our band. Would you be interested in auditioning?"

Ronnie folded his hands. "No."

"Why not?" Danny asked.

"Don't want the hassle."

"James says you've played with a band before."

"I played with the school band once."

"How about you audition us?" John said.

Ronnie tilted his head.

"You give us a chance to show you what we can do, then you decide if you want to play with us. Sound fair?"

Ronnie reflected for a moment. "I don't know."

"If you're worried about not fitting in or playing too fast, don't," John said. "There is no judgment here. None of us are perfect, and we all have our handicaps. For us, it's about making music. I'm not going to lie to you, Ronnie. We are in a bind and desperately need your talent. If you could see your way clear to help us out for this one show, we would be forever in your debt," John said.

"He's right, Ronnie, I'm in trouble, and I could use your help," Danny said. "Please let us show you who we are before you judge us?"

Ronnie looked at his hands briefly, while concerned looks passed between James, John, and Danny.

Finally, Ronnie nodded. "Okay."

John and Danny slapped hands across the table.

"Thank you, Ronnie. You won't regret this, I promise," Danny said, placing his hand on Ronnie's shoulder.

Marcy returned to the table. "Well, you all seem happy."

"Ronnie's agreed to give us an audition," Danny said.

Marcy smiled. "That's wonderful."

"Wait until you see our rehearsal space. You're going to love it," Danny said.

"You have your own place?" Ronnie asked.

"Yep."

"Wow."

"I would love to see the space too," Marcy hinted.

"No females allowed," John said.

Marcy raised her eyebrow. "Says who?"

"Says me," John answered.

"That's discrimination."

"That's my rule."

"James," Marcy said, nudging James.

"What?"

"Tell him that isn't fair."

James looked from John to Marcy, both of them frowning at him. "Danny, help me out here."

"No way am I getting involved in this," Danny said.

"Females tend to distract a male's attention from their objectives, therefore, causing a rise in testosterone and a drop in mental reasoning and judgment. So, it only makes sense that an attractive female should not be present so that a man can stay focused and do his best work," Ronnie said.

Marcy blinked at Ronnie, and John smiled. Puffing her cheeks out, Marcy turned on her heel and left in a huff.

John grinned at Ronnie and stood up. "Shall we go then, gentlemen?"

Ronnie hesitated; he led a simple predictable life within the confines of the familiar and the comfortable. He very rarely ventured far from his home. Going to The Beat with the boys was beyond Ronnie's level of comfort. A familiar tingling sensation crept up his spine and sprouted into perspiration under his arms and on his neck.

"You okay, Ronnie?" James asked.

"I don't think I should go."

"Why not?" John asked.

"I need to be home in time for supper."

"Heck, I can take you home," Danny said, rising out of his chair.

"I know you might feel some anxiety about coming with us, but I promise is will be fun," James said.

"You can even ride shotgun," Danny said.

Ronnie looked from one face to the other with uncertainty.

"Your chariot awaits you, my liege," John said with a low sweeping bow.

Ronnie grinned, breaking the ice everyone was standing on. He rose to his feet, and the boys followed him out the door.

18

ONNIE'S HEAD BARELY CLEARED The Beat's small doorway. A mellow Nat King Cole tune soothed the tension of being in an unfamiliar place. Stepping slowly down the front of the counter, Ronnie's eyes flit from one corner of the store to the other. The vibrant displays of records and posters on the walls delighted his senses.

"Welcome to my uncle's record store, Ronnie," Danny said.

"Pretty cool, huh?" John said.

Ronnie nodded with his mouth open.

"Wait until you see the posters upstairs," Danny said.

"You mean there's more?" Ronnie blinked.

The boys laughed.

Eddie came out of the back room and stopped short. His mouth began to widen slowly.

"Hey, Eddie, I have someone here I would like you to meet," Danny said, stepping into Eddie's line of sight.

Eddie was mesmerized by Ronnie.

"Eddie?" Danny said, annoyed.

"Huh?" Eddie said.

"I want you to meet Ronnie. Ronnie, this is my cousin Eddie."

Ronnie and Eddie stared at each other.

"It's not polite to stare," John said, nudging Eddie.

"I ain't staring. I am just amazed," Eddie said.

"Amazed?" Danny said.

"Yeah, I try to get my hair to stick up like that, and I can't do it. What's your secret?" Eddie asked.

"Bacon grease," Ronnie answered.

Danny smiled at John.

"Really?" Eddie said in disbelief.

"No."

Slowly, Eddie realized the joke. "Oh. Ha ha."

"We're going upstairs," Danny said.

"Cool," Eddie said.

"Bring up something to drink for our guest," John said.

"Sure."

"You all right with the stairs, Ronnie?" Danny said.

"Yup." Ronnie climbed the stairs quicker than anyone expected.

"Hey, Dan," Eddie said, pulling his cousin aside. "Is he the new drummer?"

"With any luck, by the end of the afternoon, he will be," Danny said with a smile and ran up the stairs.

◻◼◻◼◻◼◻◼◻◼◻◼◻◼◻◼◻◼◻

Like most people who saw the rehearsal space for the first time, Ronnie was attracted to the posters on the wall. Seeing the large color prints comforted him, and he forgot all about being in a new space.

"Where is the picture of Marylin?" Ronnie asked.

"We don't have one," Danny answered.

"Why not?"

"Don't know."

"You don't have any pictures of Chopin, either," Ronnie remarked.

"Who?" Danny said.

"Chopin was a composer and virtuoso pianist," James said.

"Oh," Danny shrugged.

"You ready to hear us play, Ronnie?" John asked him.

Ronnie nodded and sat down on the couch. James brought over a stool for him to rest his leg on.

Eddie brought each of them a soda.

"You have any requests?" John asked Ronnie.

"As long as it isn't Chopin," Danny said.

"Guess you could play me the song that inspired your name," Ronnie said.

"Actually, Eds gave us that name," John said.

"Because the Crickets was already taken?" Ronnie asked Eddie.

Eddie smiled widely. "Yeah. You like Buddy Holly?"

"Do Buffalo Gals dance under the moon?"

Eddie scratched his head while the others laughed.

It was impossible to tell by the look on Ronnie's face if he was enjoying the music the boys were playing, but his left foot hit the pedal of an imaginary drum while his hands slapped his legs in tune with the music.

When the song finished, Ronnie lifted his hand, signifying the strike of the symbol.

"So, what do you think?" Danny asked Ronnie.

Ronnie held his thumb up but didn't say anything.

"So, I assume that means you like our audition?" John asked Ronnie.

Ronnie crossed his arms and was silent. John had never been on the receiving end of the silent answer, leaving him unsure of what to think.

"What we're wondering is, are you willing to join the group?" James asked.

Ronnie glanced at each one of them with a blank stare. "We will consider it."

Danny sat his guitar up against a chair. "You have to consult your folks?"

"I don't have any *folks*," Ronnie said.

Danny's mouth dropped. "Oh, um, I'm sorry."

Ronnie shook his head. "There's no need to be."

John picked up his soda and straddled a stool. "All right, Ronnie, who are you consulting with?"

"Otis."

"And who is Otis?"

Ronnie folded his hands in his lap. "My best friend."

Danny sat on the floor next to John. "You don't think he will like us?"

"Dunno."

"Can we meet him?" John asked.

Ronnie's thumbs rolled over each other.

James sat on the arm of the couch. "Ronnie, your best friend—is he kind of like your girlfriend?"

"Not exactly."

"Who is your girlfriend?" Danny said.

"Marylin Monroe," John said.

"What?" Danny said, looking at John, who smiled and nodded slowly.

Danny began to nod his head too. "Oh, okay, yeah."

John sat his soda bottle down and leaned forward, resting his elbows on his knees. "Ronnie, I understand why you're cautious about joining our band. You've been hurt, and you don't trust people. So, to protect yourself, you've created a private world where you can be alone and safe from ridicule and cruelties, and it works if you want to live a misanthropic existence. I can't even begin to imagine what it must be like to live the life you have, but believe me when I say we see you for who you really are: a drummer."

Danny moved close to Ronnie. "We desperately need your talent. We have to play in a contest against another band, and they have a lot of advantages over us. If you refuse to join us, we're doomed."

"Please, Ronnie, give us a chance," James said.

Ronnie reflected for a moment. "Okay, we're in."

"You mean it?" Danny said.

"Yes."

"Oh man, Ronnie, you're our hero!"

Ronnie smiled widely. "I've never been a hero."

"Get used to it," John said, setting his hand on Ronnie's shoulder.

"Does Ronnie get an initiation, John?" James asked.

John felt his chin. "I don't know. What do you think, Danny?"

"I think we wait until the whole group is here."

"Agreed. On our next rehearsal, Ronnie becomes an initiated member," John said.

"You like beer, Ronnie?" Danny asked.

"The kind that comes from a root," Ronnie said.

"Works for me," John said.

"Works for me too. I'm not fond of barley myself," James said.

"I like barley soup," Ronnie said.

Danny tilted his head. "What does barley soup have to do with anything?"

"It was a joke, Dan," John said.

Danny squinted his eyes.

"I didn't say it was a good joke," John said.

"I thought it was funny," James said.

"That's because your head is square root," John said.

Ronnie and Danny laughed.

"Now that was funny," Danny said.

The corners of James's mouth twisted, and John joined the laughter.

Ronnie spent the rest of the afternoon hanging out at the rehearsal space. As the afternoon passed, he began to relax and for the first time in his life he felt like one of the group and not like a misfit who never belonged. Maybe this time would be different, and it would be worth taking a chance. He glowed inside.

19

IT WAS ONLY TEN AM, and Monica already had a headache. The pencil tip rested against her lips as she read the want ads at the back of the Sunday paper. She had no idea what type of position she was looking for, and the task seemed daunting.

"How goes the search?" Monica's sister asked while chopping apples at the counter.

"Not so great, I'm afraid."

"What's the matter?"

Monica sighed. "I have no idea what I'm looking for."

"I think it's called a job."

"Very funny," Monica said, rubbing her eyes.

"Maybe a cup of coffee would help."

"It wouldn't hurt."

Monica adored her older sister Gina. She was her confidant and best friend.

Married with two children and one on the way, Gina's life was not easy. Living two-bedroom house with one bathroom, the couple struggled to make ends meet. Monica paid Gina what she could for letting her stay, but Gina's husband wasn't happy about the intrusion. Gina reasoned with him that they could use the extra money, and he eventually agreed Monica could stay, but only for one month.

Gina brought Monica a cup of coffee and sat down across from her with her own cup. Her hair was pulled back in a loose braid, and she was wearing a faded dress. The fatigue of being pregnant and managing a family aged the edges of Gina's once rosy cheeks, but her pleasant disposition managed to shine through.

"They're looking for help at the department store," Gina said, turning the paper toward her.

"What kind of help?" Monica asked.

Gina pointed to the ad. "Says, sales clerk, here."

"What does that mean?"

"It means you would probably be assigned a department where you would help sell the merchandise."

Monica's cheeks rose. "What kind of merchandise?"

Gina laughed. "I don't know, you would have to answer the ad."

"Would I have to put up with fussy old ladies who don't have a clue what they want or what they're looking for? And then when you suggest something, they turn up their nose in the air and scold you because you didn't give them what they wanted?"

Gina grinned over her cup. "Maybe."

Monica waved her hand in the air. "Forget it. What else?"

"A beautician?"

"Same problem, next."

Gina sighed. "Do you have any idea what you would like to do?"

Monica twitched her foot. "Be in a rock 'n' roll group."

"Uh-huh, isn't that what put you in this situation in the first place?"

Monica adverted her eyes back to the paper.

"Oh, looks like the florist is looking for help. You could make pretty flower arrangements," Gina said.

Monica contemplated the thought.

Gina took the pencil out of Monica's hand and circled the ad.

"What else?" Monica sighed.

"Here is one for a nanny."

"Obviously, I am not cut out to take care of children."

Gina and Monica paused, their words sinking below the surface.

Gina set down her coffee cup and touched Monica's forearm. "Oh Monica, how stupid of me. I didn't mean . . ."

"Don't give it another thought," Monica said, and pushing her hair behind her ear, she turned the page. "Now where were we?"

The doorbell rang, and the loud excited screams of Gina's toddlers bounced down the hall.

"Who could that be?" Gina said.

"A traveling salesman?" Monica joked.

Gina pulled herself out of her chair. "On a Sunday?"

"You want me to answer?"

"No, you keep looking."

Monica frowned and looked back at the paper. A few minutes passed before Gina returned to the kitchen with her son in her arms and her daughter clinging to the bottom of her dress.

"Who was it?" Monica asked.

"You have a visitor," Gina said.

"A visitor?"

"Yep."

Monica frowned. "Who is it?"

"Who do you think?"

Monica closed her eyes.

"You can't avoid him forever."

Monica ran her hand over her hair. "I look a fright."

"He's in the living room," Gina said with a wry smile.

Monica slowly entered the living room and found Joe dressed in jeans, a casual sweater and sunglasses. "Hello, Monica."

"Joe," Monica whispered.

"Can we talk?"

Monica clasped her hands in front of her. "Sure."

"In private?" Joe said, acknowledging the little faces that were peeking around the corner.

"Yes," Monica said, following Joe out onto the front porch.

Monica smoothed her dress and sat down on the small wooden bench by the window.

Joe removed his sunglasses and put them in his jacket pocket. "You could have at least told me where you were going."

"I was going to call you."

"When?" Joe said, turning to her.

"When I was ready."

"I know you're mad at me for hiring a replacement for Daniel, but I told you when you filled in that it wasn't going to be permanent."

Monica averted her eyes and turned her hands over each other. "I just thought maybe after you saw how much the crowd loved me, you would change your mind."

Joe folded his arms. "You know, if I made you a permanent member of the group, it would cause all kinds of problems."

"Why? Because Will would quit?"

"Yes."

Monica crossed her legs. "And he is more important to you than I am?"

"Don't start that again, Monica," Joe said, softening his tone. "You know how important you are to me."

"No, I don't. You avoided me like you always do when you think I'm upset."

Joe took a small step forward. "I didn't want to fight with you."

"I didn't want to fight with you, either. I just wanted you to talk to me."

"I would have been more than open to talking to you about something other than your disappointment and feelings of rejection. We have been over all of this before."

Monica sighed and turned away.

Joe sat down by her. "Why don't you stop this foolishness and come home?"

Monica rested her hand against her mouth.

"I miss you," Joe said, setting his hand on her knee. "We could go away for a few days like we used to."

"You can't get away; you have a contest coming up."

Joe slowly removed his hand. "I know you saw him."

"You're spying on me?" Monica said, moving away from Joe.

"Did you sleep with him?"

"What if I did?" Monica said over her shoulder.

"I would kill him," Joe said, curling his fingers.

Monica raised her eyebrow and turned to face him. "Oh, so now you're jealous?"

Joe rose to his feet. "You best not forget who you belong to."

"I'm not a possession, Joe. I'm a human being with feelings and dreams that I've neglected for far too long. This is good for us. You don't love me anymore," Monica said, retreating to the other side of the porch.

"That's not true."

Monica whirled around to face Joe. "Yes, it is. When was the last time you paid any attention to me? We don't spend any time together, and when we do, we fight. We don't make love . . ."

"You're the one who moved out of the bedroom. What did you expect me to do? Live like a monk?"

Monica folded her arms. "I think you need to go now."

"Not without you."

"I'm not going back there. I need some time to think and figure out my life."

"Your life is with me," Joe said, crossing to her.

"Don't you understand? If I go back there, nothing will have changed. Things will just go back to the way they were."

"No, they won't. I promise," Joe said, gently touching her cheek.

She wanted so badly to believe him. She wanted things to be different. Maybe things would change. Then, summoning all her courage, she took a step backward. "I'm sorry, Joe. I need some time on my own. I'm staying here."

Joe's eyes narrowed into a cold glare, but Monica didn't flinch. "Fine, if this is what you want. You stay here and have your little holiday, but I don't want you seeing him anymore."

Monica raised her chin. "I'll see whoever I want to."

"You think that little farmer boy can make you happy? Huh? Do you think he can take care of you? What is he going to do when he finds out who you really are underneath all the makeup and pretty clothes?" Joe said, waving his hand. "You forget I have known you for a very long time, and there is no way in hell he can replace who I am to you. You need me, and you know it."

Monica's jaw clenched. "I'm going to get a job."

Joe scoffed. "Doing what?"

Monica crossed her arms. "I don't know yet. Maybe I'll go work for the florist."

"The florist?" Joe laughed, making Monica's lip quiver. "There is no way you would survive on that pittance. You would need at least two jobs to pay the rent on the hovel you could afford. And then what will you do when you have broken nails, coarse hair, and callouses on your feet? You won't be wearing any satin or silk unless you're standing on a street corner."

"Get out," Monica hissed through her snarled lip.

A hateful glare ignited the inches between them.

Joe tightened his aching jaw. "I'm leaving *for now*, but you better think long and hard about your actions and the decisions you make. Because the longer you play these games with me, the harder it will be to come back to me. Am I clear?"

"Crystal," Monica said, raising her chin.

Joe turned and left the porch. Trembling, Monica went inside the house, fled down the stairs to her tiny cot, and clutched her pillow tightly to her chest. Rocking back and forth, desperation wracked her body. Joe's hateful words echoed in her head, and as much as she didn't want to admit it, he was right. How would she ever survive with hardly any money? She had no idea how to keep one job, let alone two. What would she do when she couldn't dress nicely or go to the beauty salon? She would be right back where she was when Joe met her, hopeless.

Lying down and pulling her knees up to her chest, Monica hid under the covers and cried.

20

THE BELL RANG OUT ITS resounding chime, marking the official start of summer break. Students poured out the doors in an exhilarating rush. Exclamations, cheers, and paper hung in the air as their burden was left behind them.

Oblivious to the excitement around her, Anne celebrated her own delight at finally being with John. He held her hand as they strolled slowly through the park. His usual brusque disposition was relaxed, and his affectionate essence showed through.

"Well, Miss Prim, here we are strolling through the park on a warm, sunny afternoon. The pressure of the day is over, and you're lookin' rather fetchin' today."

Rose flushed Anne's cheek. "Thank you."

"I like you in that color."

Anne glanced at her dress. "What? Light blue?"

"Not necessarily light blue, just anything but pink."

She frowned at him. "So, where are we headed?"

"I don't know. Are you hungry?"

"Do you know any place special?"

"Special?"

"Well, you know of a lot of cool places that aren't mainstream."

John laughed. "Are you implying you don't want to go to Be-Bops?"

"Well, it would be rather crowded there."

"I was thinking we could eat a hot dog in the park."

"Under the big oak tree?"

John chuckled. "Which one?"

"The one where I returned your notebook."

"Ah, that one."

"I think it's the biggest one in the park," Anne said.

"It's a historical landmark, you know," John said, stopping at the crosswalk.

"Really?"

"Yep. Legend has it that Elroy Madison planted it himself."

Holding Anne's hand firmly, they crossed the street and headed toward the hot dog vendor whose cart was set up on the corner.

"Do you know the legend?" Anne asked.

"Hmmm, that I do."

Anne waited anxiously for him to continue, but he said nothing further.

"Well? Are you going to tell me?"

"I thought, being a native to the area, you would know its history."

Anne shrugged. "Sadly, I don't."

"I see your education is lacking."

Procuring lunch, they returned to the park and sat under the formidable oak tree, which offered an abundance of welcome shade.

"I really do want to hear its history," Anne implored.

John looked thoughtfully up at the canopy of leaves. "Well, people are under the delusion that Madison claimed this land without a problem, but that's not true. This land was inhabited by a small rebel tribe of Potawatomi Indians, and they didn't take too kindly to Madison and his corporate cronies coming in here and disrupting their way of life."

Anne licked the catsup off her fingers. "So, what happened?"

John leaned back on his arm. "Well, the tribe's shaman threatened to curse Madison's family if he didn't move on, but, of course, everyone laughed and dismissed the threat as nothing more than hokum. But one night, shortly after the construction crew broke ground on the site, Madison's son got sick. At first, it looked like he had a common cold, but by the second day, he was burning up with a fever. Madison snuck out of camp that night and paid a visit to the shaman, begging him to lift the curse and spare his son's life."

"He did, of course," Anne hoped.

John sat up and crossed his hands in front of him. "He did. Under one condition."

"What was the condition?"

"That this land would forever remain untouched and sacred. It was a huge ask, but Madison agreed to the terms. Madison sealed the contract by making a blood oath with the Chief of the tribe, and he planted this tree so that he would always remember where the plot of land was."

"So, he's responsible for the tree and the park?" Anne asked.

John nodded.

The corners of Anne's lips lifted. "Is that story written down somewhere?"

John shrugged. "Dunno."

"Where did you hear it?"

John leaned closer to her. "Do you know you ask a heck of a lot of questions?"

Anne's finger lazily circled in the grass. "I just found the story interesting, is all."

A light breeze pushed a stray strand of hair across Anne's forehead. John reached up, pushing the hair away from her face, and caught the slight shimmer of infatuation in her gaze. Resting his hand on her neck, he closed the void between them. Anne closed her eyes as he pressed his lips to hers, lifting her to suspended animation above the clouds. John pulled away and gazed at her closed eyes. Smiling, he tapped the tip of her nose, causing her eyes to flutter open, as if waking up from a dream.

"You all right?" John asked.

"Of course I am," Anne said, sitting up straight.

John chuckled.

"What's so funny?"

"You."

"Me?"

"Yes, you. You look like you're twelve years old and just kissed a boy for the first time."

Anne pushed her hair back. "I'll have you know that I have kissed plenty of boys."

"Is that right?"

"Yes."

John watched her fiddling with the hem of her skirt. "How many is plenty? Two?"

Anne frowned. "No."

"Okay, three."

Anne stuck her bottom lip out at him.

"So, you must know how to French kiss?"

Anne snorted. "What? Of course I do."

Setting his hand on the ground, he leaned forward. "Show me."

Anne's breath escaped in tiny gasps as muddled thoughts tried to form an answer. John inched closer to her, making her breath labored. His free hand touched her arm, causing her to almost jump out of her skin. "You can confess, I won't judge you."

"I . . ., I. . . ."

John didn't wait for her to finish stuttering or let her brain form another conclusion. He set his hand firmly on the back of her neck and claimed her mouth as he eased his tongue between her parted lips.

The new sensation was a surprising shock, and Anne's first reaction was to pull away. Still, John held her fast and continued to pursue her tongue until the moment's pleasure began to register, and the playful entanglement eased her resistance. Pulling away was harder this time, and Anne wasn't the only one with hazy eyes.

"Did you hate it?" John whispered.

Anne shook her head and bit her lip as the corners of her mouth rose.

John reluctantly pulled away from the heat and rubbed the back of his neck. "I hate to cut this short, but I am meeting a friend today."

"Oh?"

"Yeah, there are things about me that you don't know yet."

Anne tilted her head. "Like what?"

"Like I play guitar in a rock 'n' roll band."

"You do?"

"Yep."

Anne smiled. "Wow, that sounds exciting."

"It can be."

"My goodness, I can't even get up in front of the class to read a chapter out of a book."

"You do fine. It's only when you've stolen someone's notebook that you get nervous."

"It was worth it," Anne said, sipping from her soda bottle.

"Was it?"

"It got your attention, didn't it?"

He smiled. "That it did."

"I can't wait to see you play."

"You like rock 'n' roll, Miss Prim?" John asked.

"You seem so surprised?"

John set his hands on his knees. "Okay, name an Elvis tune."

"'That's All Right.'"

"Name a Fats Domino tune."

"'Blueberry Hill.' Now I get to ask you one."

John rested his head on his hand. "You think you can stump me?"

"I bet I can."

"How much?"

She didn't answer.

"Come on, you started this."

"Okay, a soda."

John reflected. "All right, you're on."

"Priscilla Wright."

"I wouldn't consider her song to be a rock 'n' roll tune."

Anne shrugged.

"Nice try, though."

"You haven't said it yet."

"Do I have to?"

Anne lifted her chin. "If you want me to buy you a soda."

"'The Man in the Raincoat.'"

Anne curled her lip. "You win."

"I always do," John said.

Standing up, John helped Anne to her feet and headed for the bus stop.

"So, where does this lady you're going to be staying with live?" John asked.

"On 2470 Clover Street," Anne answered.

"Not that far from here."

"No, it will make it easier for us to see each other. I won't have to worry about running to catch a bus."

He turned to her and pulled her into his arms. "I am pretty busy for the next couple of days, but I was thinkin' maybe we could go out Saturday night, like on a proper date."

"That sounds so formal."

"Yeah, well, don't expect too much."

She sat her hands on his chest. "I just want to be with you."

He felt the side of her face, and they kissed, not wanting to let go. She rested her head on his arm until the bus came.

"I will see you on Saturday. I'll come by, say six?" John said.

Anne smiled. "I can't wait."

"Me either."

They kissed one more time before she got on the bus. She didn't want to go home, but she knew she would be staying at Mrs. Brewster's house and wouldn't have to worry about her parents or Steve. Her conscience's tiny voice began to mutter, disrupting her peace. Closing her eyes, she pressed the voice into silence by telling herself more lies, and it worked for now.

21

RONNIE RECLINED ON THE STEPS of Barnhardt House, waiting for John and Danny to pick him up.

The Barnhardt House was the place Ronnie had called home for the last sixteen years.

Abandoned and orphaned at three-years-old, Ronnie only had fragmented memories of his mother. A petite, soft-spoken woman, she loved Ronnie despite his imperfections, but his wealthy aristocratic father did not share his wife's feelings. When Ronnie was born, he rejected the tiny infant and exiled him to a wing in the house he never visited. Confined to his nursery, Ronnie was never allowed to grow and play like normal children. The only people he ever saw were his nurse and occasionally his mother. Spending most nights strapped down in his bed, Ronnie would scream and cry himself to sleep. One night, Ronnie escaped his prison and snuck downstairs, where his parents were hosting a large dinner party. Thrilled to see his mother, Ronnie cried out and attempted to run to her without his leg brace. His deformed limb was exposed, and Ronnie's father was enraged. Snatched up and carried back to his room, Ronnie cried out to his mother, but all she could do was cry. It was the last time he ever saw her.

Resting his arm on Otis, Ronnie tried to relax while he waited, but he had no concept of time and grew impatient. People passing by cast questionable glances, causing Ronnie's anxiety to heighten. What if they had forgotten about him? Or what if they rejected him like so many had before? Drumming his fingers against Otis's black surface helped to ease the agitation.

Danny pulled up to the curb moments after the designated time, but Ronnie thought it had been longer.

"So, you ready for your first day as an official member of the group?" Danny asked.

"I thought you weren't coming," Ronnie said.

"Why? John said.

"It's late," Ronnie snapped.

"We may be a few minutes late, but that's all," John said.

Ronnie blinked at them.

"Don't you have a watch, Ronnie?" Danny asked.

"I did, but I got frustrated with it," Ronnie answered.

"Oh?"

Ronnie nodded. "It never showed the time I wanted it to."

"I think we have all been frustrated with the time, but you can't ignore it," John said. "You just learn to work with it."

Danny put his hand on Ronnie's shoulder. "And this is coming from a man who's always late."

"Very funny," John said.

"So, when do we get to meet Otis?" Danny asked Ronnie.

"He's right here next to me," Ronnie said, patting his bass drum.

"Otis, is your drum?" John said.

"Yes. My best friend. He's afraid to leave here, you know? He's been here his whole life. What if something happens to him?"

John placed his foot on the stair and leaned on it. "What is he thinking is going to happen to him?"

Ronnie shrugged. "Any number of things."

"Like he might be mistreated and disrespected?"

"Maybe," Ronnie said, running his fingers along the edge of the drum.

"That ain't gonna happen, Ronnie. You can trust us when we say he will be treated with the utmost respect," Danny said.

"Nothing bad is going to happen. I promise," John said.

Ronnie looked at them and then nodded. "Okay."

When the boys arrived at the record store, John and Danny carried Ronnie's drum kit upstairs. While Danny and John talked on the couch, Ronnie fussed and positioned his drums in the right spot. Satisfied, Ronnie took the sticks out of his pocket and sat behind his drums.

"You don't mind if I play, do you?" Ronnie asked. "I want to ensure Otis wasn't damaged in the move."

"Be our guest," John said.

Ronnie twirled the right drumstick over his fingers and then began to play. It only took a few hard-hitting beats for John and Danny to be in heaven. Soaking up Ronnie's energy, Danny joined in. Letting his fingers pick their own rockin' course, Ronnie and Danny traveled down a rhythmically charged path.

The intriguing sound brought Eddie upstairs to enjoy the show. People passing the street could hear the tune coming from the shop's open door, and without Eddie to control them, they were quickly filling up the small space.

When the song finished, the crowd clapped with enthusiasm. The boys smiled at them as an annoyed Eddie struggled to shoo the crowd down the steps and out of the store.

James saw Jerry crossing the street a block from the record store with a new guitar case in his hand. Jerry had changed a lot since James first met him. His hair was combed in a wavy combover, and his clothes were clean and pressed.

"Hey, Jerry," James called out.

Jerry turned to see James trotting up to him. "Hey, Professor."

"Gosh, it feels like forever since I've seen you," James said, placing his hand on Jerry's shoulder.

"Yeah, it's been a while," Jerry said with an insignificant grin.

"How are things going?" James asked.

"Okay, I guess."

"You still like your job?"

"Yeah."

"How's Betty?"

"Fine," Jerry said, placing his hand in his pants pocket.

James glanced sideways at Jerry. "Are you sure everything is all right?"

"Yes. Why?"

"I don't know. You don't seem like yourself."

"I am just tired. Been working a lot of hours."

"Ah," James said with a nod.

"How are you, Professor?"

"Good. Classes are completed, and I'm looking for summer work."

"You aren't even going to take a break and have any fun?" Jerry asked.

James smiled. "Maybe a small one."

A few feet away from the store, James and Jerry saw Eddie standing on the sidewalk, waving people out of the store.

"I wonder what's going on?" James said.

"Looks like Eddie is excited about something," Jerry answered.

"Hey, Eds," James said, "what's all the hubbub about?"

"The fellas were playing a tune, and when the people heard them, they came into the store thinking there was a free concert," Eddie snapped.

"Wow," James said.

Ushering the last people out the door, Eddie took a deep breath. "You can go in now."

"Thanks," James said.

Jerry followed James upstairs. Danny, John, and Ronnie were talking when the two walked in.

"Looks like the party started without us," James said.

"Yeah, Ronnie and Danny brought in a crowd," John said.

"Eddie wasn't happy," James said.

"Eddie is just fussy," Danny said.

"Hey, Jerry," John said, smiling widely at his friend. "How have you been?"

"Okay," Jerry shrugged.

"Come here. I want you to meet Ronnie."

Jerry walked over to John.

"Jerry, this is Ronnie, our new drummer. Ronnie, this is Jerry."

"Hello," Jerry said with a polite smile. "Welcome to the group."

"Thanks," Ronnie said.

"I should probably get out my guitar. I hoped to fuss with the tuning this week but have been busy," Jerry said, sitting on the floor.

"Are we starting soon, Barnaby?" Danny asked John.

"Yeah, as soon as Stu gets here."

"Perfect. I'm gonna check on Eddie. Make sure everything is all right," Danny said, exiting the room.

James hesitated a moment before approaching John. "Hey John, I don't know if Stu is coming tonight."

"Oh?"

"Yeah, I haven't seen him in a while. I've been focused on finals."

"He did know about the practice, though, right?" John asked.

"Well, yeah, I mean, I think so. I left a message for him."

"He's got five minutes, and if he isn't here, we are going on without him," John said, picking up his guitar.

James sighed, placing his hands on his hips. "Look, I'm sorry I didn't talk to him. You want me to try and call him now?"

John adjusted his guitar strap. "Nope."

"You could have called him, you know? I'm not his keeper," James groused.

John sat on the stool closest to him. "Don't worry about it, okay? I'll talk to him."

James reflected. "I will go and find him tomorrow, all right?"

"I thought you said you weren't his keeper."

"I know it, but I feel responsible."

John rested his arm on his guitar. "Well, you're not. Stu is a big boy, and if he is going to be a part of this group, then it's time he took responsibility for himself."

"Are you going to yell at him?"

John frowned. "No, I'm not gonna yell at him."

"I will talk to him, okay? He can be so sensitive."

John gave James an even look. "Well, all right. You just need to clarify that this is important, and he needs to stay in touch with one of us."

James nodded. "Okay."

"You better strap up because we need to get started."

James took a deep breath and strapped on his guitar.

Gathered in a half circle around Ronnie, the group decided to start rehearsal with "Hound Dog" so that Ronnie could get a feel for the group's dynamic. Even before the first note, Ronnie noticed the song's almost mundane familiarity to the group. Holding his drumsticks poised, Ronnie waited for the number four to pass James's lips before giving the room a jolt with his explosive opening drum roll. Ignited by the shockwave, John's fierce opening lyric sent tremors of excitement through the collective spine of the group. Each member, spurred on by the energetic start, poured forth their creativity, progressing the song to new heights. It was both a rush and fun to feel like they were a real rock 'n' roll band.

"That was fantastic!" Danny exclaimed, crossing his hands behind his head.

"I didn't know we could sound that good," James remarked.

"I didn't know Barnaby could sing on key," Danny chuckled.

John took a playful swipe at Danny as he caught his breath.

Ronnie beamed and playfully hit the cymbal a couple of times.

John pushing back his hair breathed out. "Phew, that was almost better than . . ."

"What? Jerry asked.

John blinked, mouth half open.

"Moving on," Danny intervened, leaning closer to John, "Whadda ya say we introduce Ronnie to the dog?"

John rubbed his jaw. "Hmm, I don't know. You think he's ready?"

Danny nodded. "I think maybe so."

"What dog?" Ronnie asked.

"It's a song John wrote," Jerry explained.

Ronnie bobbed his head. "Nice."

"It's a basic twelve bar blues song," Danny said, strumming a few chords.

"With a little rock 'n' roll for good measure," John said, strumming the following two chords.

Ronnie played a few impromptu beats of his own, earning a smile from Danny.

"The song has never had an official drum part, so just sit back and see what you think. Sound good?" Danny said to Ronnie.

"Sure thing, Danny-O," Ronnie said, flipping one of his sticks.

"Okay, boys, let's crawl the dog," John declared.

With a resounding howl, the song began. Ronnie sat and patiently absorbed the initial bars, tapping out the rhythm on his leg and bobbing his head. Like Danny, Ronnie couldn't sit back and just watch. The tune was moving him and he had to join in. Jumping in on the first beat of the next bar, Ronnie's rhythmic accent gave the song the boost it needed to form the perfect song.

With the last piece of the puzzle in place, victory seemed possible.

When the song ended, John showed his approval by clapping, and the rest joined in cheering.

"I am going to say, I have never heard that song sound so sweet," Danny complimented.

John grinned at Ronnie. "I agree. You complete us, Ronnie."

Ronnie's smile radiated his pride.

John set his guitar aside. "You know, I think it's time we initiate our newest member."

"Here, here," James and Danny hooted.

"What do I have to do?" Ronnie asked.

"You need to come sit on this stool," John said, setting a stool in the middle of the room.

Ronnie got up and sat on the designated stool. James and Danny sat on the couch, and Jerry sat on the floor.

John placed his hands on Ronnie's shoulders. "Normally, the new member takes us all out for a beer, but since you aren't into that sort of thing, we did bring in some root beer."

Ronnie's grin expressed his appreciation.

"Ronnie, I can't tell you how much your agreeing to be a part of this group means to all of us. The chance of us winning the challenge we are facing seems possible now. Put your left hand on your head and hold your drumstick up with your right."

Ronnie complied.

"Do you, Ronnie . . ."

"Crocket," Ronnie finished.

"Crocket," John repeated. "Do you swear by a salmon that you promise to uphold every ruler set forth behind you, to howl at the moon regardless of its phase, to be a scoundrel whenever necessary, and to run with your pack when your liege calls for you?"

"Forsooth!"

"Then, by the power invested in me by the state of Hullyabalabooby, I now pronounce you Ronnie Crocket, a member of the misunderstanding of the Hound Dogs. May Carl Perkins forever guide your blue suede shoes."

James and Jerry clapped, while Danny opened a bottle of root beer he had been shaking. A burst of foaming bronze-colored fizz shot through the air and spattered onto everything in its path.

"Daniel!" John hollered.

"Whoops," Danny said. "I didn't think it would shoot up that far."

"Eddie's gonna throw a fit," Jerry said, looking up at the ceiling.

Ronnie began to laugh loudly, and its boisterous sound infected the rest as they all started laughing, including John, whose hair was soaked in goo.

22

J AMES ASSUMED THE LOGICAL EXPLANATION for why Stu hadn't returned his calls was because he wasn't receiving messages from his mother and sister. Stu only ignored James if he was mad at him, which was possible. James had been so wrapped up in finals and seeing Marcy that he had neglected their friendship. John told James it wasn't his fault, but he still felt guilty. The upcoming show was extremely important, and James didn't want to make the tension between John and Stu worse.

James had no clue what Stu's working hours were, so he figured early morning was his best chance to catch him at home.

James knocked on the door and waited until Carly answered the door. She was still in her pink pajamas with rosebuds on the pants. Her hair was on top of her head, held in place by a faded red ribbon with a faint trace of milk on her mouth.

"Morning, Carly," James said.

"What are you doing here so early?" Carly asked.

"I'm here to see Stu."

"He's still in bed."

"I figured as much, but I need to speak with him."

Carly wrinkled her nose. "I'm not goin' down to his stinky old room to wake him."

"I don't mind going down there," James said.

"Mama is still sleeping, so you will have to be quiet."

"I will be, I promise."

Carly opened the screen door. "I warn you, Stu doesn't always wear pajamas."

"Good to know," James said, stepping into the house.

Carly returned to her bowl of cereal in front of the TV.

James made his way down the stairs to the basement. The main room was dark, and the door to Stu's room was ajar. Thankfully, he was still in his clothes with one shoe off and one on. Lying on his stomach with his pillow over his head, Stu snored. James wasn't sure how to wake him without scaring him.

"Stu," James muttered.

Stu snorted, shifted and resumed snoring.

Reaching out, James gently shook Stu. "Stu, wake up."

"Leave me alone, you little brat," Stu said, waving his hand.

James lifted the pillow. "Stu, it's me, James."

Stu peered at James with one eye. "James?"

"Yeah, buddy, it's me."

Stu frowned. "What the hell time is it?"

"It's a little before eight."

"Like morning eight?"

"Yeah."

Stu groaned. "Why are you here so early?"

"Because I need to talk to you. It's important."

Stu turned back over. "Nothing is that important. I'll call you later."

James sighed and sat on the corner of the bed. "You'll forget to call me later."

Stu squinted at him. "You're worse than my mother, you know that?"

James smiled.

Sitting up, Stu ran his hands over his messy hair. "Why don't you go make me some breakfast?"

"What?"

"Well, you woke me up. You might as well put yourself to some good use."

James wrinkled his lips. "I'm not making you breakfast."

"Fine," Stu said, getting out of bed. Stumbling out into the main room, he went to the bathroom.

James went upstairs and waited at the kitchen table.

Stu came up a while later, his eyes half closed. He shuffled to the cupboard and pulled out a cereal bowl.

"So, what is so damn important that you had to get me out of bed?"

"You missed practice last night."

Stu poured cereal into a bowl. Several tiny pieces missed the bowl and landed on the counter. "Huh?"

"I know you didn't know about it, and that is my fault."

"When did they decide to have practice?"

James felt his temple. "Last week."

Stu straddled a chair at the table. "I'm surprised they even missed me."

"Why do you think we wouldn't miss you?"

Stu spooned out a heaping spoon of sugar and put it on his cereal. "Oh, I don't know. Call it a hunch."

"Honestly, we missed you."

"Maybe *you* did, but that is about it."

James's shoulders fell. "Is this about Danny? I know you weren't happy the night he was initiated."

Stu shrugged and put more sugar in his cereal.

"I know you don't like him."

Stu chewed a giant spoonful of cereal, leaving a trace of milk at the corner of his mouth like his sister.

"Are you going to say anything?" James asked.

"There's nothing to say."

"Look, it won't do us any good if you continue to hold this resentment. Sooner or later, you won't be able to hide it anymore, and then there will be real trouble."

Stu snorted. "You think he cares about what I want or how I feel? All he cares about is that his precious Danny is in the group. Danny is the only one he needs."

James shook his head. "That's not true."

"Oh, come on, James, who are you trying to kid? He may keep you around because you at least have some talent, but he doesn't care about me or Jerry."

"Remember what things were like when I first started to go to practice? Huh? Remember how John defended you and Jerry to Patrick? You were certain John would dump you then, but he didn't."

Stu stirred his cereal.

"I admit those two have a special relationship, but he cares about all of us. Now we have a drummer, and it's even better."

Stu lifted his eyes. "There's a drummer?"

"Yeah, he started last night."

"Cool," Stu rocked back in his chair.

"So, can you make it this afternoon?"

"Nah, I've been doing some double shifts. We're short staffed."

"When do you think you'll be back?" James asked.

Another spoonful went into Stu's mouth, and he waited until he finished chewing to answer. "I don't know, maybe Wednesday. Tuesday is my day off."

James crossed his hands. "You know, Tuesday would be better."

Stu shook his head. "Nah, I got stuff to do Tuesday."

"Like what?"

Stu shrugged. "I dunno. Stuff."

James sighed. "You know we've been rehearsing 'Johnny B. Goode' for the show. You need to be rehearsing your part."

Stu waved his hand. "I'll be fine. One run through an' I'll have it down."

"Then you need to tell John you're not coming back until Wednesday."

"Why should I have to tell him? You're the one that has been sitting here," Stu said, slurping the milk out of the bottom of his bowl.

"I think you should tell him."

Stu stood up. "You do know how much he hates phone calls, don't you?"

James groaned. "All right, I'll tell him."

"Gee thanks, buddy."

"Sure," James murmured.

Stu set his dirty bowl on the kitchen counter. "I need to get ready for work. You need anything else?"

"No, that will cover it," James said, standing. "I guess I'll talk to you later."

"Yeah. See you later."

James left the house. Stu breathed a sigh of relief and ran his hand over his hair.

□■□■□■□■□■□■□■□■□■□■□

Carly stepped into the kitchen with her bowl in her hand. "You better clean up your crumbs and wash out your bowl. Mom doesn't want to have to clean up after you anymore."

"Yeah, well, maybe I won't live here much longer, and she won't have to worry about me."

Carly blinked at Stu. "What does that mean?"

"It means I'm movin' out, little sister," Stu said, patting her on the head and moving toward the stairs.

"But what about me and mom?"

"What about you?"

Carly put her hands behind her back. "Who will watch me at night?"

"That I do not know, but I am sure she will find someone," Stu said, going down the stairs whistling.

Carly stood alone in the empty kitchen, twisting her hands. Then, slowly turning, she returned to her cartoons.

23

Anne compared the name on the street sign to the instructions her mother had written on a piece of paper. The bus had dropped her off a few blocks back, and she wanted to confirm she was headed in the right direction. Picking up her suitcase, Anne crossed the street. The heavy humid air clung to her dress as she walked through the unfamiliar neighborhood. Children running through a sprinkler in the park made her long for a spray from the cool water, but Anne decided not even the oppressive heat could ruin her cheerful mood.

The last few days before her trip had been trying. Her parents were expecting an announcement about the wedding, and Steve's patience waiting for an answer was wearing thin. Anne almost cracked under the pressure after their date the previous evening. Steve parked in the driveway and demanded an answer, but Anne batted her eyelashes and held his hands while she reasoned with him in a soothing voice. Anne hated resorting to such tactics, but it worked, and by the time Steve kissed her goodnight, he had agreed to give her more time.

The street at the edge of the park was marked Clover Street, and Anne hesitated before crossing the street that led to Mrs. Brewster's house. She had tried to forget her mother's comments about Mrs. Brewster being an invalid who could barely get out of bed. The idea of spending the next two weeks caring for the cantankerous, feebleminded, old woman worried Anne. What if she fell? Or spent all her time moaning and ordering Anne about? Pushing the disturbing thought aside, Anne squared her shoulders and crossed the street. Carefully checking the addresses as she walked down the street, Anne finally stopped outside a picket fence. Surely her mother had written down the wrong address. How could an ill old woman maintain such a charming home? Anne double checked the number before lifting the gate latch and stepping onto the cobblestone walkway.

Radiant red, white, and pink rose bush branches wound around stout trellises in front of the white clapboard house. Unable to resist, Anne felt the satin edges of a perfect pink rose. Its soporific fragrance kissed the humidity and turned the moisture to perfume. With a rejuvenated confidence, Anne stepped onto the porch and knocked on the door. No one answered. Maybe the old woman couldn't hear her knocking, so she tried again. Still no answer. Anne stepped off the porch and followed the cobblestone path to the back of the house. A woman wearing a wide-brimmed straw hat was bent over, pulling weeds out of a vegetable garden. Dressed in a blue and green checkered house dress with green rubber boots, the woman hummed. Anne was afraid she might startle her, so she spoke softly.

"Hello?"

The woman continued to hum.

"Excuse me," Anne said louder. This caught the woman's attention, and she turned to look at Anne with large brown eyes.

"Hello, I didn't mean to startle you. I am looking for a Mrs. Brewster. I am Anne Clark."

The older woman stood up straight. "Oh, my goodness, is it noon already?"

"Yes, ma'am."

"Oh, for heaven's sake, call me Mildred," Mildred said, extending a dirt-covered gardening glove.

Anne blinked.

"Forgive me, I wasn't thinking," Mildred said, wiping her hand on her dress before offering it again.

Anne smiled and shook Mildred's hand.

"Will you please hand me my cane?" Mildred said, pointing to a garden chair with a wooden cane leaning against it.

"Of course," Anne said, handing Mildred the cane.

"Thank you. Just think, if it was later in the summer, we would eat fresh vegetables."

"Indeed, we would."

"Come along, dear, let's go inside," Mildred said, stepping out of the garden. "Do you like lemonade? I made some fresh this morning."

"I would love some."

Anne followed Mildred into the mudroom, where Mildred took off her hat and gloves before entering a cheery kitchen. Yellow curtains with white eye lace borders hung in the window. A small round table and chairs sat on a lime green area rug.

"Go ahead and sit down while I pour the lemonade," Mildred said. "Do you like gingersnaps? I made them yesterday."

"Yes, please." Anne sat at the table and admired the small vase of wildflowers.

"Did you have any problems finding the house?" Mildred asked.

"No."

Mildred handed Anne a glass of lemonade. "That's good."

"Thank you," Anne said, sipping the tart drink.

"Of course, dearie."

Mildred brought over a plate of cookies and napkins.

Anne picked up the delicately embroidered napkin that matched the tablecloth. "Your napkins are lovely."

"Thank you," Mildred said, sitting with her glass of lemonade.

"Did you make them?"

"Yes, a long time ago."

Anne admired the handiwork. "I wish I knew how to sew like this."

"Do you like to sew?"

Anne shrugged. "Sewing isn't exactly my mother's favorite hobby."

Mildred laughed. "Well, I can show you if you like."

"I would like that."

"Good," Mildred said, sipping her lemonade.

Anne nibbled on her cookie. "You have a lovely home."

"I like to think so. It's small, but I don't need a lot of room now that it's just Boots and me."

"Boots?"

"Yes, he is my cat. Do you like cats?"

"Yes. We don't have any pets at home, but someday I hope to have one," Anne said, wiping her hand on the tiny napkin.

"Boots is shy at first, but once he gets to know you, he will be purring beside you."

"I look forward to meeting him."

Mildred took a cookie from the plate. "So, Emogene didn't tell me much about you. All she said was you were young and attending college."

"Yes, I attend the Junior College in Madison."

"What are you studying?" Mildred inquired.

"I hope to be a teacher someday."

Mildred smiled. "That is a fine career. I taught school at one time."

"You did?"

"Yes. It was rewarding at times, but it could also be very challenging. Especially if you had little rascals causing trouble."

Anne chuckled. "Yes, I realize children can be mischievous."

"You want to teach grade school?"

"Yes."

Mildred took another cookie.. "Emogene told me that you're engaged?"

The question surprised Anne, and she almost choked on her drink.

"My goodness, dear. Are you all right?"

Anne wiped her mouth with a napkin. "Yes, I just swallowed wrong. I'm not engaged."

"Oh, but there is a special young man?"

Anne looked at the napkin in her lap. "Actually, I hope to see a young man in town while I'm here. If it's all right with you, of course. I don't want you to think I will be inattentive to your needs. After all, I did promise to look after you."

Mildred waved her hand. "My goodness, child, of course, it's all right with me. I am perfectly capable of spending an afternoon or evening here by myself."

"It would only be a couple of times."

"Listen, my daughter doesn't think I can care for myself. She fusses over me all the time. Constantly calling and checking up on me. You would think I needed a babysitter."

Anne laughed.

"True, I am older than I used to be, and sometimes my arthritis acts up, or my knee hurts, but I manage."

"Well, I want to help you as much as possible."

"I know, dearie," Mildred said, patting Anne's hand. "Now, why don't you come with me, and I will show you around? Then you can settle into your room."

"All right," Anne agreed.

The rest of the house was just as welcoming as the kitchen. Handmade decorations with light pastel accents complimented the home's country-themed rooms. The guest room's brass bed had a handmade patchwork quilt. A nightstand, a small dresser, and a white wicker chair completed the furnishings, but the open window that brought in the smell of roses was the room's best feature. Anne settled into the room by putting some things in the small closet and dresser. Slipping into a light pink sweater, Anne secured the pearl buttons. Her earlier fears had disappeared, and the next two weeks seemed brighter and full of promise. Checking her beaming reflection in the mirror, Anne left the room to join Mildred on the porch, where they would spend a quiet afternoon chatting, laughing, and enjoying the smell of the roses.

24

JOE BUTTONED HIS SUIT JACKET and stepped onto the curb in front of The Beat. His sleek black Jaguar was already attracting curious pedestrians and shopkeepers along Mulberry Street.

Eddie recognized the car right away because he still dreamt about the night when he went for a ride in it. Forgetting that Joe was considered the enemy, Eddie rushed to meet him at the door.

"Hey, Mr. Delaney," Eddie said with a squeak in his voice.

Joe glanced at the magnified eyes and wide smile. "Hello, Eddie."

Eddie couldn't believe Joe remembered his name, and he was over the moon.

"Mind if I come inside?" Joe asked Eddie, who was blocking the door.

"Oh, yeah, sure, of course, come in!" Eddie stepped back and swept his hand out like he was welcoming a king.

Joe stepped into the store and tucked his sunglasses into his jacket pocket.

"Welcome to The Beat!"

Joe walked slowly into the store and quietly observed his surroundings.

"Pretty neat, huh?" Eddie said, puffing his chest out.

Joe nodded coolly.

"Can I get you a soda?"

Joe turned to Eddie and chuckled, "I haven't had a *soda* since I was fifteen."

"Oh, yeah," Eddie said, his face turning red.

Joe casually walked down the first row of records, glancing at album titles. "You got any jazz, Eddie?"

"What? Of course! About halfway up the next aisle."

"You like jazz?"

Eddie followed behind Joe as he continued his stroll. "Of course I do."

"Chet Baker?" Joe asked.

"Yeah, and Billie Holiday."

Joe smiled. "I knew you had good taste."

Eddie jutted his chin out, and his cheeks hurt from smiling.

Joe stopped to flip through some records. "So, is Danny here?"

"No, he isn't here yet."

"You are expecting him?"

"Yes, anytime."

Joe nodded. "What's upstairs?"

"The group's rehearsal space."

"Do you mind if I go up and look around?"

Eddie opened his mouth when a group of curious spectators wandered into the store. Annoyed, Eddie crossed to them. "Can I help you?"

"Who is that?" an older woman asked in a quiet voice.

"Is it Frank Sinatra?" another asked.

"No, it's not."

"He must be famous if he drives a car like that," the first woman asked.

"As a matter of fact, he is a friend of mine, and he is a guest in my store. So, if you all wouldn't mind waiting outside." The group groaned and left the store. Eddie turned to Joe. "Sorry about that. I know it's hard to have crazed fans following you around."

Joe chuckled. "If it's all right, I will wait for Danny upstairs."

"Okay, you need me to show you around?"

"No, I'll be fine," Joe said, ascending the stairs.

Eddie smiled and went outside to deal with the people that were gathering out front.

□■□■□■□■□■□■□■□■□■□■□

Danny figured he was hallucinating when he saw the Jaguar parked in front of The Beat. He wanted to believe that it wasn't Joe's, but who else would drive such an expensive, exclusive car?

John let out a low whistle. "My gosh, will you look at that sweet piece of tail pipe? You think Bob decided to get a new car?"

Danny paid no attention while he parallel parked his car.

"Hey, Dan, are you all right?" John asked.

"Sure, why wouldn't I be?"

"Well, I dunno. I thought you would be impressed by that car."

"I am," Danny said, opening up his car door and getting out.

"I wonder who it belongs to?" John remarked as followed Danny into the store.

The sound of piano music stopped Danny and John abruptly at the door.

"Do you hear that?" John asked Danny.

Danny hesitated and rubbed his neck. "Yeah, I hear it."

Lost in a spellbound daze, John followed the notes to the bottom of the stairs and listened intently. The piano was obviously being played by someone with skill, and the oddest part of all was the piano was in tune.

John cast his eyes toward Eddie, who was cowering behind a magazine. John stepped over and snatched the magazine out of Eddie's hands.

Eddie smiled at John's glare. "Oh, hello, I didn't hear you come in."

"Why do I hear piano music coming from upstairs?" John asked.

"Umm . . ." Eddie sputtered.

"Did I or did I not say no *women* are allowed in the rehearsal space?" John said, glancing at Danny, then Eddie, then back to Danny.

"You did?" Eddie said.

John narrowed his eyes at Eddie, who shrugged.

"I am going up those stairs and escorting her little blond behind to the door, and no one better try and stop me." With those words, John ascended the stairs.

Eddie looked at Danny with wide eyes.

"Barnaby," Danny said, racing to the bottom of the stairs, but he was too late. John was already at the top and walking in through the door.

"Oh boy," Eddie said.

◻◼◻◼◻◼◻◼◻◼◻◼◻◼◻◼◻◼◻◼◻

With stern words aching to leave his mouth, John's determined footsteps entered the rehearsal space.

"All right, you've had your fun. This isn't your personal playroom, and you don't have my permission to be here. So, get on your feet because I am escorting you to the door. Now!"

Stopping short with his anger in full bloom, John realized the person he was yelling at was not Monica. His mind couldn't register the grinning image before him, and he blinked his eyes in disbelief.

"Dildothorpe, fancy meeting you here," Joe said.

By now, Danny had caught up to John, who was still speechless.

"Hello, Danny," Joe said.

Danny's breath turned to a rock in his throat.

"What? No greeting for me?" Joe remarked with a small smile.

John gritted his teeth. "Dalamey. What ill wind blew you in here?"

Joe pushed away from the piano and stood up. "I was in the neighborhood and thought I would drop in on some old friends."

John's fingers tensed. "Cut the crap, what do you want?"

Joe brushed past John and stood in the middle of the room. "What I want is to talk to Danny alone."

Danny shut his eyes.

"If you think I'm leaving you alone with Danny for one second, you can think again," John growled.

Joe looked at the tips of his fingers. "What I have to say to Danny would be best said in private, but if he wants you to stay, that is totally his decision."

"Maybe you better step out for a few minutes," Danny said to John.

John blinked. "What?"

"Please," Danny said, averting his eyes.

John paused, daring to face Joe's complacent grin. John turned and left the room, closing the door after him.

The unsettling silence fought to suffocate Danny. He wasn't sure why Joe was so quiet. If he thought it would make him more intimidating, he was right.

"You know why I'm here, Danny?" Joe asked, withholding eye contact.

"I can guess," Danny answered.

Joe took a few steps forward and studied the poster in front of him. "I know you took Monica out the other night."

"She stopped by the store earlier and looked like she could use a friend."

Joe crossed his arms and slowly turned. "Is that what you consider yourself to be? Her friend?"

"Well, yes, of course," Danny said, folding his arms for comfort from Joe's glower.

"She told you we separated, and you just figured you would be a shoulder to cry on, is that it?"

"Something like that."

Joe took a taunting step forward. "I am only going to say this to you once, and I would recommend that you listen very closely. I want you to stay away from her."

Danny anchored his feet. "You know, she may have been your girlfriend, but you can't tell her what to do."

Joe narrowed his eyes. "Is that right?"

"Yes. She's her own woman and can choose to spend time with whoever she pleases. It's not like she has a ring on her finger."

"That's because she doesn't wear it."

Danny's mind went blank, and words failed him. "What?"

"Judging by the look on your face, you understood what I said just fine."

Like a deflated balloon, Danny let his breath out and sank onto the piano bench. "I had no idea."

"Of course, you didn't know, but now that you do, you will put her out of your life period."

Danny lifted his chin and looked Joe square in the eye. "I will not see her anymore. You have my word."

Joe observed Danny's granite features before shifting his position. "You know, despite our differences, I admire your chivalry, your code of honor. Young men with morals like you are rare. Don't let the cruelties of this world change you."

Joe walked to the door, then, taking something out of his pocket, he turned to Danny. "I did what I could, but you will still need a professional to come in and finish the job." Joe tossed Danny the piano's tuning hammer.

"Thanks," Danny said.

Joe nodded and left the room. Going down the stairs, he saw Eddie sorting magazines at the front counter.

"Everything all right, Mr. Delaney?" Eddie asked.

"Eddie, when are you going to call me Joe?"

"I just was trying to be respectable."

Joe chuckled. "That is quite a refreshing change, considering who your friends are."

Eddie shrugged as Joe coolly set his hand on the counter.

"I look forward to seeing you at the community center show. You will be there?"

"Of course," Eddie said.

Joe paused. "Oh, I forgot. You will be with the losers. We can still be friends, though, right, Eddie?"

"Well, yeah, sure," Eddie replied.

Joe smiled. "I knew you were better than the rest. Someday, you and I will need to discuss your future."

"My future?"

"You are wanting to go into the management side of the business, right?"

Eddie nodded with wide eyes.

Joe winked. "Talk to you later, Eddie."

Eddie was dumfounded as Joe left the store.

Joe reached into his pocket for his sunglasses when he saw John casually leaning up against the wall. "Admiring my car, Dildothorpe?"

"Actually, I was contemplating how long it would take for the air to leak out of your tires."

Joe narrowed his eyes.

"It's a dangerous neighborhood, you know."

"How I would love to wipe that smug look off of your face," Joe said through his teeth.

"What is stopping you?"

Joe cracked his knuckles.

John ginned. "Come on, Dalamey. One punch, and I put us all out of our misery."

Joe stood his ground, his focus like a bull looking at a red cape. "You think you're better than me, don't you? You think I'm too old to lay your punk ass out, but you're wrong. I used to box in high school."

John laughed. "Those matches have rules, but out here, there are no rules. You see, I was trained in a different ring. One where nothing is fair. People hold you down and let others beat you senseless until you bleed so much you think you're gonna die. Then they leave you lying there in filth, with your pants down and no dignity left. If you're lucky, they might leave you alone for a week, but it's usually more like a couple of days before they wait to pounce on you again, because once is never enough."

Joe's eyes stayed focused, but they were losing their malice as he relaxed his shoulders.

John turned his head and rested it on the wall.

Joe put his sunglasses on. "We settle this at the community center, then."

"You better hope your group plays fair, no tricks," John said.

"It will be fair. You have my word on it," Joe said, offering his hand.

John looked at Joe's hand and then stared through the covering over Joe's eyes, but Joe didn't withdraw his gesture of honor. John relented and shook Joe's hand.

Joe withdrew and walked to the driver's door, gave John one last look before getting in the car, and disappeared up the street.

25

EVER SINCE SHE WAS OLD enough to hold a pencil, Nancy Calhoun dreamed of being a newspaper reporter. The breathtaking stories, the sound of a clacking typewriter, shouting voices, and the smell of ink on the paper thrilled Nancy.

Every day she waited for the newspaper boy to deliver the paper. Then, sitting at the kitchen table, she carefully took the rubber band off and settled down with a pencil and paper to make notes of worthy news stories. The smell of the printed page transformed the kitchen into a busy newsroom. Pretending to be the editor, she combed every page with a critical eye.

"Looks like your story about the trash fire behind the market is weak, Mr. Pomboy," she said, shaking her pencil at the teddy bear on the table. "Details, we need details!"

With its red felt tongue and crooked eye, the bear always listened intently.

"I need to smell the fire! I need to feel the heat from the flames! You need to work on your imagery," Nancy ordered.

After critiquing the paper, she refolded it perfectly and set it on the end table next to her father's easy chair.

With notes in hand and Mr. Pomboy under her arm, she would go to her room and cut out stories and pictures to paste into her scrapbooks.

By the time Nancy turned seventeen, she knew everything there was to know about Madison and the local paper: from the editor's name to the reporters and the ladies who wrote the society columns. It felt like a dream come true when she was hired as a copygirl. She couldn't wait to start working for the paper, and once they saw her talents, she would be a reporter!

Unfortunately, the editor of the paper and the other reporters didn't share her enthusiasm. They laughed at her story ideas and told her that her job was to be quiet and do what she was told, but the rejections didn't faze Nancy. She knew there was a newsworthy story in Madison. She just had to find it.

<hr>

The boisterous frenzied chatter and the infectious beat pulsing from the jukebox ignited the atmosphere at Be-Bops. The restaurant was filled with teens coming in for a soda, malt, or just to mingle with friends.

Lucky enough to find a table, Nancy sat in a booth with her girlfriends. Their conversation about the latest fashion trends, nail polish, Elvis, and boys bored Nancy. A thin, short girl with blunt cut wavy sandy blond hair and cat eyeglasses, Nancy had no interest in any of those subjects. To her, fashion was a waste of time when she was perfectly happy wearing a plaid skirt, knee-high socks, and saddle shoes. Concentrating on current events and observing the activity on the street was way more interesting.

"Are you going to eat your French fries, Nancy?" her best friend, Carol, asked.

Nancy's soda straw was still in her mouth as she daydreamed.

"Earth to Nancy," Lois said, waving her hand in front of Nancy's face.

Nancy blinked. "Wha'?"

Carol dipped a French fry in the ketchup.

"For heaven's sake, Nancy. Have you not been listening to us?" Lois said, disgusted.

"Elvis could walk right in here, and Nancy would never know," Carol said, traces of ketchup on the edge of her mouth.

"Of course I would," Nancy said, chasing the cherry around the bottom of her empty dish.

"Okay, tell us the name of our waiter?" Lois asked.

Carol nibbled on the tip of another French fry. "He's so dreamy."

"Who? Todd Kramer?" Nancy said.

"You know him?" Lois said.

Nancy adjusted her glasses. "Yes, unfortunately."

Lois fluffed the lime green scarf around her neck. "Do you think you could introduce him to me?"

"I guess so," Nancy sighed and sat back.

Lois. Poor delusional Lois. Just because she wore pretty clothes and had long, brown hair, she thought every boy within twenty miles wanted to date her. The problem was, Lois had a big nose and wore too much makeup, trying to draw attention from it. And Carol, well, Carol had been Nancy's friend since middle school. Carol pretended to care about fashion trends and boys, but Carol's first love was food. If she cared as much about her appearance as she cared about food, she would have been quite pretty, but instead acne plagued her pleasant, round face.

With her mouth open, Lois picked up a menu and sat it on the table. "Oh no! She's here!"

"Who?" Nancy said.

"Susan," Lois mouthed.

"Where?" Carol said, sticking her head up.

Lois grabbed her sweater and pulled her forward. "Stay down! I don't want to talk to Miss Smarty Pants!"

"Hello, girls."

Lois looked up to see the judgmental glance of Susan Edwards. Susan was a pretty girl with thick blond, shoulder-length hair and petite features. Her strong, opinionated attitude made most girls think she was a snob. Nancy was the only friend Susan hadn't managed to ostracize since grade school. So, wherever Nancy was, Susan would join, invited or not.

Lois forced a smile. "Hello, Susan."

Susan nudged her way beside Lois on the bench. She looked across the table at Carol.

"What are you eating?"

"Nothing," Carol said with a full mouth.

"You're going to have a new crop of pimples in the morning," Susan said, tossing her hair.

Todd came over, dressed in his official light blue Be-Bops uniform. He smiled at Susan. "Hey, Susan, whadda ya have?"

Susan twirled her hair around her finger and glanced at the menu she had seen a hundred times.

Lois kicked Nancy under the table and tilted her head toward Todd.

"Hey, Todd," Nancy said.

He looked over at her. "Hey, Nancy."

"This is my friend, Lois," Nancy said, pointing at Lois, who scowled at her.

"I'll have a Bubble Up," Susan said.

"Sure thing," Todd said, winking at her as he walked away.

Susan paid no attention to the wink, and Lois fumed over it.

"So, what's new, Susan?" Nancy said, wanting to lighten the mood.

"Oh, you know, the same old boring thing."

"I like your sweater," Carol said. "Is it Angora?"

Susan ran her hand over the luxurious baby blue material. "Yes, but I'm not sure if I like it."

Carol looked at her old torn cardigan and ate another cold French fry.

"You're crazy," Lois said. "Anyone in their right mind would love that sweater."

"I suppose it's all right."

Todd returned with Susan's soda and sat it in front of her. "Here you go. Can I get you girls anything else?"

"How long have you been working here?" Lois asked.

"Not long. I'm just trying to make a few dollars before I head to college in the fall."

Lois batted her eyes. "Oh, a college man. How ginchy."

Nancy rolled her eyes.

"Can we get the check?" Carol said. "I have a baby sittin' job tonight."

"Sure," Todd said, reaching into his pocket and laying the check on the table. "I'll be back," he said, walking away.

Carol looked at the check, opened her tiny coin purse, and fished out her money.

"So, what movie is showing at the theater Friday night?" Lois asked Nancy.

"I think it's *South Pacific*."

Lois looked at her reflection in her compact. "I get so tired of the same boring thing week after week. Why I've seen that movie so many times, I think I could recite the lines."

"Oh, I don't know," Susan said, "if you're with the right boy, the movies can be kinda fun."

Lois giggled, Nancy wasn't listening again, and Carol's face fell, having never been on a date.

"Most of the handsome boys in this town are taken. The average ones are working and the others, well, the others are a waste of time," Lois said.

"Oh, I don't know. Todd isn't that bad-looking," Susan said, glancing over at Todd, who was taking an order at another table.

Lois tore off the corners of a napkin. "Do you know him?"

"Not intimately," Susan said.

Carol blushed and sunk down further in her seat.

"Still, this town is so boring," Lois complained. "I feel like I will be fifty before something exciting happens."

Susan sipped on her straw coolly. "Well, there will be a rock 'n' roll show at the community center in a few weeks."

Lois's eyes lit up. "The community center? Are you joking?"

"No joke." Susan said.

"Why didn't you say something sooner?"

Susan shrugged. "I guess it slipped my mind."

Nancy knew it hadn't slipped her mind. She just wanted to drop it at the right moment.

Lois shifted in her seat. "Give us the details?"

"It's just two local bands putting on a show."

"What two local bands?" Nancy said, gaining interest.

Susan swung her foot. "I don't recall, exactly."

Todd came back. "Are we set?"

"Say, Todd, have you heard about two local groups playing at the community center?" Lois asked.

"Oh yeah, there's a flyer posted by the bathrooms and one hanging by the door."

"Would you mind bringing it over here?" Nancy asked.

Todd chuckled. "I can't just rip it off the wall."

Susan lowered her eyelashes. "Please."

"Oh yeah, sure," Todd said, tripping over his feet to do her bidding.

When he returned with the flyer, Nancy snatched it away from Lois.

"The Hound Dogs and Joey and the Moon Rockers?" Nancy said.

Carol looked over Nancy's shoulder. "Who are they?"

"Who cares? They're playing a live show at the community center. Tickets are only a quarter!" Lois said.

"Have you heard of them, Todd?" Nancy asked.

Todd folded his arms. "I've heard of the Hound Dogs. They played at Len's birthday party."

"Oh, I remember now," Lois said. "There was some guy there wearing a leather jacket. So dreamy."

"Yeah, I remember hearing something about it," Carol said.

Nancy stared at the flyer. "I remember that show too."

"You were there?" Carol said.

"Well, no, but I heard about it."

"It was in the paper?"

Nancy looked at Carol. "Not everything that happens in this town makes the papers, Carol. That's why I work so hard looking in all the places where a news story might be hiding."

Carol closed her eyes and shook her head.

Lois snatched the flyer back. "Well, I, for one, am going. How about you, Todd?"

Todd looked at Susan. "I don't know. Maybe I will."

Susan looked at him over the rim of her soda bottle.

"I wish I could go to the show," Carol said, slightly shrugging her shoulders.

"You probably could if you wore a nice dress," Susan said.

"What about you, Nancy?" Lois asked.

"Her parents won't let her go," Carol whispered.

Nancy frowned at Carol, snatched the flyer back, and stared at it. "Your mother wouldn't let you, either. They say shocking things happen at those rock 'n' roll shows."

"Like what?" Carol said, her eyes wide.

"I can't say."

"Oh no, Miss Newspaper Reporter, you started this. What's the dirt?" Lois said.

Todd leaned on the table. "Yeah, don't hold out on us now, Nan."

Nancy looked over her shoulder and then leaned forward. "Well, I read that the music draws an unruly crowd, and dancers move in suggestive ways."

"Really?" Carol said, chewing on her straw.

"Yeah, and there is booze, smoking, and dark corners where couples can, you know," Nancy said, nodding and moving her eyebrows up and down.

"Neck?" Todd chuckled. "You can do that in the balcony at the movie theater."

"Unchaperoned?" Nancy whispered.

Todd whistled.

"Sounds dangerous," Carol said.

"I am totally going," Lois squealed.

Lois's prattle drifted into background noise as Nancy studied the crude drawing of a dog looking up at the smiling moon. How could there possibly be a group in town that she had never heard of? She knew about the Hound Dogs but had never heard of Joey and Moon Rockers. A glimmer of excitement flicked in Nancy's mind. This could be the break she had been waiting for her whole life! A mystery right here in boring, old Madison! Just think, if she uncovered something big, Mr. Cummings would have no other choice but to print her story. It may even make the front page! Smiling to herself, Nancy pulled out an old pencil from her purse and started to make notes on the back of a Be-Bops napkin.

26

J ERRY SUCKED ON THE STRAW, but not even one little shard of crushed ice remained at the bottom of the cup. Betty had drunk all the soda. Disgusted, Jerry glanced at her sideways. Her tiny hands clenched the popcorn container that rested close to her blue chiffon dress. One by one, Betty

popped delectable butter-covered kernels past her pouty lips. With every tormenting crunch, the wrinkle on Jerry's forehead pulled tighter. Buttered popcorn was one of his favorite treats, and she was intentionally needling him.

Pressed against the armrest, Jerry knocked the hollow cup against his knee. How could sweet, kind, shy Betty be so aggravating? Had he not been devoted to her? He loved coming home after work and spending his free time with her. It was when he started to go to band practice that Betty became unhappy, moody, and snippy. He hoped that a romantic evening at the movies would make it easier to talk to her, but her unwavering mood only added to the weight of the unspoken conflict between them.

Betty dropped the empty popcorn container on the floor with a thud. Then, shifting in her seat, she sighed loudly. Jerry ignored her attempt for attention and kept his eyes glued to the screen.

"Go get me another soda," Betty finally said to him.

Jerry looked over at her. "No."

"What?" Betty snapped.

"You drank the last one by yourself. You've had more than enough sugar for one night."

Betty's eyes narrowed, and she glared at the side of Jerry's head, but he kept his eyes glued to the screen. Crossing her arms tightly across her chest, Betty sulked in her seat.

The couple sitting in the row in front of them were necking heavily. It was impossible to ignore them because they were blocking Betty's view. The passionate, entangled pair annoyed Betty because they reminded her of what she was missing out on.

"I want to move," Betty said to Jerry.

"What?"

"I can't see from this seat and want to move."

"Betty, the movie has started, and no more seats are available."

"Shhh," the man sitting beside Jerry hissed.

"There are seats in the front row," Betty said.

"Sitting that close hurts my neck."

"Then stay here." Betty got out of her seat and disrupted the couple sitting beside her by almost knocking their popcorn into their laps.

Jerry sighed.

The young man leaned over Betty's seat. "Your date needs to be taught some manners."

Jerry looked at him, then turning his eyes forward, he clicked his tongue. Standing up, Jerry stepped next to the young man, thumped the bottom of the popcorn container, sending it into orbit. Popcorn rained down on the young man and his date, and while she was shrieking, Jerry exited the row.

❑■❑■❑■❑■❑■❑■❑■❑■❑■❑■❑

The rest of the movie passed without incident, and the two left the theater. If it had been a typical Saturday night, Jerry would have taken Betty to Be-Bops to share a hot fudge sundae, but

Betty hadn't made any further conversation with Jerry, and his neck was cramped. He hated confrontation, but he knew he would lose sleep again if he didn't find out what was bothering her.

They were crossing the street corner before the house when Jerry stopped under a streetlight. "Betty, we need to talk."

Betty turned to him with her chin jutted out.

Jerry sighed. "Will you please tell me why you're so mad?"

"You know why I'm mad," Betty spat.

"I suppose I do."

"You suppose?"

"Well, it's not like you told me."

Betty whirled around and started to walk forward.

Groaning, Jerry followed behind her and stepped in front of her. "Betty, I think I deserve an explanation."

Betty folded her arms. "I am mad because you've been neglecting me."

"I have not been neglecting you!"

"You have left me at home alone for the last two nights!"

"You know I had rehearsal."

Betty tapped her foot.

"What do you want me to do? Quit the group?"

Betty reflected, her foot still tapping. "I think I should be your number one priority."

Jerry sat his hands on her arms. "You know you are."

"Well, then, I shouldn't have to sit at home alone."

Jerry pulled his hands away. "You're being unreasonable."

"Am I?"

"Yes, you are."

"Fine then, maybe I will just find someone who wants to put me first!"

Jerry folded his arm. "Maybe you should, then."

Betty's eyes flashed. "At least I won't be wasting time waiting on you!"

"If that's what you want."

Betty's fingers clenched into tight balls. "I don't ever want to see you again!"

"Good luck because I live here too," Jerry said.

"Oooo!" Red-faced, Betty stormed up the walkway and inside the house.

Jerry took a deep breath and leaned up against the fence. Looking up at the night sky, he wondered if Betty would really start dating other guys. He couldn't bear the thought of it, but it wasn't fair of her to make him choose. If he gave in to her demands, he would be doing it for the rest of his life, and he would be back in the prison he had just gotten out of. It would be hard to not to cave and beg her to take him back, but it was time that Betty learned she couldn't get her way by throwing a tantrum. Sighing, Jerry completed his walk to the house alone.

27

IFE WITH MILDRED WAS QUIET and simple. With no studies and no stressors, Anne was free to be herself and relax. Each day, she learned something new, from planting in the garden, to helping prepare the meals and sewing lessons. It was easy to learn from Mildred because she was patient and guided Anne's hands while she learned each new skill. In the evenings, they would sit in the living room, sewing and listening to the radio, or Mildred would share one of her extraordinary life stories. Boots warmed up to Anne and sometimes stretched out on the back of the couch. His large, fluffy grey tail would sway while he watched the needle pull the string.

Every night before bed, Anne would sit on the window seat in her room and write an accurate narrative of the day's events in her diary. She wanted to remember the stories for comfort when she was back at home.

◻◼◻◼◻◼◻◼◻◼◻◼◻◼◻◼◻◼◻◼◻

Saturday afternoon, Anne fussed over finding the perfect outfit for her date with John. Being with him was always an adventure, and she wanted to be ready for anything. Deciding on a pair of houndstooth pedal pushers, tennis shoes, and a red pullover sweater, she swept her blonde hair back in a curly ponytail. With a polka-dot scarf around her neck, she added a faint touch of makeup, then sprayed on a hint of perfume behind each ear. Satisfied, she left her room to join Mildred, who was reading in the sunroom.

"Well, how do I look?" Anne asked, twirling around in a circle.

Mildred looked up from her book. "You look lovely."

"You don't think it's too casual, do you?"

"Where is he taking you?"

Anne bounced on the balls of her feet. "I'm not entirely sure. John is a bit unconventional."

"Oh?"

"Like an explorer of sorts."

"Ah, then you should be just fine. Is tonight your first date?" Mildred said, setting her book aside.

Anne swung her arms. "Sort of. Are you sure you will be all right here by yourself tonight?"

"For heaven's sake, child. I have told you a hundred times, I will be fine. I have lived alone for many years, you know."

Anne clasped her hands in front of her. "I know. It's just that I made a promise to look after you."

"And you have been doing a wonderful job. I just know that I will have a bountiful harvest come fall."

Anne twisted her hands. "I wish I could be here to see it."

"You know you can come and visit any time you like."

Like a wilted flower, Anne sat on the couch.

"What is it, dearie?" Mildred asked.

"Oh, nothing."

"You can't kid an old woman. You were lit up like a firefly, and now you look like the sun's being choked by rain clouds. Now come here and sit by me."

Anne moved to the footstool next to Mildred.

"Why the gloomy face?"

Anne shrugged. "I don't know. I guess I'm just not looking forward to the fall."

"Why not?"

Anne wished she could share her thoughts and feelings with Mildred, but she had to keep her secret safe inside.

Mildred sat her hand on Anne's shoulder. "It's all right if you don't feel like talking about it."

Anne glanced up at Mildred. "I do want to talk about it—just not right now."

Mildred patted Anne's hand. "I understand. We can talk about it any time you like."

Anne smiled and looked at the clock. "Oh, my goodness, he'll be here any minute. I better grab my purse!"

Mildred smiled as Anne's exuberance returned, and she bounced out of the room.

❑■❑■❑■❑■❑■❑■❑■❑■❑■❑

Anne sat on the porch, patiently waiting for John to arrive. She knew he was always late, but she thought it was their first date, and he might have made an effort to be on time. Thoughts of doubt that he might not show at all began to creep into Anne's mind when she heard the low rumbling of a small motor.

Walking out to the sidewalk, she saw John coming down the street on a motorcycle. He pulled up along the curb, lifted the goggles from his eyes, and rested them on his head with a smile.

"My goodness, I didn't know you had a motorcycle," Anne said.

John shut off the engine and got off the bike. "I don't. A friend of mine has been tuning the engine and wanted me to take it out for a spin."

"Oh," Anne said with a quick nod.

"I see you're wearing pants," John said.

"Is that all right?"

John tilted his head. "I don't know. Why don't you turn around in a circle for me?"

Anne turned around.

"Okay, but slower this time. I want to ensure those are the proper pants for riding on a motorcycle."

Anne slowly turned around, and he had a roughish grin when she turned back to face him.

"I assume they meet with your approval?" Anne asked with blushed cheeks.

"Anything that is not pink meets my approval."

Anne twitched her nose.

"So, have you ever ridden on a motorcycle before?"

"No. I've heard they're dangerous."

"Well, if you don't sit properly and hold on tight, then yeah, they can be." Taking a step closer to her, he handed her his goggles. "Put these on."

Anne frowned at them.

"What's the matter?"

"Are you sure I have to wear these?"

"It will help to protect your face. Now put them on."

Anne didn't like the thought of her hair getting mussed or her makeup smearing, but judging by the stern look on John's face, she decided to comply.

John straddled the bike. "Now, all you need to do is wrap your arms around me and hold on tight. You think you can do that?"

"Yes."

John helped her climb on behind him, and she placed her arms around his middle.

"Tighter," John said. "I don't want you falling off."

Anne moved closer and squeezed tighter. "Where are we going?"

"You'll see."

John started the bike and pulled away from the curb.

The loud rumbling engine and the fast-forward motion robbed Anne of her breath as she held onto John with all her strength.

Reaching down, John gave her hand a reassuring squeeze that eased her fear. Anne assumed they were going to downtown Madison, but when the bike turned down an unfamiliar road headed in the opposite direction, a slight adrenaline spike flashed through her veins. Anne had never traveled north to the edge of town, and a new adventure lay before her as the bike turned left onto a narrow road that curved and turned till it followed the creek on its rippling path. Straight ahead, the large ominous structure of the steel mill dominated the darkening skyline. Clouds of thick, dark smoke choked out the last rays of the setting sun. All signs of nature had been exterminated by the cruel conditions, leaving the mill on a lifeless, decimated hill.

Dipping down, the road went under a viaduct before rising once more to curve around to the east side of the mill. Then a right turn on an unmarked driveway led them up a hill and to the other side of a tall, uneven wooden fence that ran the perimeter of an unfamiliar property. John slowed down as he pulled up to the gate and turned off the bike.

"Where are we?" Anne asked him.

John smiled. "The shores of forgotten treasure."

28

T HE LARGE CLOSED, PADLOCKED GATE with a *No Trespassing* and a
Beware of Dog sign nailed to a wooden plank was not a welcoming
message to Anne or anyone else that might approach the derelict
property. Ringlets of barbed wire bordered the top of the fence as a
threat to anyone who may try to climb it.

"What is this place?" Anne asked.

John pointed to a faded wooden sign caked with mud and dirt
that concealed the words. "Sheppard's Salvage and Junk Yard."

Anne blinked at him in disbelief. "You brought me to a *junkyard?*"

John smiled. "Yeah."

Anne frowned. "This is your plan to impress me?"

"Excuse me?"

"Well, this is our first date, and most boys take a girl out to dinner
or a movie."

John folded his arms. "Would that have impressed you?"

"Well, yes, because . . ."

"It's ordinary?"

Anne bit her lip.

"True, I could have taken you on a dull, ordinary date, or I could
take you on a date you will never forget."

John pulled on the rope that hung outside a large wooden door. A rusted bell that hung from a tall lamp post made a loud clanking noise. A few moments later, the door opened, and an elderly man stepped out.

"Chandy," the man greeted John.

"Hello, Captain."

"How'd she do?" the Captain said, pointing his finger at the motorcycle.

"Good."

"No black smoke this time?"

"Not that I saw."

The Captain smiled and looked at Anne. "And who is the lovely young lady?"

"This is Anne. Anne, meet Captain Sheppard."

At first glance, Anne was apprehensive of the Captain's rugged appearance. His grey hair stuck out from under a faded Greek fisherman's hat, most of his teeth were missing, and his scraggly beard covered his tan leather chin. But his snapping green eyes were pleasant, and his charming smile was welcoming.

Sheppard rubbed his dirty hands on his ragged coveralls. "I would offer ye me hand, but I'm afraid I've been workin' on an ol' truck."

"It's a pleasure to meet you, sir," Anne said.

Sheppard's eyes widened. "My, my, I can't remember the last time someone was pleased to meet me!"

John laughed.

"Well, no sense a standin' around out 'ere—come on inside."

Taking John's hand, Anne crossed the threshold to an unusual world.

With her mouth open and eyes widening, her mind struggled to process the complicated scene before her. The property was covered with various pieces of junk and broken rusting vehicles of all makes and models spread as far as the eye could see, but something was different. Something in the way the items were arranged and organized made the scene look more like art than forgotten castaways. Fountains made of various pieces of rusted metal and car parts landmarked the two main pathways that led toward the back of the yard. A yellow front-end loader with missing front tires rested on large metal barrels with lovely pansies growing in the bucket. A small trailer sat next to the weather-beaten barn that housed the Captain's workshop.

Sheppard sat in a lawn chair on an old rug outside the trailer. John sat beside him on a wooden crate as Anne wandered the front area, enjoying the novelties.

Sheppard packed his pipe. "Pretty girl."

"Thanks," John said.

"She looks like she comes from uptown."

John nodded, his elbows on his knees.

Sheppard lit his pipe and leaned back in his chair. "I'm sure ye don't need me to tell ye how the well-to-do tend to coddle their daughters."

"I know," John said.

A bark rang out from a distance, and John whistled. An exuberant three-legged dog came galloping around the corner.

John held his arm's out. "Scout!"

Scout ran up to John, wagging his tail. "How you doin', boy?"

Scout showered John with kisses.

"He's doing well," Sheppard said.

"I can see that."

Anne had walked over and smiled at Scout as he wagged his tail at her.

"What a sweet dog," Anne said, petting his head.

John sat on the ground with Scout. "His name is Scout,"

"Chandy wrote a song about him, ye know," Sheppard said.

Anne sat on John's crate and continued to pet the dog. "No, I didn't."

"She hasn't seen me play yet," John said.

"You're in for a treat, then."

Anne smiled. "You have an extraordinary place here, Mr. Sheppard."

"Please, call me Captain, and thank ya."

Sheppard, watching Scout absorb all the attention, smiled. "Did I tell you that Lucky may be coming here?"

"You mean the old clown that sits on top of the arcade?" John said.

"Yup."

"Why?"

Sheppard shrugged. "Apparently, the city council thinks he is an eyesore, and he scares away the tourists."

John shook his head. "Brother, all he needs is some paint. It's not like his voice box works anymore."

"I'm thinkin' if he comes out here, I might just fix up his ol' voice box and sit him on top of the barn. That way, at night, I can turn him on, and he can scare all the kids away who try and break in."

"Kids try and break in here?" Anne asked.

"Oh yeah, they like to dare each other to see if any of 'um are brave enough to come in and pull one over on the junkyard man. I got an old stuffed bear and a couple of other props set around to scare um, but it only works for a while. Then I got to think up new stuff. I thought about gettin' another dog, you know, one that will bite their britches when they try and scurry outta 'ere."

John laughed. "That would do it."

"Well, I reckon ya young folks don't wanna spend your evenin' jawin' with an old man. I turned on the tent lights for you, Chandy."

"I don't think Scout wants Anne to go anywhere," John said.

Scout's head was contently resting on Anne's knee as she scratched his ears.

"He can go with ya if ya don't mind some extra company," Sheppard said.

"Whadda, you think, Scout? You wanna come out to the tent with us?" John said to the dog.

His ears perked up, and he looked at Anne, who smiled at him, and he trotted forward, eager to show the way.

John took Anne's hand, and they followed Scout down the path toward the back half of the property. The sun had set, and various lights illuminated their path.

"So, what do you think of this place?" John asked.

"I think it's amazing. One could spend hours in here just exploring all the different pathways. Why you could get lost in here," Anne said, moving closer to John.

"Very true."

"Have you got lost in here?"

John laughed. "It took me a while to get used to the place, but I was lucky to have Scout for a compass."

"So how did you meet the Captain?" Anne asked.

John chuckled. "Well, it's kind of a long story."

"One you don't want to share?"

John shifted his gaze. "Not right now."

"I understand. You don't like to share your private life."

John didn't respond, and she let the topic drop as a red and white striped canvas circus tent with strings of Christmas lights wrapped around two plastic palm trees came into view.

Anne stopped, flabbergasted. "Oh my! Is that a real circus tent?"

"Yep. It had been damaged in a bad storm, and Barnum & Bailey didn't want anymore, so they left it behind."

"And the Captain took it?"

"It passed through a few hands before it finally ended up here."

She blinked her wide eyes at John. "It's so . . ."

"Magnificent."

Scout trotted inside the tent.

"You ready?" John asked.

"Yes," Anne said, holding onto his arm.

John pulled back the flap, and Anne went inside. A faded red velvet couch sat in front of a projection screen. The smell of fresh buttered popcorn wafted from a popcorn cart sitting in the corner. Scout sat on the area rug with his tongue hanging out.

"Have a seat," John told Anne.

She smiled as she sat on the couch. Scout moved closer to her, and she patted his head.

John brought over the popcorn and soda.

"What movie are we going to see?" Anne asked.

"I thought it would be fun to start with a few Chaplin films."

"Silent film?"

"Yes," John turned on the player piano sitting on the opposite side of the tent, then dimming the light, he turned on the projector and sat next to Anne.

Traveling back to the early age of film, Anne and John appreciated the art and talents of Charlie Chaplin and other icons of the time. Laughing, sharing popcorn with Scout, and enjoying the atmosphere, the hours flew by like autumn leaves.

When the last piece of film rolled past the light, the piano was silent, the popcorn was gone, and Scout was sleeping peacefully on the rug. Anne was cuddled up against John with her head on his shoulder, watching the projection of stars from a zoetrope skip along the top of the circus tent.

"This place is magical," Anne murmured.

"It is," John said.

"I don't want to leave."

John turned and gazed at her in the dancing light. "Neither do I."

Reaching up, he felt her chin with his thumb as his fingers stretched back, touching the base of her hairline. Being drawn in by the gentle pull of the arm behind her head, Anne shut her eyes and melted into the sensation she longed for. Burying her hands in the fullness of John's hair and placing her other hand around his middle, she pulled him closer. His arms obliged her movement until not an inch separated them.

All timidness was cast aside as she claimed his tongue and tasted him fully. Lost in the moment and the desire, she gave no thought about her position or where John's hands were. She was totally lost in the power of filling a need that she didn't understand. John pulled away, and she heard a faint moan from afar. His lips tantalized her neck sending a tingle down her spine. Sinking into the delicious wave, she felt his left-hand touch her bare lower back, and though it shocked her for a second, it was only a second. Warm, persuasive fingers meandered up her back and unclasped her bra. Before this sensation had fully registered, the hand was headed for her chest and brushed against flesh that no one had ever touched. Her eyes flew open, and she pulled back with a jolt.

"What's the matter?" John said through his haze.

"Wha . . . what . . . are you doing?" Anne mumbled, clasping her hand over her chest.

"What does it feel like I'm doing?" John said, his gaze locked on her lips.

Anne pushed him back with both hands and this time, he focused on her terror-filled face.

John sat up. "Anne? What's the matter?"

Fretful and scared, Anne scrambled away from John's arms and moved to the other side of the tent.

John stood up. "Anne . . ."

"Don't come any closer," Anne cried, holding her hand out.

John held up his hands. "All right, all right. I'm going to go outside and get some fresh air. Take a moment, and come out and join me when you're ready, okay?"

Anne nodded, not daring to look at him.

John turned and left the tent.

Anne's heart plummeted, and she sank onto the couch in shame.

29

WHAT THE HELL JUST HAPPENED? John thought, while running his hand over his hair. One moment, he held Anne's pleasing form close in his arms, and the next, she pushed him away like poison. Had he read the signals wrong? Had she not moaned only moments before? Baffled, John sat on a tree stump and tried to make sense of Anne's behavior. He had been with several girls, and none of them had ever been so daring as to let them take what they needed. He was always in charge, the one with the cool head, but her overpowering desire and sensual moan had swept away all rational thought, and he moved forward with his own sensations.

He thought it was what she wanted too.

He was wrong.

A while later, Anne came out of the tent, Scout beside her. John stood up but held back to not overwhelm her. Her lashes fluttered, and she looked up at him through sheepish eyes.

"Are you okay?" John asked.

"Yes," Anne said, hugging her body.

"Can you tell me what I did wrong?"

Anne's eyes fell, and she shifted her weight.

"I scared you, didn't I?" John asked.

Anne bit her lip.

"It wasn't my intention."

"I know that."

John stepped closer. "I thought you wanted me to touch you."

"I did," Anne whispered.

"Well, then, what's the matter?"

Anne tried to hide a blush.

John gently tipped her chin up. "Talk to me."

"I'm just not ready to . . . you know."

John shook his head. "No."

She looked up at him, and in the instant when her tear-filled eyes met his, he knew.

John closed his eyes tight. "Oh."

"Are you mad at me?" Anne said, her voice trembling.

John looked at her standing there, clutching tightly to the sides of her sweater. "Of course not."

"You mean it?"

John pulled her in his arms and held her close. "I do."

Anne's trembling arms wrapped around him. "I know you've been with girls that are experienced."

"Other girls, aren't you."

"I would understand if you didn't want to see me anymore."

John pulled back. "Stop talkin' nonsense. Nothin' has changed between us. Do you hear me?"

Anne nodded.

"Don't spoil this perfect night by crying," John said, wiping the tears off her cheek. "Everything is all right, right, Scout?"

Scout barked, and Anne laughed.

"See? That's better. I best be takin' you home," John said, slipping his arm around her. She leaned against him and soaked up their last few moments together.

The ride back to Mildred's was chilly, and John let her wear his jacket. Its warmth held her like his arms, and she wished she could keep it. John pulled up to the curb and helped Anne off the bike. He kissed her gently goodbye and promised he would see her again soon. She parted with his jacket, and he waited for her to be safe inside before leaving.

Anne locked up for the night and went into her room. The soft ticking of the clock next to her bed was comforting. She lay on the bed and looked up at the dim halo of light on he ceiling. What was wrong with her? The moment had been so intense and like nothing she had ever experienced before. It had warmed her to her core, yet she froze and pushed it away. When was she ever going to have another chance like this one? The days before she had to go home were already short.

Turning on her side and pulling her knees up to her chest, she wished she could stay here with Mildred and never have to leave a place that made her so happy and so alive. There had to be an answer. There had to be some way to escape the fate that waited for her at home. She just needed to stand up to Steve and her parents. Sadly, she knew that wouldn't be easy, but being without John would be impossible. She had to escape this mess somehow or be miserable for the rest of her life.

30

FLIPPING THROUGH MAGAZINE PAGES, MONICA wiggled her toes to the beat of the music on the radio. Her sister was out with her family for the afternoon, and Monica decided to pamper herself. First, she took a long, warm bath, rolled her hair in curlers, and finished painting her fingers and toes. She was fixing herself a glass of iced tea when she heard a knock at the door. Who could that be? One of the nosey neighbors, no doubt. Monica walked to the door on her heels because she didn't want to mess up her freshly painted toenails. She opened the door, and her eyes widened when she saw Joe standing there. He was dressed in a dark blue turtleneck with a tan blazer and jeans while she was still in her baby doll pajamas.

"Joe," she said, her voice squeaking.

He lifted his eyebrow as he observed her attire. "Monica."

"What are you doing here?"

"I was in the neighborhood and thought I would drop by to see you."

Monica absently felt the edges of the scarf that hid her curlers. "If I knew you were coming, I would have . . ."

"Put some clothes on?"

Monica frowned.

"I certainly hope you don't parade around the house like that in front of Scott."

"No, they're out."

Joe put his hands in his jean's pockets. "Are you going to invite me in?"

"Oh, yeah, come in."

Monica opened the door, and Joe stepped into the small living room.

"I would offer you some coffee, but there isn't a fresh pot."

Joe took off his sunglasses. "I'm fine."

"Do you want to sit down?"

Joe nodded, removed a forgotten doll, and sat on the worn, overstuffed chair.

Monica sat on the couch and began to tidy up the mess she had made on the coffee table. "So, how are you?"

Joe crossed his legs and undid the button on his blazer. "I am well. How are things with you?"

Monica secured the lid to the nail polish. "Oh fine. I can't complain, really. Gina has made me feel at home."

"Hmm," Joe said, running his finger over his lips. "I'm sure that can't be easy, seeing as how the house is so small."

"I heard on the radio that you have a show on Friday night."

"We do."

"Your new guitarist must be working out well, then," Monica said, resting her feet on a footstool.

"He's doing exceptionally well."

"Good."

An awkward silence fell between them as Monica looked at her nails, and Joe's foot swayed.

"So, how goes the job search?" Joe asked.

"Good. I have a job now."

Joe lifted his eyebrow. "Oh?"

"Yes."

"Doing what?"

Monica paused. "I'm a waitress."

Joe tightened his hands in his lap. "Really? Do you like working?"

"I am saving up money for my own place."

Joe chuckled. "You know, it's hard to find a nice place on a waitress's wage."

"I know."

"When did you last go out and have a decent meal?"

Monica pulled on her scarf. "I don't remember."

"Why don't you get dressed and let me take you to dinner? It's a beautiful day, and I would hate to see you waste it in this dreary . . . room."

Monica shifted. "I don't know if that would be a good idea."

"Come on, it's just dinner. I promise I will be a gentleman."

Monica laughed.

"What?"

"I don't think you have ever been a gentleman, Joe."

Joe tilted his head. "Maybe I've changed."

Monica rolled her eyes. "Yeah, right, and the cow jumped over the moon."

Joe's face fell. "Please, Monica, I really am trying."

Monica gave him a small smile. "Well, all right. Let me get ready."

Monica left the room, and Joe sat back and smiled.

31

THE WARM SUNLIGHT FILTERED THROUGH the canopy of trees, casting mosaic shadows on the red convertible as it passed. Songs from chirping birds blended harmoniously with the soft hum of the engine as the car followed the meandering road. Joe's hand rested on the steering wheel and observed the vibrant landscape. The rolling hills with colorful wildflowers and quaint farmhouses drifted by like a dream. Glancing over at Monica leaning back comfortably in her seat, Joe admired her natural beauty. Dressed in a light blue sundress and sandals, Monica's hair flowed around her like a wild horse's mane. Thoughts of when they first met flowed through his mind like the water in the creek. Long drives, listening to music, and playing guitars in a field with a bottle of wine were common back then. Love was new, and their future was bright. Nothing could have come between them.

Driving on the city's outskirts and up along the coast of Lake Michigan, Joe stopped at a restaurant close to the waterfront. Sitting on the deck, their table looked out over the still water. Joe ordered a bottle of champagne, and its delightful texture and taste alleviated Monica's stress.

"Do you remember the first time I took you out for seafood?" Joe asked.

"Yes," she said with a shy smile.

"You had never eaten crab before, and you were shocked when we had to crack the legs open. I thought you might turn green."

Monica laughed. "I felt green!"

He gazed at her over his glass; the smile lingering on his lips.

"We used to spend a lot of time by the water, didn't we?" Monica reflected.

"Yes."

"Ian loved playing in the water." Monica said.

Joe's smile evaporated, and his features hardened, and he leaned back in his chair.

"He had that little sky-blue pail with the starfish on it and a seahorse, remember?" Monica said, facing Joe.

He stared at the water, his elbow resting on the armchair and his hand covering his mouth.

Monica realized the champagne was going to her head, and she had said too much. Making tiny circles with her finger on the table, the ever-present heartache crept between them.

▢■▢■▢■▢■▢■▢■▢■▢■▢■▢■▢

After dinner, Monica assumed Joe would take her home, but he drove up a dirt road and stopped at the top of a hill overlooking the water.

"What are we doing here?" Monica asked.

"Enjoying the view. I have memories, too, you know," Joe said, turning to Monica. "I remember sitting with you on a hill like this one. The moon was bright, and no soul was around for at least ten miles or more. It was just the two of us and a blanket. Your hair was windswept, hanging down to your shoulder," Joe said, gently pushing Monica's hair away from her face. "You were the most beautiful girl I had ever seen, and I was nervous sitting there with you."

Monica turned toward Joe, his thumb rubbing her chin. "I know that I haven't done right by you. I know that I have made a lot of mistakes, and I'm sorry."

Monica's eyes threatened to close as Joe's comforting fingers caressed her aching neck.

"I know that words don't mean much, but I want to try and make things up to you. I'm miserable without you and want you to come home."

The champagne and the tingle in her veins were muddling Monica's thoughts. "Joe, I . . ."

Joe pressed his finger to her lips. "Shh, don't say anything tonight. Tonight, you belong to me."

All the sleepless nights spent on a stiff cot with aching feet and back, all the tears that stained her pillow from missing Joe were swept away like footprints in the shifting sand. Held in a feverish embrace, Monica surrendered to their passion, and there would be peace for tonight.

32

WHILE RIDING IN THE BACK seat of Danny's car, Jerry observed busy commuters returning to work on Monday morning. Danny and John were discussing the song on the radio, but Jerry was half listening because he was thinking about Betty. Sunday was always a pleasant day at the Bruer house. The day started by going to church, followed by a delicious meal that ended with a freshly baked pie. Then the rest of the day, Bob would play games with the boys, while Mable and Betty sewed or read. The family would gather in the living room and watch TV in the evening while eating sandwiches and chips, but yesterday was different. Betty didn't sit with Jerry at church, dinner, or on the loveseat that night. There was no handholding, no snuggling, sweet talking, or kisses. Just complete avoidance and sour looks. Now he was driving to face a dreary day with no hopes of loving arms to greet him later.

The boys pulled into the hospital parking lot, and Danny parked the car. John turned and glanced at Jerry, who looked like he was on the verge of tears.

"Hey Jerry, we're here," John said.

Jerry didn't respond.

"Hey Jerry, are you all right?" Danny asked.

Jerry looked up to see both Danny and John staring at him. "Huh?"

"We're at the hospital," John said.

"Oh, yeah."

"What's with him?" John asked Danny after Jerry got out of the car.

"I'm not sure, but I think he might have quarreled with Betty. She was kinda mean to him yesterday."

John frowned. "Betty?"

Danny nodded. "Yup. She can be a pain sometimes."

John gave a slight smile and got out of the car.

❑■❑■❑■❑■❑■❑■❑■❑■❑■❑■❑

Stepping through the doors into the sterile, white, dreary hospital instantly changed the boy's disposition. The women dressed in white with pointy short hats made Jerry feel uneasy. The memories of being repressed within these walls were still fresh, and he hated visiting the dreadful place.

The nurse at the counter smiled at Jerry as he stepped up to the counter to check in for his visit.

"Hello, I'm here to see Mrs. Palmer," Jerry said.

The nurse looked at the clipboard beside her. "Did you say, Mrs. Palmer?"

"Yes."

"I'm sorry, but it looks like she was discharged yesterday."

Jerry's forehead wrinkled. "What do you mean, she was discharged yesterday?"

"Her husband came in, and she was discharged to his care," the nurse said.

The color drained from Jerry's face, and fear gripped his heart. "Her husband? Are you sure?"

"Yes, he signed all the release forms."

John and Danny joined Jerry at the counter.

"What's goin' on, Jer?" John asked.

Jerry turned to John, devastated. "Gus came and took Mom!"

"What? Are you sure?"

Jerry ran his hands over his hair. "She was discharged to his care yesterday."

"Excuse me, did Mr. Palmer say where he was takin' her?" John asked the nurse.

"No."

"You didn't ask?"

"It isn't our business."

Jerry's hands were trembling. "John, what am I gonna do?"

"First, you're not gonna panic. We'll find her."

"Where do we start?" Jerry said.

"Do you think there's a chance he took her back out to the house?" Danny asked Jerry.

"I dunno. Maybe."

"It's a place to start," John said.

The boys left the hospital as quickly as they could travel to the dreaded destination.

$$33$$

THE WISPY COTTON CLOUD WRAPPED around Monica like a warm, safe cocoon. Not wanting to open her eyes, Monica teetered on the edge of her subconscious. The luxurious bed and beating of Joe's heart coaxed Monica to stay in the arms of forgetfulness. As long as she held onto the dream, reality would remain in the shadows. Last night's reminder of how blissful things had once been wooed Monica's exhausted reason. Joe's low hot voice in her ear and his attentive love had chased away the weeks of heartache and discontent. She was home, and as long as she could keep the truth buried, she could stay there, but deep in her heart, the unresolved conflicts would surface, and discontent would rule her life once more.

Joe grumbled in his sleep and turned over and Monica slipped out of bed.

Walking across the thick white carpet to Joe's large walk-in closet, Monica slipped on one of his robes and walked into the bathroom. Humming, she secured her hair on top of her head, then opening a drawer, she fished for a hair tie. Her searching fingers brushed up against something latex and she froze. Looking inside the drawer, she saw the coiled latex strap. Pulling her hand out as if she had been bitten by a snake, Monica slammed the drawer shut. Shuddering, she steadied herself against the vanity. Taking a deep breath, she left the bathroom.

Monica walked downstairs into the kitchen, where Madge was making coffee.

"Miss Monica!" the older lady said with delight.

"Hello, Madge," Monica said, hugging her.

"My, it's good to see you!"

"You too."

"Are you coming home?"

"Did you make some coffee?" Monica asked, avoiding the question.

"Yes, ma'am."

Monica poured herself a warm cup. "Oh, Madge, how I've missed your coffee."

"You want me to make you breakfast?"

Monica leaned against the counter. "I don't want to put you to any extra work."

"There's fresh cantaloupe."

"Oh, you know how to melt a girl's heart."

Madge smiled and crossed to the refrigerator.

"So, Madge, how is Joe doing?"

"Fine," she said, pulling the eggs from the refrigerator.

"He's not eating right, is he?"

Madge shook her head.

Monica walked over to the double glass doors overlooking the back patio. "I can tell he's not taking care of himself."

"I rarely see him, ma'am."

Monica sighed.

"He misses you terribly."

She mulled Madge's comment internally, finally responding, "I am going to sit outside and enjoy the crisp morning."

"I'll bring your breakfast out to you."

"Thank you, Madge."

Monica went outside, sat in her favorite chair, and slowly drank coffee while listening to the birds. Madge brought Monica's breakfast of eggs, cantaloupe, and toast. She ate it slowly, relishing every delectable bite. After breakfast, Monica went up to her room. It was just as she left it: cast-off clothes and shoes had been tossed aside like forgotten toys. The bed was wrinkled, and the latest fashion magazine lay on her nightstand beside her favorite spangled bracelet. Taking off her robe, Monica went into her private bathroom and took a rejuvenating shower.

Stepping out of the bathroom wrapped in a robe, she rubbed a towel over her hair.

"Good morning."

Monica looked up to see Joe sitting in one of the large blue and white striped armchairs that occupied her dressing area.

"Good morning," Monica said sitting down at her dressing table.

"I trust you slept well?" Joe inquired, nonchalantly crossing his legs.

Monica picked at her snarled hair. "I did."

"You had breakfast?"

"Yes, Madge was kind enough to make my favorite."

Leisurely shifting in his chair, Joe continued. "So, what are your plans for the day?"

Monica paused. "Well, I thought I might tidy up and pack a few more things."

Joe averted his gaze and stroked his chin, prompting Monica to add, "I hope you know I'm not trying to upset you. Last night was wonderful, and—"

"No," Joe said, raising his hand. "I understand."

"You do?"

"Yes. I think this time apart has been good for us. I want you to come home, of course, but I realize it will do no good unless you are ready."

Monica blinked in surprise. "You mean it, Joe?"

"I do. This experience will be good for you, and I am willing to wait. Take as much time as you need."

Monica beamed. "Oh Joe, you don't know what that means to me!"

"I hope we can continue to renew our relationship."

"You mean date?"

Joe shrugged. "Why not? We really didn't have a chance to date much before. . ."

Monica watched Joe retreat into his shell. Reaching out, she set her hand on his knee. "It's all right to talk about him. We can't ignore the fact that he existed. I know you still hurt as much as I do."

Joe's jaw tightened.

"It might help if we—"

"No," Joe snapped.

"But I think . . ."

"The discussion is closed."

The air suddenly turned frigid. Monica turned away and returned to brushing her hair.

Joe stood up. "I will inform Clive that you require a ride to your sister's."

Joe stepped toward the door, but Monica's voice stopped him.

"I know what's in the bathroom vanity drawer."

Joe stopped short.

"You're using again, aren't you? Don't try and deny it when I can see it in your body."

Joe turned to her. "Don't start with me."

"I'm worried about you, Joe. Can't you see that?"

"No, I can't see anything."

"Joe," Monica said, deflated.

"You talk about how much I have ruined our relationship. Well, what about you? Huh? Let's talk about what you've done that hurt me."

"I don't know what you're talking about."

Joe chuckled. "Of course, you don't know what I'm talking about. What's happened between us was magically born out of the air!"

Monica stood up. "You know what? You're right. I have made some mistakes, but maybe if you hadn't shut me out when it happened and turned to someone else to comfort you, maybe I would still be sleeping in your bed."

"Turn to someone else? I didn't turn to someone else!"

"Don't insult me, Joe. You think I don't know about those late nights when you didn't come home, how your suits smelled of perfume that wasn't mine!"

"Here it comes. The accusations. The doubt. The judgment!" Joe snarled.

Monica stepped up to him. "Look me in the eye and tell me you didn't sleep with her."

"I've had enough," Joe said, turning.

"Why can't you just be a man and admit it?"

Joe slowly turned around. "Why don't you admit to your indiscretions?"

Monica took a step back. "What?"

"Now, who is insulted?"

Monica returned to her dressing table. "I don't know what you're talking about."

"Don't you?" Joe said, stepping behind her. "You think I don't know who you keep company with?"

Monica looked at Joe's taunting reflection in the mirror. "Now, who doesn't want to talk?"

"You're crazy."

Joe bent forward and placed his hands on the dressing table, trapping Monica.

"Dennis," Joe hissed in her ear.

Monica stared straight ahead, her body shaking. "Nothing happened."

"Lies don't become you, my dear."

"It's not a lie. We were just friends."

"Like you and Danny are friends?"

Monica whirled around. "You know I haven't been with Danny!"

"I know you say you haven't, but you said you weren't with Dennis either."

"I wasn't!"

"You want me to admit to the things I've done but you won't admit yours. You're a hypocrite."

"I don't have to sit here and listen to this," Monica said rising from her seat, but Joe pushed her back down roughly.

"Oh, but I think you do. I think it's time that you admit this situation isn't all my fault!"

Monica started to weep. "Please, I don't want to talk about it anymore."

"How convenient."

"All right, so I did have a tryst with Dennis. Are you happy now?" Monica spat in Joe's face. "But I never touched Danny Bruer!"

Joe leaned in, his heated breath close to her face. "But you wanted him to. Only Danny and his precious code of honor kept him from giving in to a treacherous temptress like you!"

Monica turned her distorted face to Joe and lashed her hand out toward his face, but he caught her wrist in his hand and tightened his fingers making her call out. "Joe, you're hurting me!"

"You should be glad you didn't scratch my face because if you had, the weight of my wrath would have crushed you."

Monica's sobs wracked her body.

Slowly Joe removed his hand and Monica held her throbbing wrist close to her body. Void of compassion and remorse, Joe's wounded pride surged with a false vindication as he glanced at her broken spirit. Turning on his heel Joe left the room, closing the door behind him.

34

THE HOUSE AND THE PROPERTY it sat on had been neglected for years, and an ominous essence created an unsettling feeling of dread to anyone who stood in its shadow. Tall, overgrown weeds crept through the yard, wrapping their spindly stems around every unoccupied surface. The screen door hung off its hinges and banged against the house. Stepping up onto the sinking porch, Jerry reached for the doorknob, but his hand recoiled.

"What's the matter, Jerry?" John asked.

"The door—it's ajar."

"You think he's in there?" Danny asked.

"Maybe," Jerry squeaked.

"Let me go first," John said. "That way, if he's going to jump out and attack someone, it will be me."

Jerry didn't argue, and he stepped back.

John flexed his fingers and took a deep breath before pushing the door. A rancid odor was the only thing that greeted him. He leaned back and tried not to gag.

"Whew, that's terrible," Danny said, waving his hand in front of his face.

"You think he brought her here?" John asked Jerry.

"I don't know, but I have to find out."

"I can wait out here in case someone shows up," Danny said.

"Chicken," John said.

"I'm goin' in," Jerry said, covering his mouth.

"We're right behind you," John said, grabbing Danny's arm.

"Oh, man, do I gotta?" Danny said.

"You're a Hound Dog, ain't ya?" John said.

Danny groaned and covered his mouth.

Squinting their eyes, the boys entered the dimly lit living room.

"What happened in here?" John said.

The room looked like a cyclone had blown through it. Papers, books, unopened mail, and empty liquor bottles were strewn everywhere. The TV was on, making loud hissing noises as chaotic white and black static covered the screen like ants.

Jerry cautiously stepped over strewn debris. "Mom?"

John kicked bottles and trash out of the way, crossing over to the TV and turning off the annoying noise. An unsettling silence took place as Danny and John followed Jerry toward the back of the house.

The door to Jerry's room was closed, the door to his mother's room was ajar, and the bathroom door was closed.

"You think someone's in the bathroom?" Danny whispered.

"You couldn't pay me to go in there," John said.

Jerry tiptoed to his mother's bedroom door.

"Careful, Jerry," Danny said.

Jerry pushed the door open and jumped back like he had touched fire.

"Well?" John said.

"The only thing in there is another mess."

"Who is going to check, you know, the bathroom?" Danny said.

"It's your turn to open a door," John told Danny.

Danny shook his head. "Oh, no. Not me, no, no, no!"

"Oh, for heaven's sake," Jerry said, reaching for the doorknob.

They all heard the click at once, and slowly turning, they saw Gus standing in the doorway to Jerry's room with a rifle in his hand.

A jagged snarl curled his lips. "Lookee, what we got here. Some juveenile delinquents a trespessin' on my land."

"Your property? This is my mother's house, not yours," Jerry snapped.

"She's my wife, and everythin' that belongs to her belongs to me."

"You better put that gun down before I take it away and beat you over the head with it," John threatened.

Gus cocked the rifle. "You take one step toward me, boy, and I will blow a hole in ya as big as a dinner plate, and I would be well within my rights seein' as how yous is a breakin' the law and all."

Jerry clenched his teeth. "Where's my mother?"

Gus chortled. "Somewhere's safe where I can take good care of her."

"You're not going to take care of her! You're trying to kill her!" Jerry said, stepping forward, but John took hold of his shoulder and held him firm.

"Where is she?" John hissed.

"I ain't tellin' ya. Now ya best all be a clearin' on out a here before I call the poeleece!"

Jerry clenched his fists. "You can't do this! She's my mother! I have a right to know where she is."

"You gave up your *rights* when you moved outta here! Now get outta here before I get trigger-happy!" Gus hissed.

John stepped forward. "Fine, we're leavin', but this ain't over."

Gus grimaced. "Are you a threatnin' me?"

John narrowed his eyes. "I don't make threats."

"What does that mean?"

"It means that if somethin' has happened to my mother, you're gonna wish I sent you to hell," Jerry said, giving Gus one more hateful glare before leaving the house, John and Danny behind him.

◻◼◻◼◻◼◻◼◻◼◻◼◻◼◻◼◻◼◻◼◻

Jerry hugged his stomach and rocked back and forth in the backseat of the car.

"Jerry, we're going to find her," John said.

"This is all my fault!" Jerry wailed.

"No, it's not."

"Yes, it is! If I had stayed and hadn't left home, none of this would have happened!"

Danny looked in the rearview mirror at Jerry. "If you would have stayed in that house, your life would have never changed. It would have only been a matter of time before he would have beaten you again."

"Danny's right, Jerry, and you know it," John said.

"I can only imagine what he's done to her!"

"We are going to find her. Danny and I have a friend that will help us. You just have to trust us. Now, you need to calm down."

Jerry ran his finger under his nose. "I want to come with you."

"You need to go to work," Danny said. "Uncle Bob is counting on you. Let Barnaby and me take care of this."

"We got your back, Jerry. I promise," John said.

Jerry nodded and calmed down when Danny and John dropped him off at the mercantile.

"You think he'll be all right?" Danny asked John.

John sighed. "I hope so."

35

LOCATED ON THE OUTSKIRTS OF town on the floor above a cheap Chinese restaurant, Lou's cramped office resembled a clothes closet. The Asian couple that owned the restaurant spoke little English but were very kind and the rent was affordable.

Lou munched stale popcorn while listening to the radio and reading *Man's Life* magazine. An old squeaky fan labored to circulate air around the cramped space. The knock on his door scared him half to death. The only people who knocked on Lou's door were bill collectors or Mrs. Chen from downstairs.

"Hey Lou, are you in there?" a voice he didn't recognize said.

"No," he said. Then, realizing he had answered, he hit himself upside the head.

"We need to talk to you. It's important."

"Hold on a minute," Lou said, readjusting his toupee, brushing crumbs off his shirt, and shoving the magazine in an overstuffed drawer. Lou opened the door to see John and Danny. Lou's eyes widened.

"Hey Lou, you look guilty of somethin'," John said.

"It wasn't my idea, I swear it!"

"What are you talkin' about?"

Lou looked at John and then at Danny. "You're not here about the other night?"

"What happened the other night?" John said.

"Mr. Delany was looking for his wife."

"And you saw us together," Danny said.

Lou scratched his head. "Yeah, but I had found her before that happened."

"Don't worry about it," Danny said.

Lou sighed.

"We actually came here because we need your help," John said.

"You do?"

"Yeah."

"Oh."

"Can we come in, or are we gonna talk in the hall?" John asked.

"Oh yeah, come in," Lou said, opening the door. "Just push that stuff off the chairs."

Danny and John moved papers, books, and empty Chinese carryout containers that occupied the two chairs in front of Lou's desk.

"You need a cleaning lady," Danny said.

"He needs a bulldozer," John said.

"I don't normally have clients come to the office," Lou said, sitting in his overstressed office chair that creaked under the weight.

"That's probably a good thing," John said.

"What can I do for you, fellas?"

"Well, we need help finding a missing person," Danny said.

"Wait a second," Lou said, shifting through his stacks of paper and looking for a notepad. Finding one, he pulled it out, causing an avalanche of items to fall to the floor. Smiling sheepishly, he dug through his desk drawer until he found a pen. "Okay, now I'm ready. What's the name?"

"Martha Palmer," John answered.

"Where was she last seen?"

"She was a patient at Madison Central."

Lou glanced up from his paper. "Are you sure she didn't just wander off? Patients do that all the time."

"No. Her husband said he would take care of her. So, they discharged her."

"And that's a problem?"

John leaned on Lou's desk. "Her husband has a history of beatin' her regularly. He is the one that put her in the hospital in the first place."

"Oh."

"She isn't in her right mind," Danny added.

"We aren't sure why he would even want to take her out of there except to beat her some more," John said.

"He didn't take her home?" Lou asked.

"No. We checked there."

"Do you mind writing down the address, anyway?" Lou asked John, giving him the paper and pen.

"Can you describe her?" Lou continued.

"She's about five-foot-two, maybe three. One hundred ten pounds with mousey brown hair. She's in her early forties but looks a lot older."

"What's the husband's name?"

John handed the pad back to Lou. "Gus Palmer. We're unsure if he still has a job, but he worked at the steel mill. His favorite hangout is the bar on Decatur Road."

"What does he look like?"

"Besides ugly, balding, rotting teeth, and body odor?" John jeered.

Lou cleared his throat. "How tall?"

"Under six, and he weighs close to one hundred forty pounds, maybe."

"I think he has an anchor tattoo on his left forearm," Danny added.

"Does she have any friends or relatives that might know anything?" Lou asked.

"She worked at the diner on Grover," Danny said. "But no one has seen her since he put her in the hospital."

Lou tapped the end of his pen on the desk. "Well, this gives me something to get started on. I do have one more question. Do you know if she had a life insurance policy?"

"No. There is a house, but it's in pretty bad shape," John said.

Lou rubbed his chin. "How about the land?"

"It does sit on a fairly large lot."

"Sometimes the house isn't worth much, but the lot it sits on is."

Both Danny and John groaned.

"How can I get in touch with you?" Lou asked.

Danny wrote down the number for the house and record store. "We will more than likely be at the store. My cousin normally answers the phone. Just tell him you're Lou calling for Danny, and don't let him ask you a hundred questions."

"'Cause he will," John said.

"I will contact you as soon as I know something," Lou said.

"This woman is our friend's mother. It is important that we find her as soon as possible," John said. "She is in a lot of danger."

"I won't let you down," Lou said, offering his hand.

John shook it and felt a bit of a greasy residue but didn't say anything.

"Okay, we'll let you get to work, then," John said.

Danny shook Lou's hand too. They left the office and headed down the hallway.

"You think there's a washroom someplace close?" Danny said. "I need to wash my hands."

"Me too," John said.

36

HERE WAS NO QUESTION THAT with each passing day, Joe was slipping, and Will's patience shortened. Like a calculating vulture, Patrick sat back and observed each character in the drama while his mind made notes. Will was a reactionary narcissist, and Boyd, well, Boyd was a simpleton. Boyd only cared about playing the drums, food, and his girlfriend, Doris. As long as Boyd had a delicious lunch plate in front of him, he could listen to Will rant on for hours.

It was Joe that Patrick found to be the most fascinating and complicated. On the outside, Joe was the perfect picture of finesse and style. Other than the occasional squabble with Will, Joe was calm and reserved. Always in control of every situation, he kept his humanity guarded. So why was he coming to rehearsal late, in clothes that looked like they had been slept in? His temper was short, and he snapped at everyone. Will and Boyd dismissed it as Joe being moody, but Patrick noticed the trembling hands that made mistakes in chord progressions and a jaw that never stopped grinding. A crack was forming under Joe's domineering personality, and it was spreading.

Like a pendulum, Will paced the floor. His eyes were transfixed on the closed door.

"Why don't you sit down?" Boyd said. "Staring at the door is only making your blood pressure rise."

"Maybe he's not coming today," Patrick commented from his relaxed position on the floor.

"Joe never misses rehearsal. He probably just got hung up somewhere," Boyd reasoned.

"Maybe he's meeting with the record producers?" Patrick offered.

Will stopped pacing and glowered at Patrick.

Patrick glanced at Boyd. "What? Did I say something wrong? That is the plan, isn't it? To make a record?"

"I say we wait a while longer, and if he doesn't show, we go to lunch," Boyd said.

"Will, did I step out of line?" Patrick asked.

Will's eyes shifted toward the door. "No. It's just Joe is too busy thinking about this ridiculous contest to think about making a record."

"I did offer an alternative, you know. What did you fellas think of my song?"

"I like it. It had a catchy tune," Boyd said.

"What about you, Will?" Patrick asked.

Will shrugged. "I liked it. I thought the lyrics were well written. I would probably change the rhythm some."

"Yeah? Like, what would you suggest?"

"Well, I would pick up the tempo. I understand it is a love song, but giving the rhythm a bit of bounce wouldn't hurt."

"Can you show me?"

Will chuckled. "Me?"

Patrick stood up and grabbed his guitar. "Yeah, why not? It'll be fun to do something creative for a change. It beats the hell out of waiting and pacing. Right?"

Will grinned. "Right."

Working on composing a song together gave Will and Boyd a chance to branch out and use their talents to try something new. Patrick consulted Will on what sounded good and what might work, and the process energized Will's waning desire to play music.

The unfamiliar sound of laughter and conversation greeted Joe when he entered the rehearsal space. Boyd was playing a steady beat while Will fiddled with the bass line. Patrick was counting the beats and making notes. When Boyd spotted Joe, he stopped playing.

Patrick looked up at Boyd. "I like how that sounded, but you missed the last beat."

Boyd nodded toward the door. Will and Patrick turned to see Joe. Sunglasses covered his eyes, but they could tell by his tight lips that he wasn't in good humor.

"Well, look who decided to show up," Will said.

"I don't need your crap, Will," Joe said, crossing to the piano.

"I can only imagine the crap you would give one of us if we sauntered in here whenever we felt like it."

Joe took off his coat. "I had some unexpected business to attend to."

"And you couldn't call?"

"It was last minute. What are you three doing?" Joe asked.

"We were working on a song," Patrick said.

Joe laughed. "Oh really? And what song is that?"

"The one I played for you the other day," Patrick said.

"Oh."

"You know you never did give me your opinion."

Joe picked up his Stratocaster. "I thought it needs work."

Patrick's shoulders fell.

"It's not a bad song, Joe," Will said.

"I didn't say it was a bad song. I just said it needs work."

Will stood up. "I think it might be the better choice."

Joe plugged his guitar into the amplifier. "What are you talking about?"

"I think it might be a better song to record."

"I have to agree with Will on that, Joe," Boyd said.

"Can we at least show you the changes we made?" Patrick asked.

Joe paused. "I don't have time for that nonsense right now. We have a show to rehearse."

Patrick shared a glance with Will.

"Take your place, Patrick. You're out of step and out of time," Joe said. "I want to see a significant improvement today."

"Of course, Joe," Patrick said, standing on his mark.

Will stood frozen, his patience and resolve threatening to leave him.

"Are you waiting for something, Will?" Joe asked.

"No."

Will walked over to his mark, and the rehearsal commenced, but for Will, this rehearsal was different. For the first time in eons, he didn't just go through the motions like some mindless puppet. This time, his mind had been opened to the possibilities of contributing something meaningful to his music career.

After practice had finished, Will approached Patrick.

"Hey, Pat."

Patrick latched his guitar case. "Hey."

"Do you have any plans for the evening?"

Patrick shook his head. "Not really."

"Would you like to have a drink with me?"

Patrick shrugged. "Sure."

Patrick put his coat on and walked with Will toward the door when Boyd stopped them.

"Hey Will, where you headed?" Boyd asked.

"The Cornby Club."

"Without me?" Boyd chortled.

Will tilted his head. "Don't you have a girlfriend?"

Boyd blinked at Will. "Well, yeah, but I can still have a drink with friends."

"When did you and I just have a drink?"

Boyd rubbed the back of his neck.

"I'll see you tomorrow, Boyd," Will said. Boyd looked crestfallen as the door closed behind Will and Patrick, their laughter echoing through the hall.

"Everything all right, Boyd?" Joe asked.

"Yeah, sure," Boyd said, retrieving his coat from the peg on the wall.

"I didn't realize Will and Patrick were so chummy," Joe said, disconnecting his guitar from the amplifier.

Boyd adjusted the collar on his coat. "Will's been giving me the cold shoulder ever since I started dating Doris."

Joe picked up a dust rag. "I wouldn't take it personal. He's probably just jealous."

"Oh, I don't know," Boyd said, burying his hands in his coat pockets. "I don't think Will wants to settle down."

Joe raised an eyebrow. "And you do?"

Boyd shrugged. "I don't know. I'm not getting any younger, and Doris is an amazing cook."

Joe chuckled. "That is important."

"I'm going to go ahead and take off. I'll see you tomorrow?"

"I'll be here."

Boyd saluted Joe and left the studio.

Alone in the cavernous space, Joe rubbed smudges and fingerprints off his guitar. Then, stepping over to its case, he placed it on the velvet. Like a low, slithering fog, the nagging parasite that haunted Joe's existence stirred beneath the surface. Its icy tendrils trailed up Joe's spine, leaving an undeniable impulse to scratch. Joe painfully wrapped his fingers around his arm in an attempt to stifle the urge.

Resting his hand against the piano, Joe steadied himself. Its polished smooth keys tantalized Joe's fingertips. Having played piano since he was a small child, this one constant brought him solace.

Sitting down on the bench, Joe's trembling fingers hovered inches above the keys. With a deep breath, Joe closed his eyes, and his fingers began to play Bach's "French Suite No.2 In C Minor." Each note of the flawless progression soothed his tormented mind as he floated on a cloud of pure bliss. Then like a hard slap the horrid sound of a misguided chord splintered the illusion. Joe's eyes flew open, he must have let his mind wander too far and his fingers faltered. Calming his nerves, Joe flexed his fingers and began the suite again. Once more his fingers betrayed him, and he made the same glaring error. How was this possible? He was a brilliant classical pianist. He hadn't been incompetent in his playing since he was five. Placing his elbows on the keys, the dreadful noise echoed from the walls. Joe ran his hands through his hair, his breathing labored. What was wrong with him? What had happened to his focus? His discipline? Then a far-off, distant voice whispered the answer. *Monica. Monica is to blame for all of your problems.*

Joe placed his hands over his ears and tried to ignore the tormentor's voice.

None of this would have happened if she would have listened to you and remembered her place. She is the reason your whole world is falling apart. Ungrateful shrew!

Sobs rose in Joe's throat, threatening to choke him.

You don't need her, Joe. She is nothing but a reminder of the past. I am the one who can make all of the pain disappear. I am the only one who can give you true happiness. Trust me.

Joe pounded his fists against his head as tears burned for release.

You know I'm your only friend, Joe. I am the only one who understands you. Stop this foolishness and come home to me.

But Joe didn't want to go home. All that was there were memories of a life that was. A love that was and a ghost of a small boy that was.

Joe's shoulders shook. Defeated tears splashed on the piano keys like rain.

Come home, Joe, come home to me . I promise to make it all better. You won't feel a thing, you will be . . . numb.

Joe stared at the dark before his closed eyes. His skin crawling with hundreds of insects, driving him to the edge of madness. He knew he had no other choice but to give in. To go home and pay the tormentor and spend another night in its arms of bottomless oblivion.

37

THE AROMA OF DINNER WELCOMED Bob and Jerry at the door. Jerry missed Betty's welcome kiss and hug, and he could sure use some comfort right now.

Mable exited the kitchen, wiping her hands on a dish towel.

"Hello, dear," Mable said to Bob.

"Hello," Bob replied, kissing Mable on the cheek.

"Did you have a good day?"

Bob hung up his coat. "It wasn't bad."

Jerry was silent as he hung up his coat.

"Dinner should be ready in about ten minutes if you want to wash up," Mable told Jerry.

"I'm not hungry," Jerry said.

"Not even for fresh-baked cookies?"

Jerry pushed his hair back. "No, I'm just tired."

"Are you feeling ill?" Mable asked, setting her hand on his shoulder.

"No. I just need to lie down. Good night."

"Good night, son," Bob said.

Jerry slumped his shoulders and trudged up the stairs.

Mable turned to Bob. "Is this because of the quarrel he had with Betty?"

"His mother is missing."

Martha gasped. "*What?*"

"Apparently, the hospital discharged her into Gus's care."

"Did he take her home?"

Bob shook his head.

Mable wrung her hands. "Oh, that evil man! What are we going to do?"

"Danny and John said they know someone who might be able to help."

Mable sighed. "Poor Jerry. I will make a tray for him."

"I think that's a wonderful idea," Bob said.

Mable returned to the kitchen, and Bob went into the living room. Betty stepped out of the dining room where she had been setting the table. She wanted to go up and talk to Jerry, but for some reason, she couldn't convince her feet to move. Instead, Betty joined her mother who was preparing a dinner tray for Jerry.

"I finished setting the dinner table, Mama."

"Thank you, dear," Martha said placing a glass of cold milk on the tray.

"If it's all right, I want to take the tray to Jerry," Betty said.

Mable paused and glanced at Betty. "I think that would be very nice."

Betty gave her a small smile, grabbed a cookie to set on the tray, and then headed up the stairs.

❖❖❖❖❖❖❖❖❖❖❖❖❖❖❖❖

Jerry was lying on his bed, trying to fight back the waves of grief and guilt that added to his headache. He had taken a couple of aspirin, but so far, they had not helped. A quiet knock pulled him off the bed. Jerry opened the door to see Betty with a dinner tray in her hand. His expression held no hint of joy.

"Hi," Betty whispered.

"Hi," Jerry answered, unmoving.

"May I come in?"

Jerry stepped back and let Betty into the room. She walked over to the small table by the window and set the tray down.

"It's roast beef, carrots, and potatoes," Betty said.

Jerry remained standing, like a sentinel by the door.

Betty turned to him. "I put a cookie on your plate. I know they're your favorite."

Jerry's cold stare hadn't thawed one degree.

Betty wanted to hug and comfort him, but her hand gripped her skirt instead. "I'm sorry to hear about your mother."

Jerry's eyes fell to the floor.

"I know how much she means to you."

Jerry pulled the door as wide as it would go. "Thank Mable for me, please."

"I will," Betty said, pausing in hopes that something more would be said, but Jerry wasn't making any gesture of kindness toward her, and his rigid pose made Betty's heart sink. Lowering her eyes, she left the room. The door closed and locked behind her, and she wiped a tear away.

38

WILL RARELY WENT TO THE Cornby Club, but it was the best place to have a casual drink with Patrick and unwind. The small, discreet club didn't have the extra entertainment and excitement that Will craved, but he wanted to avoid taking the chance of running into someone he knew.

Patrick looked around the elegant lobby and pulled on his tie. "Are you sure I'm not underdressed?

"Of course. You look fine," Will said.

A dark-haired hostess in a long burgundy dress showed them to a quiet table in the lounge.

"How is this table?" the hostess asked Will.

"Fine, doll," Will said, slipping her a tip.

"Thank you," she said, batting her long lashes at him.

He winked at her as she walked away. She glanced over her shoulder twice at him before she greeted the next guests. Relaxing piano music wafted over the dull clamor of chatting customers. A cocktail waitress in a skimpy black cocktail dress approached their table.

"Good evening, gentlemen. What can I get for you?"

"I'll have a scotch on the rocks," Will said.

"Same," Patrick said.

"Coming right up."

Patrick watched her saunter away, the flared tulle on her dress rubbing against the taffeta.

"Pretty girl," Will said.

"Hmm," Patrick hummed.

. Will crossed his legs and leaned back in his chair. "You know if you play your cards right, she might grant you some favors."

Patrick grinned. "That's all right. I'm not interested in any favors."

The waitress returned, and stooping down, she served their drinks.

"So, what's your name, doll?" Will asked.

"Connie," she answered in a nasal voice.

"Nice to meet you, Connie. I am Will, and this is my friend Patrick."

Patrick made eye contact with her. "Hello."

"Hi," she said with an eager smile.

An awkward moment passed before Will said something. "We will let you know when we need another round."

"Okay." She walked away.

Will took a smooth drink from the glass, as Patrick eyed his warily. The amber in the glass resembled a beer, so how harsh could it be? Taking a confident, hearty swallow, Patrick paused as the burning sensation filled his throat and eyes. Gripping the chair arm, Patrick blinked rapidly and did his best not to choke.

Will smiled as he swirled the glass in his hand. "I guess I should have warned you about the bite."

Patrick opened and closed his mouth, trying to catch his breath. "Excuse me."

"Of course."

Patrick got up and headed toward the men's washroom, leaving Will with a humorous grin. Twirling his swizzle stick in the glass, Will observed the room, and for the first time that day, he felt at ease, and then he noticed her. Sitting up straight, Will shook his head. His eyes had to be lying to him. There was no way it was her. Squinting, Will leaned forward, and when she turned and walked toward the bar, he could see her perfectly. His pupils dilated, and every muscle tightened. His eyes locked on her as he observed her with great interest.

"Are you ready for another round?" Connie inquired.

Will turned to her with a glower.

"Is something wrong?"

Will regained his composure and rubbed his hands together. "No, everything is fine. Tell me, the blond waitress standing at the table by the piano—is she new?"

"Yes, she started about a week ago."

Will nodded. "Ah."

"Do you know her?"

"We share a mutual acquaintance."

"Oh.

"Listen, would you mind doing me a favor?" Will asked.

"Of course."

❑■❑■❑■❑■❑■❑■❑■❑■❑■❑■❑

Monica shifted from one foot to the other while waiting for the bartender to fill her drink order. Everything about her skimpy work uniform was uncomfortable, from the low-cut dress that was too short to the pinching heels. It was only seven o'clock, and she already had a headache and a backache. Pulling at the unforgiving stockings, she tried to straighten the seam for the third time.

"Did you lose something?" the bartender said, setting drinks on her tray.

She looked up at the young man. "No. I've just been battling my stockings."

"I'm sure glad I don't have to wear those."

"Hey, Mike. Two gin and tonics for table six," Connie said, setting her tray on the bar.

"Sure thing," Mike said, walking away.

Monica was arranging things on her tray.

"Rough night?" Connie said.

"Oh, I'm just having trouble keeping my stocking seams straight."

"So, the gentleman at table nine says hello, and he would like for you to serve the next round."

Monica looked over at table nine, and the minute she saw him, her throat tightened.

"Just so we're clear, I'm not sharing the tip," Connie commented and walked away.

39

PATRICK RETURNED TO THE TABLE and casually sat down. "Sorry about that. I didn't realize I was so anxious."

"That's perfectly all right," Will said.

Patrick picked up his glass. "I wanted to apologize if I ruined practice today."

"Why would you think that?"

"Well, obviously, Boyd was right. Starting practice without Joe was a mistake."

Will scoffed. "Joe wasn't upset that we started without him. What upset him was we didn't need him."

Patrick sat back. "I agree with that. I don't think he wants things to change. I think he likes the status quo. Writing your own material is not the status quo."

Will suspended the glass by his fingertips. "You think writing our own material is the right direction?"

"Don't you? Look at it this way. After the single becomes successful, the group will be signed to record an album. Now how long do you think we can hold on to an audience if we're playing other group's material? We want groups copying us, right?"

Will nodded. "Right."

Patrick set his glass on the table. "I say we sit down and write the song together. Then we present it to Joe. It could be a hit single. He would be a fool to turn us down. What do you say?"

Will twitched his foot. "It's better than waiting to see how this contest turns out."

"This contest is a joke, in my opinion. A contract is a contract," Patrick said, sitting back in his chair.

"It's not about the contract, it's about Joe's ego," Will said, draining his glass.

Patrick chuckled. "Let me ask you something. You consider yourself to be a good bass player, right?"

"Of course I do."

"Would you have a contest with some pimple-faced, ignorant bumpkin who played a washtub bass to satisfy your ego?"

"Hell no," Will chortled.

"Exactly. Because you already know you're the better man."

Will rested his elbow on the armchair and regarded Patrick for a few moments.

Patrick sat forward in his chair. "When you're the best, you don't need to prove it. So, I guess the question is, do you want to be the best or do you want to continue to be crushed by someone who knows they're not?"

Patrick sat back in his chair and finished his drink, and Will longed for another one.

❑■❑■❑■❑■❑■❑■❑■❑■❑■❑■❑

Monica waited until her thoughts were clear before approaching Will and Patrick's table.

Smiling, she forced the greeting from her mouth. "Good evening, gentlemen."

Relaxed in his chair, Will's dark eyes roamed up Monica's legs. "Hello, Monica."

"Will," Monica said.

Will steepled his fingers. "Imagine my surprise when I look across the room and observe you serving drinks to a table of drooling businessmen. Whatever made you decide to take a job as a cocktail waitress?"

Monica removed Will's drink from her tray and set it in front of him. "I needed the work."

"Why?"

Monica picked up Patrick's empty glass. "You can stop pretending, Will. You know damn well why I needed a job."

His lips stretched slowly. "So, did you two split the sheets?"

Monica placed Patrick's drink in front of him. "We're separated, yes."

Will set his hand on his heart. "Ah, how sad is that? I feel heartbroken for you."

Monica kept her attention on Patrick. "Will there be anything else?"

"I do have one question," Will said, sitting forward.

Monica gripped her tray tight against her chest before meeting Will's sneer.

"How does it feel to have greedy old men gawking at your cleavage and pinching your plump fanny?"

Monica shrugged. "I wouldn't know anything about that."

"Oh, come now, surely you want them to tip you well? Or maybe it's not the tip you're looking for, but an invitation to let them take you to a private room."

Monica leaned forward and looked Will square in the eye. "You're just jealous because I would rather be with a lecherous old man than be with you."

Will's face screwed up into an enraged scowl as his mouth dropped. Satisfied, Monica tossed her hair and walked away.

40

JERRY ATE A SMALL AMOUNT of his dinner before crawling into bed. Sleep visited him briefly, but all too soon, he was awake again and staring at the ceiling. He glanced at the clock on his nightstand. It was only 11:30 p.m. Groaning, he turned over and rubbed his eyes. The single, horrible question he had contemplated for hours resounded in his head. What did Gus do with his mother? Jerry couldn't imagine that he had taken her very far. She was so sick and would only be a burden to him. He had never cared for her before and surely wouldn't start now. They had to be somewhere close, but where? Moonlight was shining through the lace curtains, casting creepy webbed shadows on the wall like ghastly faces, cobwebs, and . . . spiders. Crawling, creeping, terrifying spiders.

Jerry sprang upright on the bed, his eyes darting around the room. Of course! How could he have been so stupid? Jerry threw back the covers, jumped out of bed, and pulled on his clothes. Then, running down the stairs, he retrieved a flashlight from the kitchen drawer, grabbed his jacket, and left the house, running as fast as his legs would carry him.

The chilly night air prickled the hair on the back of Jerry's neck as he made the long trek out to the house. He contemplated taking a shortcut through a vacant lot that was marked with large no-trespassing signs. Not wanting to waste more time, Jerry ignored the warnings and climbed through the barbed-wire fence that threatened to tear holes in his flesh. The faint flashlight beam bobbed along the thick weeds, rocks, and holes that littered the landscape. When Jerry reached the fence perimeter, his body ached from his tight muscles. Passing through a hole in the clipped wires, Jerry climbed the ravine to the main road.

After another half mile, the foreboding house came into view. The full moon cast an eerie glow over the tortured landscape of the front yard. Jerry stopped, wishing he could turn around and go back. He summoned his courage and approached the hole in the ground that was the cellar. A new chain and padlock hung from the dilapidated doors. Jerry yanked on the formidable chain, but it wouldn't budge. Falling to his knees, Jerry placed his ear as close as he could to the jagged hole in the door. All he could hear was the pounding of his heart.

"Mom, are you down there?" Jerry cried as loud as he dared. Returning his ear to the hole, Jerry prayed to hear something. What if she was unconscious? What if she was . . . Jerry shook the dreadful thought out of his head. Standing, he searched the yard for something to try and break the chain, but among all the junk, he found nothing. Jerry began to panic. There had to be something! Then he thought of the garage. Horrific memories of being tied to a chair in the putrid-smelling space tormented his brain, but he couldn't afford to be paralyzed by fear. He had made it this far; he had to move forward. Gripping the flashlight till his knuckles were white, Jerry slowly descended the path. The dead tree that bent over the grey cinder block garage was in view now. Its long barren branches choked out the only window, and a large padlock hung from the door. Jerry choked down the large lump in his throat and stepped forward. An unfamiliar sound froze him in his tracks. At first, he thought he was imagining things, but one more slight move of his foot and the sound was confirmed. It was a growl. A low, deep, guttural growl. Adrenaline flooded Jerry's veins. What was out there in the dark? A coyote? A demon? Slowly, oh so slowly, Jerry lifted the flashlight to illuminate the creature. Its eyes reflected the light like two silver orbs, and its jowls stretched across its saliva-soaked teeth. Jerry knew one false move, and the beast would attack.

"I wondered how long it would be before ya showed up here again."

Jerry turned to see Gus leering at him. "I knew ya just couldn't resist the urge to snoop around. So I got me some security."

Jerry stared into Gus's yellow eyes. "All I want to know is where my mother is."

Gus's lips parted over his hole-filled mouth. "Where do ya think she is?"

Jerry was shaking so hard his teeth ground together. "Please, please, just let her go. Whatever you want, you can have, but please, let her go."

Gus cackled. "Let her go? Now, why would I want to do that?"

"I have money."

Gus felt his stubbly chin. "How much money?"

"I'm not sure of a definite amount. I was saving it to buy a house and a ring."

"Ah, now isn't that nice? Ya got yourself a little sweetheart, heh?"

Jerry clasped his hands. "I will give you all the money I have. I will drain my savings. Just let my mother go."

"I have to say, you have piqued my interest, boy. Yes. You have piqued it quite a bit."

"I will go to the bank first thing in the morning and bring you the money."

Gus nodded his head. "Well, now, that sounds mighty fine."

"She is . . . still alive?" Jerry asked.

Gus cocked his head. "What? You think I'm some kinda of animal?"

Jerry's nostrils flared.

"You just worry about comin' back here tomorrow with the money."

Jerry nodded.

"Oh, and don't try anything stupid, or I'll throw ya in the cellar with my new friend. He's mighty vicious when he's hungry."

Jerry looked over toward the animal that was tied to a post by a thick, ragged rope.

"Now get along before I decide to let him taste ya now," Gus hissed.

Jerry turned and ran as fast as he could down the drive. The sound of Gus's malicious laughter and the dog's ear-splitting barks followed him into the darkness.

41

S TREETLAMPS CAST SILVER SHADOWS ON pools of rainwater along
the vacant street. Monica held her coat tight as she walked to the
bus stop. Her feet and back ached, and thoughts of soaking in a
scented bubble bath with a glass of champagne teased Monica's weary
mind. But there would be no bath, only a tepid shower from a leaky
showerhead. Passing by Carter's Department Store window, Monica
admired the colorful summer dresses adorning the lifeless mannequins.
A dainty light blue handbag hung on a gold chain from one of the
mannequin's shoulders. She stopped and gazed at the perfect accessory,
like a child dreaming of a Christmas toy. Touching the glass with her
fingertips, she saw a reflection she didn't recognize. Caked-on makeup
covered the imperfections of puffy features and sticky, stiff hairspray
held the messy chignon on top of her head. The manager insisted the
girls look beautiful and pleasing for the gentlemen who frequented the
club. But the truth was, she looked cheap and easy, so the leering old
men might tip her a few extra dollars. Monica turned away from the
haggard face. A large black tear rolling down her cheek left a crooked
line like the scar on her heart. The bus had pulled up to the curb, and
she ran precariously on her high heels, hoping to catch it.

Sitting at the back of the bus, Monica noticed the spindly runs
on her new stockings that she couldn't afford to replace. More black

tears fell, and thoughts of the home she left behind made her clutch her stomach. How much longer could she live this way? She hated being a burden on her sister, she hated sleeping on a cot, and she hated herself and the role she had to play. One phone call and this nightmare would end. Sure, he would berate, admonish, and punish her in his own silent way. But she could endure it if it meant she could just go home, sleep in her own bed, feel safe, and erase this whole nightmare from her mind. Clutching her purse tightly, she leaned her head against the glass window and closed her eyes for the remainder of the bus ride. After walking four blocks to her sister's house, she would go to bed hungry and dream of a sweet little boy who stole her heart away.

42

Nancy sat on her bedroom floor, surrounded by stacks of scrapbooks containing her treasured newspaper clippings. Sighing heavily, Nancy closed the last scrapbook from her stack. She had spent the entire morning searching for information about Joey and The Moon Rockers. Maybe she had missed something. There had to be some evidence somewhere, but sadly, she had turned up empty. Twirling her pencil between her finger, Nancy stared at the flyer for the show. She knew she needed to investigate, but where would she start? Picking up her notebook, she began to write down where she could find some clues.

"Where do you think I should start, Mr. Pomboy?" Nancy asked the beloved bear that sat on her bed.

"The library? The newspaper archives? Hmmm."

Nancy's mother knocked and then opened the door. "My goodness Nancy, your floor looks like a paper bin exploded."

"I'm doing research, Mom," Nancy said, not looking up from her notebook.

"Can you tear yourself away long enough to talk to Carol? She's on the phone."

"I'm coming." Nancy stood up and stepped over the scrapbooks on her tippy toes. Following her mother into the living room, she picked up the phone and flopped on the checkered couch.

"Hey, Carol."

"Hey Nan, what you doin'?"

"Oh, not much. Just doing some research."

"What kind of research?"

Nancy wound the phone cord around her finger. "Remember that band that is playing at the community center?"

"The Hound Dogs?"

"No, the other one. Joey and The Moon Rockers."

"Oh, yeah."

Lying back on the couch, Nancy crossed her legs. "Well, it's driving me crazy! I can't find out anything about them."

"Why don't you just go to the record store?"

Nancy sat up with a start. "Oh, Carol, you're a genius! Of course, the record store! They're bound to know something!"

"Glad I could help. I was wondering if you would help me with a dress pattern?"

"We don't have time for that now! We need to go to the record store!"

"But I promised my mom."

Nancy tied the loose shoestring on her saddle shoe. "Oh, for goodness sake, of course, I will help after we go to the record store."

"But . . ."

"I'm on my way to your house."

"But . . ."

"See you then!" Nancy hung up the phone and rushed to her room, grabbing her purse, pad, and pencil. "See you later, Mr. Pomboy. I'm on the trail of a real story!" Nancy waved her pencil at the bear and left.

43

D RESSED IN HER MOTHER'S OLD green sweater with three buttons missing and baggy jeans, Carol reluctantly walked to the record store with Nancy. Carol was a shy, reserved girl with brown hair and a plump figure. Her free time was spent helping her mother with housework and watching after her two younger siblings. Going out somewhere and falling out of the routine made Carol uncomfortable and self-conscious.

"Well, you hurry up," Nancy said. "I swear, a turtle walks faster than you."

Carol shuffled her feet. "I don't know why you're in such a big hurry to get there."

"Don't you see? The answer to this mystery could be right around the corner!"

Carol rolled her eyes.

Strolling down Mulberry Street, the girls stopped across the street from The Beat.

"There it is!" Nancy said.

Carol pulled her sweater tighter. "Do I have to go in there with you? Can't I wait out here?"

"No, you can't wait out here! Now come on," Nancy said, taking hold of Carol's sleeve and dragging her across the street.

"Now remember, we are on an investigation, so we have to be cool," Nancy instructed.

"How do we act cool?"

"You know, nonchalant."

Carol wrinkled her nose. "Noncha wha?"

"Just follow my lead."

The door to the store was open, and Chuck Berry's deep voice rumbled through the store. Eddie sat behind the counter reading a newspaper with a sucker in his mouth.

Nancy walked casually into the store. Spotting Eddie, Carol turned down the first row of records. Carol walked as close to Nancy as she could without bumping into her. Nancy leafed through some records as she surveyed her surroundings.

"Look at some albums," Nancy whispered to Carol.

"Why?"

"Because we want the clerk to think we're customers."

"Okay," Carol said, pretending to be interested in the displayed records. "Look, Nancy, there is a magazine rack."

Nancy walked over and stood in front of the display.

"Maybe there is something in one of these." Carol picked up a magazine.

"Don't be silly. They're not famous."

"How do you know?"

Nancy frowned at Carol and put the magazine back on the rack. "If they were famous, we wouldn't be here."

"Oh. Maybe the clerk knows something," Carol said.

"Maybe, but I have to be cool. I can't just walk up to the counter and start asking a bunch of questions. He'll know something is up."

A middle-aged man who was browsing albums turned to Nancy. "Hey, have you listened to this album before?" he asked, passing the record to Nancy. "I'm shopping for a birthday present for my daughter, and I have no idea what you young kids listen to these days."

Nancy glanced at the Lawrence Welk album in her hands. "Well, honestly, I don't know many contemporary artists myself."

"I know Elvis," Carol said.

The man looked down his nose at Carol and took the album back from Nancy. "That is one young man I do *not* want my daughter to listen to."

"Hello," Eddie said, walking up to the customer. "Is there something that I can help you with?"

The man turned his back to Nancy and Carol. "Yes, I am looking for some *wholesome* music that I can buy for my daughter's birthday."

"Of course, sir. May I ask what album you have in your hand?"

The man showed the record to Eddie.

"Excellent choice, sir, but I think I have something she might like better."

"It's not going to be someone like *Elvis*, is it?"

Eddie put the record back in its spot. "No, sir, if you will follow me."

The man, Nancy, and Carol followed Eddie to another row of records.

Eddie's fingers flipped nimbly through some albums. "Ah yes, here it is." Eddie pulled out an album and handed it to the man.

The man smiled.

"Better?" Eddie asked.

"Much. Thank you so much, young man."

"Of course."

The man followed Eddie to the counter, and Eddie chatted with the customer while he rang up his purchase.

"What album did he choose?" Carol asked Nancy.

"Doris Day," Nancy answered.

"Oh, my mother loves Doris," Carol said.

The man walked out the door with a smile on his face, and Eddie went back to his newspaper. Nancy stepped up to the counter, with Carol hiding behind her. Eddie didn't look up right away, so Nancy cleared her throat.

Eddie looked up. "May I help you?"

"Yes. I was wondering if you had ever seen this flyer," Nancy said, pulling it out of her purse and laying it on the counter.

Eddie turned the flyer toward him. "Oh yes, there is one in our window and a few extras by the register."

Nancy pulled her pad and paper out of her purse. "Good. So, what can you tell me about Joey and The Moon Rockers?"

Eddie wrinkled his lip. "Um, not much, really."

"You mean you don't know who they are?"

"Nope, can't say as I do."

"You mean to tell me that you work at a record store and don't know about the local talent?"

Eddie raised an eyebrow. "How do you know they're local?"

"Because a friend told me."

Eddie placed his left hand on the counter and put his right on his hip. "Hmm, then maybe you should ask your friend about them."

Nancy pursed her lips. "Well, she's never actually seen them play."

"Oh, so she is *assuming* they're local."

Nancy tapped her finger on the counter. "So, I suppose you don't know who the Hound Dogs are, either?"

"Let me think," Eddie said, tapping his finger on his chin. "You know, I do know who the Hound Dogs are."

"All right then, what can you tell me about them?" Nancy said, poising her pencil over the paper.

"I can tell you they're one hell of a good rock 'n' roll band."

"And do you happen to know any of the members?"

Eddie frowned as he watched Nancy writing in her notebook. "You know, I have a question for you, actually. Who are you, and why are you asking me so many questions?"

Nancy looked up at Eddie and paused before answering. "I am Nancy Calhoun, a reporter for *The Madison Herald.*"

"Nancy!" Carol gasped.

Nancy shot Carol a stern look.

"You're a reporter?" Eddie asked.

"Yes."

"For *The Madison Herald?*"

Nancy folded her arms. "Yes."

Eddie laughed.

Nancy folded her arms. "I fail to see what you find so amusing."

"I just have never seen a reporter in pedal pushers and saddle shoes."

"It's my day off."

"Is that a fact?"

"Yes, it is. Now are you going to answer my questions, or will I have to note in my article how uncooperative and rude you are?"

Eddie blinked his eyes. "Excuse me?"

Nancy stuck her chin out. "You heard me."

"Oh, I heard you. I just can't believe my ears is all."

"Well, believe them. Now, can we resume our interview?"

Eddie shook his head. "No. I don't think so."

Nancy opened her mouth in surprise. "Wha-what?"

"I said, I don't think so."

"Why not?"

Eddie folded his arms on the counter. "Because I don't believe you are really a reporter."

"Are you calling me a liar?" Nancy squeaked.

"Yeah. I think I am."

"How dare you call me a liar! Why, this is slander!"

Eddie grinned at her, making her face puff out.

"You . . . you . . . just wait until I finish my article!" Nancy said, picking up her pencil and notepad. "Why, by the time I finished writing about how arrogant and horrible you are, you'll be sorry!" Flouncing her hair and turning on her heel, Nancy stormed out the door, almost knocking Danny and John over.

"Woah, where is she goin' in such a hurry?" Danny said.

"She is on some kinda mission," John said, going inside the store with Danny behind him.

"Another satisfied customer, hey Eds?" John asked Eddie.

Eddie shook his head. "That one sure is a piece of work."

"Oh?" Danny said, taking a piece of candy from the jar on the counter.

"Yeah, she was telling me some cockamamie story about being a newspaper reporter."

"A newspaper reporter here? That's kinda funny, don't you think, Barnaby?" Danny said, stepping up behind John, who was looking at the wide-eyed girl standing in front of him. Danny set his hand on John's shoulder. "Scarin' the customers again?"

"Apparently," John said.

"Hey there," Danny said. "Can we help you with something?"

Carol shifted her wide eyes to Danny.

"Eds, do you know this girl?" John asked.

"She was with the *reporter*," Eddie answered.

"Are you a reporter?" John asked Carol.

Carol slowly shook her head.

John leaned forward. "You know we can't help you if you don't say something."

"I . . . I should go," Carol stuttered.

"So soon?"

Carol twisted her hands in front of her. "I should catch up with my friend."

"The reporter?" Danny asked.

Carol sighed. "I guess so."

"She's not a reporter?" John asked.

Carol pulled on her hair. "Do I have to answer that?"

John glanced at Danny, who shrugged.

"I guess not," John said.

"May I go now?" Carol asked.

"Sure," John said.

Carol headed toward the door.

"Hey, I like your sweater," John said.

Carol paused long enough to glance back at John. He winked at her, and she ran out of the store, her face as red as a tomato.

44

Tension and nerves tightened as the community center show drew near. With only a handful of days left, the boys immersed themselves in rehearsals, determined to polish their act. Danny, John, and Ronnie convened early to strategize on the two best songs for the performance. The band had undeniably improved, but the challenge remained—Jerry struggled with certain tunes, and spotlighting Danny's talents on easier songs proved to be a tough balancing act.

"I wish we knew what songs they were playing," Danny said, tapping his pencil on top of the coffee table.

"Well, knowing Joe, they will be showstoppers," John replied.

Danny rested his head on his hand. "I know it, but 'Johnny B. Goode' isn't an option, right?"

John rubbed his temples. "I don't think Jerry could handle it."

"Why don't we just have Jerry play a few simple chords, kind of like a bass line? Have him stand close enough to the drums, and if things get too bad, I can drown him out," Ronnie suggested.

"That's not a terrible idea. What do you think, Barnaby?" Danny asked.

John, leaning back against the couch with bent knees, tapped his knee with his thumb. "Yeah, that might work. As long as Jerry doesn't catch on. Are things improving between him and Betty?"

Danny shook his head. "No."

"What's her problem?"

"I have no idea. All I know is she is stomping her foot and being snippy. I stay clear of her when she gets like that," Danny said.

"You mean she's done it before?" John questioned.

"Oh yeah, whenever she gets mad, she becomes a little tyrant."

"Sounds like the headmistress, except she ain't little," Ronnie remarked.

"Sounds like someone needs to have a talk with Betty," John suggested.

"You volunteering?" Danny scoffed.

"I could, but she wouldn't get away with stomping her foot at me."

"Never mind," Danny said.

"What time is it, anyway?" John asked.

"Nap time," Ronnie declared, his hands crossed over his stomach.

"You know what, Barnaby? I got an idea," Danny said.

"Oh no, you don't."

"What?"

"Any time you get an idea, I somehow end up getting involved in some crazy situation," John remarked.

"We should have a pre-show party."

John scowled at Danny.

"Nothing big or fancy, just a small gathering of our close friends. It would give us a chance to perform in front of a small audience."

John grunted.

"Come on, Barnaby, it would be fun and relieve some of the tension."

"And just where would we have this little party?" John inquired.

"We could have it right here. Of course, I would have to clear it with Uncle Bob."

"I think it sounds like a great idea," Ronnie added.

"We could have some sodas and pizza or something," Danny continued.

Ronnie nudged John with his foot. "Come on, boss, all work and no play makes Hound Dogs bite."

John snarled at Ronnie.

"Point proven," Danny said.

"All right, I guess it does sound like it might be fun," John grumbled.

Danny jumped up off the floor. "Awesome! I'll go tell Eddie."

"Hey now, wait a second," John said, slowing down Danny's enthusiasm. "You make sure that he understands this is a private party and not blab it to the whole town. Got it?"

"Understood." Danny left the room.

John stretched out his legs.

"Everything is going to work out," Ronnie said, lazily twirling his drum stick.

John sighed. "I sure hope so. I will be so glad when this whole mess is behind us."

A little while later, Danny returned. "Hey, look who's here."

Lou walked into the rehearsal space with a broad smile.

"Hey Lou," John greeted.

"Hey. Nice place you have here," Lou said admiring the space.

"Thanks," Danny said.

"Lou, this is our drummer, Ronnie. Ronnie, this is Lou," John introduced.

"Nice to meet you, Ronnie," Lou said.

Ronnie saluted him.

"So, I am assuming that you have news?" John asked.

Lou put his hands in his pockets. "I do."

John sat up. "Let's hear it."

"I went out to the house and checked things out."

Danny sat on a stool. "And?"

"I observed some activity that leads me to believe Mrs. Palmer is still there."

John's brow furrowed. "But we went out there looking for her."

Lou rocked back on his heels. "I know, but I don't think she's in the house. I think he might be keeping her in the garage."

Danny raised his eyebrow. "Why the garage?" .

"I saw Gus making several trips back and forth from the house to the garage, and there's a dog tied outside the garage door."

"Jerry told me horror stories about the garage," John said, rubbing the back of his neck.

"What do we do, Lou? Call the police?" Danny asked.

"I'm not sure. At this point, we have no proof that she is in the garage. If the police go out there, who knows what story Gus would tell them. It could put her life in danger."

"We need proof that she's in that garage," John concluded.

"What about the dog?" Danny asked.

Ronnie sat up. "I can handle the dog."

"No, Ronnie, it's too dangerous," John said.

"Do you want to know if she's in the garage or not?" Ronnie said.

John sighed. "All right, we go check things out, and if this dog looks too dangerous, we devise another plan. Agreed?"

They all agreed, and leaving the rehearsal space, they headed out to Jerry's house.

45

FAINT BREEZE PRICKLED THE PERSPIRATION that seeped into the collar of Jerry's shirt. Even in the noonday sun, the foreboding shadow that loomed over the garage was terrifying. Jerry licked his dry lips. His fatigued mind had conjured up more fear and apprehension as he walked the arduous miles out of the house. Visions of unspeakable things Gus may have done to his mother clenched Jerry's stomach. Facing Gus by himself was a stupid idea, but Jerry didn't want to give him any excuse to alter the terms of their agreement. Finding his mother alive and safe was Jerry's top priority. With his hand in his pocket, resting on his money, Jerry murmured a quick prayer and knocked on the door.

Gus opened the door with a jagged grin. "I was beginning to think you weren't comin'."

Jerry stepped through the entryway but hovered by the door. "I had to make up an excuse to leave work early."

Gus rolled his greedy hands. "Did you bring it?"

Jerry nodded and slowly took the money out of his pocket.

Gus snatched it and counted it with greedy shaking hands. "What's this? A measly hundred bucks?"

"It's all the money I have."

"You expect me to believe that?" Gus spat.

"It's the truth."

Gus groaned. "Well, it ain't enough. I need more."

"I haven't got any more!" Jerry snapped.

"I think you're a liar."

Jerry threw up his hands. "You can think whatever you want, but it's true."

Gus grunted and walked over to a small table next to the couch.

"I gave you my money. Now, where is my mother?"

Gus took the bottle off the table and pulled the cork out with his broken front tooth. "I thought there would be more money."

"Sorry to disappoint you," Jerry sneered.

Gus poured his drink into a smudged cracked glass. "How much do they pay ya, anyways?"

"None of your business."

"Well, I was just thinkin' ya must pull a decent wage if ya's a thinkin' about buyin' a house and all."

Jerry shifted his weight. "I have a couple of years to save."

Gus scoffed. "At this rate, you will need at least five."

"All right, cut the crap. How much money will it take for you to release my mother?"

Gus felt his stubbly chin. "Oh, I don't know. I figure maybe another three hundred dollars."

"Three hundred dollars! Where am I supposed to come up with that kind of money?" Jerry asked.

"I don't know, but I'm sure you'll figure it out. Maybe ya can take it from those rich folks ya been a livin' with." Gus watched Jerry's fingers roll up into fists. "I would advise you not to do somethin' real stupid, boy. You wouldn't want any harm to come to your mama, now would ya?"

Jerry breathed heavily through his flared nostrils.

"Now, run along and get the hell out of here before I beat you within an inch of your life," Gus sputtered.

Loud, sharp barks came from outside, causing Gus to turn his head. Thrusting all his weight forward, Jerry jumped on Gus, knocking him backward. Gus moaned as his head crashed on the floor.

Jerry sat on top of Gus, his hands wrapped tightly around his throat. "I am going to kill you!"

The pressure on Gus's throat was intense, causing him to choke, but Jerry was light, and Gus flung him across the room. Jerry crashed into the overstuffed chair, hitting his head hard on the end table. Newspapers, magazines, empty bottles, and dirty dishes rained down on top of Jerry. Gus staggered to his wobbly feet and walked over to Jerry, who was groaning with his hands gripping his head.

Gus took off his belt and wrapped it around his grimy hand. "I told you not to do anything stupid, now, didn't I? When I get through whippin' ya, you're gonna wish ya was dead."

Gus lifted the belt, but before it struck Jerry, something hard hit Gus on the back of the head.

"Arggg!" Gus grunted, stumbling into the wall.

Jerry looked up to see his mother with a pot clenched in her hand. "You leave him be!"

Gus turned to her. "You little bitch! I'm gonna gut ya!"

"You take one more step; it will be your last."

Everyone turned to see Lou standing in the front doorway with a gun pointed straight at Gus.

"Who the hell are you!" Gus snarled.

"Someone who would like nothing better than to blow your head off!" Lou growled.

Jerry looked up to see John and Danny come in behind Lou.

Jerry's eyes closed. "John, thank God."

"Jerry, are you all right?" John said, stepping over the trash on the floor.

Jerry rubbed his head. "I've been better."

John helped Jerry off the floor.

"Take the mealy mouth brat and get outta my house!" Gus bellowed.

"No one is goin' anywhere until the cops get here," John said.

Gus raised his eyebrows. "What cops?"

"The ones that are comin' to haul your ass to jail."

"On what charge?"

"Wife abuse," John hissed.

Gus scoffed. "You can't prove nothin'."

"Look at her," Jerry said, crossing to his mother. "She's starvin', dirty, and I bet they would find more than one bruise if she was examined." Jerry put his arms around his mother. "It's all gonna be all right, Mom. I promise."

Gus ran his shaking hand over his head. "Look, I don't want no trouble. Maybe there is some deal we can make."

"Are you serious?" John tittered.

"All I want is what's comin' to me," Gus said.

"And just what is it that you think you have comin' to you?" John asked.

"My share of her money."

"You want half of zero?" Danny asked.

"She has more than zero. This house has got to be worth somethin'," Gus spat.

"Your name isn't on the house, Einstein," Jerry scoffed.

"No, but hers is, and she's my wife."

"Say you get your *share*, then what?" John inquired.

"I'll move out of the house," Gus said, lifting his chin.

Jerry squinted his eyes. "Oh, no, if you get your share, it means you sign the divorce papers and you leave this town *forever*."

Gus wiped his sleeve over his nose. "All right, deal."

"It's going to take me some time to pull three hundred dollars together," Jerry said.

"Oh no, that was then—now I want five."

"Five?" Jerry gasped.

"Five," Gus hissed.

"I gave you a hundred, so four and you leave the house today," Jerry sneered.

Gus raised his eyes, and his sweaty palms rubbed on his pants. The wail of a siren shrieked in the distance, adding urgency to the moment.

"Do we have a deal?" Jerry asked.

Gus fervently nodded his head while his eyes darted around the room.

"I will meet you here in a week and we finish this," Jerry said.

"A week? I ain't got a week! I need that money now!" Gus yelled, his body shaking.

"You know I don't have the money now. I gave you all I had!"

Gus grunted and peered out the window to see the cop cars coming up the street. "All right, one damn week!"

"I'll be here," Jerry said.

Gus didn't say another word. He ran through the room, toppling over another pile of papers.

The sirens stopped wailing as the police pulled into the driveway and the backdoor slammed.

46

RONNIE MUNCHED ON SOME CRACKERS that he took from the kitchen that morning. He had told Danny that he would wait in the car, but he couldn't stop wondering about the dog.

Ronnie ambled up the driveway expecting to find a large ruthless dog, but the dog he saw lying in the dirt, with a heavy, thick rope tied around its neck, was medium-sized. Its parched tongue hung from the side of its mouth and goo gathered at the corner of its eyes. Hearing the crunch of the dirt under Ronnie's boots, the dog turned its head. Its black eyes locked onto Ronnie with a glare. Ronnie dared to move closer, and the dog lowered its ears and head. Its intimidating growls rumbled deep inside his belly. Ronnie stopped a few feet in front of the dog and tilted his head to the right and left. Leaning forward from the waist, Ronnie made a guttural chirping noise. The dog stopped its growling and blinked. Ronnie removed his brace and sat on the ground. The dog wasn't growling, but he wasn't relaxing either. His eye remained fixated on Ronnie.

"I know you're hurt and scared, but I don't want to hurt you. I want to be your friend," Ronnie said, rummaging through his pocket. The dog's focus shifted, and it licked its nose when Ronnie produced a cracker.

"It's not much, but it's all I have," Ronnie said, tossing cracker. The dog caught it before it hit the ground. Ronnie smiled.

The dog devoured the cracker without a hint of hostility.

"I hate seeing you tied up, thirsty, and starving. But I can tell you this much, you're not alone. You have me now and I'm going to help you," Ronnie said, giving the dog another cracker.

The shriek of a siren in the distance raised the dog's ears.

"Sounds like help is on its way," Ronnie said, leaning back on his hands.

The dog's attention stayed focused on the horizon until Gus came running out of the back door. Even then, the dog didn't make a sound or movement; he just watched as Gus disappeared over the hill.

47

J ERRY SAT NEXT TO HIS mother while the police officers questioned her about her ordeal. Her addled mind couldn't follow the questions, and if she did manage to answer, her replies were fragmented. Jerry explained her illness to the police officers, so they directed their questions to him. Unable to keep her weary eyes open, Martha laid her head on Lou's shoulder and went to sleep.

Danny and John escaped the suffocating atmosphere by leaving the house to check on Ronnie.

"Boy, am I glad to get out of there," Danny said, glancing back over his shoulder. "Cops make me nervous."

"Me too," John agreed.

"I know they have a job to do, but I would just as soon stay as far away from them as I can."

John put his hands in his pockets. "You never did tell me how you got in trouble."

"There's not much to tell, really. I was young and dumb, end of story."

John chuckled. "I'm pretty sure there is more to the story than that."

Danny nodded. "I suppose so. I promise to tell you the whole story some other time, okay?"

"That's fair."

Danny and John stopped in front of Danny's empty car.

"You did say you left Ronnie in the car, right, Danny?" John asked.

Danny sighed. "I did."

The two reflected in silence for a few more moments.

"Are you thinking what I'm thinking?" Danny asked.

John rubbed his chin. "I don't know. What are you thinking?"

"I think Ronnie went for a walk."

"To visit, oh I don't know, a dog?" John asked, his eyes still focused on the car.

"Yep, that's what I'm thinking."

"I guess we're walking to the garage."

"I guess so," Danny said, as he followed John up the driveway.

Ronnie was petting the dog's head that was resting on his knee when John and Danny approached them.

"Hey, Ronnie," John said. "Looks like you made a new friend."

"I did," Ronnie beamed.

"This is the vicious dog?" Danny asked John.

John shrugged.

"He's not vicious," Ronnie said. "He's just scared and lonely."

"What should we do about him?" Danny asked John.

"I don't know," John said. "Call animal control, I guess."

Ronnie's head snapped up and his brow furrowed. "Animal control? What are you talking about?"

"Well, we can't leave the dog here and we can't take him with us." John said.

"Why can't we take him with us?" Ronnie asked.

"Because he's a stray dog that is a victim of animal abuse. He needs to be taken to a facility where they can care for him and find him a proper home," John reasoned.

Ronnie shook his head. "I'm not letting animal control take him anywhere."

John crouched next to Ronnie. "Ronnie, those people are professionals and know how to handle sick dogs."

"I told you—he's not sick," Ronnie growled.

John rolled his tongue. "And you told me that he was scared, right?"

"I did."

"Well, scared dogs can be very dangerous. He could easily bite you."

"Yeah, and what if he has rabies?" Danny added.

"He already has fleas," John remarked.

"I don't care," Ronnie said, refusing to look John in the eye.

"Yes, you do, and I know you want him to get the care he needs."

Ronnie slowly turned his head. "I do, but I want to be the one to take him in. He's not some stray we found on the side of the road. He's got someone who cares about him."

John stood up. "Fair enough. Danny, go get a blanket from inside the house," John said.

"But . . ."

"Go on."

Danny turned and walked to the house, shaking his head.

Ronnie put his brace on, and John helped him up. Danny returned with the blanket and handed it to Ronnie.

Ronnie chittered at the dog and gave him another cracker.

"You think he will bite him?" Danny asked John.

"I hope not."

Placing the blanket over the dog, Ronnie removed the callous rope, exposing red sores and blisters. "It's okay, buddy. You're safe with me."

The dog didn't protest when Ronnie picked him up and carried him down the driveway to the car.

"Barnaby, he isn't going to want to let that dog go," Danny said.

"We will deal with it as it comes," John replied, and Danny nodded.

48

Fter the police left, it was decided that Lou would take Jerry and his mother to the hospital, while John and Danny took Ronnie and the dog to the animal shelter. It wasn't the resolution Ronnie wanted, but John and Danny explained that it was in the dog's best interest for the shelter to treat his ailments and find him a good home.

It was late afternoon when they arrived at the city animal shelter. The yellow brick building with a picture of a dog chasing a ball on the side brought no comfort to Ronnie. Danny went inside to inform the staff that he had an abused, homeless dog that needed medical attention.

The pleasant young shelter worker followed Danny to the car, and Danny opened the passenger door.

Ronnie held the dog closer and glared at the young woman.

"Ronnie, this is Tammy, and she is here to take care of the dog," Danny said.

Tammy's blue eyes twinkled at Ronnie from behind her small red glasses. "Hello, Ronnie. Danny tells me this little guy is hurt and needs our help."

Ronnie was silent.

"Can I take a look at him?" Tammy asked.

"He doesn't like strangers."

Tammy squatted. "Oh, I understand that. It's hard to meet new people."

Ronnie's features softened.

"If you lift the blanket, I can see him."

Ronnie lifted the corner of the blanket. The dog looked at Tammy, and his lip curled.

"Hey, there," Tammy said. "You're not happy to be here, are you?"

The dog buried his head in the blanket.

Tammy stood up. "The dog seems to be stressed and maybe a bit hostile."

"He's scared," Ronnie said.

"I agree," Tammy said. "You need to bring him inside so Doctor Canfield can examine him tomorrow morning."

Ronnie's face fell. "You mean he has to spend the night alone?"

"I promise to do what I can to ensure his comfort," Tammy said.

"Will you leave on a light and talk to him?"

"I will," Tammy said, touching Ronnie's knee.

Ronnie looked at Tammy's hand like it was a spider. Tammy pulled her hand back. Reluctantly, Ronnie got out of the car and carried the dog inside.

Tammy looked dismayed at John. "I was only trying to comfort Ronnie."

"He's just hypersensitive," John said.

"He'll be fine," Danny said.

"I hope so," Tammy said, heading for the door.

John and Danny followed her inside.

❖❖❖❖❖❖❖❖❖❖❖❖❖❖

Surrendering the dog to Tammy was heart-wrenching for Ronnie. Even though Tammy explained that the intake area was restricted, Ronnie didn't understand why he couldn't go with the dog to his kennel. Tammy promised Ronnie that the dog was in good hands, but Ronnie was still anxious and remained vigilant at the front counter until Tammy returned.

"He's all settled in and ready for a nap," Tammy said.

"When can I see him again?" Ronnie asked Tammy.

"Well, the doctor will give the dog a thorough examination. Then he will be treated for his ailments. Once this is done, the dog's temperament can be evaluated, and the doctor will determine if the dog is adoptable."

Ronnie's forehead wrinkled. "Why wouldn't he be?"

Tammy sat her clipboard down. "Honestly, the dog has had a rough life and may not overcome his hostilities."

Ronnie blinked at Tammy. "What if he can't overcome them?"

Danny set his hand on Ronnie's shoulder. "Let's not think about that right now. The important thing is he is someplace safe and will be taken care of."

"That's right," Tammy said, her smile returning.

Ronnie reflected for a few long moments. "He wasn't hostile to me. I could comfort him, and then he might pass the tests."

Tammy paused. "It's not up to me. It's up to the doctor."

"Then I want to talk to the doctor."

"Ronnie, the dog is resting now and needs to recover," John said. "Who knows, maybe once he starts to feel better, he might not be so hostile."

"I still want to see him."

Tammy sighed. "I tell you what, I can't make any promises, but you come back in a couple of days, and I'll see what I can do."

"Anytime Buddy is upset, do this." Ronnie made a clicking noise with his tongue.

Tammy blinked at him.

"Try it."

Tammy did her best to mimic the sound.

"He knows what it means," Ronnie said, putting his hand inside his jacket pocket. "And give him one of these," Ronnie said, handing Tammy some crackers. "He will know they're from me."

"Okay," Tammy said.

"We can go now," Ronnie said to Danny and John.

John hung back and waited for Danny and Ronnie to leave.
"Thanks for your patience," John told Tammy. "It means a lot."
"Do you really think it works?" Tammy asked.
John lifted an eyebrow.
"You know, the clicking of the tongue?"
"The dog is here, isn't he?"
Tammy reflected, while tapping her chin.
John grinned and left the shelter.

49

THE BUZZING FROM THE OVERHEAD florescent bulb sounded like an annoying, large fly in the newspaper's archive room. Located in the basement of the building, the room was full of ancient papers, rolls of microfiche, and dust. Rumors of rats, spiders, and a one-eyed creature with drooling teeth terrorized the newbies sent down there to retrieve information, but Nancy liked the gigantic cave of a room. She had spent the last few hours searching through rolls of microfiche, looking for a story that might point to the identity of Joey and the Moon Rockers. After viewing the last reel of microfiche from 1956, her eyes felt like two burnt holes. It made no sense to go back another year. There was simply no information about the mysterious band anywhere. Flipping the switch on the microfiche machine, the screen went dark, and Nancy returned the reel to its box on the shelf. Gathering her things, Nancy walked to the door and entered the dimly lit hallway. When she heard the voice behind her, she almost jumped out of her skin.

"What are you doing down here in the underbelly of the paper?"

Turning with her hand on her throat, Nancy saw the janitor, Mr. Trimble. "Oh, it's you."

"I was concerned when I saw the light on. No one ever comes down here but me," Trimble said.

"I was doing some research, actually."

Trimble leaned on his mop. "Were you now? What kind of research?"

"Well, it sounds kind of silly, really. I've been looking for information regarding a band playing at the community center this weekend, but I came up empty," Nancy sighed.

"What's the name of the group?"

"Joey and the Moon Rockers."

"Now, there's a name I haven't heard in years."

Nancy tilted her head. "You mean you have actually heard of them?"

"As a matter of fact, I have."

Nancy fumbled around in her bag for her paper and pencil. "Oh, boy, Mr. Trimble, I can't believe it! What can you tell me about them?"

"Well, let me see," Trimble said, stroking his chin. "It's been a long time, about six years or so."

Nancy nodded with rapt attention.

"It was my senior year in high school, and I asked Rosalie Cummings to the homecoming dance. I remember the gymnasium was decked out in the school's colors, red and gold crepe paper. Anyway, a couple of boys from my class had formed a rock 'n' roll group, and they performed at the dance that night, and everybody loved them. After that night, they played every dance and party for the rest of the year."

"And this group, they were Joey and the Moon Rockers?" Nancy asked.

Trimble nodded. "Yep, that was their name, at least back then it was."

Nancy put the tip of her pencil to her mouth. "Do you think they changed their name?"

"I know they did."

"What is their name now?"

"The Dice."

50

Bored and apathetic, Stu relished in trampling through the weeds, where hundreds of olive-green bodies burst up like droplets from a sprinkler head. It wasn't necessary to walk through the vacant lot to get to The Beat, but something about disturbing the grasshoppers appeased Stu's mood. He wished he was headed home instead of practice. Watching John fawn over Danny made Stu's stomach lurch. James didn't want to believe that John was biased, but Stu knew better. Like a parasite, Danny wormed his way into John's life by feeding his ego, supporting Jerry, and providing the rehearsal space. Before long, Danny would be taking over the group and calling the shots. Well, Stu wasn't going to stand around and be some kind of patsy. He was working on polishing his talents and building a better future with Patrick. Smiling, Stu thought about the humiliation coming for both John and Danny. He would enjoy watching it, he would enjoy it very much.

❖❖❖❖❖❖❖❖❖❖❖❖❖❖❖

The group was gathered in the rehearsal space when Stu stepped through the door. John was sitting on the couch, talking with someone Stu didn't recognize. Stu squinted his eyes. Was his mind playing tricks on him, or was the stranger wearing a leg brace? Without even realizing it, Stu's mouth dropped open, and he stared.

"Well, well, look who decided to join us," John said from his reclined position on the couch.

Stu's mind refused to register the comment.

Noticing that Stu appeared to be in some sort of stupor, James signaled Stu to come closer. "Hey, Stu, come over here and meet the newest member of the group."

Stu's cheek lifted, and his eye squinted. *A member of the group?*

"Stu?" James said.

Stu heard James, but his mouth was frozen.

John sat forward on the couch, his eyes narrowing.

"Stewy," Jerry said, reaching out and pinching Stu's arm.

"Ow!"

"It's good to see you."

Stu rubbed his arm. "That hurt, you little twerp!"

Jerry took Stu's elbow and guided him toward the couch. "Ronnie, let me introduce you to the joker in our group, Stu."

"Hell-o," Ronnie said.

"Stu, this is our new drummer, Ronnie," Jerry said.

Stu hesitated, his response stuck in his throat.

James broke the lingering silence. "Aren't you going to say something?"

"Hey," Stu said, bobbing his chin.

John's brow slowly rumpled.

Danny clapped his hands together, distracting the tension. "Well, it's been a long time since we have all played together, so this will be a treat. Nothing like jumping right in and getting the night rolling. Right, James?"

"Right," James said, nodding.

John's eyes hadn't lost their dark focus.

James stepped into John's line of sight, facing Stu. "Come help me strap on my guitar."

"You don't need my . . ."

James didn't let Stu finish his sentence. He just pulled him across the room.

"What the hell is wrong with everyone tonight?" Stu said, yanking his arm away from James.

"What's wrong with us? What's wrong with you?"

"What do you mean?" Stu asked.

"Why did you stare at Ronnie?"

Stu set his guitar on the table. "I didn't stare at him."

"Well, it's not like you gave him a warm welcome."

Stu shrugged. "It threw me off guard, is all. You could have warned me."

"About?"

"*Him.*"

James's mouth dropped aghast. "Are you talking about his brace?"

Stu pulled his guitar strap over his head. "I guess."

"You sound like you're biased."

"No. I mean, I admit I am having a hard time picturing him fitting in."

"Because he's handicapped?" James asked.

"Come on, James, you know how the record business is. They want to record and promote what sells, and right now, that's perfection."

James ran his hand over his hair. "I can't believe you're acting this way."

"I'm simply stating a fact. Look at any magazine or record cover down in the store, and you'll see."

James glanced over at John, who was talking to Ronnie. "You better not let him hear you talk that way."

"Who? John?"

"Yeah."

Stu chuckled. "I'm not afraid of him."

"Maybe you should be."

Stu sneered at James and walked away.

Guitars tuned and ready, James, Stu, and Jerry stood on the right side of the drums.

Danny and John engaged in conversation out of earshot before John addressed the group.

"All right, fellas," John began, "Danny and I have been talking, and we think it would be good for some of us to switch places. James, you and I need to switch."

"Okay," James said, moving to the far left.

"Stu, you need to switch places with Jerry," John instructed.

Stu raised a brow. "What for?"

"Because we think it would be better if Jerry stood closer to the drums."

"But I like where I'm standing."

"I don't care," John asserted, folding his arms. "I told you to move."

"We just think it would sound better," Danny added.

Stu mumbled as he moved to Jerry's left side.

"You have something you want to share?" John asked.

"No," Stu replied, averting his eyes.

"Are we starting with 'Johnny B. Goode'?" James asked John.

"Since this is Stu's first time with us, let's do something simple," John suggested.

Stu huffed. "Wait a second, are you implying that I don't know how to play 'Johnny B. Goode'?"

"You've never played it with us," Danny clarified.

"So? I know what I'm doing," Stu retorted, sticking his chest out.

Danny turned to John. "Let's try it."

Taking his mark, John nodded to James, who began the count, and the music started.

Danny started the song with a flawless riff, complemented by Ronnie's powerful drum strike. For the first time, Jerry was keeping in time, and John's smile encouraged Jerry to continue. The song progressed perfectly until there was a discordant note. Stu was off. John hated to cut the song short, because Jerry was finally in time, but he had no choice.

Taking a deep breath, John turned to Stu. "Stu, when was the last time you tuned your guitar?"

Stu glanced around at the straight faces. "This week, why?"

"Because you're not in tune with the rest of us," John explained.

"It sounds like his hand is lying too flat on the guitar neck," Danny said, crossing to Stu. "You need to curl your fingers, so your tips are what is pressing on the string. See, watch," Danny said, demonstrating the technique. "Do you hear the difference in the chord when I use my fingertips?"

Stu's lips pressed tight as he barely nodded.

"Now, give it a try," Danny said.

"I know how to strum a chord, Danny," Stu snapped.

"Humor us," John added, his tone dry.

With a firm grip on his guitar, Stu strummed the chord.

Danny smiled. "See, it sounds better, huh?"

Stu's lips twitched slightly. "Sure."

Danny walked over to his spot. "You want to start from the top again, John?"

John's gaze was still on Stu. "That's fine, Danny."

Danny turned to James who begun the count, and the song started for the second time. Stu knew he needed to fall in line and go through the motions. After all, he was only there to be a spy for Patrick, but for some reason, he couldn't. He had to push the boundary. As the second guitar solo approached, Stu strutted forward before Danny could.

Leaning back, Stu played his version of the solo, which was some random combination of chords. Stunned by what was happening, James shared a confused look with Jerry. John's mouth opened, but Danny shook his head and mouthed the words, "Let him finish."

John closed his mouth, but his rigid stance showed his disapproval.

When the horrible song finally ended, Stu turned to the rest of the group with a triumphant grin on his face. No one dared to offer a comment as John ground his teeth.

"I think it's time for a break," Danny offered.

John unstrapped his guitar and went down the stairs.

Danny turned to James. "What is going on with Stu?"

"I wish I knew."

Stu stepped over to them. "I hope you're not sore that I kind of stepped in and played the last solo, Danny. I just wanted to show you how much my playing has improved."

Danny rubbed the back of his neck as he struggled to find a gentle answer. "Well, I think your playing has improved, but I don't think it's the right fit for this song."

Stu's face fell. "What do you mean?"

"I mean, it's fragmented and in the wrong key."

"What did you think, James?" Stu said, folding his arms.

"Well, I think Danny's right. I don't think it quite fits the song."

Stu stepped back. "Oh, so you think Danny's better than me?"

"I didn't say that," James clarified.

"That's not what this is about," Danny added.

"Everyone knows you think you're better than everybody else," Stu snapped.

"That's not true," Danny protested.

"Isn't it? Just because John thinks you have golden fingers doesn't mean you do."

"Stu! That's enough!" The voice rumbled through the room like an echo of a bomb. John had come back upstairs. His patience and good humor were at the end.

Stu turned to face him.

John's jaw was set, and his posture was rigid. "You apologize to Danny right now."

"Barnaby, he doesn't have to apologize," Danny said.

John's eyes were locked on Stu, and they didn't waiver. "He does if he wants to stay in my band."

"Maybe I don't want to stay in *your* band," Stu spat.

"Then you know where the door is."

Stu slowly unstrapped his guitar. "You know you treat Danny better than the rest of us. Ever since he joined us, all you have done is kiss his ass."

John's eyes narrowed. "You need to leave."

"I'm going," Stu said, turning to the rest of the group. "Good luck with your little *contest*. You're gonna need it."

Stu headed for the door, but John was blocking his path. His cold glare crushed Stu's confidence, and he averted his eyes. "Are you going to let me pass?"

John didn't move at first, but he finally let Stu pass. A long, dark silence fell over the room.

"Well, that's really stickin' your head in rotted pumpkin," Ronnie said.

"What?" Danny said with a chuckle.

Ronnie shrugged. "Well, someone had to say something."

John shook his head, and James laughed.

Ronnie stepped out into the room. "If someone is foolish, let um go, and if they come back, forgive um, and if they don't come back, then you were right to let the dunderhead go in the first place."

John was the first to start laughing, and the rest joined in while Ronnie smiled.

51

A MILE PAST THE DEAD-END SIGN at the edge of Decatur Road stood a small bar named the Dead Spot. A haven for steel mill workers and other nefarious characters, the dreadful, dimly lit establishment offered cheap drinks and asked no questions.

Dressed in dirty jeans and a woolen cap, Patrick rubbed a small clump of mud over his face and hands. The sensation of the grime on his skin reminded him of working in the sweltering cornfields. With only the moon to light his way, Patrick trudged the crooked road to the bar. The crunching sound of twigs and dirt under his feet caused Patrick to constantly look over his shoulder.

A single light fixture hung above the door, casting a dim halo over several patrons who were smoking, playing craps, or engaging in some other foul activity that Patrick didn't want to acknowledge. Pulling up the collar of his dark blue pea coat, Patrick pulled his arms in close and entered the bar without incident.

The overwhelming smell of rotten eggs, cigarette smoke, and cheap liquor threatened to suffocate Patrick. He stayed close to the doorway and squinted his eyes. He had almost lost hope of finding the person he was looking for when he spotted him hunched over a beer at the bar. Patrick squeezed through the crowd until he was standing next to the man.

"Hello, Finley," Patrick said, placing his arms on the bar.

Finley turned his head. In his late twenties, Finley's thick, leathery skin made him look like he was closer to forty. Tufts of greasy hair stuck out from under his soot-coated cap. He took a hardy swallow from his mug as he sized Patrick up. "McNeil. I thought they only let men in this place."

"Funny."

A bald bartender leaned against the bar. "Who's the maggot, Finney?"

Finley turned sideways, leaning on the bar. "This 'ere is the brother of an ol' friend of mine. McNeil, this is Ned."

"Nice to meet you, Ned," Patrick said.

Ned laughed and slapped his hand on the bar. "Nice to meet you?"

Embarrassment washed Patrick's cheeks.

Finley smiled. "Give this boy a drink, Ned. It's time he got some hair on his peaches."

Ned set a shot glass on the counter and filled it with liquid from a dingy bottle with no label.

"Bottoms up," Finley sneered.

Patrick glimpsed at Ned's gold-capped grimace. Then, glancing at Finley, he drank back the shot. Grasping the bar's edge, Patrick clenched his jaw tightly and held back his spittle.

Ned's boisterous laughter filled Patrick's ear again.

Finley slapped Patrick on the back. "Well, I'll be. Ya got more grit than I gave ya credit for!"

Ned lifted the bottle. "Ya want another?"

Patrick shook his head and wiped his mouth on his sleeve.

"Bring me and the boy a beer," Finley said.

Ned slapped his hand on the bar, fraying Patrick's nerves.

Finley rested his foot on the foot rail. "So, tell me, McNeil, how's your brother?"

"As far as I know, he's okay."

"Still workin' for Uncle Sam?"

"Yeah."

"He's a good lad, your brother."

Patrick nodded, hating the reminder.

Ned returned and put two fresh beers on the counter.

Finley held his mug up. "To Ryan McNeil, a right pain in me ass!"

Patrick fully agreed as he tapped Finley's mug.

Finley drank back half his mug in one gulp. Setting the mug down with a thud, he burped loudly. Several of the men standing around cheered.

"I'm sure ya didn't come down 'ere just to give me a good laugh," Finley said.

"That's true."

"Then why are ya here?"

"I have a proposition for you," Patrick said.

Finley wrinkled his nose. "A what?"

"An offer. How would you like to make some easy money?"

Finley cracked his thumb knuckle. "How much money?"

"Oh, say roughly around a couple hundred dollars."

Finley's eyes narrowed, and he rubbed his greasy hand over his mug. "Is this some kinda joke?"

Patrick reached into his pocket, pulled out a hundred-dollar bill, and slapped it on the bar.

Finley licked his lips and then slowly looked at Patrick. "Whadda I got to do?"

A dark grimace crossed Patrick's beer-glazed lips.

52

Betty watched Jerry get in Danny's car from her bedroom window. She knew he was on his way to the hospital to see his mother, and then later, he would be going to a party at the rehearsal space. Danny had invited her, but it wouldn't be much fun if she wasn't with Jerry. Wiping another tear away, she returned to her bed, littered with crumpled tissues. Holding her favorite stuffed dog, Noodles, she fought the urge to cry again.

A quiet knock came from the door, and then a comforting voice. "May I come in?"

"Yes," Betty squeaked.

Mable entered the room and gazed at her bewildered daughter, who was blowing her nose into a tattered tissue. Mable shut the door, walked to the small chair in front of Betty's desk, and sat down. "Betty, I think it's time for you and me to have a mother-daughter talk."

Betty hid a blush. "I already know about the birds and the bees, Mama."

"That is not what this is about."

"Oh."

Mable folded her hands in her lap. "I want you to tell me what your fight with Jerry is about?"

"He was being unfair to me."

"How so?"

"Well, we always spend Friday nights together, and he decided that rehearsal with the band was more important than spending time with me!" Betty spat.

"Didn't he take you to the movies on Saturday night?" Mable asked.

"Well, yeah, but that's not the point."

"What's the point?"

Betty pulled on Noodle's ear. "Well, I should be his number one priority. He should be focused on spending time with me, not them."

Mable reflected for a moment. "Do you think it's unfair that your father is on the City Council and has to go to a meeting once or twice a month?"

Betty's shoulders fell. "Well, no."

"Do you think it's unfair that he spends time with the boy's youth group at the church on the third Thursday of the month?"

Betty stared at Noodle's head. "No."

"Don't you think that maybe you are being a bit unfair to Jerry? How would you feel if he told you that you couldn't spend time helping with the toddlers during Sunday school or help me with bake sales or go to sewing circles?"

Betty pulled her knees up close to her chest.

"I know you're young, and you want to spend as much time with him as possible, but you need to understand that he's a young man trying to make his way in this world. Also, remember, he is stressed about dealing with his mother's situation. I think Jerry needs your support, not your scorn."

Betty sniffled and wiped her nose.

"You know, when I first met your father, I felt the same way. I wanted to spend every moment with him, but he was popular and involved in almost every school committee or activity. I used to hate when those obligations took time away from me, but I learned that if I tried to smother him, I would lose him. Pursuing other interests and spending time with others is a healthy part of any relationship."

"Do you think I've lost Jerry?" Betty whispered.

"No, but I do think you owe him an apology. Don't you?"

Betty nodded her head.

Mable stood up and sat on the edge of Betty's bed. "Jerry is a good boy, Betty, and he is very devoted to you. Why, every time he sees you, his admiration shines in his eyes. It is rare to find a boy like that. You are a fortunate girl, believe me. Now dry your eyes and throw the tissues away. I'm making a cake for the party tonight, and I could use your help."

"Thank you, Mama," Betty said, hugging her mother.

"You're welcome, dear."

Betty slid off her bed, cleaned up her bed, put Noodles back on her pillow, and followed her mother downstairs with a new resolution in her heart.

53

"*You what?*" Patrick said, running his hand through his hair. Surely, he hadn't heard Stu's last statement correctly.

"I quit," Stu repeated.

Patrick turned his back to Stu and put his hands on the stereo console for support. "Stu, we talked about this."

"I know, but I don't need to tolerate being treated like an idiot anymore. Besides, this will give me more time to spend with you working on our future."

Patrick closed his eyes tightly and ran his tongue over his teeth.

"Right?" Stu finished.

Patrick took a deep breath before turning to face Stu's crestfallen look. "Stu, I know you're anxious to move on, but being a part of the Hound Dogs is crucial right now."

"But I don't want to be a member anymore, Patrick. Besides, I told you everything I know."

Patrick sat on the footstool that was close to Stu. "I know you have. The information you shared with me today is invaluable. You are a vital part of the plan right now. I can't pull this off without you. You know that, right?"

Stu nodded and looked at his hands.

"We're so close. Only a few more days and you will be home free," Patrick said, setting his hand on Stu's knee.

Stu looked up. "Patrick, I can't go back there."

"You have to."

"No, I don't," Stu said, moving across the room.

Patrick sighed. "Look, let me go upstairs and get another soda, okay?"

Stu nodded, and Patrick went upstairs. Sitting on the floor next to the stereo, Stu browsed Patrick's record collection. He had looked at his records many times, but dreaming of being on the cover someday never got old.

Patrick returned downstairs and handed Stu a bottle before sitting on the couch. "So, they really have a handicapped drummer?"

"Yep."

Patrick shook his head. "Is he any good?"

"I guess so."

"You didn't pay attention?"

"Not really. I was concentrating on my solo."

Patrick's eyebrow lifted. "Your solo?"

Stu nodded. "Yeah, I played the solo on—"

"And John was okay with that?"

Stu turned to Patrick. "Yeah."

"Wow," Patrick said, setting his foot on top of his knee.

"Danny said it wasn't good enough, of course."

Patrick sat up. "I really need you to try and stick it out, at least until the performance."

Stu absently picked at the corner of a record jacket. "I don't think John will let me come back."

"Of course he will. All you need to do is apologize."

Stu's eyebrows pulled together.

"Come on, don't you want a front-row seat for the fireworks?"

"I will do it on one condition," Stu said.

"Name it."

"I want to play a solo in our band."

Patrick chuckled. "Of course."

Stu returned his attention to the albums. "All right, I will go back."

Patrick sat back on the couch, breathed a sigh of relief, and finished his soda in one swallow.

54

Aᴀғᴛᴇʀ ᴘʀᴏᴍɪsɪɴɢ ᴛᴏ ʙᴇ ᴀ gentleman and not tease John, Danny agreed to go with John to pick up Anne. Danny had known John to never let anything rattle him and to always be cool, but tonight, he sat in the seat next to Danny, fussing with his hair and buttoning the cuffs on his shirt.

John glanced at Danny, who had a smirk on his face. "What?"

"Nothing," Danny said.

John scowled. "What did I tell you about giving me a hard time?"

"I didn't say anything," Danny said.

"You don't have to. I see that sly smirk on your face."

Danny scoffed. "I've just never seen you like this before. I didn't think you even owned a comb."

"You're a real comedian. Do I look all right?"

"Yeah, you look fine."

John sat back and tried to see himself in the rearview mirror.

"You must really like this girl to be puttin' on such a fuss," Danny said.

"Yeah, I like her," John murmured.

"I'm happy for you."

John wrinkled his lip.

"No, I mean it. I think it's good that you found someone, you know, steady."

"We are not going steady," John growled.

"Okay, sure."

John was silent, and Danny covered his mouth to hide another smirk.

Danny turned down the block to Mrs. Brewster's house, and when John told him to pull over, he got out of the car. Anne was waiting for him on the porch steps.

"Hi," she said.

"Hey. How am I supposed to come to the door proper when you're always waiting for me on the porch?" John groused.

Anne stood up. "Because I'm excited. I hardly ever get to go to a party."

Dressed in a light sweater with a peach sundress and matching headband, Anne's hair fell in perfect curls down her back. Her sparkling eyes looked up at John, warming his heart.

At that moment, he knew it wasn't her pleasing form, brown doe eyes, or shiny blond hair that captivated him. It was the way her face shined when she saw him, the way her childlike sense of wonder made the adventure more fun, but above all else, she made him feel like he was enough.

"Does my dress meet your approval?" Anne said, swaying the skirt.

"Yes, you look beautiful."

Her cheeks flushed with the color of the roses.

He took her hand, and they walked out of the gate together.

Danny expected some made-up girl in tight pants and a low-cut sweater. He never expected a petite girl in a sundress with quirky dimples.

John walked up to the driver's side. "Anne, this is my good friend Danny. Danny, this is Anne."

"Hello, Anne," Danny said with his dashing smile.

"Hi," she said, with a hint of red on her cheeks.

John opened the door and Anne climbed in. John climbed in next to her and closed the door.

"We're going to pick up another friend of ours," John told Anne.

"Okay," Anne said.

John slid close to her on the seat and put his arm around her.

"Why don't you turn on the radio, Danny?" John said.

"Sure."

Danny flipped on the radio. He felt odd being up in the front seat by himself, but glimpsing in the rearview mirror, he watched John whisper something in Anne's ear. A faint giggle escaped from her stretched mouth as the tops of her cheeks flushed pink. John gazed at her like a pubescent boy before she whispered something back. He chuckled in amusement as their hands twisted around each other.

Ronnie was waiting when Danny pulled up in front of the house.

"Your taxi is here," Danny said to Ronnie when he opened the passenger door.

Sitting on the seat, Ronnie lifted his leg into the car and shut the door.

"Hey Ronnie," John said.

Ronnie turned to see John with his arm around Anne.

"Anne, this is Ronnie. Ronnie, this is Anne," John said.

"How do you do, ma'am?" Ronnie said, tipping his hat.

Anne smiled. "Hello Ronnie."

The car pulled away from the curb, and they headed to the record store.

"So, John, are you going to tell me what instruments Danny and Ronnie play?" Anne asked.

"Well, Danny is the lead guitarist, and Ronnie plays drums," John explained.

Anne tilted her head. "How many more members are there?"

"Currently two. James and Jerry."

"Oh, yeah. You've mentioned Jerry," Anne answered.

"So, how did you two meet?" Ronnie asked.

Anne laughed. "Well, it's an interesting story. Why don't you tell him, John?"

"Me?" John balked.

"Yes."

"Why me?"

"Because I don't know which version of the story you'll tell."

"You mean there is more than one?" Danny asked.

"We met in composition class," John said dryly.

"Yes, and he borrowed a pencil from me, and when he broke it, he tried to tell me it was defective," Anne teased.

Danny laughed. "That sounds like Barnaby."

Anne's eyebrows rose. "Barnaby?"

Danny laughed. "Now there is a story."

"Oh, I want to hear it," Anne said, clasping her hands together.

"No, you don't," John said.

Anne patted John's hand. "Oh, come on—it sounds amusing."

"Well . . ." Danny began.

"Remember our agreement, Danny," John warned.

"What agreement?" Anne said.

"I promised him I wouldn't embarrass him," Danny said.

"I didn't make that agreement," Ronnie said with a grin.

Danny and Anne laughed, and John frowned.

55

R ONNIE, DANNY, JOHN, AND ANNE arrived to find Molly and Marcy setting out the food and Jerry sitting on the arm of the couch, talking with James.

Anne felt slightly overwhelmed, so she held tightly to John's hand.

"You okay?" John asked Anne.

"Yes."

"But you're shy?"

A hint of red brushed the top of Anne's cheeks. John squeezed her hand. "I know they look like they might bite, but they won't."

Anne laughed.

John led Anne over to the couch. Danny, Ronnie, James, and Jerry stopped talking.

"Anne, allow me to introduce the rest of my merry men. This is the Professor, sometimes known as James, and this is Jerry."

"Hello," Anne said.

"Hello," Jerry said with a slight wave.

"So, you're dating him on purpose?" James asked.

"Even hound dogs need love, Professor," Ronnie said.

Danny and Jerry laughed.

"Laugh it up, funny boys," John said.

"It's nice to meet you, Anne," James said.

"You too, Professor," Anne said.

"Come on, I'll introduce you to the girls." John steered Anne to the other side of the room.

"So, what do you guys think?" Danny asked in a hushed tone.

"She's pretty," Jerry said.

"She seems nice," James said.

"She's not what I expected," Danny said. "I thought we had gone to the wrong house."

"Now that you mention it," James said. "She doesn't seem like his type."

"I think she will be good for him," Jerry said. "He needs a nice girl."

"Speaking of nice girls, where is Betty?" James inquired.

"Yeah, what happened between you two?" Danny asked.

"Do we have to talk about it right now, fellas?" Jerry said.

John came over to join them. "I know you're talking about me."

They all shook their heads.

"Liars," John said, making Danny move off the stool.

Danny sat on the floor. "Actually, we were asking Jerry what was up with him and Betty."

"Yeah, where is the little lady tonight?" John asked.

"He doesn't want to talk about it," James said.

"Come on, Jerry, you can tell us. We're your brothers," John said.

"We should respect his wishes," Ronnie said.

"Thanks, Ronnie," Jerry said.

"Okay, you can all respect his wishes, but he can't hide from me all night," John said.

Jerry curled his lip. "You're like the older brother I'm glad I never had."

John grinned.

❑■❑■❑■❑■❑■❑■❑■❑■❑■❑

Anne was anxious being away from John. He had encouraged her to mingle with the girls while he joined the boys, but she didn't know

258

how. She had always been quiet and reserved and had no idea how to start a conversation. Marcy observed Anne biting her nails and looking like a lost waif.

"Hey Anne, you want to help me bring up the rest of the party supplies from downstairs?" Marcy asked.

Anne yanked her hand away from her mouth. "Sure."

Anne followed Marcy down the stairs. Her eyes lingered on the rows of records as they passed. "I've never seen so many records before," Anne remarked.

"Is this your first time in the shop?" Marcy asked.

"Yes."

"You need to ask John to show you around later," Marcy said, opening the door.

"I will," Anne answered, passing through the door.

Marcy pulled the car keys out of her pocket. "So, how long have you known John?"

"A few months. We had a class together."

"Oh, which one?"

"Composition."

Marcy opened the trunk of Mollie's car. "I never was good at that kind of stuff."

"Are you going to school?" Anne asked, taking the paper plates from Marcy.

"No, I have a full-time job."

"Oh? Where?"

Marcy handed Anne the napkins. "I work at the coffee shop across from the campus."

"Do you like it?"

"I do. Somedays, it's busy, but for the most part, it's easygoing."

Marcy grabbed the cups and closed the trunk. Then, heading toward the door, Marcy saw Eddie walking toward them.

"Hi, Eddie," Marcy said.

"Hello," Eddie said.

"Anne, this is Eddie," Marcy said.

"Hello," Anne said.

"This is Anne, Eddie. She is John's girlfriend," Marcy said.

Eddie blinked. "You're John's girlfriend?"

"Yes," Anne said.

"Wow."

"Are you Danny's brother?" Anne asked.

Eddie opened the door for the girls. "No, I am his cousin."

"Eddie manages the store," Marcy said.

"Oh, that sounds like fun," Anne said, following Marcy into the store.

"Anything you want to know about the record business, just ask Eddie," Marcy said.

Eddie's chest puffed out. "Yeah, I want to pursue a career in the biz."

"Oh?" Anne said.

Eddie grinned widely. "Yep, I'm gonna be a record producer."

"Are you going to produce the Hound Dogs?" Anne asked.

"You never know."

"Are you coming up soon, Eddie?" Marcy asked.

"Yep. I'm going to grab some records," Eddie said.

"Okay."

Marcy and Anne returned upstairs. Mollie stood by the table gazing at Danny.

Marcy set the cups down. "Has he come over to say hi yet?"

"No," Mollie said, crestfallen.

"Who?" Anne asked.

"Mollie has a crush on Danny," Marcy whispered.

"But he doesn't even know I'm alive," Mollie said.

Marcy patted Mollie on the shoulder. "I'm sure he will say something soon. The night is just starting."

"I hope so. I bought a new dress, after all," Mollie said, flouncing the blue skirt on her A-line dress.

"It's a very pretty dress," Anne said.

"Thank you."

Marcy picked up a cracker. "I'm sure he will dance with you tonight."

Mollie sighed. "Do you really think so?"

"I do. Men can be so clueless sometimes. Would you agree, Anne?" Marcy asked.

"Yes."

"How did you get John to notice you?" Marcy asked.

Anne absently touched her hair. "Is it all right to have a cup of punch?"

"Help yourself," Mollie said.

Eddie came upstairs with an armful of records.

"Hey Eddie, do you think Mollie looks nice tonight?" Marcy asked.

Eddie glanced over his shoulder and shrugged. "Sure."

"Goodness, Eddie, how many records do you think we need?" Danny said.

Eddie sat the stack down next to the turntable. "You never know what someone might want to hear, Dan. A good DJ is always prepared for the mood."

"Yeah, Danny, don't you know anything?" James teased.

"All right, boys. We didn't come here to drink root beer and eat peanuts all night," John said. "We have a show to do!"

"Let's do it!" Danny said.

The boys jumped up. Eddie sat on the stool, and the girls sat on the couch.

"Before we start the show. I have an announcement to make," Danny said. "I want everyone to note that Barnaby has broken one of his golden rules tonight."

"Oh yeah, Danny, and what is that?" James asked.

Danny slapped his hands together. "Well, let me tell you. I think it was the night of our first rehearsal here in our new space that our fearless leader told us that his number one rule was that no girls were allowed in the space. Am I correct, Professor?"

"Yes," James affirmed.

"Am I correct, Jerry?"

"Yes," Jerry said.

Danny looked at John, who had a scowl on his face. "I think it's only fair to mention that things suddenly changed once he got a girlfriend. I find that peculiar, don't you, Professor?"

"I do."

Danny waved his finger. "That having been said, there will be absolutely, positively, no hanky-panky of any kind in this rehearsal space. Right, fellas?"

"Right," James and Jerry said together.

John drummed his fingers on the guitar's body. "You thinkin' about havin' your head dunked in the punch bowl tonight, Danny?"

Danny rubbed the back of his neck. "Um, no, not really."

John stepped forward. "Now that you have had your fun, let's start with 'Johnny B. Goode.'"

The boys started to play, and the dynamic changes in the band were evident to Mollie, Marcy, and Eddie. Having Ronnie's strong drum beat made all the difference in the world. Their playing and confidence had improved, and even with Jerry's few missed chords, they played the song perfectly. The next song they played was "Blue Suede Shoes." Danny was having fun bopping around and showing off for his audience.

The girls clapped and giggled at an unspoken urge that made them kick their legs and bounce on the couch. Eddie rolled his eyes at the silly girls, but he was swaying and tapping his feet. The energy in the small space was intoxicating, and the boys, loving the attention, didn't want to stop playing.

❑■❑■❑■❑■❑■❑■❑■❑■❑■❑■❑

After their fifth song, the boys decided it was time for a break and let Eddie spin some records. Digging into the snacks and passing around sodas and punch, everyone began to relax.

Danny was laughing and talking to James when Mollie came up with a cup of punch for him. He turned to her and grinned.

"Hey, Mollie."

"Hey Danny, I brought you some punch."

"Gee, thanks," he said, taking the cup from her.

"I'll catch you later," James said.

Danny nodded at James and turned back to Mollie. "So, what did you think about the set?"

"I thought it was terrific."

"Yeah?"

"Yeah, I can tell you guys have been working hard to perfect your sound."

He smiled and took a drink from his cup. "We have been working hard."

"I just know you're going to blow their socks off on Saturday."

"You think so?"

Mollie tilted her head and swung her hips. "I know so."

"You are coming to the show, right?"

"I hope to."

Danny placed his arm around her shoulders. "You better be there, you know? You've been a fan from the start."

"Of course I will be there."

Danny's arm lingered, and Mollie's eyes glittered. "That punch was really great."

"You want me to get you another cup?" Mollie offered.

"Nah, I can do it myself."

"It would be no trouble."

He felt her chin. "You are so sweet, but I can help myself. What have we got for eats over here, anyway?" Danny said, crossing to the refreshment table, Mollie close on his heels.

John walked over to Anne and sat next to her on the couch.

"So, what's the verdict?"

Anne tilted her head. "The verdict?"

"Yeah, what did you think about the band?"

"The band or you?" Anne said, looping her arm through his.

John rolled his eyes up. "Gee, I don't know."

"The band was good, but you were amazing."

He turned to her with a grin. "Aw, shucks."

Anne grinned.

John stood up and took Anne's hand. "So, what do you say we get some food?"

"Okay."

Jerry spotted John coming toward him, but he was with Anne, so Jerry was sure he could dodge him until John intercepted him.

"You ready to talk to me yet?" John asked.

"No," Jerry said, trying to pass him, but John stepped in front of him.

"Too bad."

"I have nothing to say."

John shrugged. "I guess I could hold you upside down and shake it out of you."

Jerry sighed. "There isn't much to tell, really. She just is upset because she thinks I am neglecting her."

"Why does she think that?"

"Because I haven't been home every night. I've been here practicing with the group."

John shifted his weight. "Have you talked to her about it?"

"Kinda."

"What does kinda mean?"

"It means I don't like confrontation."

"Who does?"

Jerry shuffled his feet.

"If you are seriously thinking about making her your wife, you need to find a way to communicate with her. This is not the time to be timid. If she can't have a reasonable conversation with you, there is a big problem."

Jerry shook his head. "I don't know how to make her listen."

"You tell her you need to have a serious talk with her. She will listen to you if she cares about you like you care about her."

"She can be so stubborn."

John smiled. "Yeah, she's a bit of a firecracker, but she is also is crazy about you."

Jerry nodded. "I'll talk to her."

John sat his hand on Jerry's shoulder. "You can do it."

Anne stood next to John with a plate in her hand.

"You brought me a plate? Oh, aren't you sweet?" John said, reaching for the plate.

Anne held onto the plate firmly. "I fixed it for me."

John covered her hand with his. "But I want this one."

"Too bad."

John leaned in. "I will give you a kiss for it."

Anne lowered her lashes. "What if I want more than one?"

John widened his eyes. "Well, well, Miss Prim, what kind of a guy do you think I am?"

"A bad one."

"That's just a rumor."

"Is it?"

John gently touched her chin. "Well now, I guess you'll have to wait and find out."

Anne bit her lip, and John eased the plate out of her hand.

"I'm going to make another plate," Anne said, turning away.

"Oh, and bring me a root beer," John said.

Anne shook her head and sighed.

56

THE GROUP SAT AROUND EATING and talking while Eddie played some records.

Mollie was on the floor next to Danny, hanging on his every word. He smiled at her several times, making her wish she was his.

"We should play a game," Marcy said.

The boys groaned.

"What game?" Jerry asked.

"I don't know. Charades?"

More groaning.

Marcy crossed her arms. "You boys are no fun."

"We could tell ghost stories," Mollie said.

"There's no campfire," Eddie said.

"Too bad we don't have a candle," Jerry said.

"No way," Eddie said, sitting next to Danny. "Ain't nobody gonna burn down the record store."

"He's got a point," Ronnie said.

John sat up. "How 'bout truth or dare?"

"What? Are you serious?" Marcy said.

"Why not?" James said.

"James!" Marcy said.

"Yeah, why not Marcy? Are you scared?" John said, leering at her.

Marcy scoffed. "I was just thinking of Mollie and Anne."

Mollie bounced. "I'm in!"

"Anne?" Marcy said.

Anne looked at John's rakish grin. "I'm in."

"All right, but if we're going to play this, everyone has to sit on the floor in a circle, and we dim the lights," Danny said.

"It's not a séance, Danny," James said.

"If we dim the lights, the girls will get scared," Eddie said.

"Don't worry, I'll protect you," James said, putting his arm around Marcy and kissing her.

"Hey! No kissing, remember?" Danny teased.

"Where are we gonna find an empty bottle?" Jerry asked.

"I got one," Ronnie said, holding up his empty root beer bottle.

"All right, kiddies, everyone on the floor," John said, sitting on the floor. Anne sat beside him.

Ronnie sat down and put the bottle in the middle of the circle, and Jerry turned off the bright overhead lights.

"Now what?" Jerry said, sitting next to Eddie.

"Here are the rules," John said. "Someone spins the bottle, and whoever the mouth of the bottle points to has a choice of either telling the truth or taking a dare."

"Who thinks up the dare?" Mollie asked.

"The person who spun the bottle," John answered.

"Sounds simple enough," James said, sitting next to Anne.

John held up his index finger. "There is one other rule. If you choose the truth, but you lie, and someone in the circle knows you're lying, you have to take a dare. Understand?"

Everyone nodded.

"These are going to be clean dares, right John?" James said, making room for Marcy to sit next to him.

"Where is the fun in that?" John said.

"How do we know who spins first?" Jerry asked.

"I guess we do, weenie meanie teeny mole," John said.

Jerry shook his head. "*What?*"

John ignored him and began pointing at everyone in the circle, starting with Jerry, sitting on his right side. "Weenie, meanie, teeny, mole, ran around the crawdad hole. Out popped a badger mean as could be he said, 'Come inside the crawdad hole with me.' 'I may be a meanie, teeny, mole, but I ain't goin' in no crawdad hole.' So, the weenie, meanie, teeny mole ran away to eat his weenie rolls by the bay." John's finger landed on Ronnie.

"Looks like you spin the bottle, Ronnie," Danny said.

Ronnie rubbed his hands together and spun the bottle. Around and around it went until the mouth landed on Jerry, whose arms were wrapped around his legs.

"Truth or dare, Jerry?" Ronnie said.

"Truth," Jerry said.

Ronnie looked at Jerry for a long moment, rubbing his chin. "Is it true you wear Bozo the Clown pajamas?"

"No, it's not," Jerry said.

"He's on his underwear," John said.

Everyone started to laugh, and Jerry thumped John on the head. John rubbed his head. "Hey!"

"That's what you get for telling a lie," Jerry said.

"Okay, Jerry, spin the bottle," Danny said.

Jerry spun the bottle, and this time, it landed on Eddie.

"Truth or dare, Eddie?" Jerry asked.

"Truth," Eddie said.

"Chicken," John said.

"Is it true that you had a crush on Polly Brown in middle school?" Jerry asked.

Eddie's face went blank. "Who?"

"That's not the question," John said.

"I don't know a Polly Brown."

"He's lying," Jerry said.

"I am not!"

"You are too. Everyone knows you tried to kiss her in the lunchroom, and she threw her milk in your face," Jerry scoffed.

"Oh yeah, I remember hearing about that," Danny said.

"From whom?" Eddie demanded.

"Betty."

Eddie's face turned red.

Everyone laughed.

"All right, Jerry, what is Eddie's dare?" John asked.

"I dare Eddie to draw a mustache on the Buddy Holly poster in the store," Jerry said with a smirk.

"Woo, Jerry, you're cold-blooded," Danny laughed.

"I refuse to defile the picture of my idol!" Eddie said.

"We could just draw the mustache on Eddie's face," Ronnie suggested.

"And if I refuse?" Eddie said.

"Then Danny and I depants you in front of everyone," John said.

"You wouldn't do that! Would you, Dan?" Eddie squeaked.

Danny grinned widely.

Eddie sighed and closed his eyes. "All right, I accept."

"I'll go get the marker," Danny said, jumping up and running downstairs. A few moments later, he came back with a black marker. "Who draws the mustache?"

John shrugged.

"I want you to, Dan," Eddie said.

"All right." Danny knelt in front of Eddie and drew a thin black mustache on his face. "Dare satisfied."

Everyone cheered, and Eddie gave a crooked smile.

"Your turn to spin, Eddie," Danny said.

Eddie spun the bottle, and it landed on John.

"Truth or dare, John?" Eddie asked.

"Oh gee, gosh, what do I say? Dare," John said.

Eddie tapped his chin with his index finger. "I dare you to go and spit out the window."

"What? Oh, come on, Eds, you can do better than that," John said.

Danny whispered in Eddie's ear.

"Hey, no coaching," John protested.

"I dare you to go across the street, knock on old lady Taylor's door and kiss her when she answers." Eddie's mustache stretched with his grin.

Everyone's mouth opened, and their eyes turned to John.

"Oh Eddie, that is . . . horrible," Danny said.

"Are you chicken?" Eddie taunted.

John stood up, smiled at Eddie, and went downstairs. Tripping over themselves, everyone except Anne and Ronnie ran to the windows to witness the action below.

"Did he knock on the door, Eddie?" Jerry said, trying to wedge between Marcy and James.

"Yeah, he knocked, but she hasn't answered."

Everyone was anxious for Mrs. Taylor to open the door. They had almost given up hope when the door opened, and Mrs. Taylor poked her head out.

"Oh!" Danny yelled, clapping his hands. "I can't believe he did it!"

"She is pissed too!" James laughed.

"What if she calls the cops?" Jerry said.

"Eddie can take care of them," Danny said between bouts of laughter. "It was his dare!"

John returned upstairs, and the boys circled around him, slapping him on the back and expressing their congratulations.

"I can't believe you kissed old sourpuss," Eddie said.

John shrugged. "I've done worse."

Once everyone was settled back in the circle. John spun the bottle. Everyone held their breath, hoping it wouldn't land on them. Watching the bottle slowdown was pure torture. No one wanted to be John's victim. The bottle finally landed on Marcy. She swallowed hard as John gave her an evil grin. "Truth or dare, Marcy?"

"Truth," Marcy said.

"Chicken."

Marcy pulled at her dress. "Just ask the question."

John tilted his head to one side and squinted at Marcy. "What is the color of your panties?"

Marcy closed her eyes. "How did I know you would ask something so personal?"

John folded his hands in front of him. "You can refuse to answer the question."

"And fall prey to your dare?"

John spread out his hands. "It's your choice."

Marcy sat up straight and tossed back her hair. "They're white."

A quiet moment passed before Mollie said, "She's lying."

A side-splitting laughter broke out from the group. Even Anne covered her mouth.

"*Mollie!*" Marcy squealed.

"Are you lying, Marcy?" Danny asked.

"She is," James said.

John was laughing so hard that his arms were wrapped around his stomach and he was lying on the floor.

Marcy was playfully beating up on James, but he didn't care. He was laughing too.

"John," Jerry said.

John wiped the tears from his eyes. "What, Jerry?"

Jerry pointed toward the door. John sat up and looked over in the direction of the door. The lively moment evaporated, and a humorless glower appeared on John's face.

One by one, everyone looked toward the door, and the room became silent.

"Hey, fellas," Stu said, stepping into the room. It was anybody's guess how long he had been standing there, witnessing the hilarity.

Everyone exchanged a blank look before turning their attention to John.

"What are you doing here?" John asked.

"I wanted to talk to you," Stu said.

"About?"

Stu scratched his head. "The other night."

"What about it?"

"Can we talk about this downstairs?"

"Nope."

Stu chuckled and wiped his hands on his pants. "You sure don't make things easy, do you?"

John held his glare.

"Look, I realize I made a mistake, okay? I shouldn't have disrespected Danny, and I should have apologized."

John didn't move or say a word.

Stu shrugged. "What do you want me to say?"

"I told you what I wanted you to say," John said.

Stu walked over to Danny, who stood up. "I'm sorry, Danny, for what I said to you. You are right. My solo wasn't right for the song."

"I never wanted there to be a problem, Stu. I am more than open to giving you a chance to branch out. If you are willing to work with me, we can find the right song for you to showcase your talents. Okay?" Danny said.

Stu lowered his eyes and nodded.

Danny stuck out his hand. "Friends?"

Stu acknowledged Danny's hand and shook it.

James and Jerry cheered.

John slowly stood up. "Just because Danny forgives you doesn't mean I have."

"Barnaby . . ." Danny started.

"Stay out of this, Dan," John said.

Danny paused, then took a step backward.

John stepped up to Stu. "If you want your place back in this group, you're gonna have to earn it."

Stu's eyes fluttered, and he shoved his trembling hands into his pockets. "What do you want me to do?"

"For starters, you can look me in the eye when I'm talkin' to you."

Reluctantly, Stu met John's ominous glare.

"Are you workin' tomorrow?" John asked.

"Yes."

"Okay. After your shift, you come here and start cleaning up this space. That means you sweep, scrub the floors, take out the trash, beat the dust out of the area rug, and whatever else I can think of for you to do. Is that clear?" John said.

Stu's hands balled into fists in his pockets. "Yes."

"Then I guess we will see you tomorrow. We have a lot of work to do before Saturday," John said, resting his hands on his hips.

"I'll see you all tomorrow," Stu said to the group and left the room.

John sighed and turned back to the group that was looking at him. "Well, kids, it's getting late, and we should all get a good night's rest. We have a hard couple of days ahead of us."

"Hey John, are you going to let Stu play the show on Saturday?" Jerry asked.

John looked over his shoulder at the door and didn't answer Jerry.

57

JERRY BRUSHED HIS HAIR AND straightened the collar on his new blue shirt before heading for practice. He picked up his dirty clothes from the floor and headed for the laundry room. His mood was light as he whistled down the main staircase, and then, cutting through the kitchen, he headed down to the basement to drop them in the clothes hamper. He entered the laundry room to find Betty folding towels at the small table. Her hair was pulled with a light pink scarf and curled tendrils formed soft waves around her cheeks.

"Hey," Jerry said.

Betty looked up at Jerry. A lazy curl fell across his forehead, and the fading freckles highlighted his smile.

"Hey," Betty said in a hushed tone.

"I just came down to drop off my laundry before I head out, you know, for rehearsal."

"Oh, sure," Betty said, lowering her lashes, but her eyes watched Jerry drop off his clothes in the hamper. He then turned to watch her fold a peach towel.

Jerry put his hands in his pants' pockets. "So, how have you been?"

"All right. You?"

"Okay, I guess."

She set the towel aside and picked up a lime-colored one. "So, tomorrow is the big show, huh?"

"Yeah, we've been practicing hard, and I think things are coming together."

"That's good."

An awkward silence fell between them.

"Well, I guess I should get going," Jerry said.

Betty nodded. "Oh, yeah."

Jerry took a couple of steps and then stopped.

Betty's heart beat in her ear.

"Are you coming to the show tomorrow night?" Jerry asked.

She stared at the towel. "I um . . . wasn't invited."

"You should come to the show tomorrow night. I mean, Danny could use all the support he can get."

Betty looked at him. "Just Danny?"

Jerry rubbed the back of his neck. "Well, we all could, really."

Betty nodded. "Oh."

"Please say you'll come."

A small smile lifted Betty's cheek. "I will be there."

Jerry smiled at her. "I'll see you later, then."

"Okay."

Jerry went up the stairs, and Betty's excitement made her whirl around, hugging the towel.

58

Nancy stood with her hands behind her back in front of Mr. Cummings' desk. The large balding man sat back in his creaking office chair while he read the article Nancy had written. Occasionally, Cummings would grunt from deep in his throat but said nothing further. The fact that he had even agreed to talk to her had surprised Nancy because most people that came to his office unannounced were dismissed with a grunt and wave of his flabby hand. The shiny gold surface of the nameplate on the desk mesmerized Nancy while she daydreamed of the day when she would be the editor.

Mr. Cummings finally sat forward in his chair and turned to Nancy. "Not bad for your first time, Calhoun."

Nancy grinned until her cheeks hurt.

"But, unfortunately, I can't use it," Cummings said, throwing the paper on top of all the other rejected articles on his desk.

Nancy's cheeks deflated. "But Mr. Cummings, The Dice are popular in this town, and I'm sure their fans will be curious to know why they are playing a show at the community center under an assumed name."

"Listen, kid, I'm going to be honest with you, most people in this community don't want to read any stories about rock 'n' roll, let alone the people that play it. Parents want their kids to go to school, attend church, become productive members of society, and pay taxes.

Rock 'n' roll does nothing but promote juvenile delinquency and other nefarious activities. Now, I suggest you return to your copy duties and let me go back to mine," Mr. Cumming said, picking up a magazine and his French cruller.

Nancy paused, trying to think of something to say to change Cumming's mind, but nothing came. Slumping her shoulders, Nancy passed a young man on her way out the door.

"Mornin', D.C.," the young man said.

"Mornin' Jim," Cummings said, not looking up from his magazine.

Jim put his hands in his pockets. "Who's the little girl?"

Cummings rolled his eyes. "One of the copy runners wants to be a reporter."

Jim chuckled. "She wrote an article?"

Cummings nodded.

"Was it any good?"

Cummings pointed at the stack on his desk. "Read it for yourself."

Jim picked up the paper and started reading while leaning against the wall.

A woman dressed in a navy blue fitted dress and heels entered the room. "Would you like some more coffee, Mr. Cummings?"

"No thanks, Pam," Mr. Cummings said.

"Here's your messages, sir," Pam said, setting a small stack of papers on his desk.

"Thanks, Pam."

Pam turned and smiled at Jim. "Morning, Jim."

"Morning, Pam," Jim said with a polite nod as Pam left the office.

Jim perched his foot on one of the chairs in front of Mr. Cummings' desk. "You know, this article isn't half bad."

Cummings rumpled his lip. "The last thing I need is the ladies from the church committee calling me and preaching about the evils of rock 'n' roll."

"It's about more than that. Would you mind if I took a crack at it? It's kind of a slow news day."

"Sure, go ahead, but I'll have Pam send you the calls."

Jim laughed. "Okay. I'll try not to make it too offensive."

Cummings waved his hand in the air, and Jim left his office.

59

FLIPPING ON THE LIGHT SWITCH, the evidence of the party from the night before was illuminated in a grey halo. Empty cups, bottles, rumpled napkins, and other bits of trash littered the rehearsal space. It was obvious to Stu no attempt had been made to tidy the area before everyone went home. They left the space a mess on purpose.

After an hour of intense cleaning, the trash was cleared and the floor was swept clean. John had ordered Stu to beat the dirt out of the rug, and he would do that later. Right now, he needed a break. Sitting on the couch, Stu stretched the fingers on his sore hand. The dull pain reminded him of his rage from the night before. Seeking release from the tension, Stu had slammed his fist against a rotted wooden board. At the time, he thought the board would crack, but it didn't, and he was left with an injured hand. Stu rested his head on the back of the couch and stared up at the ceiling. Whenever he thought about John's condescending attitude, his rage threatened to reignite. How would he ever make it through the day without letting his attitude show? Patrick and his stupid ideas be damned. After all, Patrick wasn't there having to do all this menial work to soothe John's ego. Rolling his head to the side, Stu's gaze rested on the guitars that sat where their owners carelessly discarded them.

One guitar in particular captured Stu's attention. Danny's precious guitar was leaning against the stool he usually sat on. Its worn leather strap fell limp at the side. His most prized possession, sitting there vulnerable, naked, alone.

Stu sat forward with slumped shoulders; his fatigued eyes narrowed as he glared at the instrument. Rising onto his feet, Stu stepped over to the guitar. Aching fingers trailed over perfectly tuned strings. Picking it up, Stu sat on the stool and cradled the instrument in his arms. His fevered touch played his wailing solo. Each note seduced Stu's eardrums like the song of a distant siren.

It should have been him playing lead guitar. It should have been him playing the solo.

The corners of Stu's lips twitched. If only there was some way to silence the guitar, to silence . . . Danny. Running his finger up the guitar's neck, the tip of his index finger touched the low E string's tuning peg. The crack of Stu's lips spread into a fiendish grimace, and the siren laughed.

60

THE FRIDAY NIGHT SHOW AT The Beaumont was sold out. The exuberant audience waited in anticipation of the rising curtain. Will, Patrick, and Boyd waited in the wings, but Joe had yet to join them. It wasn't like Joe to be late for the opening curtain. He was always there early, rounding everyone up and ensuring everything was perfect before the curtain went up.

"Where is Joe?" Patrick asked.

Boyd shrugged.

"He is here, isn't he?" Patrick asked Will.

Before Will could answer, the stage manager walked up to him.

"Are you ready?" the nervous man asked.

"No, give us a minute," Will said.

The stage manager looked at his watch.

"I am aware of the time," Will snapped.

Shaking his head, the stage manager walked away, mumbling to himself.

"You want me to look for him?" Patrick asked.

"No, I will." Will unstrapped his bass and walked toward Joe's dressing room. He knocked on the door. "Joe, it's Will. Are you in there?"

Will didn't hear anything. "Joe, are you in there?"

No noise. Will tried the doorknob, and it was locked. "Joe, I'm not messin' around. Now open this damn door!"

The fact that there wasn't a noise or a returned explanation began to concern Will. He walked up to one of the stagehands. "Where is the key to Joe's dressing room?"

The young man looked confused. "I don't know. I can go try and find it."

"There isn't time for that." Storming toward the door, Will's adrenaline rose in his veins. Lifting his foot he kicked the door open.

Joe was slumped over on the dressing table. His shirt sleeves rolled up with the rubber tube still tied around his arm. Will rushed to him and lifted Joe's head. Drool was on his lips.

"Joe!" Will slapped Joe's face, trying to revive him.

"Will, what's going on?" Boyd said, stepping into the room.

"Leave us alone!" Will snapped.

"But . . ." Boyd stammered.

"I said, leave us alone!" Will shoved Boyd out of the room and slammed the door shut. Stepping to a side table, Will poured a glass of water and threw it into Joe's face. Joe moved his head and moaned.

"Joe?" Will said, squatting beside him. "Joe, come on and wake up!"

Joe opened his heavy eyelids and looked through a haze at Will. "Hey, Willie," he said.

"Come on, Joe, you need to get up and move around. The show was supposed to start ten minutes ago."

Joe's head rolled around. "I don't want to get up."

"I don't care," Will said, pulling him off the chair.

Joe stood on his wobbly feet. Water dripped off his forehead.

"You need to walk around with me," Will ordered, putting his arm around Joe.

Joe was swaying. "I can't."

"How much of that shit did you shoot? Are you trying to kill yourself?"

"Do you remember when we first started to play together?" Joe asked.

"Joe—"

"Remember how fun it used to be? We didn't have any cares back then. Nothing mattered but playing music. When did that all change?"

Will looked at the dazed, swaying head of his friend. "I don't know, man."

"It was her, wasn't it?"

"You need to start walking, or you won't make it."

"I know I've been an asshole, but I never meant to hurt you. Can you ever forgive me?" Joe said, setting his hand on Will's chest.

"Joe, this isn't the time to bring up ghosts from the past."

"It's hard to forget them when every time I close my eyes, I see him standing there. Looking at me with those big blue eyes." Translucent tears formed in the corners of Joe's drooping eyes. "I should have been there. I should have never let him out of my sight."

"Joe, it wasn't your fault. It was nobody's fault," Will reasoned.

"I can't forgive myself, Will. I loved him. He was my son."

Will held Joe securely as guilt was exposed, and tears failed to wash it away. Words didn't seem adequate, so Will didn't say anything as he offered the supportive arms Joe needed.

"You want me to cancel the show?" Will asked.

Joe shook his weary head. "This is all I have left, Will. The audience and music are all I have left to live for. I just need one more bump."

"No, you don't need another bump. Let's get you cleaned up. Splash cold water on your face and change into a clean shirt and jacket."

Will helped Joe to the bathroom, and ten minutes later, The Dice was ready for the show. The clean shirt and jacket didn't hide the dark circles and fatigue that Joe harbored, but when the house manager introduced the band, the sultry spotlight stripped away his agony. The showman emerged with a charismatic charge that electrified the atmosphere. Joe poured what was left of his energy into the performance, and everyone who witnessed was mesmerized.

Covered with sweat and short of breath, Joe left the stage. The crowd's echoing cheers for the second encore followed him. The Dice had reached a brilliant zenith. With the rest of the band celebrating around him, Joe Delaney saw the sweet cherub face and the innocent smile that had defined his life. Wanting to touch him, wanting to hold him, Joe took one final step forward and collapsed.

Rock 'n' Roll Show in Madison: Ethical or Immoral?

News of disruptive juvenile delinquents and rowdy rock 'n' roll shows headline the newspapers of this country every day. While parents struggle to give their children the best education and stable home life, these terrifying maladies creep into our communities, causing corruption of teenagers, unprepared schools, churches, and homes of the hard-working class. Our small community of Madison has done a stellar job keeping the youth of our town entertained and happy. When I learned about a rock 'n' roll show at our very own community center, I was completely shocked. A flyer advertising the event has been circulating at popular youth hangouts like Lucky's Arcade, Be-Bops, and The Beat record store. The show headliners are Joey and the Moon Rockers and The Hound Dogs.

I personally had never heard of these two groups, but if they're playing rock 'n' roll music, they're obviously of low moral character.

The Hound Dogs are a newly formed band that performed at a friend's birthday party a few months ago. The performance was struggling when a young man joined them on stage. It turns out the young man is the former rhythm guitarist for The Dice, Daniel Bruer. It is rumored that Bruer quit The Dice due to jealousy of front man Joe Delaney. Joe Delaney was unavailable for comment.

Teenagers in the immediate area have never heard of Joey and the Moon Rockers. Which raises the question, who are Joey and the Moon Rockers? I started my investigation at the local record store, The Beat. The salesclerk refused to answer any questions or offer any useful information. He was, in fact, a rude, obstinate individual who was dismissive and disrespectful to customers. I then turned my attention to the Madison Harold archives. Being blessed by pure luck and perseverance, an informant who wishes to remain anonymous saw Joey and the Moon Rockers perform six years ago when he attended high school. When asked if he knew what happened to the group, he replied that they changed their name to The Dice.

So, what exactly is the story behind this group who dares to call themselves Joey and the Moon Rockers? Is it some kind of prank? Is it a publicity stunt to bring in an audience? Or do the imposters not know where the name originated?

Whatever the reason, our goals must be clear. Remain diligent with your youngsters. Make sure you meet their friends, monitor their activities, and set a curfew. An event planned by undisciplined minors looking for an excuse to stray away from morals and family values is on a fast track to juvenile delinquency. It is the opinion of this reporter that whoever is responsible for authorizing such a nefarious activity in our reputable community should be thoroughly investigated.

Jim Robbins, Reporter

61

D RESSED IN BRIGHT PARTY DRESSES with curled hair and a light touch of makeup, Mollie, Marcy, and Anne traveled to the community center in Mollie's mother's car. Their exuberant laughing and singing drowned out The Platters on the car radio. Anne was surprised when Marcy invited her to a slumber party at Mollie's house. She didn't have many girlfriends and being included filled her with joy. Mrs. Brewster was spending the evening playing bridge with friends, so Anne was free to enjoy the evening without responsibility.

"Wow, look at all the crowd," Mollie said when the community center appeared.

"I don't think the boys were expecting this many people," Marcy commented.

"You think we will have a problem finding them?" Anne asked.

"Maybe. We need to stick close together so we don't get separated," Marcy said.

Molly parked the car having finally found a parking spot a few blocks away from the building.

Several carloads full of excited teens clamored past them and a group of boys walking across the street whistled at them.

"Don't wave back," Marcy said. "We don't want them to think we're interested."

"Speak for yourself," Mollie said.

"What about Danny?" Anne asked.

"Danny isn't Mollie's boyfriend… yet," Marcy said, wanting to stay away from the subject.

"He seemed attentive the other night," Anne said.

Mollie's spirits perked up. "Oh, you really think so, Anne?"

"Well, yeah."

"He hasn't asked her on a date or kissed her yet," Marcy commented.

Mollie folded her arms. "Gee, thanks, Marcy."

"I just don't want you to get your hopes up."

"Too late."

The overwhelming crowd pushed toward the front door while Eddie and his friend tried to take tickets and maintain order.

"Goodness, look at the line. We will never make it inside." Mollie wined.

"We can try the side door," Marcy suggested.

"Anything is better than being trampled."

The girls plowed through the crowd and made their way to the locked side entrance. Marcy knocked on the door persistently.

A harried young man with a scowl on his face opened the door. "This isn't an entrance."

He pulled the door to close it, but Marcy grabbed hold. "Wait! Our boyfriends are waiting for us."

"So?"

"So, they're in the band," Anne said.

"Likely story," he said, slamming the door closed.

Mollie's shoulders fell. "Now, what do we do?"

"He's just going to have to listen to reason," Marcy said, banging on the door with her fist until the young man opened the door. This time, he was scowling, and his swollen cheeks dwarfed his eyes. "I thought I told you to get lost!"

"And I told you our boyfriends are in there!"

"You're a little liar who thinks you can bat your eyelashes and cut the line."

Marcy's cheeks puffed out and looked like she might punch him. "How dare you!"

"Hey, hey, what's going on over here?"

Another young man from inside the building came to the door. He was dressed in jeans, a dark green shirt, and a slim black tie. His calming demeanor comforted the girls.

"These girlies think they can sweet talk their way past the line," the first young man said.

"Is that right, ladies?" the second young man said, making eye contact with Mollie.

"No, it's not," Marcy snapped. "We already told him our boyfriends are in the band and are waiting for us."

"Does your boyfriend have a name?" the second young man asked.

"James," Marcy said.

"And you?" he asked Mollie.

"I don't have a boyfriend," Mollie answered.

"And her boyfriend is John," Marcy finished, trying to move the process along.

The young man's smile left as his critical gaze evaluated Anne in one uncomfortable sweep.

"You know, Nik, I think these girls are telling the truth. Let them pass."

"Sure thing, Patrick," Nik said, opening the door for the girls.

The name rang a bell for Marcy, but she didn't waiver. "Thank you."

"No worries," Patrick said, his smooth grin returning. "I'm sure your boyfriends will be happy to see you."

"Do you think there are any free tables?" Anne asked Marcy.

"I can find a place for you ladies to sit," Patrick said.

"Really?" Marcy said.

"Sure," he said, smiling at Mollie. "I'll be right back."

Mollie watched Patrick walk away. "He seems nice."

"For a scoundrel, maybe," Marcy said.

Patrick returned a few minutes later and escorted the girls to a table close to the platform.

"Is this table all right?" Patrick asked Mollie.

"Yes," Mollie answered.

Patrick pulled out a chair for Mollie.

Mollie tucked her dress under her and sat down. "Thank you,"

Patrick sat his hand on the back of Mollie's chair. "I don't think I caught your name."

Mollie lowered her lashes. "It's Mollie."

"It's nice to meet you, Mollie. I'm Patrick."

"I heard," she said with a timid smile.

"I should head backstage," Patrick said.

"Oh, are you in the show?"

"As a matter-of-fact, I am."

Mollie grinned. "That's exciting."

"I take it you are a Hound Dog fan?" Patrick asked.

Mollie ran her thumb over the edge of the table. "I am."

"Hmm, well, maybe I can change your mind."

Mollie placed her hand on her chin. "Maybe."

"I will talk to you later, then," Patrick said, letting his hand linger on the back of Mollie's chair.

Mollie nodded and held Patrick's gaze before he finally turned and walked away.

Marcy rested her arms on the table and glanced over her shoulder. "This crowd is much different from the one at Len's party. Huh, Mollie?"

Mollie nodded, disinterested.

"How so?" Anne asked.

"I can't quite put my finger on it. Some of them seem to be a bit . . ."

"Rough?" Mollie said.

"Yeah, that's it."

"Do you think we will see the boys before the show?" Anne asked Marcy.

"I wonder if they are even here yet," Marcy said.

"Hey, look, I think I see Stu," Mollie said, pointing her finger at the platform.

"Oh, thank goodness," Marcy said, getting up and crossing to Stu. "Hi, stranger."

Stu turned to see Marcy's thankful smile. "Hey, Marcy."

Marcy gently touched Stu's hand. "Boy, am I glad to see you."

Marcy noticed the bandage on Stu's hand before he pulled it away. "Is something wrong?"

Stu held his hand. "No."

"What happened to your hand?"

"Nothing," Stu said, keeping his hand close to his body.

Marcy reached her hand forward. "Come on, let me see it."

"No!" Stu growled, catching Marcy off guard.

"I'm sorry. I was only trying to help."

"Did you need something, Marcy? I have work to do," Stu said.

"Yes, I was hoping to see James before the show. Can you let him know I'm here with Anne and Mollie?"

"Sure," Stu said with a slight nod.

By Stu's brooding features and rigid stance, Marcy could tell that he wasn't in the mood for small talk. "Thanks for your help."

"I'll tell James," Stu said flatly.

"It is good to see you, Stu."

"Yeah, you too," Stu said, walking away.

Marcy's brow wrinkled. After the incident at the party, she could understand why Stu was in a bad mood, but there was something else. Stu had never been curt or rude to anyone. Something was wrong with Stu. Very wrong.

62

TANDING BETWEEN LOIS AND NANCY, Carol wanted to turn around and go home. She hated crowds and waiting in what appeared to be an endless line hardly seemed worth it. Lois was busy flirting with any boy within three feet, and Nancy pouted, with her arms folded across her chest and her face pinched into a tight scowl. Nancy had ranted on the phone to Carol for a half hour about the article in the newspaper. Then, when she walked with Lois and Carol to the community center, she started the rant again from the beginning. Carol was already exhausted.

The line crept forward at a sluggish pace, and Carol shifted from foot to foot in shoes that were too small for her.

"How come you can't seem to stand in one place?" Lois complained.

"It's her shoes," Nancy said. "They're too small for her."

"They're the only nice shoes I have," Carol said.

Lois looked at Carol's feet. "I bet if you took those socks off, you might have more room."

Nancy looked down at Carol's thick wool socks. "She's right, Carol. Those are your winter socks."

"Why aren't you wearing nylon stockings?" Lois asked.

"Because my mother said nice girls don't wear nylons."

Lois raised her eyebrow.

290

Carol smiled sheepishly.

"You are going to have to take those stockings off or be uncomfortable all night," Nancy said.

"But I can't take them off," Carol wined.

"Why not?" Nancy said.

"Because then I will be naked."

"Oh, for heaven's sake, Carol, you will not be naked!"

Nancy's voice carried, and the two girls and three boys ahead turned around with astonished faces.

"I was talking about her feet, for cryin' out loud. Get your minds out of the gutter," Nancy snapped.

The five chattered among themselves and turned forward.

Carol finally removed her socks, and her feet felt better. Not sure where to put them,

Carol stuffed them between her shirt and skirt, making her look as if she had a lumpy middle.

Lois struck up a conversation with a young man behind her. He didn't look anything like most of the young men she went for. As a matter of fact, he was rather plain. His dark hair was combed neatly to one side, and he wore a cardigan with loafers. With his hands behind his back, he listened intently to Lois's chatter. Most young men tired of listening to her and then moved on quickly, but this one smiled and nodded, making her talk more.

They were almost to the front door when Nancy stopped. "Oh no."

"What's wrong, Nan?" Carol said.

"It's him!"

Carol looked around. "Who?"

Nancy pointed at Eddie. "The clerk from the record store."

Carol looked around a few people to see him.

"I can't let him see me!" Nancy said, ducking behind Carol.

"What do you mean you can't let him see you?" Carol said.

"He'll recognize me."

"So?"

"So! I'm too embarrassed to face him."

Carol shrugged. "So, what do you suggest we do? Go home?"

Nancy bit her thumbnail.

"Maybe if you tie your scarf over your hair, he may not recognize you."

"Oh, that's the perfect idea, Carol!" Nancy removed the scarf tied around her neck and put it over her head. Then, reaching into her purse, she pulled out a pair of sunglasses and put them on. "Well, how do I look?"

"Good."

Nancy handed her ticket to Carol. "Okay, now give him this ticket, and I will hide my face. Okay?"

"Sure," Carol said.

"Hey, girls," Lois whispered to them. "I hope you don't mind, but Theo has asked me to sit with him. You understand, don't you?"

"Lois—" Nancy started, but she already left with Theo.

Carol sighed. "Some girls have all the luck."

Nancy grabbed onto Carol's arm. "Now, pay attention, we're next."

Stepping up to Eddie, Nancy put her head down.

"Ticket?" Eddie said to Carol.

Carol held the tickets out with a lopsided grin.

Eddie looked at her oddly and shifted his gaze to Nancy. "What's wrong with your friend?"

"Huh?" Carol said.

"I asked what's wrong with your friend?"

"My friend?"

Eddie wrinkled his brow.

"Oh, this friend," Carol giggled. "She's just shy is all."

Eddie tried to look down to see Nancy's face, but she turned away. Eddie looked back at Carol, who still had an odd smirk on her face. Eddie rubbed his chin. "Hey, have I seen you before?"

"Who me?" Carol said.

"Yes."

"I don't think so."

Eddie looked back at Nancy. "I think I would feel better seeing your friend's face."

Nancy tightened her grip on Carol's arm.

Carol grimaced. "Ow! Oh, I don't think that's a good idea. She might faint."

Eddie folded his arms. "Faint?"

"Yes."

Eddie drummed his fingers on his arm. "Does she realize she's going into a noisy venue where there will be loud live music?"

"I think so."

Eddie rumpled his lip. "All right, you can go in."

Carol and Nancy passed by Eddie. Eddie noticed Nancy's scuffed saddle shoes as they walked away and smiled to himself.

63

He joy and confidence Friday night brought had quickly evaporated like dew on a desert cactus.

Staring in disbelief at the small building, the occupants of Danny's car were dumbfounded. The magnitude of the morning's newspaper article ignited excitement and curiosity from the community's youth. What should have been an inconsequential event had turned into a major attraction.

Young men and women waited in a ticket line wound around the parking lot and down the sidewalk. The show sold out quickly, and several disappointed teenagers hung around, hoping to sneak in.

"Where in the world did all of these people come from?" Danny said in disbelief.

"There is no way all these people can fit community center," Jerry remarked from the back seat.

"So, what are all those people doing milling around?" James said, glancing out the passenger's side back window.

"Good question," John said, peering out the driver's side back window.

Betty sat in the front seat between Danny and Ronnie. She noticed Ronnie was despondent and tapping his thumbs on his knees.

"You know the show will be terrific tonight, don't you?" Betty said.

Lost in their own thoughts, the boys ignored the question.

Betty sighed. "Can I turn on the radio, Danny?"

"No," Danny answered.

"Boy, you are tense if you don't want to listen to the radio."

Danny's fingers tightened around the steering wheel. "I just got a lot on my mind. This is it, really it."

"What does that mean?" Betty asked.

"It means tonight decides if I'm still under contract," Danny said glancing at John in the rearview mirror and didn't finish his sentence.

Betty sat her hand on Danny's knee. "I believe in you. I believe in all of you. This will all be behind us in a few hours, and we'll celebrate. Right, John?"

John looked at her with a slight grin.

◻◼◻◼◻◼◻◼◻◼◻◼◻◼◻◼◻◼◻

The boys walked the blocks to the building before stopping across the street.

"We need to keep Betty in the middle, so she doesn't get trampled," John said.

Jerry took Betty's hand. "I have a hold of her."

Betty grinned.

John took a deep breath "Okay, here we go."

Huddled tight together, the group crossed the street and John forged toward one of the side doors. The additional entrances were flooded with teens trying to force their way inside. Quickly changing course, John worked his way toward the front. Darting and squeezing through small openings, John inadvertently was shoved into a large young man with a buzz cut.

"Excuse me," John said.

"Hey, who the hell do you think you are tryin' to cut the line?" buzz cut asked John.

"I'm not tryin' to cut the line."

"The back of the line is back there," the young man beside the buzz cut said, pointing behind him.

"We belong inside," James said.

"We're the band," Danny said.

"You look like a bunch of goobers to me," the second boy said.

"Well, you look like a dunce, Elmer," Betty said, stepping in front of John.

Elmer wrinkled his nose. "Well, if it ain't Betty bug eyes. What's a prude like you doin' at a rock 'n' roll show? Don't you have some knittin' to do?"

Buzz cut laughed and punched Elmer in the shoulder, almost knocking him over.

"Hey, careful there, slug-o," Elmer said, rubbing his arm.

Betty stepped up to Elmer. "Listen here, you big dummy, these fellas have a show do, and you and the ape are blocking their way. So, step aside and let the band inside the building!"

Elmer folded his arms. "And what if we refuse?"

"Then I am going to tell Pastor Tomkins that you and Timothy Dugan mooned the girl's youth group last Sunday."

Elmer laughed. "You don't know that was me."

"No, but your sister does."

Elmer's jaw dropped, and his eyes widened.

Betty put her hands on her hips. "So, are you gettin' the hell out of the way or what?"

Hanging his head down and rubbing the back of his neck, Elmer and his large friend stepped aside.

John set his hand on Jerry's shoulder. "Boy, you got your hands full with that one."

"Tell me about it," Jerry sighed.

Eddie stood vigilant by the front door with a friend, trying to hold the crowd back. He looked harried and exhausted when Betty walked up to the door with the boys.

"Hey, Eds," John said.

"Boy, am I glad to see you guys. This place is a madhouse!"

"No kiddin'," Danny said.

"Have you seen the girls?" James asked.

Eddie shook his head. "I haven't had time to see anything. It's all I can do to watch the door."

"Where's the equipment?" John asked.

"Behind the sheet with Stu."

"Did you say a sheet?" Jerry asked.

"There was no curtain, so Len and I hung a sheet."

"Swanky," Danny commented.

"Come on, fellas," John said, stepping inside the building.

"Thanks, Eds," Danny said.

Seconds after the boys went inside, the crowd began to scream and wave their hands in the air as they ran toward the street.

"Now what?" Eddie said.

A baby blue shiny 57 Chevy pulled up to the curb. A bright paisley sock and a black and white loafer stepped onto the bare space on the sidewalk. The tall, slim man with wavy golden hair adjusted the lapels of his pink jacket. Placing a pair of sunglasses on the bridge of his narrow nose, he greeted his fans with a smooth white smile.

"Oh, my goodness, I can't believe it's him," Eddie gasped.

"Who is it?" Eddie's friend asked.

"Digsby."

64

STEPPING INSIDE THE BUILDING, THE boys transitioned from one chaotic situation to another. The only air came in through the doors, and oppressive heat threatened to steal oxygen from their lungs. Teens lined the walls, girls sat in boys' laps and the fortunate few who secured a table let their friends sit on the table.

"I can't see anything," Danny complained.

"One more person touches me, and they're meeting the floor," John groused.

"Do you see anything, Ronnie?" James asked.

With a height of six-foot-one, it was easy for Ronnie to rise above the crowd. "I see Marcy."

"You do?" James said.

"Anne and Mollie, too."

"Great, show us the way," Danny said.

Ronnie pushed forward, and once the girls came into view, John's frazzled nerves began to calm. Anne's demure smile and bounce when she saw him blocked out any negative thoughts or frustration he had.

"Hi," she chimed when he came up to her. Without a word, he pulled her in his arms and held her close like a life vest in a raging river.

Anne touched his cheek. "Are you okay?"

"I am now," he whispered in her ear.

James put his arm around Marcy. "This crowd is insane."

"It took us a while to even make it inside," Mollie said.

"They are tenacious," Danny said, smiling at her.

"Hey, Betty," Marcy said.

"Hey, Marcy, Mollie," Betty said with a slight nod.

John's arm was securely around Anne's waist, and he wasn't paying attention to anything else.

"John, aren't you going to introduce Anne to Betty?" Marcy prompted.

"I am," John said, sneering at Marcy. "Betty, this is Anne. Anne, this is Betty—Eddie's sister."

"It's nice to meet you," Anne said.

"Likewise," Betty said.

Ronnie's head moved from side to side. "I need to find Otis. He's scared."

"Otis is just fine," Danny said, reassuring Ronnie's anxiety.

Ronnie ignored Danny and walked toward the platform.

"I better follow him before he is overwhelmed. It's good to see you, Mollie," Danny said, taking off after Ronnie.

"We better get up front," James said to John.

"I'll be there in a minute," John said.

"You coming, Jerry?" James said.

"Yeah."

"We'll see you ladies later," James said.

"Good luck," Marcy said, kissing James's cheek.

"Good luck," Betty said to Jerry, keeping her hands folded.

"Thanks," Jerry said.

James and Jerry walked away, and John led Anne a few feet from the girls.

"I'm so thankful you're here," John said.

"I wouldn't miss it," Anne said, straightening John's collar.

John leaned in. "You look very pretty tonight."

"I'm sorry, my dress is pink. I know you don't like it."

John's arm tightened around Anne's waist. "Your dress could be purple with green spots for all I care."

"Are you sure?"

"Okay, maybe not green spots."

Anne's wistful laugh charmed John, and he gently touched her chin. "I can't wait to be alone with you after the show tonight."

Anne's heart skipped as she gazed into his intensified eyes. "I think Mollie's folks are out, and she wants the gang to come over for a small party."

"Is that what you want to do?" John asked.

Anne nodded fervently. "I think it would be fun."

"All right," John agreed, and Anne let her breath out. "We can stay for a while, and then we will leave."

"And go where?" Anne squeaked.

"Somewhere private."

Anne swallowed hard, her mouth turning dry. "Are you sure that's a good idea?"

John chuckled. "Why wouldn't it be?"

"Um . . . well I just meant that ... what if I'm not . . ."

"Shh," John said, kissing her words away.

Behind her closed eyes, the sound faded, the room emptied, and all that was left was the tremor of anticipation.

John loosened his grip and put his mouth close to her ear. "I need to go, but I'll see you later."

Anne opened her eyes. "Good luck. I know you're going to do great."

John winked at her and keeping his eyes on her for as long as possible, he walked away. Anne reached out and steadied herself against a nearby chair.

"Are you all right, Anne?" Marcy asked.

"Yes, I just feel a bit lightheaded from the heat."

Marcy pulled out the chair. "Sit down, and I will see if I can find you some water."

Anne nodded, and Marcy left her alone with her new companions, gnawing guilt and endless dread.

John joined James, Jerry, Danny, and Stu behind the makeshift curtain.

Ronnie was sitting with his arm around Otis like a protective brother.

"Has he calmed down?" John asked Danny.

"Yeah, once he saw that Otis was okay, he was fine."

"I think the crowd makes him nervous," James said.

"It's makin' us all nervous," John said.

"Have you been sitting with the equipment this whole time?" James asked Stu.

Stu nodded. "I have. Once people started to come in, I haven't even taken a break to hit the head."

"For heaven's sake, take a break," John said.

"I'm afraid to venture into that mob," Stu said.

"You need me to hold your hand?" James said.

"That's not what needs to be held," Stu said.

James turned red and swiped at Stu as he passed through the curtain.

"I wonder where Joey and the Moon Rockers are," Jerry said.

"Knowing Dalamey, he's probably waiting to make a grand entrance," John said, sitting on a trunk.

"He surely has the crowd for it," Danny said.

Len came behind the curtain with some root beers in his hand.

"Our savior has arrived," Danny said.

"I wouldn't go that far," Len said, passing the bottles around.

"It's good to see you, Len," John said.

"You as well."

"Has the crowd out front died down at all?" James asked.

"I don't think so. A local celebrity pulled up in a 57 Chevy."

"What local celebrity?" Danny asked.

Len took the top off his root beer bottle. "Digsby."

"You got to be kidding," Jerry said.

Len tilted his bottle back. "Nope."

John shook his head. "Could this night get any worse?"

65

THERE WASN'T A TEENAGER IN town who didn't know who Digsby was. His smooth voice came over the airwaves of KTWB almost every day. Quick with witty quips and knowledge of rock 'n' roll, Digsby was a teenage idol in the small town of Madison. Standing calmly on the sidewalk, Digsby signed autographs for the swooning girls that crowded around him. The last of the sun's sinking rays danced across the sequins on his jacket, giving him an extra flash of star quality.

"What are you doin' here, Digsby?" one of the annoyed boyfriends asked.

"I thought I would coast down here and see what all the fuss is about. I mean, a rock 'n' roll show happenin' right here in my own hometown that I don't know about? That's all kinds of crazy!" Digsby said, swinging his hips.

There was more screaming and jumping from excited girls. Digsby sauntered up the path to the doors, and the crowd parted like fans along the red carpet on Oscar night.

Digsby stepped up to Eddie at the door and removed his sunglasses. "What's up, cat? I'm here to see the show."

"Do you have a ticket?" Eddie's friend asked.

Eddie frowned. "Forgive my co-worker, Mr. Digsby. You don't need a ticket."

Digsby raised his eyebrow. "Mr. Disgsby? I ain't no mister, just Digsby."

The crowd laughed, and Eddie's cheeks burned.

Digsby shook his finger at Eddie. "Say, aren't you the kid that manages The Beat?"

Eddie rubbed the back of his neck. "Yeah."

Digsby nodded his head like a bobblehead. "Yeah, you're the kid who calls always wantin' to hear Buddy Holly."

Eddie nodded. "That's me."

Digsby leaned on the podium that was between Eddie and his friend. "You know, I know old Buddy."

Eddie's eyes widened. "You do?"

"Oh, yeah. I met him when he performed in Texas. He's a real nice guy. Heck of a performer too."

All Eddie could do was blink dumbfounded.

Digsby stood up straight and adjusted his jacket. "I bet you'd like to see him, huh?"

"I would give anything," Eddie said.

Digsby smiled and tapped Eddie on the nose. "I'll see what I can do for you kid."

"Wow," Eddie muttered.

Digsby smiled and went inside, leaving a speechless Eddie at the door.

◻◼◻◼◻◼◻◼◻◼◻◼◻◼◻◼◻◼◻

"I feel like an idiot," Will groused, pulling on the sleeves of his plain grey jacket. "What if someone sees me in these ridiculous clothes?"

"I don't see what the problem is," Patrick said. "You look fine."

Will scratched his arms. "Well, I don't feel fine. Wool makes me itch, and jeans are for farmers."

Patrick leaned against the wall. "I worked on a farm."

Will wrinkled his nose. "On purpose?"

Patrick shrugged. "Money is money."

"Agreed, but there are other ways to make it other than being close to cows."

"Don't forget the pigs and chickens."

Will huffed with disgust. "I need a drink."

"I do too, but there isn't a drop in the place."

Will patted his jacket pocket. "Care to join me in the washroom?"

"No thanks. I want to have my wits about me when I step on stage."

Will lifted his eyebrow. "This show is important to you, isn't it?"

Patrick pulled on sleeves of his shirt. "I just want to make a good impression on the crowd."

Will chuckled. "It isn't difficult to impress teenagers."

Patrick folded his arms. "You do realize they buy a lot of records, and sales means money, and money means we work for ourselves and not with pigs."

Will straightened his tie. "You have a point."

Voices could be heard coming around the sheet, and Patrick turned to see Boyd holding a curvy young lady's hand. An attractive blond, wearing an orange front-fitted dress with puffy drop shoulders, was with them. Her high cheekbones and pursed red lips made her resemble a pinup. Will's eyes locked onto her pleasing figure, and his disingenuous interest changed.

"Hey, fellas," Boyd said. "What a crazy crowd."

"Yes, it is," Patrick said. "I was beginning to worry about you."

"Sorry, Mae was late," Boyd grumbled.

"Is it my fault you were early?" Mae said, folding her arms.

Boyd opened his mouth to respond, but Doris pressed her finger to his lips, blocking further comment.

Patrick pushed away from the wall. "So, who are the lovely ladies with you tonight?"

"This is my girlfriend, Doris, and her friend, Mae," Boyd said. "These two gentlemen are Patrick and Will."

"It's nice to meet you, Patrick," Doris said. "Boyd has told me good things about you."

"Has he now?" Patrick smiled.

"He thinks you're a good fit."

"Well, I think he's pretty terrific too," Patrick said.

Boyd grinned.

Pushing past Boyd and Doris, Will casually stood next to Mae. "Well, hello there. I don't believe we've met."

Will's smooth grin and musk aftershave captivated Mae's attention. "No, I don't believe we have."

"The name's Will."

"Mae," Mae said, offering her hand.

Without breaking eye contact, Will captured her manicured hand. "What a refreshing pleasure to see such a delicate lady." Mae lowered her lashes, and Will kissed her hand.

Doris rolled her eyes.

"Have you talked to the Hound Dogs yet?" Boyd asked Patrick.

"Not yet. We've been waiting for you," Patrick said.

"Well, I guess it's time we get this party started," Boyd said.

"Yes, I know Will is anxious for the night to be over," Patrick said, shifting his weight.

Will was still boldly gazing at Mae. "Oh, I don't know. I think this evening is looking up."

"I saved a table for you ladies by the stage," Patrick said.

"Great," Doris said, anxious to move away from Will, but Mae was soaking up his attention.

"Come on, Mae. Let's let the boys work, huh?"

Mae flashed Doris an annoyed look, but a syrupy smile returned when she gazed back at Will. "I guess you're right, Doris. I wouldn't want to hold up the show."

Will tightened his fingers before Mae pulled away. "I will see you later, won't I?"

"Well, I don't know, I guess that's up to you," Mae purred.

Will's grin spread his thin lips and he released her hand. Holding his eyes, Mae walked away with Doris, but before she was out of sight, she gave Will a small wave.

Patrick folded his arms. "Things are looking up, hey Will?"

Will turned to Patrick, and his wicked grin gave Patrick his answer.

The longer it took for the show to start, the more unsettled the crowd became. Eddie's door duties were concluded, and he started spinning some records, which helped to appease the crowd.

Betty, Mollie, Marcy, and Anne were swinging their feet and engaged in idle girl talk when Doris and Mae walked up to their table.

"Hey, chickens."

It had been a long time since Marcy and Mollie had seen Doris, and they hardly recognized her. With a few extra pounds, Doris had always been conservative and reserved in her appearance, but now she was wearing a yellow chiffon A-line dress with puffy sleeves and ruffles. Her dark brown hair was in perfect soft waves that framed her face, and a trace of makeup complimented her almond eyes.

"Doris, is that you?" Mollie asked.

Doris chortled. "Of course, it is silly."

"You look so different," Marcy said.

"She looks like a doll," Mae said, putting her arm around Doris.

"I do not," Doris said, fanning her hand that showed her painted pink nails.

"Where are you two sitting?" Mollie asked.

"Over there, not far from the side door," Doris said.

"Why don't you come sit with us?"

"Yes, why don't you?" Marcy said.

"Well, I don't know how that would look. Seeing how my man is with The Dice and yours is well . . ."

"With the Hound Dogs," Mae finished.

Marcy's face fell.

"That shouldn't matter. We're all friends," Betty said.

"Yeah. We can cheer together," Mollie said.

"I don't know. What do you think Mae?" Doris asked.

Mae shrugged. "It does seem silly to let men break up a friendship."

"Okay," Doris said with a smile.

Mollie and Anne moved over, making room for Doris and Mae.

Mae sat down next to Marcy. "So, who is your new friend?"

"This is Anne. John's girlfriend," Marcy said.

Mae's eyes narrowed. "Is that right?"

"Yes," Anne said.

"You look like a big fluff of cotton candy. Syrupy sweet," Mae drawled.

"Thank you," Anne said with a reserved smile.

"How are things going for you, Marcy?" Doris asked.

Marcy folded her hands. "Oh, fine. Things are busy at the shop. I really can't complain."

"It looks like you're happy with Boyd, Doris," Mollie said.

"I am," Doris beamed.

"You should show them your necklace," Mae urged.

Doris's hand fluttered to her neck. "Oh, I hate to brag,"

"Come on, Doris. I want to see," Mollie urged.

"Well, if you insist." Doris pulled out a gold chain with an exquisite diamond heart pendant that sparkled in the light.

Mollie gasped, putting her hand to her chest. "Oh, Doris, that's gorgeous!"

"Wow," Betty said.

"It must have cost a fortune," Mollie said, fawning over the stone.

"It did," Mae said.

"I've never seen a diamond that big," Betty said.

"Things sound serious," Marcy said.

Doris shrugged while admiring her treasure.

"He spoils her rotten," Mae said.

"Well, good for you," Mollie said. "You deserve to be spoiled. Doesn't she, Marcy?"

Marcy nodded. "Yes."

"I bet it won't be long until Marcy has a diamond," Mollie said.

"Oh, I don't think so, Mollie," Marcy chuckled.

Mae spread her hands. "I doubt James could afford it."

Doris scowled at Mae.

"What? I mean, he doesn't even have a job, does he, Marcy?" May asked.

Marcy's hand clenched under the table. "No."

"But he will," Betty said. "He's going to be an accountant. They make good money."

"Yes, they do," Doris said, nudging Mae.

Mae sat back in her chair. "Don't worry about it, Marcy. I am sure James will buy you a small ring sooner or later."

Marcy's hand tightened on her dress as her jaw clenched.

"Don't listen to her," Anne whispered to Marcy. "James is a good man with a good heart. Believe me, that is worth more than money."

"Thanks, Anne," Marcy said, squeezing Anne's hand under the table.

"Of course."

"I sincerely hope we have a chance to get to know each other better," Marcy said.

"Oh, so do I. I don't have any girlfriends."

"Well, you do now."

Anne returned Marcy's squeeze, and they smiled.

66

As the minutes ticked by, the tension behind the sheet heightened while the boys waited to confront The Dice. Naturally, everyone expected to see Joe first, but when Patrick emerged, followed by Will and Boyd, confusion and apprehension brought the boys to a defensive stance.

A lengthy, bleak glare passed between band members like sharp needles.

"Hello, John," Patrick said, breaking the silence.

"Patrick," John said in a dull tone. "What are you doin' here?"

Patrick jutted his chin. "Haven't you heard? I'm a member of The Dice now."

John allowed a faint smile and remained calm on the surface.

"Congratulations," Danny said. "I'm sure you fit in perfectly."

Will scoffed. "We are very pleased with his refined talents. Aren't we, Boyd?"

"Yes," Boyd said, putting his hands in his pockets.

"Shall we discuss the rules for tonight?" Patrick asked.

"Wait a minute—where's Dalamey?" John asked.

"Joe is in the hospital," Will answered.

"*What?*" Danny said in disbelief.

"What happened?" John asked.

"He collapsed after last night's show."

Danny's head shook. "Collapsed? Why?"

"We're not sure yet."

"So, I guess this means you're canceling the show," John said.

"On the contrary," Patrick said. "We talked things over ourselves and see no reason to cancel. There's a decent crowd, and we know the material. We don't need Joe here to put you in your place."

John's jaw tightened, and his head tilted back.

"From what we understand, whoever gets the most audience appreciation wins the contest," Will stated.

"Yes," Danny answered.

Patrick tilted his head. "Then I get my song back?"

John stepped up to Patrick. "What did you say?"

Patrick squared his shoulders. "You heard me."

John's eyes narrowed. "You know damn well I wrote that song."

"The lyrics, yes. But everyone knows you aren't talented enough to compose music of that caliber."

Grabbing Patrick by the lapels of his jacket, John slammed Patrick into the wall, jarring his neck.

A long thin grin split Patrick's lip. "Go ahead, John, what's stopping you? I know you want to show everyone what a brute you are."

John clenched his fingers, and his chest was heaving.

Patrick chuckled, feeling the death grip on his throat. "All I have to lose is blood, but you? Once I walk on stage and tell everyone in Madison who you really are, you'll be finished. No one will want anything more to do with you once they learn you're a coward who spent time in juvenile hall."

John's rage ran roughshod through his muscles, making him shake. "I doubt you'll be able to say much with a broken jaw."

Patrick's eyes widened as he grasped the iron hands that threatened to crush him.

James's reassuring hand grasped John's shoulder. "John, let him go. He's not worth it."

Gazing at Patrick's wide eyes and red face, John knew he could bring Patrick to his knees, and it sated him somehow. Releasing his hold, Patrick stumbled backward, coughing.

"Are you all right?" Will asked Patrick.

Patrick nodded, wiping his chin with the back of his hand.

Will turned to say something to John, but his menacing eyes changed Will's mind.

Danny stepped forward. "Let's decide who is going on first and end this."

Patrick adjusted his collar. "We're going first."

Will raised his brow. "We are?"

"Do you object?" Patrick asked Danny.

Danny shook his head. "Nope."

"May the best band win," Patrick said, extending his hand to Danny.

Danny firmly shook Patrick's hand. Then Patrick walked away, Will and Boyd close behind.

"Are you sure going first was a wise choice?" Boyd asked Patrick.

Patrick stopped. "Why? Are you afraid they might win?"

"Well, no, but we don't have . . . Joe."

Patrick grimaced. "Trust me. We could win this competition without you, Boyd."

Boyd's cheeks rose, his mouth dropping.

"Let's not get crazy," Will tittered.

Patrick glanced at Boyd's ashen face. "I was only joking. I merely meant that we could play ukuleles and a tin can and win this. Trust me."

Will's gaze lingered long enough to notice the disappointment and sorrow on Boyd's stalwart face. Denying his conscience, Will dropped his eyes and followed Patrick toward the platform.

❑◼❑◼❑◼❑◼❑◼❑◼❑◼❑◼❑◼❑◼❑

The restless crowd forgot about the show's delayed start when Digsby stepped onto the platform and stretched out his long arms. Cheers of enthusiasm and screams from exuberant girls brought the audience to their feet.

Throwing kisses, punching the air, and showing his perfect white teeth, Digsby soaked up the spotlight.

"Woah, what a night? Huh? I had no idea I would be standing on a platform in the community center, opening a show for two local groups. Wild!" Digsby roared.

Boisterous applause abrupted.

Digsby paced the small platform. "I personally have never heard of these two groups before the article in today's paper, but I have a feeling everyone in Madison will know who they are by the end of the night. Would you agree?"

A resounding agreement flowed from the crowd.

Digsby clapped his hands together. "First up tonight is a group with a bit of a mysterious past, but I think the article in today's paper alluded that they might have transformed into The Dice. So please, put your hands together for Joey and the Moon Rockers!"

Digsby jumped off the platform, and once the crowd saw Will and Boyd, they started to scream. "It's The Dice!"

Cheers and deafening screams crackled in the air.

Patrick commanded center stage. "Good evening, Madison! It looks like you're all ready for a shot of rock-n-roll!"

"Where's Joe?" a few audience members shouted.

Will stepped up to the microphone. "Well folks, sadly, Joe can't be with us tonight. As I am sure some of you know, he collapsed after last night's show."

A chaotic chatter traveled through the crowd.

Will held his hands up. "But not to worry, he is in the hands of the best doctor in the county. You know Joe wouldn't want anyone to be sad. He would want the show to go on! So, let's kick it off with 'Johnny B. Goode'!"

Patrick stepped forward, playing the familiar riff of the popular song, and the crowd came undone. Without missing a step or a note, Patrick wooed the crowd like a proficient lover. His confidence and charisma transfixed the crowd, and Joe's absence was quickly forgotten.

From the sidelines, the boys watched the events unfold like a horrifying nightmare. It was bad enough that Patrick was a sensation with the crowd, but their opening song had been lost to them. Patrick bowed at the song's end and ran his hands over his damp brow. The crowd's booming acceptance echoed off the walls.

"Wow, what a rush!" Patrick said. "What a great audience you are!"

Several shouts of love and admiration came from the crowd.

"For our next number, we thought we would slow things down a bit and play a song I wrote a few years back. Will and I have worked on the composition, and we hope you enjoy it. It's called 'Walkin' with Baby.'"

The first notes penetrated John's ears like sharp razors, his fragile constitution threatening to crack along with his rationality. The atmosphere suffocated him, and he turned and left the group.

"Where's he going?" Danny asked James.

"I don't know. Maybe he just needs some fresh air," James said.

"We're on in a few minutes!"

"Calm down, Danny. I'll go after him."

James left after John, and Danny's eyes closed, and his knees threatened to buckle.

❑∎❑∎❑∎❑∎❑∎❑∎❑∎❑∎❑∎❑

The cool night penetrated John's strain as he bent over and touched his knees. The struggle to calm the clamor was impossible.

James came out the back door and walked up beside John. "John, are you going to be all right?"

John was silent, and James didn't push him for an answer. He just let him breathe.

"You have any idea what song to open with now?" John muttered.

"We could do 'Hound Dog.' After all, it is our name, and we all know how to play it well."

"Danny wanted a chance to shine."

"Danny can make 'Ring around the Rosie' shine."

John chuckled.

"Besides, we still have 'Crawlin' Dog' to impress the crowd with. We'll be fine."

John stood upright. "I really felt like this time we were confident and prepared to give a top-notch show. I really thought we could win this."

James touched John's arm. "We still can. We can't let that jackass intimidate us. We're ready for this."

"I know it," John said, running his hand through his hair.

"We better get back inside before Danny loses his mind. Then we are sunk."

"I'll be right there."

James patted John's shoulder and went inside.

John turned his strained eyes to the sky, recited the only prayer he knew, and returned inside.

◻◼◻◼◻◼◻◼◻◼◻◼◻◼◻◼◻◼◻

The Dice finished playing their second song, and everyone took a short break while the two groups switched places on the platform. Patrick handed his guitar to a Dice stagehand.

"Great set, man!" the stagehand gushed.

"Thanks. Make sure once the equipment is secured that you take it back to the studio as soon as possible."

"Sure thing, Mr. McNeil."

Patrick nodded, and then, turning, he noticed Mollie sitting at the table by herself. Her fingers turned absently over each other while she observed the nameless faces around her.

Casually, Patrick strolled over to her. "Hey."

Mollie looked up at the dashing, thin smile. "Hey."

Patrick leaned on the table. "So, what did you think of our performance?"

Mollie held her hands still. "I thought it was terrific."

"Did I win you over?"

Mollie's lashes lowered. "Maybe."

Patrick sat down in the chair next to her. "So, tell me about yourself?"

Mollie averted her eyes and pushed back a stray strand of hair. "There isn't much to tell."

Patrick perched his foot on the rail under her chair. "Oh, come now, you're being modest."

"Currently, I'm working in the children's department at Carter's Department store."

"Do you like it?"

Mollie shrugged. "It's okay. The little ones can get kinda rowdy sometimes."

"I bet. I know I couldn't handle a department full of ankle biters."

Mollie laughed.

Patrick draped his arm on the back of his chair. "So, what are you doing after the show tonight?"

"I'm having a slumber party with my girlfriends."

"Sounds fun."

"What are you doing?" Mollie asked.

"I don't know yet. I guess it depends on who wins the contest."

Mollie bit her lip. "Oh."

Patrick leaned forward, resting his arms on the table. "You know, it sure would make me feel good if I thought you were in my corner."

Mollie glimpsed into Patrick's shining green eyes. "Well, I don't want to be fickle."

"Of course not. I respect loyalty."

Mollie beamed and tilted her head back.

Patrick stood and gently grazed Mollie's chin with his fingertips. "I'll just have to find another way to win your admiration."

Mollie's cheeks flushed, and her lashes lowered over her shy eyes.

Patrick put his hands in his pockets, winked at her, and walked away.

◻◼◻◼◻◼◻◼◻◼◻◼◻◼◻◼◻◼◻◼◻

Anne, Betty, and Marcy visited the ladies' washroom during the break. Anne brushed her hair while Betty watched Marcy freshen her lipstick.

"Wow, that sure is a pretty color, Marcy. It makes you look so glamorous," Betty said.

Marcy ran the lush red stick across her bottom lip. "Thank you. I just bought it this week."

Anne adjusted her headband. "It is pretty."

"It's called red passion," Marcy said, reading the label.

"Oh my," Betty said, her cheeks growing warm.

Marcy laughed. "What color do you wear, Betty?"

Betty clutched her purse. "Mama won't let me wear lipstick. She says I'm too young."

"How old are you?"

Betty stood up straight. "Seventeen."

"Really?"

"Almost."

"Do you think she's too young, Anne?" Marcy asked.

Anne shrugged. "Oh, I don't know. My mother doesn't like me to wear it either, but I sneak it in my purse sometimes. I just have to wipe it off before I get home."

Marcy fished around in her purse and pulled out another lipstick. "Here, try this one, Betty. It's brand new, and it's a lighter shade."

Betty shook her head. "Oh no, I couldn't."

"Oh, come on, it's a party."

"But what will my mother say?"

"Like Anne suggested, make sure it is cleaned off before you go home."

Betty gazed at the temptation.

"Go ahead," Marcy urged.

Betty looked at Anne, who nodded. Taking the stick from Marcy, Betty leaned in as close to the mirror as she could and put on the lipstick.

"How do I look?" Betty said, turning to Marcy and Anne.

Marcy smiled. "It's a little crooked."

"It is?"

"Here, let me help."

After Marcy fixed Betty's lipstick, the girls left the washroom laughing. Eddie was standing at a nearby table selling sodas. They walked over to him.

"Hey, handsome," Marcy said to him.

Eddie turned his head quickly. "Hey, girlies."

"Can you hook us up with some sodas?" Marcy asked.

"Sure."

"I want grape," Marcy said.

"I'll take cherry," Anne said.

"Me too," Betty said.

Eddie handed each of them their choice.

"Thanks, Eds," Marcy said, kissing Eddie's cheek.

Eddie's eyes widened. "Marcy!"

"Wow, Eddie's cheeks are redder than my soda," Betty said.

The girls walked away laughing, and Eddie shook his head. Pulling out his handkerchief, he wiped his cheek while his eyes browsed the room. A girl talking to a couple of friends grabbed his attention. Something about her was familiar, but he couldn't place it until his eyes fell on her scuffed saddle shoes. Smiling to himself, he walked over to her. "Well, well, if it isn't the reporter."

Nancy whirled around to come face to face with Eddie's wide smirk. "What do you think you're doing, sneaking up on people!"

"If anyone is sneaking, it's you," Eddie said, folding his arms.

Nancy's eyes widened. "Me?"

"That was you wearing that scarf over your head and keeping your head down."

"That wasn't me."

Eddie touched the edge of Nancy's scarf. "Who else owns a bright yellow scarf with white flowers?"

Nancy snatched the scarf out of Eddie's grasp. "I was trying to keep the sun out of my eyes."

Eddie laughed. "I knew you were nothing but trouble from the first day I met you. You must have enjoyed feeding all that malarkey to some ignorant newspaper reporter."

Nancy's fingers rolled up into fists. "I did no such thing!"

"Oh really? You were the only one that asked about Joey and the Moon Rockers. Thanks to you, this night has turned into a three-ring circus."

Nancy's eyes were squinted, and her bottom lip was pouted out. "For your information, that reporter *stole* my article and twisted it all around to suit his needs! I didn't write half of what he said!" Nancy pounded her finger into her chest. "I'm the one who has been slandered here! I am the one that has been double-crossed!"

Eddie leaned back, watching Nancy's cheeks puff in and out like bellows.

"You do believe me, don't you?" Nancy sputtered.

"It doesn't matter what I believe. All I have to say is, do me a favor and stay away from my store." Turning on his heel, Eddie stalked away, and Nancy groaned.

67

I F ANYONE NOTICED THEM COMING in, they didn't pay any attention. Like obscure, slithering snakes, the unruly gang entered the congested space with thin, sinister grins. Draped in sullied clothes and dirty boots, they shoved people aside like flies. Walking up to the center table, they evicted the innocent patrons and commandeered the space. Stained fisherman hats covered their unkempt hair, and they sneered at anyone who dared look at them.

Finley put his muddy boots up on the table and chewed on a toothpick. It was easy for him to spot Patrick because of his hair color.

"Look at all the young girlies, flitin' around 'ere," one of Finley's cronies said with a smirk.

"Don't go gettin' ideas, Maxie. We focus on what we came 'ere for," Finley warned.

"Maxie was only wanting a bit of fun, Fin," the third man said.

The fourth man's tongue licked his yellow teeth. "I like the one in 'ellow dress, I do. Nice and plump, she is."

The men snickered.

"Where's the beer in this place?" Maxie grumbled.

"There ain' no beer," the third man said.

"That's a dirty rotten shame, that is," the fourth man said, running his hand over his stubble chin.

"Can it, ye dimwits. Once we collect our fee, we can drink all the beer we want," Finley said.

"Takin' down these bumpkins is gonna be like knockin' down dominoes," Maxie said, cracking his knuckles.

"It won't take much to make the little chickies scream," the third man said, licking his lips.

"Goosin' um would be even more fun," the fourth man said.

The three vile men guffawed. Fin succeeded at capturing Patrick's attention from across the room. They nodded slightly, and Patrick stepped back and disappeared into the crowd.

❑■❑■❑■❑■❑■❑■❑■❑■❑■❑

Tension gripped Danny's body while he tapped his finger on the side of his guitar. He always thought himself to be the backbone of the group, the one the others could lean on when things were rough. But The Dice's successful performance weighed heavy on the group's shoulders, and Danny's confidence was shaken. Walking up to the platform while Digsby once more excited the crowd, John turned to the sullen faces around him.

"Well, this is it, boys. You know we've come a long way since that night we stood here shaking in our boots. Our best performance is still ahead of us. So, let's go out there and howl like the Hound Dogs we are."

Throwing his head back, Danny howled, and the rest joined him, surprising Digsby.

Digsby laughed. "When the group said their name was The Hound Dogs, I didn't realize actual dogs were coming up here to play!"

The crowd laughed, and Digsby stomped his foot. "All right, everybody, put your paws together for The Hound Dogs!" Digsby howled as loud as he could and jumped off the stage.

"Let's open with 'Blue Suede Shoes,'" Danny said to John as they stepped on the platform.

John opened his mouth, but Danny was already up front with his guitar in the air. He shouted to the crowd. "You all wearin' your blue suede tonight?"

The enthusiastic cheer came from the crowd.

"What is he doing?" James asked John.

"He wants to open with 'Blue Suede Shoes,' " John sighed.

"What happened to 'Hound Dog'?"

John shook his head.

"I don't know this song very well," Jerry admitted.

John took his shoulder. "Do the best you can. You okay, Ronnie?"

Ronnie nodded, twirling his drumstick.

With his fingers on the opening chord, John turned forward just as Danny began the opening riff.

Danny started his routine, and the crowd cheered their love for him. The electric charge in the air fed Danny's ego, and he executed his first turn without a hitch, but halfway through the second turn, Danny's high E string broke, throwing his timing off. Attempting to improvise, two bridge pins popped out, releasing two more strings. Thoughts of what could have happened fired rapidly through Danny's confused mind.

The song came to an abrupt halt, and the once receptive audience's cheers turned to jeers. Sinking in a vortex, Danny shifted his line of sight to look at John, but for a frozen second, he spotted Stu standing by the side of the platform. His relaxed stance, crossed arms, and smug grimace caused paralysis to choke Danny's senses.

John rushed to Danny, his grave voice slapping time back into place. "Danny, what's the matter?"

"My guitar . . . it's broken!" Danny stammered.

"Calm down," John said.

Danny painfully pulled his hair. "Why is this happening?"

Jerry ran up to Danny. "Here, Danny, take my guitar!"

"I can't play *that*," Danny snapped.

John unstrapped his guitar. "Here, take mine."

Danny's face was contorted. "And lose you?"

"I'll take Jerry's," John said, taking Jerry's from him.

Jerry shuffled off the platform, passing Stu.

Danny strapped on John's guitar. "What do I say?"

"I got it." John stepped up to the mic. "Sorry for the delay, folks. We had a bit of trouble, but we've recovered and are ready to resume the show."

"Why don't ye do us all a favor and get the hell off the stage!" Maxie shouted from the crowd.

"Ye obviously can't play for shit!" the third man in Finley's gang shouted.

Wanting desperately to recover and produce a miracle, Danny stepped forward and played the first few chords of "Crawling Dog." The group stepped in line, but it was too late. More obscenities and booing rose from the crowd.

Finley and his gang got out of their chairs and approached the platform.

"We came to see a show, we did, and so far, all we've seen is a bunch of bumbling idiots," Finnley sneered.

"Yeah, go home, why don't ye?" Maxie yelled.

"You need to shut up and let the group recover," a young man with broad shoulders in a letterman's jacket shouted at Finley.

"Yeah, you're stinkin' up the joint," another young man in a matching jacket said.

"Are you talkin' to me, little boy?" the sizeable third man said, lumbering toward the younger man.

"Look at you. You haven't even had a bath, you mongrel," the letterman said to the third man.

The third man slugged the letterman with that remark, sending him sprawling into a table.

"Brent, are you all right?" his friend said, kneeling by him.

Brent was the quarterback for the high school football team, and several of his teammates gathered.

"Who the hell do you think you are?" one of the tight ends said, stepping up to the man who had punched Brent.

Eddie appeared from out of the crowd. "You all need to settle down and let the show resume."

"You need to get out of my way, ye peewee," Finley said, shoving Eddie aside.

Having recovered, Brent got up off the ground and, walking up to the third man, punched him square in the jaw. The punch barely fazed the rock-hard man.

"Ye should have stayed down, ye muttonhead." Lifting back his fist, the ugly man punched Brent again. This time, there would be no more talk. Fists started flying, and a full-on brawl began. Chairs, bottles, and other debris flew through the air. Girls screamed, and people began to flee the building.

"Come on, fellas, we need to get off the platform before someone gets hurt," John said.

Without any kind of barrier, the crowd moved closer, and as the last word left John's mouth, the jagged end of a broken bottle grazed his forehead.

"John!" Danny cried.

John was dazed and didn't even feel the blood on his forehead.

Danny handed John his handkerchief. "You're bleeding!"

John put his hand up to his forehead. Feeling the moisture, he looked at his red hand. "I am."

"Come on, Ronnie, let's go," James said.

"I'm not leaving Otis," Ronnie cried.

"Ronnie, be reasonable," James pleaded.

"No!"

"John, Ronnie won't leave," James said.

"Ronnie," John said firmly. "We need to leave."

"I'm not leaving my friend!"

John bent over to console Ronnie further when the unthinkable happened. From the right side of the platform, a rock was thrown, and it smashed into the bass drum, leaving a large dark hole in its wake.

Flabbergasted, Danny and James stared at the gaping hole. Ronnie slowly rose to his feet and stormed to the end of the platform with gritted teeth and blazing eyes.

"Ronnie, where are you going?" Danny said, trying to stop him, but Ronnie shoved Danny aside and stepped off the platform. Having seen the young man who threw the rock, Ronnie's eyes locked on his target.

"Ronnie!" Danny yelled, taking after him.

Ronnie quickly closed the gap between himself and the young man who threw the rock. His hand shot out and grabbed hold of the teen by the neck of his shirt.

"What the—" the youth started, but all he could see was Ronnie's twisted grimace before he hit the table behind him. In the blink of an eye, Ronnie's deadly switchblade was up against the boy's throat.

"Oh my God!" the boy bawled.

"God isn't going to save you now," Ronnie growled.

"Ronnie!" Danny yelled, having caught up. "Let him go!"

"Not a chance," Ronnie hissed. "He's gonna pay for what he done."

The young man's eyes bulged. "What . . . what . . . did I do?"

Ronnie's grip tightened. "You know what you did."

"I don't. I swear it!"

"Your rock killed my best friend!"

"*What?*"

Ronnie trailed the blade down the side of the teen's throat. "Now I'm gonna see what your insides look like."

"Ronnie!" Danny pleaded.

One by one, Ronnie cut the buttons from the boy's shirt.

Tears flooded the boy's face as he sputtered. "Please, mister! I didn't mean to. It was an accident!"

John, James, Jerry, and the girls came running over to where Danny was pleading with Ronnie to put down the knife.

"Holy cow!" James exclaimed.

A sound of wailing sirens shattered the chaotic air, and the rest of the crowd began to scatter.

Danny began to shake, and beads of perspiration formed on his forehead. "Oh, no, no, this can't be happening. The cops can't find me here!"

"Get out of here, Danny," John said.

"But . . . I can't just leave you," Danny sobbed, holding John's arms.

"Get the hell out of here before everything you have worked for is gone!"

"But John . . . .."

"Get him out of here, Jerry!" John roared.

Jerry grabbed hold of Danny. "Come on, Danny, let's get out of here."

Danny hesitated, his fortitude crushed. Giving John one last glance, he left with Jerry and Betty.

"The rest of you beat it too," John ordered.

"But John, you're hurt," James said.

"Get the girls to safety."

"John!" Anne cried.

"Now, damn it!"

By now, the cops had arrived and were surrounding the building. James and the girls ran out the side door, barely escaping. John turned back to Ronnie, who was leaning over the young man with his blade, teasing his stomach.

"Drop the damn knife, Ronnie," John growled.

Ronnie didn't move. John grabbed Ronnie's chin roughly and turned his head. "Give me the knife, Ronnie."

Ronnie glared at John through his veil of grief.

John's fingers tightened on Ronnie's jaw, and he stepped forward. "I said, give me the knife."

Tears rolled down Ronnie's cheeks as he regarded the grave eyes in front of him. Defeated, Ronnie surrendered his blade to John.

The teen, seeing two police officers, cried out for help. Turning, they saw John with a knife in his hand.

A police officer, who looked barely older than John, pulled out his gun. "Drop the knife!"

John held up his hand and dropped the knife.

Without asking questions, the cop holstered his gun and ran to John. Grabbing him roughly, the police officer yanked John's arms behind him and cuffed him.

"Are you okay?" another cop asked the shaking youth.

"That . . . guy is a crazed maniac! He tried to kill me!" the teen said, pointing at Ronnie.

The policeman turned to Ronnie. "You're under arrest!"

Ronnie didn't struggle or fight as they put the cuffs on him. He stared straight ahead, unresponsive, while they read him his rights.

The remainder of Madison's small police force rounded up frightened teenagers who were not lucky enough to escape the dreadful scene. Loaded into police cars, they were taken to the police station to await their parents' conviction.

Ronnie and John left the community center in handcuffs. Several cameramen were out front, snapping pictures for the paper. As the police car pulled away, a lone figure watched from the shadows of the ransacked community center, a sadistic grimace on his lips.

68

RED AND BLUE FLASHING LIGHTS illuminated Stu's solemn face. From his vantage point across the street from the community center, he watched the ugly scene unfold. He had dreamed of this moment for a long time, and the night could not have played out more perfectly. The look of devastation on Danny's face when they made eye contact was priceless. Tonight, he would celebrate his victory, and Danny and John would feel the agony of defeat he experienced daily. So why wasn't his spirit rejoicing? Why didn't he feel vindicated? He had gotten what he wanted, yet he still felt empty.

❑■❑■❑■❑■❑■❑■❑■❑■❑■❑■❑

Will and Patrick walked across the street laughing.

"You were brilliant tonight," Will exclaimed.

Patrick shrugged. "I don't know if I would go that far."

"Why not? You nailed the performance, and not only that, but we also crushed the competition! They are done!"

The corners of Patrick's mouth slightly lifted.

Will put his arm around Patrick's shoulders. "I say you and I go out and whoop it up tonight. The sky is the limit. You in?"

"All right, but what about Boyd?" Patrick asked.

"What about him?"

"You are inviting him?"

Will frowned and pulled his arm away. "Boyd's no fun anymore."

"Why? Because he has a girlfriend?"

Will ignored the question.

"Her blond friend is pretty."

Will grinned. "Yes, she is."

"If they come with us, so would she."

Will turned his head. "Are you interested?"

"Me? No," Patrick said, shaking his head.

"Why not?"

Patrick shrugged. "She's not my type."

Will chuckled. "What is your type? Betty Crocker?"

"Maybe."

"Ah ha, I saw you talkin' to the little mousey brunette."

Patrick's brow furrowed. "She's not mousey."

"She sure ain't no beauty queen."

"Exactly."

Will raised his eyebrow. "You don't like beauty queens?"

"I like them fine, but when it comes to dating a girl, I like a girl with simple needs. Someone who will please me and not count zeros in my bank account."

"Dating? Who said anything about dating?" Will scoffed.

"You're not interested in settling down, Will?"

"Hell no. I've got too much living to do to be tied down to that kind of hassle."

Patrick nodded. "Then I would say you and the blond have a lot in common."

"Exactly, my boy!"

Patrick saw Stu standing on the sidewalk with his hands in his pockets. "Hey Stewy, what are you doing over here?"

"Waiting for you."

"Me?" Patrick said with a nervous laugh.

"Well, yeah. I thought we were celebrating."

"Oh?"

"Do you know this person?" Will said to Patrick.

Patrick nodded. "Uh, yes. Will meet an old friend of mine, Stu. Stu, this is Will."

"We've met already," Stu said dryly.

"We did?" Will said.

"Sure, the night at the Beaumont, when Danny was still a member of The Dice."

"Oh," Will chuckled. "I met so many people that night."

Stu rocked on his heels. "Sure, you did. So, where are we headed?"

"Well . . ." Patrick's eyes shifted between Will and Stu. "I actually accepted Will's invitation."

Stu blinked. "Oh."

"You understand, right?"

Stu rubbed the back of his neck. "Uh, yeah, sure."

"I would invite you to come, but the Cornby Club does have a dress code, and I'm afraid unkempt hair and tattered clothes are not it," Will said with a smug grin.

"We can go out some other time," Patrick said.

"Oh, yeah, sure. Some other time," Stu said, putting his hands in his pockets.

"Good man," Patrick said, patting Stu on the shoulder. "I'll see you later?"

Stu looked at the ground and nodded. "Yeah, yeah, sure."

"Good night, Drew," Will said.

"It's Stu," Stu said.

"Oh, yeah, sure," Will said, pointing at him and giving him one of his snide smiles.

Will and Patrick walked away. The sound of their laughter gradually faded into the chill of the night air. Stu pulled his arms tighter against his body and began to walk home along the desolate street. The pang of rejection tugged at Stu's heart, but he resolved to push it aside. He understood the importance of Patrick's social connections and the need to mingle with influential people. It was all part of the plan. Once Stu joined Patrick's band, he would have expensive suits, drive a flashy car, and have any girl he desired. The false assurance brightened Stu's outlook for the moment, no matter how brief it was.

69

Chief of Police Sherman Bronson was not happy to be called away from his Saturday night bridge game to deal with a bunch of disruptive teenagers.

Bronson was proud of Madison's low crime rate. An occasional disturbance of the peace or domestic dispute made up the majority of the offenses. Teenagers from surrounding counties might wander into town and try to stir up trouble, but the situation was quickly handled, and everything returned to normal. Tonight, the situation was anything but normal.

Loud shouting, angry parents, and ringing telephones greeted Bronson when he entered his normally quiet station. The thought of turning around and going back to his peaceful home seemed attractive. Shoving his way through the mob surrounding the front counter, Bronson passed through the tiny swinging gate and headed toward his office. His hand was on the doorknob when he noticed a young man sitting inside. Cursing under his breath, Captain Bronson crossed to the front counter.

Deputy Murphy was filling out a form at the front counter while an enraged mother struck the counter with her fist.

"This is an outrage!" she bellowed. "Terrance is a good boy. There is no way he could be involved with those hoodlums!"

Murphy looked up from the paper. His sleeves were rolled up to his elbows, and distress highlighted the folds on his damp forehead. "I'm sorry, Mrs. Wadsworth, but we had to question everyone because we are trying to gather information about who started the incident."

"Obviously, it's the boys who are dressed in jeans and put grease in their hair! They have bad manners and listen to rock 'n' roll music. Those are the boys that should be prosecuted!"

Murphy sighed. "Yes, ma'am. You have my word that we are working diligently to uncover the truth."

"See that you do," Mrs. Wadsworth said, turning to her son and grabbing him by his ear. "Come along, Terrance."

"Ma!" Terrance protested behind his mother.

Bronson walked up to Murphy. "Evening, Murphy."

Murphy turned around, his mouth half open. "Oh, Captain, am I glad to see you."

Bronson leaned on the counter. "You mind telling me why a young man is sitting in my office?"

"We think he might be one of the young men responsible for starting the disturbance this evening."

"What makes you think that?"

Murphy pulled up on his belt loops. "Because he had a switchblade in his hand."

"Was he using it?"

"No, but the young man sitting on the bench told me that the young man in your office and his friend were threatening him with it. Said they were going to kill him."

Bronson turned to see a young man sitting on a bench with his head in his hand. An oversized stern man sat next to him. "Who is the man sitting next to him?"

"His father."

"Have you taken his statement?" Bronson asked.

"Yes."

Bronson sighed. "Where is the other boy?"

"In cell two."

"Where is the knife now?"

Murphy opened a small drawer in the table behind the front counter and handed the switchblade to Bronson. "We caught him with it red-handed."

Bronson looked at the pearl-handled casing in his hand. "You started a file on him yet?"

Murphy picked up a folder off the table and handed it to Bronson. "Me and Harve are betting he's the ringleader. The top cheese."

Bronson lifted an eyebrow.

Murphy leaned in. "You can always spot the troublemakers."

Bronson turned the knife over in his hand. "Did you contact Mr. Chandler's parents?"

"He's nineteen, sir."

Bronson rubbed his neck. "Is there any coffee?"

"There hasn't been time to make any."

"Make the time. It's going to be a long night."

70

AVING ESCAPED FROM THE HORRIFYING scene at the community center, the group gasped for breath while anchoring themselves to the solidity of Danny's car. Their whirling minds struggled to process the chaos of the evening's events. Each idea of how to help was quickly dismissed by the lurking fear of potential dangers that bound them in invisible ropes of helplessness. With no visible course of action, Mollie suggested that her disheartened friends come over to her house for companionship and support.

Danny didn't want to go. He wanted to retreat to the confines of his room and hide from his grief. Running out and leaving John alone to face the cops brought back dark memories of being caught, restrained, and prosecuted. Confessing and accepting the consequences of his action had been the easy part. It was facing the disappointment and disdain from his father that had crushed Danny. He would forever remain a disappointment in his father's eyes.

Relenting to the pressure from his friends, Danny decided to join them. Lamenting alone in a dark room without his guitar for comfort was not a good idea. Being with his friends would occupy his mind, at least for a while.

Once back at Mollie's house, the girls prepared sandwiches in the kitchen while the boys waited in the living room.

Jerry and James occupied themselves by looking at Mollie's meager record collection, while Danny moped on the couch.

"Boy, this selection is dull," Jerry commented.

"They're probably her parent's records," James said.

"I don't know, Mollie is kind of . . ." Jerry said, casting his eyes to Danny.

Danny wasn't paying attention to their conversation. His interest had been drawn to the liquor cart, and he poured himself a drink.

"You know that isn't going to solve anything," James said.

Danny turned to James. "Probably not, but right now, I don't give a damn."

Jerry glanced at James as the first glass went down without hesitation.

"Would you boys like to join me? Danny asked.

"I would," Jerry said.

Danny poured Jerry a glass and passed it to him. Jerry had never drunk anything besides a beer, and the whiskey took his breath away.

Danny grinned and poured himself another glass.

Jerry's face contorted. "That stuff is awful! I can't believe people drink this on purpose."

"You going to join us, Professor?" Danny asked James.

James turned over the record jacket in his hand. "I'm fine."

"Suit yourself," Danny said, finishing his second glass.

"One more," Jerry said, holding out his glass.

Danny obliged him.

"You know, Mollie's father is not going to be happy when he finds out that his bottle of whiskey is almost empty," James warned.

"How is he even going to know?" Danny said. "I mean, look at all these bottles. I take one of the full bottles and put some of it into this bottle, and he will never know the difference."

"Hit me again," Jerry said with a wide, sappy grin.

Danny took Jerry's glass and set it on the cart. "I don't think that's a good idea."

Jerry frowned. "Oh, so you can have as much as you want, but you're monitoring me?"

"Uncle Bob would kill me if he knew you drank hard liquor."

"You're younger than me," Jerry groused.

"Let's just say I have more experience than you," Danny said, sitting on the couch.

"Oh, you're saying I can't hold my liquor?"

Danny propped his feet up on the coffee table. "I don't want you puking in my car later."

"Maybe I won't be in your car later. Maybe I will walk home," Jerry said, folding his arms.

"Fine," Danny said, laying his arm over his eyes.

"I'm going to go see what is keeping the girls," James said, setting the record down and entering the kitchen.

The girls were finishing up making sandwiches and putting them on plates. Setting his hands on Marcy's hips, James rested his chin on her shoulder.

"What are you doing?" Marcy asked.

"Watching you make my sandwich."

"Who said this is your sandwich?" Mollie said, cutting a sandwich in half.

"I did," James said, nuzzling Marcy's ear.

"James, behave," Marcy said.

"You girls better hurry things up a bit," James said, stealing a chip off the plate.

"Oh?"

"Danny has had a few drinks."

"What?" Marcy said.

"Is something wrong?" Mollie asked.

"Nope," James said, backing away from Marcy.

"Come on, girls, let's feed these hungry boys," Marcy said.

71

W ITH HIS EYES CLOSED, JOHN tried to think about something other than the throbbing gash on his forehead. Sitting in the Chief of police's office wasn't ideal, but the closed door muffled the shouting and other senseless noises. Questions without answers swirled around in his mind, keeping his anxiety level heightened.

When the door finally opened, John peeked through his fingers to watch the sizeable barrel-chested man in a green button-up short-sleeved shirt move behind his desk. Pulling his chair out, Bronson sat down and plopped the folder on the desk.

"Mr. Chandler, I assume," Bronson said, putting his glasses on.

"Yes," John said in a monotone voice.

Bronson thumbed through the pages in front of him, then scrutinized John over the top of his glasses. "What happened to your forehead?"

"I was hit in the head with a broken bottle."

"Looks nasty. You may need stitches."

"Great," John said.

"My deputy tells me that this is your knife," Bronson said, throwing the weapon on his desk. "You want to tell me about it?"

"It's a switchblade."

Bronson folded his hands in front of him. "You want to tell me why you and your friend threatened Walter Johnson with the knife?"

John reflected on the question. "I don't know a Walter Johnson."

"He's the young man who claims your friend tried to kill him."

John rolled his lips. "He's mistaken."

"It says here your friend had Walter pinned against a table and tried to kill him."

John shook his head. "Ronnie was only holding him for me."

"Who's Ronnie?"

"My friend."

Bronson sat back in his chair. "Why did you want to kill Walter?"

"Because he threw a rock and put a huge hole in Ronnie's most prized possession."

Bronson picked up a pencil. "And what is his most prized possession?"

"A bass drum."

"Let me make sure I got your story straight. You're saying Walter Johnson threw a rock that ruined Ronnie's drum. Then, while Ronnie held him, you would kill him?"

"I threatened to."

"And did you cut the buttons off Walter's shirt?" Bronson asked.

"I did."

Bronson tapped his pencil on the desk and stared at John, who didn't move. "Mr. Chandler, when I talk to Ronnie, will he tell me the same story?"

"Ronnie is devastated. He loved that drum more than anything in the world. I don't know what he will tell you, but I'm telling you the truth."

Bronson got up and opened his door. "Murdock."

A young, wiry deputy came to the door. "Yeah, Captain?"

"Can you please show Mr. Chandler to cell three?"

"Right away, Captain."

"Also, let him have some time in the washroom to clean up, and he probably needs a couple of aspirin."

"Yes, sir."

Bronson watched after John as he left the office with Murdock. He knew John was lying to protect his friend. He wondered if Ronnie would tell the truth or hide behind his friend's lie. Shaking his head, Bronson went back inside his office.

72

ANNY WAS STILL RELAXING ON the couch when the girls stepped into the living room.

"Danny!" Mollie said, appalled at his appearance.

He opened his eyes to look at her, glaring at him with her hand on her hip. "What?"

"Your feet are on the coffee table."

Danny looked at his feet. "So, they are."

"Danny, sit up," James said.

"Yes, Dad," Danny grumbled.

Having regained her composure, Mollie sat on the couch next to Danny. Her knee touched his, and her eyes fluttered when she handed him the plate. Danny eyed the sandwich, and his stomach rolled.

"Would you like some punch?" Mollie chimed, rubbing her hands together.

Danny gazed at Mollie and imagined Elinor Donahue sitting there. From the high bun on the crown of her head to her fashionable patent leather flats, she was the perfect picture of a wholesome girl. His parents would have loved her. "No, thanks."

"You know everything is going to be fine, don't you?" Mollie said, taking a demure bite of her sandwich.

Danny forced a smile. "Sure."

"What happened tonight wasn't your fault. Those ruffians were looking for trouble."

Danny rubbed his chin and reflected on Mollie's comment.

Mollie noticed his untouched sandwich. "Do you not like your sandwich?"

"I'm just not very hungry."

Mollie sat her plate down. "Would you like a warm glass of milk?"

"No, I'm fine."

Mollie turned her attention to the conversation going on next to her. Anne was sitting on a footstool, talking to Jerry and Betty, who were sitting close to each other on the floor.

"You don't have to sit on a footstool, Anne. There is plenty of room by me on the couch," Mollie said.

"Thank you, but I don't mind."

"Hey James, I thought you and Jerry were going to put a record on," Marcy said to James.

"Oh, we didn't see anything that was upbeat," James said.

"Why don't you turn on the radio?" Mollie said.

James got up and flipped the radio on. Then, turning the knob to KTWB, he sat down. "I'm Walkin'" played, and the peppy song lightened the mood.

The conversation in the room became livelier as the group finished their sandwiches.

The tension between Betty and Jerry was fading and forgetting about the argument seemed like an easy solution.

"I am going to get some more punch," Anne said, wiping her hand on a napkin. "Can I get you two anything?"

"I would like some," Betty said. "How about you, Jerry?"

"I'm good," Jerry said.

"Okay." Anne got off the stool and walked to the kitchen.

"How is your sandwich?" Betty asked Jerry.

Jerry shrugged. "It's a bit dry,"

"I could put some more mayonnaise on it for you," Betty offered.

"You don't have to do that," Jerry said, gazing at Betty's mouth.

Betty noticed Jerry's intense stare, and she figured the lipstick must be working its magic. Jerry leaned forward, and Betty closed her eyes in anticipation of his kiss, but instead, he wiped a spot of mustard off the corner of her mouth with his thumb. Betty's eyes flew open, and Jerry's brow slowly creased.

"Is something wrong?" Betty asked.

Jerry rubbed his thumb against his index finger. "I'm not sure. What's the red stuff?"

Betty bit her bottom lip. "Nothing."

"I would say it might be ketchup, but we're not eating French fries."

Betty tilted her head toward the light. "It's lipstick."

Jerry paused. "Oh."

Betty fluffed her hair. "Doesn't it make me look glamorous?"

Jerry shrugged. "I guess so."

"All women wear lipstick, Jerry," Betty said, tilting her head and lifting her chin.

"If you say so," Jerry said, choking down another bite of his sandwich.

Betty's shoulders slumped, and the edges of her mouth drooped.

"Hey Betty, you want to come help out in the kitchen?" Marcy asked.

"Sure," Betty said, rising to her feet.

"Here you can take my plate. I'm finished," Jerry said, handing his plate to Betty.

She looked at the half-eaten sandwich. "It's not too late for me to put some mayo on it."

"No need," Jerry said with a half-smile.

Betty nodded, sighed, and followed Marcy into the kitchen.

73

SITTING BESIDE HIS FATHER IN Bronson's office, fifteen-year-old Walter Johnson tugged at his ear and stared at the honorable service award plaque on Bronson's wall.

"How much longer is this going to take?" Norman Johnson blustered. "My shift starts in an hour."

Bronson took a comforting drink of coffee and looked into the agitated grey eyes of the rutted face across from him. "I have some questions for your son regarding this evening's incident."

"The officer at the front desk already took his statement. What more do you need?" Norman grumbled.

"I want to make sure I have all the facts straight."

Norman snorted and folded his arms.

Bronson picked up his pen. "Okay, Walter, why don't you tell me in your own words what happened tonight?"

"You're wasting my time," Norman interjected.

"Mr. Johnson, I have all night to sit here and ask questions, but as you informed me, you have a job to report to. So, I would suggest you let your son answer my questions."

Norman pouted out his lip and pulled his arms tighter across his chest.

"Go ahead, Walter," Bronson said.

Walter looked at his father's stern profile. "What was the question?"

"Tell me what happened."

Walter twisted his hands in his lap. "I dunno. Some guy on stage had problems with his guitar, and then these big ugly guys started to boo and heckle um. Then Brent Hurley told um to shut their traps. Then the biggest, ugliest guy out of um all popped Brent right in the chops. Bam!" Walter said, slamming his fist into his open palm. "But the Cougars weren't gonna stand for that, no siree. Ain't nobody gonna punch the quarterback and get away with it."

Bronson rubbed his temple. "I know that part. What I want to know is what made you believe your life was in danger?"

"I was just tryin' to find my buddies when the giant goon attacked me."

"So, you were innocently looking for your friends when the young man attacked you for no reason?"

Walter shrugged. "Well, sure—he's crazy."

"What makes you think he's crazy?"

Walter spread his hands apart. "Because he's deformed and walks funny."

Bronson tapped his pen on the desk. "The young man I talked to said you threw a rock that put a hole in the bass drum."

Walter shook his head. "Told you he was crazy."

"You're saying you didn't throw the rock?"

"If my son says he didn't throw the rock, then he didn't throw no rock," Norman growled.

Bronson sat back in his chair. "I'm only trying to uncover the truth."

"The truth is, Walter was attacked by some crazed lunkhead who needs to be locked up somewhere," Mr. Johnson snapped.

Walter smirked at Bronson.

A knock came at the door, and Murphy popped his head in. "Sorry to bother you, Captain, but a Mrs. Mulligan is here from Barnhardt House. It's about the boy in cell two."

"Thanks, Murphy. Just have her wait."

Murphy nodded and left.

"Are we done here?" Norman said.

Bronson ignored Norman and looked straight at Water, who was kicking the chair leg. "Walter, you know it's wrong to lie to a police officer, right?"

"Of course he knows," Norman snapped.

Bronson rolled his lips. "Walter?"

"Well, yeah, sure, everyone knows that."

Bronson folded his hands. "So, the statement you gave me is the total truth. The handicapped young man threatened you with a knife for no other reason than he's crazy?"

Walter pulled on his fingers and stared at the ceiling. "Yeah."

Bronson tapped his thumb on the desktop. "All right, I guess that is all I need. You may go."

"Let's go," Norman barked at Walter. Walter jumped out of his chair and followed his father out the door.

Bronson sighed and rubbed his forehead. Picking up his cup, he noticed the black sediment at the bottom. Groaning, Bronson got up to pour a fresh cup.

74

Marcy washed the dishes while Betty dried them. Mollie arranged cookies on a plate, and Anne folded napkins.

"Do you think these cookies will lift the boys' mood?" Mollie asked the girls.

"I don't know. They're really upset," Marcy said.

"I guess we can't blame them," Mollie said, rearranging the cookies for the third time. "I just wish there was something we could do."

Marcy set another plate in the drying rack and noticed Betty, who was drying the same dish she had been for the last few minutes. "So, what do you think, Betty?"

Betty looked up. "About what?"

"Have you not been listening?"

Betty shook her head and returned to drying the dish.

"Is everything all right?" Marcy asked.

Betty set the dish down and picked up the next. "Fine."

"Did something happen with Jerry?"

Betty paused, staring at the plate.

"What happened?" Marcy asked, gently placing her arm around Betty's shoulders.

Betty looked up with wide, dull eyes. "I don't want to talk about it."

"Oh, come on, we would love to help. Wouldn't we girls?"

"Sure. What are girlfriends for?" Mollie said, sitting down at the table.

Marcy took off her apron. "Come on now, tell us all about it."

Marcy and Betty joined the girls at the table.

"You want a cookie?" Mollie said, passing one to Betty. "They always make me feel better."

Betty accepted the cookie and took a small bite.

Marcy picked up a cookie and handed it to Anne before taking one for herself. "Okay, we're listening."

Betty gazed at the cookie. "I don't think that Jerry liked the lipstick."

"Did he say something?" Marcy asked.

"He didn't have to."

"Are you sure you're just not being oversensitive? I mean, he's had a hard night," Mollie said, placing her cookie on a napkin.

Betty looked up. "No. I can read Jerry pretty well."

"Maybe you should try to talk to him. I'm sure he would appreciate some comfort," Marcy said.

"I agree with Marcy. Men like it when a woman is sweet and attentive. What do you think, Anne?" Mollie asked Anne, who was in the middle of chewing a piece of cookie.

"Me?" Anne squeaked, pressing her fingers to her lips.

Mollie dabbed her napkin on her lips. "You do have an opinion, don't you?"

Anne swallowed. "I think Betty should do what she feels comfortable with."

Mollie scoffed. "Obviously, she doesn't feel comfortable doing anything. That is why we are helping her."

Anne's chin fell slightly as her hand gripped the edge of her napkin.

"I don't think Jerry wants to talk to me," Betty said.

"Why not?" Marcy asked.

Betty's eyebrows raised, and she looked down. "We had a quarrel a while ago and we broke up. I thought that maybe if I looked more mature, he might find me irresistible, and we could make up. Obviously, I failed."

"Men can be so blind sometimes," Mollie said, rolling her eyes.

"I don't think Jerry is blind," Anne said, shifting her gaze to Betty. "I think Jerry likes you just the way you are."

"But I don't look like a woman. I've got bug eyes and a little girl's body," Betty whined.

"There is a lot more to being a woman than just looking good on the outside," Anne said. "Being a woman means being kind, patient, compassionate, smart, funny, and I can bet Jerry sees all of those qualities in you."

"We all do," Marcy said.

Betty wiped at a tear. "Thank you."

Mollie picked up the cookie plate and stood up. "I'm going to take these into the boys."

"We'll finish up out here," Marcy said, walking back to the sink.

Anne pushed away from the table.

"Hey Anne," Betty said.

"Yes?"

Betty set her arms on the table. "You know, I wasn't sure I would like you. I mean, I'm kind of protective of John."

"Oh?"

Betty nodded. "He's special."

Anne smiled. "He is."

"He's going to be all right, you know."

Anne laughed. "If there is one thing I know, John can take care of himself."

"But you're still worried?"

Anne wrinkled her nose, and holding up her hand, she spread her thumb two inches from her index finger. "Maybe just a little."

Betty smiled and laughed.

75

OF ALL THE PEOPLE BRONSON had met, Ronnie was the most relaxed. His hands folded neatly in his lap, he confidently made eye contact with Bronson.

"Mr. Crockett, I am going to ask you some questions, and I expect you to be a hundred percent honest with me. Do you understand?" Bronson asked.

"I do."

"Wonderful. From what I understand, you and your friend Mr. Chandler threatened a young man, Walter Johnson, with a knife. Is that correct?"

Ronnie didn't advert his eyes or make any other movement. "I threatened the young man with Charlie. Mr. Chandler begged me to surrender Charlie to him."

Bronson raised his eyebrow. "Did you just say Charlie?"

"Yeah."

"You gave your knife a name?"

Ronnie shrugged. "I guess so."

Bronson rubbed his chin. "Do you want to tell me why you threatened Walter's life?"

"I wasn't gonna kill him. I just wanted to scare him and maybe make him beg a little."

"And you did this because he ruined the bass drum?"

Ronnie nodded. "My bass drum, Otis. Yes."

Bronson leaned back in his chair. "Do all your possessions have names?"

"I don't have a lot of possessions, sir, but Otis was my best friend. I have had him since I was twelve. He's the only gift I was ever given."

Bronson opened the folder, read the top page, and looked up at Ronnie. "It says here that you live at the Barnhardt House. Mrs. Mulligan is the Head Mistress?"

"Yes."

Bronson made notes. "How long have you lived there?"

"Sixteen years."

Bronson set his elbows on his desk. "You know I'm going to have to contact Mrs. Mulligan and inform her of your situation."

"I know."

"Does she know you were out tonight?"

Ronnie glanced at his thumbs that were rolling over each other. "Yes."

Bronson folded his hands. "Ronnie, do you realize what you did tonight was wrong?"

Ronnie nodded. "Yes, sir."

"I can understand why you were upset, but threatening someone with a knife or any other weapon is wrong."

Ronnie held his chin high. "I understand, and I will accept my punishment, but Mr. Chandler is innocent."

Bronson sighed. "You realize I must keep you here overnight."

"Yes, sir."

"All right then, let me escort you back to your cell."

When the large door that separated the front office from the holding cells opened, John stood up as Bronson walked in with Ronnie. Bronson opened the door to cell two, and Ronnie walked in. Then Bronson turned to John.

"Well, Mr. Chandler, you are free to go."

"What?" John said.

Bronson opened the cell door. "I said you are free to go."

"But what about Ronnie?"

"Mr. Crockett is spending the night with us until he can be seen by the judge."

"The judge? I told you, I'm to blame for what happened tonight."

Bronson folded his arms. "Ronnie told me the truth."

John looked over at Ronnie, who was lying down on his bunk.

"Look, I know what you tried to do for your friend, but the truth is, he is the guilty one," Bronson said.

John closed his eyes. "What's going to happen to him?"

"Well, like I said, he's going to spend the night with us until he can see the judge."

"But that won't be until Monday."

Bronson nodded.

John ran his hand over his hair. "At least let me stay here with him tonight."

Bronson raised an eyebrow. "You want to stay? In jail?"

"He's my friend, and he's a bit . . ."

"Vulnerable?"

"Yeah."

Bronson rocked on his feet. "This is very irregular."

"I know it, but it's already late, right?"

Bronson thought for a long moment.

"Please?"

"Okay, you can stay the night."

"Thank you."

John stepped back, and Bronson closed the heavy cell door.

76

THE ATMOSPHERE IN THE LIVING room had lightened since the girls moved to the kitchen. Now that Mollie had left the room, Danny resumed his relaxed position with his eyes closed. Jerry rested his back up against the love seat where James was sitting.

"I'm worried about John and Ronnie," James said. "Do you think they were arrested?"

Danny opened his eyes and regarded James. "If they were free, they would be here."

"Do you think we should do something?" James asked.

"Like what?" Jerry said.

James rubbed his hands on his pants. "I don't know. I just feel so damn . . ."

"Guilty?" Jerry said.

James ran his hand over his head. "Yeah."

"John told you to get the girls to safety and for me to get Danny to safety. Mission accomplished."

James held his head in his hands.

"I'll talk to Uncle Bob in the morning. Hopefully, they will both be home by then," Danny said.

"One can hope," James said.

"I think I'm about ready to go," Danny said. "Do you mind telling Marcy good night?"

James rubbed his hands together. "I do mind only because I don't want to spend the night alone, but she doesn't spend enough time with her friends. Besides, I think it's good for Anne to have the girls' support tonight."

"I agree," Danny said.

James passed Mollie in the hall on his way to the kitchen. Anne and Betty were looking at a magazine at the table, and Marcy finished putting the dishes in the cupboard.

"Hey beautiful," James said, slipping his arms around Marcy's middle. The faint smell of strawberries in her hair and the warmth from her curves eased James's tension.

"Hello," Marcy said. "You need something?"

"I need you," James whispered in Marcy's ear.

"James," Marcy said, feeling the warmth in her cheeks. "We aren't alone."

"I know that, but Danny wants to leave soon, and I need enough of your attention to get me through the night."

Marcy turned to him. "Are you saying you don't want me to spend the night with the girls?"

"No, I'm just saying we need to find somewhere private to say goodnight."

"We can go sit on the slider in the backyard," Marcy said with a flirty smile.

"Perfect."

"Hey James," Betty said, stepping over to them.

"Yeah, Betty?"

"If it's all right, I am going to go wait in Danny's car."

James raised an eyebrow. "By yourself?"

"Yes."

"Okay."

Betty left the kitchen and went out the back door.

"What's with her?" James asked Marcy.

"Long story. Hey Anne, James and I are stepping outside to take in some air."

"Okay," Anne said.

James and Marcy went outside, leaving Anne alone in the kitchen. The solace of the empty room offered Anne a brief respite from the night's turmoil. She was more than just a little worried about John; she was frightened. If only she could be certain of his safety, she would feel better. Closing her eyes, she imagined being held in John's comforting embrace and his deep reassuring voice would convince her it was all a bad dream. With the days dwindling to a precious few, she resented losing time with him. Wiping away a frustrated tear, Anne resolved to stay strong. She would be carried away by one of the magazine's captivating stories and forget her present worries.

77

LYING ON HIS BACK WITH his hands crossed behind his head, John stared at his cell's faded yellow, cracked ceiling. The thin, hard mattress and the stiff pillow offered no comfort.

"You okay over there?" John called out to Ronnie in the next cell.

Ronnie hadn't made a sound or moved since John had been locked in his cell. Groaning, John sat up, and the burning pain in his forehead returned. Even though Murdock had let him clean the wound and take some aspirin, the pain was relentless. Glancing through the bars, John gazed at Ronnie, sitting in the corner of his cell. His fingers were laced behind his neck, and his head rested on his knees.

"I know you're sad about Otis, but we'll get you another drum. You know that, right?" John asked, but Ronnie made no movement or response.

"Come on, Ronnie, we don't need to have a long conversation. Just let me know if you can hear me. You're scaring me."

Ronnie still made no response, and John leaned back on his bunk and rested his head on the wall. "You know I'm just going to sit over here and bug you until you say something to me."

Ronnie remained motionless.

"Okay, you asked for it," John said, moving to the floor and sitting next to the bars that joined his cell to Ronnie's. "Once upon another time, a young lobster daddy-o named Martopulaopia lived in a rusted bucket with his crepe fish friend Portismupous. Now, Martopulaopia loved to eat seaweed, while Portismupous loved to eat regurgitated juicy squirming squidishim, which made Martopulaopia nauseous. So, four days, Martopulaopia told Portismupous that he could no longer tolerate his disgusting diet. Naturally, Portismupous was offended, and he decided to tell Martopulaopia that he didn't care for seaweed either—"

"You promised that no harm would come to Otis," Ronnie muttered.

Frigid tendrils gripped John's throat as the weight of Ronnie's words impacted his weary shoulders. Daring to meet the red-rimmed eyes across from him, John's fortitude crumbled like a castle made of sand. Words were meaningless and would never repair the damage done. John rested his elbows on his knees and steepled his fingers in front of his face.

"You're right, Ronnie. I did make that promise, and I know I let you down. If I could change things, I would, but I can't, and I'm truly sorry."

Ronnie stared at John intently, the wet ruts on his cheeks drying and John's just beginning. Ronnie observed the weight of the defeating night crush John's spirit into devastating sobs.

Ronnie crawled across the floor until he sat next to the bars that connected his cell to John's. "So, did Portismupous move out or learn to eat seaweed?"

John turned his head and looked at Ronnie. "You know what? I don't know."

"I think they accepted each other for who they were because true friendship is more valuable than anything else."

John wiped his cheeks with his sleeve. "Is that right?"

Ronnie looked John directly in the eyes. "That's right. All hound dogs for the pack leader and the pack leader for all the hound dogs."

John's sullen eyes regarded Ronnie, who licked the palm of his hand and stuck it between the cell's bars.

A thin grin rose on John's damp cheeks as he licked the palm of his hand and took Ronnie's hand. Ronnie howled, and unable to stifle a laugh, John joined him.

78

MOLLIE RETURNED TO THE LIVING room, ignored Danny's disrespectful slouch, and stepped over to Jerry. "Would you like a cookie, Jerry?"

Hearing Mollie's voice, Danny sat up, ran his hand over his head, and rested his right foot on the top of his left knee.

"No, thank you. I think I'll join the others in the kitchen," Jerry said, leaving the room.

Mollie turned and sat next to Danny on the couch. "I brought in some cookies to cheer you."

"Thanks," Danny said, taking one. "I'm glad you invited us over tonight."

Mollie crossed her hands neatly in her lap. "No problem. I just wish John and Ronnie could have been here."

"Me too," Danny said, taking a dry bite of the crumbling cookie.

Mollie handed Danny a napkin. "I hope they're all right. Anne is putting on a brave face, but I know she is very worried. She's crazy about John, you know."

Danny sat forward. "The feeling is mutual."

An awkward silence passed between them, neither one sure what to say. Mollie hummed and tapped her hand on her knee to the beat of the song on the radio.

"Would you like to dance?" Danny asked.

"What? Here?"

Danny shrugged. "Sure, why not?"

Mollie touched the back of her bun. "Well, the room is cramped."

"So? I don't need a lot of space to spin you around."

Danny stood up and offered Mollie his hand. The space was tight, but Danny could control the movement enough to keep them moving without bumping into anything.

The exhilaration from the fast steps and spinning twirls made Mollie's heart flutter. Each time she thought her feet would fail her, Danny's skill led her to the next move without missing a beat. Mollie wasn't ready for the song's end or to leave her spot in the center of Danny's arms. Breathless and dizzy, Mollie touched Danny's chest and tried to center herself. Looking up, she realized she was closer to Danny than she thought. His sparkling eyes and carefree smile had faded, and a bleak sadness aged his face. The lips Mollie longed for were inches away. All she had to do was lift her chin, and he would oblige her advance, but there was no warmth, want, or anticipation. It would mean . . . nothing. Mollie compelled her lips to smile. Taking a small step back, she let her breath out in a light laugh. "Wow, I didn't know I could move so fast in such a small space."

Danny touched her cheek, his smile thin. "Mollie . . ."

"I wonder what is keeping James and Marcy," Mollie said, smoothing her dress. "You would think they would be separated for a week." Not daring to look at Danny one more time, Mollie rushed to the kitchen before she started to cry.

79

BRONSON REGARDED THE STONE FACE in front of him. Mrs. Mulligan was a humorless older woman. Her greying hair was pulled in a tight bun, and her long nose sat above thin, pursed lips. She was dressed in a plain black dress with a stiff white collar. Her fingernails were trimmed short, and her hands were rough.

"Good evening, Mrs. Mulligan. I am Chief Sherman Bronson," Bronson said, offering his hand.

"I am aware of who you are," Mulligan said, sitting rigid in her chair.

Bronson pulled back his hand and cleared his throat.

"Can I offer you some coffee?"

"No, thank you," Mulligan replied, her eyes like two black buttons.

Bronson sighed. "I guess you know why you are here tonight."

"I do."

Bronson opened yet another file. "It says here that Ronald Meyer has been a resident at the Barnhardt house for sixteen years?"

"That is correct."

Bronson picked up his pen. "And you are the headmistress, is that correct?"

"Yes."

"You accept full responsibility for him?"

"I do."

Bronson finished writing before looking up. "I want you to know that I spoke with Ronald, and he has admitted his guilt in tonight's incident. He will need to be seen by a judge before I can release him."

"What has he been charged with?"

"Assault."

Mulligan's face did not change expression. "When will he be seen by the judge?"

"Probably Monday."

Mulligan shifted her eyes. "I assume you will call us before he is released, so we can collect him."

"Yes, ma'am."

"Well, if that is all, I will leave you, sir," Mulligan said.

"Wait, Mrs. Mulligan. If you don't mind me asking, how would you describe Ronald?" Bronson asked.

Mulligan shifted in her chair. "Ronald had a difficult start in life. He was locked up in a room for three years with minimal human contact."

Bronson blinked as his brain tried to register the impact of the story.

"He has always had difficulty learning how to interact with others. He still struggles with channeling his anger." Mulligan looked at her hands. "From what your deputy told me, this evening must have been one of those incidents. I objected when Ronald became involved with these questionable young men. We, of course, want to encourage him to make friends and to fit into society. But this staying out late and playing rock 'n' roll music has had an adverse effect on him. You can assure the judge that once Ronald returns to the House, he will be dealt with accordingly."

Bronson lifted his eyebrow. "What does 'dealt with' mean, exactly?"

Without blinking an eye, Mulligan answered. "He will be punished."

Bronson rubbed his chin.

Mrs. Mulligan stood. "Thank you for your time, Chief Bronson. I am sorry that Ronald has caused this problem."

Bronson stood. "He wasn't the cause of the whole episode."

"I certainly hope, as a concerned citizen of this community, that these reprobates are dealt with a firm hand."

Bronson placed his hands in his pockets. "They will be."

Bronson watched the red taillights of Mrs. Mulligan's car disappear down the road. He took a few extra moments to contemplate Ronnie's situation. It would be heartbreaking for anyone to see their most prized possession ruined before their eyes. Especially for somebody who had so few possessions. Was punishing and keeping him locked away in the institution the best answer? He knew better than to get involved in defendants' lives, but Mulligan's cold stare and callous words echoed in his mind. Ronnie had enough harsh punishments in his life. What he needed now was guidance if he was to become a man. An idea came to Bronson's mind. One that he wasn't sure would work, but he had to try.

80

ETTY FIDGETED WITH A LOOSE button on the bottom of her sweater. Her saddle shoes rested on the seat in front of her, and the hem on her dress skirt lay way above her knees. Her mother would be horrified by the slouched position, but Betty didn't care. She was comfortable, and she was painfully alone. "Only You" by The Platters emanating from the crackling car radio did nothing to lift her despondent mood. She was sure tonight would be the night she and Jerry would reconcile, but instead, she was moping in the backseat of Danny's car.

As she remained lost in her thoughts, the silence was abruptly broken by the creaking of the car door. Betty's heart skipped a beat as she turned her wide eyes towards the door to see Jerry.

"Hey," he said.

"Hey," Betty said.

Jerry paused for a moment as his gaze lingered on Betty's exposed legs. A flash of heat warmed his cheeks.

"Did you need something?" Betty asked.

Jerry felt the back of his neck. "James told me you were out here by yourself and I thought you may want some company."

Betty straightened her posture and smoothed her skirt. "Oh, yeah, sure."

Jerry slid into the car and shut the door. Once again, the night had taken an awkward turn, and Betty wanted to disappear.

Jerry cleared his throat. "Nice night, isn't it?"

"Yes, it is," Betty said, gazing out the window.

"It's warm, too," Jerry muttered, loosening his collar.

Betty looked sideways at him. The dimly lit interior silhouetted Jerry's kind, oval face, and Betty's heart fluttered anew. Now was the perfect time to talk to him. There was no one around, and she would have his undivided attention. Her tongue felt stiff and dry, but she knew it was now or never.

Sliding across the seat, she started the conversation. "I'm sorry about what happened tonight. I know it was upsetting."

"It was disappointing. The fellas worked hard and were confident they could knock the crowd's socks off, but we didn't even get to play a note."

Betty cocked her brow. "What do you mean the fellas worked hard? You did, too."

Jerry sighed. "Not like they did."

"What do you mean?"

"I mean, I'm just not cut out to be a rock 'n' roll star," Jerry confessed, his gaze failing.

"Oh, Jerry, don't say that," Betty said, setting her hand on his knee.

Jerry turned to her. "It's true, Betty. I can't play like John and the rest. I'm too slow."

"That's not true."

"Yes, it is. No matter how much time or concentration I put into practice, my fingers never go where they should." Jerry's eyes fell. "I'm never going to be good enough."

Reaching up, Betty gently cupped Jerry's face. "I think you're more than enough. I think you're the kindest, humble, most patient gentleman I've ever known."

Jerry lifted his eyes to meet Betty's tranquil ones.

"Jerry, I owe you an apology. I know my behavior has been abhorrent lately. I've been rude and selfish, but it's only because I was afraid of losing your attention."

"Betty," Jerry started, but she interrupted by pressing her fingers to his lips.

"Let me finish. I know I was being foolish. It's just that you're the first person who paid attention to me or made me feel special. I didn't want to share you, but that was wrong of me. I know there will be times when you have other commitments, and that's okay. I don't want you to quit the Hound Dogs or any other activity you want to pursue. It will only make our time together more special. Can you forgive me?"

Jerry reached up and touched the tips of Betty's hair. "Oh, Betty, I already have."

The corners of Betty's mouth lifted, and the moisture of forming tears glistened on the edge of her eyes.

Jerry rubbed his thumb over Betty's chin. "I love you, Betty Bruer."

"I love you, too, Jerry Price."

Slipping his arm around Betty's shoulder, Jerry closed the gap between them and pressed his lips firmly against hers. Expecting the kiss to end, Betty was surprised when a more intense kiss took her breath away. Swept up in a whirlwind of unfamiliar sensations, Betty entangled her fingers in Jerry's hair. His hand rested on the back of the car seat, while his other hand found its place on her hip. The smooth material felt good against his touch, but having caught a glimpse of what lay underneath stirred a fire within him. Moving his hand down her leg, he found her knee, and when she parted her lips, Jerry instinctively slipped his tongue inside. Having only heard whispers of the bold kiss and maybe a forbidden picture or two, both Jerry and Betty knew they were crossing an invisible barrier.

Jerry pulled back and took a deep breath. "I, um, think we need a break."

"I agree," Betty gasped.

"I think I am going to step outside and enjoy the cool air," Jerry said, opening the car door.

"Me too," Betty agreed, following Jerry out of the car.

Leaning up against the car's cool surface, Jerry and Betty silently pulled their wits about them.

"Did I mention it was a nice night?" Jerry asked.

"You did," Betty said, running her hand over her hair.

"Right," Jerry said, shoving his hands into his pockets.
"I should fix my hair," Betty said, adjusting her barrette.
Jerry closed his eyes. "I should take a cold shower."
Betty nodded. "Yeah, cold sounds good."
"Ice cold," Jerry added.
And Betty couldn't help but agree.

The ride to James's house was quiet. He had lingered with Marcy for as long as possible, and parting ways felt like leaving a warm island for a deep freeze. Seated next to Danny, James brooded, attempting to find solace in a thought that didn't exist.

Danny dropped James off in front of his house, assuring him he would be in touch the moment he knew something. Then, driving home to the Bruer's, Danny remained solemn and lost in his tumultuous thoughts.

Upon entering the house, Betty and Jerry told Danny goodnight. He mumbled something to them and climbed the stairs like some kind of zombie. Betty grabbed a soda from the refrigerator and joined Jerry on the back porch. They snuggled on the porch swing, Jerry lazily rocking it with his foot. The gentle sway was comforting as they gazed at the stars, exchanging whispered words of love. Butterfly kisses and a sense of perfect peace realigned their world, strengthening their bond on its destined course.

Rock 'n' Roll Riot at the Community Center

The Hound Dog's leader, John Chandler, and another youth were handcuffed and taken to the city jail last night after a riot broke out during the obscene rock 'n' roll show at the community center. The riot broke out around 8:00 p.m., when a group of depraved thugs decided to attack Madison High's own celebrated quarterback, Brent Hurley. Lucky for Brent and other innocent audience members, fellow heroes from the Madison High Cougars football team were in attendance. Fearlessly, they faced the perpetrators and attempted to stop the anarchy, but it was too late. The unchaperoned event quickly spun out of control, and several overstimulated youths participated in the malicious mayhem, causing property damage, trauma, and delinquency.

It can only stand to reason at the center of this atrocity are the hoodlums who play rock 'n' roll.

As I predicted in my previous article, no good would come from this event; unfortunately, I was correct. It has been proven on more than one occasion that rock 'n' roll only plants the seeds of discontent and delinquency in the minds of our young, impressionable children. Our responsibility as parents, teachers, and concerned citizens is to stop young adults like John Chandler and his ilk from wreaking havoc on our small, peaceful, law-abiding community. There is no doubt in my mind that another event like this will happen again in our town unless we become vigilant and petition the city council to ban rock 'n' roll in our peaceful, blessed town of Madison.

Jim Robbins - Reporter

81

C APTAIN BRONSON RARELY WENT INTO the precinct on a Sunday, but the situation with Ronnie had prompted him to take immediate action on a case that could typically wait until Monday. Having paid a personal visit to Judge Mullins, Bronson headed to the station to sort things out with Ronnie and Mrs. Mulligan.

Bronson was sure the excitement from the night before had calmed down, and everything would return to normal, but when he saw the crowd of young men and women outside the station, he was perplexed.

Bronson set his hand on his hips. "Good afternoon. Does someone want to explain why you're all gathered outside my station?"

"Are you someone important?" a young woman holding a small notebook and pencil asked.

"I am Captain Bronson, and you are?"

"My name is Joannie, and we're just waiting for John Chandler to be released from jail."

Bronson frowned. "John Chandler?"

Joannie nodded. "Your deputy said you were holding him on account of him being a part of that riot last night."

"Yeah, he plays with that group, The Hound Dogs," a young man added.

"He's so dreamy," Joannie said, and the rest of the girls were suddenly giggling and hopping up and down.

"All right, everyone, calm down," Bronson said, waving his hands. "You youngsters can't be hanging out in front of the police station."

"Are you releasing him today?" the girl next to Joannie asked.

Bronson observed the eager faces around him hanging on his every word. "Yes."

Boisterous shouts and more girlish giggles came from the small group.

"Now you're going to have to clear off the sidewalk, or I will be forced to call your parents."

"Come on, kids, we can wait across the street for him," Joannie told the group as they left the sidewalk.

Bronson sighed and went inside.

Murphy waved fervently at Bronson from behind the counter.

Bronson nodded to him and passed through the swinging gate. "Murphy, did you go home last night?"

Murphy smoothed his disheveled hair. "I did."

Bronson eyed his harried deputy. "You didn't go home last night."

"I was going to. There were so many reports and forms to complete."

Bronson waved his hand. "Go home, Murphy. I'm sure Clara would be mighty glad to see you. Isn't the baby due any day now?"

"Yes, sir, but I have a duty to you and the department."

Bronson set a heavy hand on Murphy's shoulder. "Go home, Murphy, please. Murdock can help me with anything I need."

"Yes, sir!" Murdock chimed.

Bronson looked at the burnt coffee at the bottom of the pot. "You can start by making a pot of fresh coffee."

Murdock hopped to his feet. "Right away, sir!"

Bronson looked at Murphy, who didn't trust the green deputy. "Murphy . . ."

"I'm leaving, sir. Mrs. Mulligan is in your office," Murphy said.

"Thank you, Murphy. I don't want to see you again until tomorrow," Bronson warned.

Murphy nodded, and Bronson headed toward his office.

82

*P*ERFECT. JOHN THOUGHT AS HE gazed at his picture on the newspaper's front page. The article was a lie, and whoever wrote it needed a sound thump on the head. Throwing the paper aside, John rubbed his face. How could everything have gone so wrong? It was bad enough to face off against Joe, but Patrick? The scenario had been playing in John's brain all night, and he was exhausted. John heard the outer door and hoped that Ronnie was coming back from talking to Bronson, but it was only Murdock. John slumped against the wall.

"Hey John," Murdock said, opening the cell door.

"Hey Murdock. Thanks for the cold coffee and the delightful front-page news," John said, handing Murdock the newspaper and a chipped mug.

"I gave you fair warning, didn't I?"

John sighed. "You did."

"It'll blow over soon enough. You'll see," Murdock said, fastening the keys to his belt.

"I wish I shared your optimism. The last thing I wanted was to bring attention to myself."

"Look on the bright side, you've been cleared of the charges, and your dad is here to pick you up."

John's forehead creased. "My dad?"

"Yeah."

"What does he look like?" John asked.

Murdock chuckled. "You don't know what your dad looks like?"

John folded his arms. "Humor me."

"I don't know, those older folks all look alike. You know? Balding, glasses, with bowler bellies."

John raised his eyebrow. "Bowler bellies?"

"Yeah, Mom said that's where my dad got his. From hangin' out at the bowlin' alley."

John laughed.

Following Murdock to the front office, John saw Bob waiting for him. His face held no expression, but John could tell he was disappointed in him, and that hurt more than any words or punishment ever could.

"Hello Bob," John said.

"John. When Danny told me your stepmother was out of town, I figured I should come and take you home."

John put his hands in his pockets. "I, um, appreciate it, but you see, I can't go just yet. Ronnie is in the office with the chief of police, and I can't leave until I know he is okay."

"I see," Bob said.

"I feel responsible for him."

Bob nodded. "Then we will wait."

John and Bob sat on the long bench in the front office. Bob rested his elbows on his knee, and John twisted his hands.

"The newspaper article is a lie," John said. "That isn't what happened last night."

"Danny told me what happened," Bob said.

"You believe him, don't you? We never wanted things to get so crazy. It all happened so fast."

Bob rubbed his hands together. "We can talk about this later when we return to the house."

John felt like an errant child waiting for a lecture from his father, but for the moment, he would focus on Ronnie. Hopefully, things wouldn't go as bad as he feared.

83

Ronnie stepped into Bronson's office to feel the weight of her judgmental gaze. He could count on one hand how many times he had seen the Barnhardt House's Headmistress smile. He would rather spend a week in the cell than listen to her berate him. Ronnie sat in the chair next to her and stared straight ahead.

"Good morning, Ronnie," Bronson started.

"Sir."

Bronson leaned forward in his chair. "I asked Mrs. Mulligan to join us this morning because you are currently in the care of the Barnhardt House. She has graciously filled me in on the details of your life since you have been at Barnhardt. She tells me it hasn't been easy for you. Apparently, there have been some anger management issues, but she said you've been working on your inappropriate outbursts. I realize last night's incident may have been traumatizing for you and contributed to your behavior. You impressed me last night when you admitted that you were wrong and were willing to accept your punishment."

Ronnie's gaze fell to the floor.

"I talked to Judge Mullins this morning about your case, and he agreed to suspend your sentence for six months, as long as I was willing to supervise your probation."

Ronnie looked up. "What does that mean?"

"Well, basically, it means you will have a deferred sentence as long as you comply with the terms of your probation. Mrs. Mulligan has agreed to these terms. So, starting this week, you will be assigned some community service work. I don't know what that means at this minute, but you will need to report here in my office this Wednesday at 8 a.m. for your assignment. Do you understand?"

"Yes," Ronnie answered.

Bronson folded his hands on the desk. "I hope this will be a good opportunity for you to spend time in the community and hopefully learn some skills."

"Yes, sir."

"Do you have any questions for me?" Bronson asked.

Ronnie shook his head.

"Do you have any questions, Mrs. Mulligan?"

Mrs. Mulligan raised her chin. "No. You have my word he will be here on Wednesday morning."

Bronson handed some papers to Mrs. Mulligan. "Please sign these documents stating you understand everything discussed here today and that I am releasing Mr. Meyer to your care."

"My last name is Crockett," Ronnie protested.

"Ronald," Mrs. Mulligan said firmly. "We have discussed this before. Your last name is Meyer."

"He didn't want me to have his name, remember? He said I brought shame to the family name. He denounced me as his son." Ronnie looked Bronson in the eye. "My last name is Crockett."

Bronson nodded. "We will work on that, Ronnie. I promise."

Mrs. Mulligan signed the documents.

Bronson stood up and stepped over to his door. "All right, Ronnie, you are free to go, and I will see you on Wednesday."

"Thank you, sir," Ronnie said.

Bronson walked Mrs. Mulligan and Ronnie out of his office.

John stood up and stepped over to the counter as Ronnie approached. "Ronnie, are you all right?"

Ronnie nodded slowly.

"Come along, Ronald, it's time to go home," Mrs. Mulligan said, taking Ronnie by the arm and glaring at John.

"What happened?" John asked Ronnie, ignoring the hostile woman.

"That, young man, is none of your business," Mrs. Mulligan snapped.

John stood his ground. "I beg to differ. I'm his friend, and I was with him last night."

Mulligan narrowed her eyes. "Oh, believe me, I am well aware of who you are, and I'm telling you now that it would be in your best interest to stay away from Ronald."

John's brow furrowed. "What?"

"You heard me. You and your reprobate friends are the cause of this mess. Ronald was doing well until he came in contact with you. I believe it is in his best interest if he never sees you again."

John's muscles stiffened as his eyes scanned the adversarial faces around him. Taking a shallow breath, John's reasoning kicked in. He had seen the tight pursed lips and blazing eyes of other authority figures. To say something now would only make matters worse and ruin his chance of ever seeing Ronnie again.

John stepped back and opened the swinging gate for Mulligan and Ronnie. "As you wish, ma'am."

Mulligan's hand tightened on Ronnie's arm as they passed through the gate. For a fraction of a moment, John met Ronnie's despondent expression and winked at him.

"Come along, Ronald," Mulligan said, pulling on Ronnie's arm.

Ronnie took a step forward to follow and winked at John.

"Hey, Captain, the crowd out front has doubled in size," Murdock said.

Bronson walked to the front window and looked at the crowd across the street.

"Uh-huh," Bronson said, putting his hands on his hips.

"What are they doing out there?" Mrs. Mulligan asked.

"Waiting for Mr. Chandler's release," Murdock said.

"What? *Me*?" John said. "But why?"

"Apparently, you're a celebrity now," Bronson said.

John closed his eyes and groaned.

84

A TRANQUIL LATE MORNING BREEZE SWAYED the daisies beside the porch. Danny sat on the steps and waited for his uncle to bring John home.

The early morning had been spent in church listening to Pastor Tomkins's sermon on the importance of placing God first in the home. Without this foundation, sinful temptations waited to corrupt the young, impressionable members of the congregation. Teenagers cringed and slumped in the pews, knowing their parents' strict, watchful eyes would only worsen.

❖ ❖ ❖ ❖ ❖ ❖ ❖ ❖ ❖ ❖

Jerry stepped out of the house and walked to the opposite side of the porch. He sat on the railing and rested his head on one of the porch's supporting posts. Danny picked a dried piece of wild grass and stuck the tip between his lips. Other than a few pleasantries, the two hadn't said much since the night before.

"Hey Jerry," Danny said.

"Danny," Jerry said, not facing him.

Danny ran his hand over his hair. "About what happened last night at the show . . ."

"You don't have to say anything. I understand."

"I was just . . . devastated. I couldn't understand what happened. One minute, I was moving with the music, and the next, my guitar fell apart. It makes no sense."

Jerry's feet twitched. "The whole incident doesn't make sense. It's like we were cursed from the minute we stepped onto the platform. I mean, at least the night of Len's party, none of us had anything to lose except our pride, but last night, that was something totally different. Someone was out to get us."

Danny met Jerry's eyes, a long silence hanging between them.

"I saw him, too, Danny. He doesn't know I saw him, but I did," Jerry said.

Danny lowered his head. "Why would he do that to me? Have I not been nothing but nice to him?"

Jerry raised his leg. "You didn't have to do anything. Stu has always been jealous of you because John liked you from the start. Stu forgets he was Patrick's friend first. It takes John a while to warm up to people. For some reason, you got lucky."

"What about you?"

Jerry shrugged. "I dunno. He rescued me from a bully. I guess I got lucky, too."

Danny leaned back and rested on his elbows.

"Are you going to say something to John?"

Danny shook his head. "I'm not convinced Stu did anything. I mean, yeah, he looked guilty as hell, but maybe I'm wrong too. You know if John thinks he did something . . ."

"It would be bad," Jerry said, setting his hand on his thigh.

"I don't even want to think about it."

Bob's car turned onto the road in front of the house.

"Let's keep this between us for now, hey Jerry?" Danny said.

"Absolutely."

Betty and Eddie came out of the house when they heard the car. Danny walked beside Jerry and put his hands in his pockets.

John barely stepped out of the car before Betty had her arms around him.

"Hey. What's all this?" John asked.

Betty pulled back. "I'm just so glad to see you. We were all so worried about you!"

John pushed the hair back off her cheek. "Aren't you sweet? But I'm fine. A little tired, maybe, and hungry."

"What happened to your head?" Eddie asked.

John gingerly touched the wound. "What? This? It's just a scratch."

Betty put her hands on her hips. "It's not just a scratch! Did a doctor look at it?"

"Well no, not yet. I cleaned it up last night."

"You better see a doctor. You don't want it to get infected."

"I'm fine."

"I'm telling Mother," Betty said, running to the house.

John sighed.

"You boys don't stand out here too long. I'm sure dinner is almost ready," Bob said.

"We're coming, Dad," Eddie said.

Bob turned and went toward the house.

"It's good to see you're all right, John," Eddie said. "I made sure everything got packed up and returned to the space."

"All of it?" John asked.

Eddie nodded.

"Stu helped, right?"

Eddie rubbed the back of his neck and glanced at Danny.

"I think he took off before the cops arrived," Jerry said.

"Of course he did," John mumbled.

"I'm gonna go get washed up," Eddie said.

"Me too," Jerry said. "Glad you're back safe."

John pulled Jerry close to him and ruffled his hair. Jerry pulled away, disgusted. "You could have just said 'thanks, Jerry.'"

"Where's the fun in that?"

Jerry rolled his eyes and walked away.

John turned his attention to Danny, who gave a weak grin. "What? I don't get a hug?"

Danny chuckled. "I don't want my hair mussed."

"So, you think standing three feet away from me makes you safe?"

Danny observed the sappy grin and glint in John's eye. "Being knocked upside the head has addled your brain."

"Oh, come on, Dan. You know my brain was already addled."

Danny nodded and laughed. "Yeah, I guess I do."

John leaned back against the car. "You want to talk about it?"

Danny pulled his arms in closer to his body. "Not yet."

"You're feeling guilty, aren't you?"

Danny shrugged. "Maybe."

"You forget I know you pretty well."

Danny shook his head. "Last night was all my fault."

John scoffed. "Don't be ridiculous."

Danny sniffled. "I could have prevented all of this if I checked the tuning. Instead, all I did was let everyone down."

"You need to stop beating yourself up."

Danny hung his head. "I can't help it. I feel so responsible."

"Stop it. No one thinks you're responsible."

Danny drug his sleeve over his face.

John stepped up to Danny and took hold of his arms. "Danny, listen to me. There is no reason for you to take the burden of last night's debacle onto your shoulders. None of us could have predicted what happened in a million years. To blame you would be ludicrous. Now, I don't want to hear any more about it. You hear me?"

Danny nodded. "I guess so."

"Don't you mean yes, sir?"

Danny smiled. "Now, let's not get carried away."

John's face held no humor. "I didn't think I was."

"You're not serious?"

John lifted his eyebrow.

"I hate when you look at me like that."

A mischievous grimace lifted the corners of John's mouth.

Danny stepped backward. "You look crazy, you know that?"

"I think we've established that fact already."

Danny continued to back up. "Are you sure you want to do this with an injured head?"

"Well, you can stand still and let me humiliate you, or you can try and outrun me."

Danny's mouth opened, but with John's last footfall, Danny knew he had to try and outrun the adolescent. The odds were not in his favor.

85

Bob hadn't said much about what had happened the night before, but everyone could sense his reflective mood. Other than the occasional request for items to be passed or trivial questions, everyone digested their thoughts and ate silently around the dining room table. John's pure enjoyment of the meal was entertainment enough for those watching him devour everything in sight.

Bob held his coffee cup, watching John close his eyes and savor the last bite of his second piece of pie. "Did you have enough to eat, John?"

John opened his eyes and noticed that everyone was looking at him. "Uh, yeah. It was delicious."

Bob leisurely finished his coffee while everyone waited patiently for him to signal the end of the meal.

"So, does someone want to tell me why you all are so quiet?" Bob asked.

"We just wanted you to have a peaceful Sunday meal, dear," Mable said.

Bob sat his cup down. Betty looked at her mother, who gave her a slight nod. Pushing away from the table, Betty and Mable began to clear away the dishes.

"Want to play a game of checkers, Jerry?" Eddie asked.

"Sure," Jerry said, leaving the room with Eddie.

Bob rubbed his hands together and looked at Danny and John. "You boys want to come into the living room with me?"

Danny and John nodded, knowing they had no choice. Stepping into the living room, John and Danny sat on the couch next to each other. Bob gazed out the window for a few moments, making the tenseness of the moment drag out. Finally, he turned to them and sat his hands on the back of the winged back chair in front of him. "I guess you boys know what I want to talk to you about."

"Yes, but it's like I told you earlier. What happened last night wasn't our fault," Danny said.

"I understand, and I agree."

Danny and John felt some relief until Bob continued, "But you can understand why I have some concerns. Number one is your safety, Danny. You are in a vulnerable position right now with only having a year left on your probation."

"We realize that, Uncle Bob. As a matter of fact, it was John who insisted that I leave and get to safety." Danny turned to John. "And for that, I am eternally grateful."

"I would have done it for any of you," John said. "I just wish I could have gotten through to Ronnie quicker. He was like a lion looking at raw meat. I couldn't stop him."

"Is it true you spent the night in jail just so he didn't have to be alone?" Danny asked.

John nodded. "It's my fault that his drum was damaged."

"It was nobody's fault. That crowd was out of control."

"Do you know who started the disturbance?" Bob said, sitting down in the chair.

"The crowd was great during The Dice performance. The ruckus didn't start until we stepped on the platform and my guitar fell apart," Danny said, his shoulders falling.

Bob blinked. "Fell apart?"

"Yeah."

"That doesn't sound possible. I mean, guitars don't just fall apart, do they?" Bob asked.

Danny averted his eyes, and his leg jogged up and down.

"No, they don't," John said.

"After that," Danny continued, "a group of ruffians started to heckle us, and when the quarterback for the high school football team defended us, all hell broke loose."

"Sounds like those boys wanted to cause trouble," Bob said.

"That's just it. They weren't boys, they were men, large men," Danny said.

"Everything happened so fast, I didn't even think about that," John said. "It does seem odd that they would waste their time on a Saturday night, causing trouble at an amateur rock 'n' roll show."

"Yeah, and there was no liquor," Danny added.

"The truth is, the community isn't going to look at the circumstances," Bob said. "The only thing they care about is that their children are safe in a wholesome environment."

"That makes sense, but rock 'n' roll isn't to blame for the trouble," Danny said.

"True, but because you were playing rock 'n' roll music when the incident occurred, they think you're troublemakers and will blame you for the incident," Bob reasoned.

Danny sighed heavily.

"Bob's right," John said, "and it doesn't help that Ronnie and my picture is on the front page of the newspaper."

"I'm sorry, boys, but I think you better keep a low profile, at least until this mess blows over," Bob said.

John and Danny nodded their agreement.

"I think it's time you boys consider your future. I understand that playing music is important to you both, and I support you, but at this point, all it has done is cause you both a lot of trouble."

"But—" Danny started.

"Let me finish."

Danny's shoulders and face fell.

"You're both growing into men, and it's time to consider how you will make a living so you can settle down and raise a family. I know this is the last piece of advice you want to hear, but under the circumstances, I think it's important. I hate to push my point, Danny, but I expect you to enroll in the GED program this week. I have been more than lenient and given you enough time to stand up to your responsibility."

"Yes, sir," Danny muttered.

"It will make a good impression on your parole officer the next time we meet with him."

Danny nodded, but he was staring at his feet.

"I have been thinking about looking for a job myself," John said. "It would be good for my stepmother if I was independent."

Bob nodded. "This is an excellent plan, John. Plus, it will prove that you are working toward becoming a productive member of society."

John was staring at his feet now.

Bob stood up. "I know it doesn't seem like it, but I am proud of you both."

John and Danny both forced smiles, and Bob patted John's shoulder as he left the room.

John and Danny sat silently for a few moments, digesting the lecture.

"Do you feel like we just can't win?" Danny said.

"My whole life."

Danny sat back on the couch and stared up at the ceiling. "You know what bugs me? After all this time and the troubles we've been through, I still don't know if I'm out of my contract with Joe. It's like we're back to square one."

John sat back and looked up at the ceiling with Danny. "I agree, Daniel."

"I guess I will have no other choice but to talk to Joe."

John folded his hands across his stomach. "It would appear so."

More silence and reflection passed.

"I don't want to talk to Joe," Danny said.

"I can't blame you there."

"I can't help but wonder if he had been there, if the night would have played out the same."

John twiddled his thumbs. "I wonder if he even knew the show went on without him."

Danny raised an eyebrow.

"Think about it. The show was his idea. The rest didn't give a damn."

Danny turned his head. "Something about the whole night was off."

John turned his head.

"Do you think it was a setup?"

John shrugged. "Maybe part of it."

Danny sighed. "What are we gonna do?"

"What we've always done."

"Figure it out together?"

John faced forward. "Yep, but not today. I have other plans for the remainder of the afternoon."

"Like?"

"Spending time with Anne."

Danny put his hands behind his head. "She was really worried about you last night. She's a sweet girl."

John didn't comment. His eyes were closed.

"I think she's good for you," Danny continued.

"I'm glad she meets with your approval."

"Well, I've been afraid to say anything because, you know, sometimes, if a guy thinks a girl is good for him, then his eye starts to roam."

John opened one eye and looked at Danny. "Maybe you should quit while you're ahead, hey Dan?"

Danny rubbed the back of his neck. "Oh, yeah."

John closed his eye, and Danny closed his.

86

Tiny droplets from the upside-down bottle traveled through a translucent tube to Joe's purple scarred arm. His eyes fluttered open slowly, and the blurry scene of an unfamiliar room distraught his fretful mind. His last memory was bowing to the applause from hundreds of adoring fans, then . . . nothing. The pungent smell of ammonia and the bottle above his bed made him realize he was in a hospital.

Grasping the bed's cold metal guard rail, Joe forced himself to a sitting position. The painful movement caused the room to spin, and a nauseating tide rose rapidly in his clenched throat. Swinging his legs over the side of the bed, he gazed at the spinning floor. Violent retching sent Joe to his knees, and the IV bottle followed with an unsettling crash. Several nurses rushed into the room. Harsh, garbled voices shouted incoherent instructions as firm hands pulled Joe off the floor. Jerking movements and prodding fingers summoned another wave of excruciating stomach pain. Desperate and alone, Joe's dignity was stripped away.

"Lay still, Mr. Delaney," a harsh voice commanded.

Any question or plea Joe cried was ignored, while nameless faces forced another sharp needle into his retreating vein.

"Do you have his chart?" a deep male voice asked.

"It's here, Doctor," a female voice responded.

"Mr. Delaney, can you hear me?"

Joe forced his eyes open to see a doctor standing above him, his stethoscope hanging from his neck.

Joe nodded numbly.

"My name is Doctor Meredith. You're very sick. You almost killed yourself Friday night. Do you remember anything?"

"No," Joe mumbled.

"I am prescribing some medication that will help with your symptoms. Your body has suffered tremendous abuse, and it will be a few days before you start to feel better. Do you understand?"

Joe nodded and closed his eyes in hopes the dizzy feeling would subside.

"Your wife and manager are here. As soon as you're stable, she can see you for a few minutes."

"All right," Joe said, trying not to move.

Doctor Meredith talked to the head nurse, and, giving his orders, he left the room.

❑■❑■❑■❑■❑■❑■❑■❑■❑■❑■❑

A half-hour later, Monica was allowed to see Joe. Sitting in a stiff chair all day, her entire body ached, but she put on a brave face as she stepped into the room. She expected that Joe wouldn't look well but seeing him in his weakened state alarmed her. He was lying on his side in the fetal position, hugging a hot water bottle against his stomach. His dark blond hair was soaked with sweat, and his pale complexion made his features look dark and sunken. Monica sat down slowly in the chair next to the bed. Her warm hand wrapped around Joe's.

"Hey," Monica whispered.

"Hey," Joe responded.

"The doctor says I can only stay for a little while."

Joe's trembling fingers tightened on Monica's hand. "I don't want you to go."

Monica pushed the damp hair from his brow. "Shh, you need to rest if you're going to beat this."

"I can't beat this, knowing you aren't there for me. I'm tired of fighting and don't want to be alone anymore," Joe cried.

Monica blinked back a tear. "I'm not going to leave you alone."

"Do you promise?"

"Yes."

Joe averted his eyes. "I know I've been a horrible husband."

"We don't need to talk about this now."

"No listen to me," Joe pleaded. "You've put up with a lot, and I have caused you so much unhappiness."

Monica sighed. "Joe . . ."

"I know you tried to get me to open up about Ian, but I don't know how."

Monica's bottom lip trembled. "And you think I do? You think I know how to open up when I know his death is my fault!"

Joe's brow furrowed. "Your fault?"

"I should have never let him out of my sight. I told him a million times to stay away from the stairs. I swear, I only turned my back for a second, a second." Monica's voice cracked, and her whole body was shaking. "I miss him every damn day!"

Joe reached out and stroked Monica's hair. "His death wasn't your fault. It was an accident."

Monica's tear-filled eyes gazed at Joe. "I thought you blamed me."

"I never blamed you. I blame myself more than anyone for not being there for you, for him. All I cared about was my career and what I had to do to get ahead. Now I realize how foolish I've been." Reaching out, he lifted Monica's chin. "We've both suffered long enough. It's time we both dealt with our grief and put this marriage back together again."

Monica searched Joe's eyes. "You mean that?"

"Yes," Joe answered.

"You know it won't be easy. To beat this, my help won't be enough."

Joe ran his thumb over her tears. "I know it."

Monica rubbed Joe's forearm. "And you would agree that we need counseling?"

"I will do whatever it takes to repair the damage. You're my wife, and I love you, Monica."

"I love you, too, Joe."

Joe pulled Monica onto the bed next to him and wrapped his arms around her. His body was cold and clammy with sweat, but she didn't care. They clung to each other for as long as they could before the nurse returned. Holding each other's hand, a glance of new understanding passed between them.

"I will see you tomorrow," Monica whispered.

Joe touched the side of her face. "Are you going to be able to get some sleep?"

"It will be challenging, but knowing you're conscious will help."

"My keys are in my coat pocket."

Monica raised both eyebrows. "You would let me drive the Jag?"

"If you bring it home to me."

"It will be there," Monica said, giving Joe's hand a reassuring squeeze before leaving the room.

The next few days would be torturous for Joe, but for the first time, he wanted to recover. He had a second chance to rebuild his life with the woman he loved, even if meant he had to walk through hell first.

87

Bɪᴛɪɴɢ ʜᴇʀ ɴᴀɪʟꜱ, Aɴɴᴇ ꜱᴛᴀʀᴇᴅ at the silent phone. Having spent the day worried sick about John, her frayed nerves refused to let her relax. Marcy promised she would call the minute she knew anything. It was almost three in the afternoon, and the phone still hadn't rung.

"Anne?" Mildred called from the kitchen.

"Coming." Anne turned away from the phone and entered the kitchen.

"I was wondering if you wouldn't mind helping me cut up some vegetables for dinner tonight?"

"Of course."

"I thought you could start with the carrots I laid on the cutting board."

Getting a paring knife from the drawer, Anne sat down at the table.

Mildred looked over at her while she cracked the peas. "Anne, are you feeling all right? You seem so distracted this afternoon. Is it because you are going home this week?"

The depressing question weighed on Anne's heart. "I am sad to be leaving you. I have enjoyed my time with you very much."

Mildred smiled. "I think you will miss your friends and the young man you have spent time with."

Anne nodded slightly and picked up another carrot.

Mildred set the peas aside and wiped her hands on a towel. "I'm sure once you're home, you will still be able to see him. It just might not be as often."

Anne concentrated on her cutting and dismissed the thought.

"Why don't you go into the living room and turn on the radio? It might help take your mind off things."

"Okay." Anne wiped her hands and went into the living room. She refused to look at the phone and turned on the radio. Soft, relaxing music replaced the silence, and Anne headed back to the kitchen when she heard a knock on the door. John! With wings on her feet, she ran to the door and then stopped cold. Her entire body went numb, and her heart stopped.

"Hello, darling."

Anne froze and couldn't move as she blinked. "Steve."

"Aren't you going to invite me in?"

Anne turned her head toward the kitchen, then opened the screen door, allowing Steve to step inside.

"What are you doing here?" Anne said, a nervous laugh escaping her tight throat.

"What kind of silly question is that? I've missed you," Steve said, placing his arms around her.

"You shouldn't have come all this way. I am going to be home in a couple of days."

Steve ran his fingers down the side of Anne's face. "I couldn't wait one moment longer. Besides, I wanted to surprise you."

"I'm definitely surprised."

Leaning in, Steve kissed Anne with her eyes wide open.

"Anne, who was at the door?" Mildred said, coming into the living room.

Anne was in Steve's arms, her face was white.

"Oh, I didn't realize your young man was here," Mildred said.

"Uh . . . Mildred Brewster, allow me to introduce you to Steve Browning."

Steve smiled warmly. "Mrs. Brewster. It's a pleasure to finally meet you."

Mildred returned the smile to the handsome young man. "Likewise, I have heard so much about you."

"Have you?" Steve said, giving Anne a squeeze. "I hope it was all good."

"Yes. I know that Anne was afraid that once she went home, you two wouldn't be able to see each other anymore."

"What?" Steve said.

Anne grabbed Steve's hand. "Why don't we go and sit on the porch for a while?"

"Would you like to stay for dinner, Steve?" Mildred asked.

"No," Anne snapped. "I mean, it's such a long drive back home."

"Nonsense. I would love to stay," Steve said.

"I will set an extra place," Mildred turned and returned to the kitchen.

"I think we need to have a long talk," Steve said, touching Anne's arms.

"What? Right now?"

"Yes, right now. I have waited long enough for an answer from you."

Anne swallowed hard. "Oh, Steve. I don't want to talk about this right now, not here."

"Then we will talk outside." Steve set his hand on the screen door latch when Anne heard a faraway rumble of a motorcycle coming down the street.

Anne grabbed Steve's hand. "Wait! I changed my mind. Let's sit inside on the sofa."

Steve didn't budge. "I think outside is the perfect place for us to talk."

"Please, Steve," Anne begged.

His eyes were hardening, so Anne kissed his cheek and gave him the sweetest smile she could muster.

"All right," he said, stepping toward the couch.

Anne looked out the screen door as John pull up to the curb.

"I'll be right back," Anne said.

"Don't be long," Steve said, sitting on the couch.

Thinking as fast as she could. Anne ran into the kitchen.

"I forgot my gloves outside," Anne said to Mildred as she ran toward the back door.

"You don't have to go get them right now."

"Yes, yes I do." Anne ran out the back door and to the front gate just in time to intercept John as he approached the front walkway.

"John," she called to him.

He turned, and she ran to him, flinging her arms around his neck.

"Hey," John said, putting his arms around Anne, "this is quite the welcome."

Taking hold of the base of his neck, Anne kissed him with a deep, frantic passion.

John grinned. "Quite the welcome, indeed."

"Oh, John, I was so worried about you," Anne said, searching his eyes.

"I'm all right."

Reaching up, she touched his forehead. "How is your head?"

"Aching."

"Oh, you poor dear," Anne said stroking John's hair.

John's index finger gently grazed her chin. "You know, my stepmother is out of town. Why don't you come to my house and be my nurse?"

Anne desperately wanted to say yes. One word, one moment, and her troubles would be behind her like the exhaust from the tailpipe.

"I . . . I . . . can't," Anne said, forcing the words from her mouth.

"What do you mean, you can't?"

"I need to stay here with Mildred. She needs me."

John pulled Anne closer, and nuzzling her ear, he whispered. "*I need you.*"

The heat from John's breath made Anne's blood tingle through her veins. "Can you come back later? I promise I can come with you then."

John's glazed eyes were locked on hers while his hungry fingers caressed her hips. Then, in one fateful second, his eyes shifted slightly, and his arms were suddenly rigid.

"Later is all right, isn't it?" Anne asked.

John's eyes shifted back to hers, but the clouds were gone, and dry ice remained.

"John?" Anne muttered.

"Why is your ex-boyfriend standing on the porch?"

Anne's eyes fluttered as John's arms pulled away from her. "I . . . I . . ."

"Anne, what is going on out here?" Steve said, storming through the gate.

Suspended in a nightmare she couldn't control, John's contemptuous eyes bored into her soul.

Steve glared at John. "Is this degenerate bothering you?"

John took a menacing step toward Steve, who backed away, almost tripping over his feet.

"John, please let me explain," Anne cried.

"Don't you think it's a little late for that?" John said, turning away.

Anne grabbed John's arm. "John, please. . ."

"Let go of me," John growled.

"I didn't mean for this to happen. I swear I didn't!"

"If you don't let go of me, I swear I'll . . ."

Anne reluctantly pulled her hand away, and John strode toward the bike.

"John!" Anne pleaded, running after him. "Please, please, I'm so, so, sorry."

John didn't dare look at her as he got on the bike and turned the key.

"John, I beg of you, please don't go. I love you!"

John's cold eyes turned to her. "That, my dear, is your misfortune."

With one last hateful glare, John pulled away from the curb, and as he disappeared down the street, Anne fell to her knees in a gut-wrenching seizure of heartache.

Steve towered over Anne with his hands on his hips. "Anne, for heaven's sake, pull yourself off the ground. You're making a spectacle of yourself."

The sound of his judgmental voice only made Anne's sob harder.

Mildred came out of the house. "My goodness, what happened?"

"I'm not entirely sure," Steve said. "But whatever it is, by the time I see her again, she better have her priorities in order and a damn good explanation as to why she decided to jeopardize her future." Turning on his heel, Steve walked to his car, climbed behind the wheel, and drove away.

Mildred bent over and put her arm around Anne. Holding tightly to the supportive arm, waves of despair wracked Anne's body.

"Come along, dearie. You best come inside and dry your eyes. I will make you a warm toddy."

Anne wanted to curl up on the sidewalk and die. Her worst nightmare had come true; without John, her life was over. Mildred wrapped her hand around Anne's arm and managed to help Anne stand. Like a condemned woman, Anne shuffled her numb feet toward the house and a loveless life in hell.

88

Anne resisted opening her swollen eyes. If she remained curled in a ball under the covers, she could pretend that last night was a dream and that she would be in John's arms again.

No matter how small, the very thought of him sent an overwhelming wave of sorrow through her core. How could she have been so stupid? What made her think she could walk away from her reality and remain in this one? Hope was gone, and a scathing heartache remained. Unable to hide any longer, Anne got out of bed and forced herself to face the harsh judgments that awaited her. She put on her yardwork dungarees and tied a scarf around her head before joining Mildred in the kitchen. Even the smell of fresh coffee brought her no joy. Sitting at the table, she transfixed her eyes on the embroidered pansies that adorned the tablecloth. If she acknowledged Mildred, she would surely break.

Mildred poured Anne a cup of coffee. "Would you like a muffin?"

Anne shook her head. "No, thank you. I'm not hungry."

Mildred picked up her breakfast plate from the counter and sat across from Anne. "You know, if you ate something, you might feel better?"

Anne sniffled. "Nothing is going to make me feel better."

Mildred buttered her muffin and patiently waited for Anne to advance the conversation.

"I'm sorry about last night, Mildred. I didn't mean to put you in the middle my mess," Anne muttered. "I thought I was in control of the situation. I never dreamt that anyone would . . ."

"Find out?" Mildred finished.

Anne nodded. "I was so wrapped up in what I wanted that I didn't care how it affected anyone else. Now I've ruined everything and lost the man I love."

Mildred handed Anne a tissue. "It's a hard lesson to learn for sure. Telling lies and being deceitful never turns out well."

Anne wiped her nose. "If I could just see him one more time and explain why I did it, maybe he would understand."

Mildred took a sip from her cup. "Maybe, but it might take some time. Right now, he's probably hurting too and doesn't know what to think."

Anne looked up at Mildred. "Oh, Mildred, what am I going to do?"

"I don't know, dear, but you'll need time to sort out what you want for your future."

Anne hesitated. "You mean Steve?"

Mildred nodded slowly.

Anne wiped away more tears. "I thought I could run away from my problems."

"I think all of us have felt that way at one time or another, but they always have a way of finding us."

A firm knock came at the front door. Anne pressed her hand to her chest.

"I'll answer it," Mildred said, going to the front door.

Mildred didn't recognize the well-dressed lady who stood on her porch, but her stern face and pursed mouth let her know it was more than likely Anne's mother.

"Hello, may I help you?" Mildred said, portraying ignorance.

"Yes, I'm here to pick up my daughter," Florence said through clenched teeth.

"Excuse me, but who are you?" Mildred asked, causing Florence more frustration.

"I'm Florence Clark, Anne's mother."

Mildred opened the door. "I'm Mildred Brewster. It's nice to meet you. Won't you come in?"

Florence stepped into the entryway. No smile or cordial conversation crossed her lips.

"Would you like a cup of coffee?" Mildred offered.

Florence pulled off her white gloves. "No, thank you. I won't be staying long. If you will please let my daughter know I'm here, I would appreciate it."

"Of course," Mildred said with a polite smile.

Returning to the kitchen, Mildred saw Anne splashing cold water on her face. She didn't need to say anything to know Anne had already heard the conversation.

Mildred wiped Anne's face with a towel. "It's going to be all right. You just need to remain calm."

Anne nodded and wiped her eyes with the back of her hand.

Following behind Mildred, Anne stepped into the living room to meet the unforgiving scowl on her mother's face.

"I'm sure you know why I'm here," Florence said.

"I do."

"Good, then you need to collect your things. I am taking you home."

"But mother, I promised to stay until Wednesday."

Florence stuck her chin out. "I don't care. You need to leave with me this instant."

"Now, hold on a minute," Mildred said. "My daughter thinks that Anne will be staying with me until Wednesday. Isn't that the promise you made?"

Florence blinked. "Well, yes, but . . ."

"There is no but. My daughter will be very displeased once she discovers that you left me all alone, with no one to care for me. Why I could fall over at any moment." Placing her hand on Anne's arm, Mildred continued. "I have come to depend on Anne, and I'm sorry,

I just can't get along without her. Now, you don't want to disappoint Emogene, especially since she speaks highly of you."

"She does?" Florence asked.

"Oh yes. She says the board couldn't get along without you. Why, your contribution to the club is invaluable."

Florence absently touched her hair. "Well, I do contribute a lot of my time and resources, you know."

"Of course you do."

Florence put her hand in her glove. "All right, since we agreed that you wouldn't come home until Wednesday, I trust there will be no further incident."

"I will keep a close eye on her," Mildred said, patting Anne's arm. "There will be no further need for worry."

Florence glared at Anne. "Don't think this means you're not in big trouble, young lady. Your father and I are outraged by your behavior. We raised you to be a virtuous, respectful young lady, not some vulgar, immoral strumpet."

Anne ground her teeth together and tried not to cry.

Florence finished putting her gloves on and stepped toward the door. "Your father will be meeting with Steve this afternoon, and I don't know if he will be able to smooth over your transgressions. It's disgraceful. Steve is an admirable, upstanding young man, and any young woman in her right mind would be honored to be his wife. I suggest you take this time to think about your actions and how you plan to set things right." Straightening her suit jacket, Florence opened the door. "I expect you to be ready when I come to collect you on Wednesday. It was very nice to meet you, Mrs. Brewster."

"Likewise, Mrs. Clark," Mildred said.

Florence left the house, closing the door behind her.

Anne leaned on Mildred. "Thank you for rescuing me, Mildred."

Mildred turned to Anne. "Well, it's only temporary, but at least you have some time to decide what to do."

"Right now, all I want to do is see John."

"You know, he may not want to see you."

"I know," Anne said, swallowing hard. "But I've got to try."

"It won't be easy."

"I know, but I'm ready to take my medicine."

Mildred patted Anne's cheek. "I want you to know that I think you are a lovely girl with a bright future, but unfortunately, the problems at home will not disappear on their own. I know your parents aren't easy to deal with, but they love you and only want what's best for you. Convincing them that what you want is in your best interest will not be easy."

Anne's shoulders fell. "It will be impossible."

"You need to start with being honest, and the more you behave like an adult, the more they will treat you like one. Understand?"

"Yes, I think I do. Thank you, Mildred," Anne said, hugging her.

"Now, you dry up and eat something. You're going to need all the strength you can get," Mildred said.

Anne chuckled. "I agree."

Anne returned to the kitchen with Mildred and tried to force down some oatmeal. It tasted like sawdust, but it did help with the ache in her stomach. Later that afternoon, Anne sat in the solace of her room and began to compose a letter. If John refused to talk to her, at least she could give him the letter. It was the only hope she had.

89

Alone, sitting cross-legged on the floor of the rehearsal space, Danny worked on repairing his guitar. He spent the morning at the college gathering information about signing up for his GED. He knew his uncle was right, and it was necessary, but he had no desire to waste his time on such trivial matters. It wasn't like he couldn't get a job at the garage anytime he felt the need to make some extra cash, but until his probation was over, he had to abide by his uncle's rules.

"I can't believe John's fans are still out there," Eddie groused as he stepped inside the room.

Danny didn't look up from his work.

Eddie looked out the window. "They're a nuisance, and they're scaring customers away."

"You could tell them to move on," Danny said.

"I tried that already. Where is John, anyway?" Eddie said, turning to Danny.

"I don't know. He told me he would meet me here. He's probably just running late."

Eddie's glance fell on the sad bass drum that looked like a wounded, gaping mouth. "Gosh, I still can't believe what happened to Ronnie's drum. He must be devastated."

"That's putting it lightly."

"I'm gonna get a soda. You want one?" Eddie asked as he headed toward the door.

"Yeah, I'll take one."

"Coming up."

"Hey, wait a second, Eddie."

Eddie turned around. "Yeah?"

Danny leaned on his guitar. "After the gear arrived on Saturday, who looked after it?"

Eddie shrugged. "Stu. Why?"

"Just curious, I guess."

Eddie nodded and jogged down the stairs. Danny ran his hand over his hair. There was no more doubt or question in his mind. He knew what had happened to his guitar. He just wasn't sure what to do about it.

A while later, Danny thought he heard Eddie step into the room.

"What took you so long?" Danny said, looking up.

Anne was standing in the doorway. Her hands were clasped in front of her, and her once bright eyes were ashen with puffy circles underneath.

"Anne?" Danny said.

"Hello, Danny," Anne said, casting her eyes to the ground.

Danny stood up. "Hey, what's goin' on?"

"I . . . um was looking for John. Is he here?"

"No, he's not."

Anne's sunken posture looked like it might collapse under her.

Danny stepped over to her. "What's the matter?"

Anne wiped her nose and tried to regain her composure. She looked up at Danny, and tears emerged from the corners of her eyes.

Danny sat his hand gently on her arm. "Why don't you come in and sit on the couch?"

"I really can't stay. I was really hoping he would be here."

"He said he was coming, but I haven't seen him. You can wait if you want to."

Anne shook her head. "No, I should go."

"Wait, I can tell something is wrong. Why don't you tell me about it?"

"Because I'm so ashamed!"

Danny put his arm around her slight shoulders, and the comfort of his arm forced her body to shake from grief. Danny walked her over slowly to the couch and sat her down.

Eddie came upstairs. "Sorry, it took so long. Mr. Evans wanted to ask me a hundred questions about the other night."

Danny took the soda. "Thanks, Eds."

Eddie noticed Anne on the couch, wiping her nose with a handkerchief. "What's she doing here?"

Danny took Eddie by the elbow and led him to the door. "I'll tell you later."

Eddie hesitated, but Danny shoved him out the door.

Danny returned to the couch and sat down. "You want a soda?"

Anne nodded. "I can't take your soda, Danny."

Danny popped off the cap. "Nonsense. You look like you could use it more than me." He held out the cool bottle to her. "Take it, I insist."

Anne took the bottle from him and took a long drink.

"Now, tell me, what's the matter?"

Anne ran her fingertips up and down the bottle. "I made a mistake, Danny. Probably the biggest mistake of my life."

"Oh, come on now, it can't be that bad."

Anne looked up and met Danny's eyes. "I lied to John."

Any words Danny thought about saying left him. His lips parted slightly, but no comments came out.

"I've lost him forever," Anne sobbed.

Danny shifted. "What kind of lie did you tell him?"

"The worst kind. I told him I had broken up with my boyfriend when I hadn't."

Danny ran his hand over his hair. "Oh, boy."

"I know it was a mistake. I didn't mean to lie to him. I honestly was going to break up with Steve. It's just that my parents are dead set on me marrying him."

"*Marry?*" Danny squeaked.

The corner of Anne's mouth trembled. "I don't want to, Danny. I don't love him, but I can't disobey my parents."

Danny sat forward, placing his elbows on his knees.

"You must think I'm horrible," Anne whispered.

Danny shook his head. "No, I don't think you're horrible. I think you're trapped. I know what it's like when you feel like you have to do whatever your parents tell you to. But, Anne, we're talking about the rest of your life. You do realize that, don't you?"

"Yes, but they only have my best interest at heart."

Danny raised an eyebrow. "Is spending the rest of your life married to a man you don't love in your best interest?"

Anne bit at her nails.

"What happens in a couple of years when you hate yourself and your life? By then, who knows what might happen. You might have a baby or two."

Anne got up and moved away from Danny.

Danny sighed. "Look, I'm only trying to help."

Anne turned around. "I wrote John a letter. Will you please promise to give it to him?"

"Of course, I will, but. . . ."

Anne pulled a letter out of her purse and handed it to Danny. "If you could make sure he gets this? I would be forever grateful."

Danny stood and took the letter from her. "Anne, are you sure this is what you want?"

"It's not about what I want. It's about what I have to do."

"There has to be another way."

"I'm sorry, Danny, I have to go."

Anne took a few steps toward the door, and Danny followed. "At least let me give you a ride somewhere."

"No, it's all right. The walk will do me good."

Reluctantly, Danny opened the door for her. "For what it's worth, your happiness is worth more than making your parents happy. At some point, you need to take charge of your own life. Don't waste it on what other people think you need or want. I know John may be angry with you right now, but believe me, he wouldn't want this for you."

Anne nodded. "Thank you, Danny."

He smiled, and Anne left, disappearing down the stairs.

90

Ronnie's gait was slow and labored as he made his way home in the heat of the afternoon sun. It was awkward and difficult to bend over after spending the day pulling weeds and picking up trash. Ronnie's entire body ached. Taking a moment to lean against a wall, Ronnie welcomed the moment to rest his right hip. It bore the weight of his burden, and it was in agony. Two young girls came out of the store giggling and drinking sodas. Seeing Ronnie, they stopped with a vacant look he was used to. Then, whispering to each other, they hurried down the street.

Summoning his strength to move forward, Ronnie continued down the block to the corner of Fifth and Lincoln. Remembering that the animal shelter was on Lincoln, his thoughts drifted to his furry friend. With everything that had happened, he hadn't had a chance to check on the dog. He would be late returning to the house, but what would Mulligan do? Give him more punishment and restrictions? At this point, he didn't care and crossed the street.

❑■❑■❑■❑■❑■❑■❑■❑■❑■❑■❑

A family was leaving with their adopted dog when Ronnie arrived at the shelter. The kids were laughing as the dog jumped and barked.

401

Watching them made Ronnie's heart ache for the unconditional love of a special furry friend. Tammy was at the counter with another young woman when Ronnie stepped up to the counter.

"Hello, Ronnie," Tammy said.

"Hello," he responded.

"It's nice to see you again."

Not one for small talk, Ronnie came right to the point. "I want to see Buddy."

Tammy turned to the girl next to her and gave her instructions. Nodding, the girl left the room, and Tammy came around the counter. "Why don't we step over here, where it's quieter?" Tammy said, steering Ronnie to one of the waiting room chairs.

Ronnie sat down, and Tammy sat by him.

"Did Buddy get adopted?" Ronnie asked.

Tammy fidgeted with her hands. "No, not exactly."

"Then what exactly?"

Tammy hesitated. "Ronnie, you know that Buddy has had a difficult life. He wasn't given the love and care he needed as a puppy. We believe that Buddy never had a real home and had lived most of his life on the streets."

Ronnie's transfixed expression wasn't making Tammy's job easier.

Taking a deep breath, Tammy continued to explain. "I want you to know that we have done all we can to socialize him, but he has major trust issues and tends to be hostile. So, after doing all we could, Doctor Canfield has decided that the dog would be better off if he didn't have to deal with the frustrations of this world."

Ronnie's forehead wrinkled. "I don't understand. Buddy isn't hostile with me."

"He does seem to have a special connection with you, but he needs to behave appropriately when he's out in the world. Do you understand?"

"No."

"Maybe the best way to think about it is to know he will be happy where he is going."

Ronnie stared at Tammy, making her shift in her seat. "Where is he going?"

Tammy had no idea how to answer the question. It would have been easier to cover the truth with a lie, but for some reason, she couldn't lie to the pure heart beside her. Squaring her shoulders, Tammy looked Ronnie in the eye. "Buddy is going to heaven, Ronnie."

Ronnie lifted his eyes. His posture gave no clues to his thinking, and Tammy twisted her hands.

Ronnie's eyes finally rested on Tammy. "Can I see him?"

"Oh, I don't think that would be possible."

"Please."

Tammy glanced over her shoulder. "I could get in big trouble."

"I just want to see him."

It was against the shelter's rules to allow a civilian into the restricted back area where the dog was. But the shelter would close soon, and Doctor Canfield had left for the day.

"All right, Ronnie, I will take you in the back, but it will have to be quick. Okay?"

Ronnie nodded.

Tammy led the way, and Ronnie followed her into the kennel area of the shelter. Cages lined the walls, and some anxious, excited dogs barked at Ronnie, but others looked up at him with wide, hopeless eyes. A large lump formed in Ronnie's throat, and memories of being locked in a small space flooded his mind.

Tammy opened the door to the restricted area. "He's in the kennel in the back corner. I will be back soon."

Ronnie stepped inside the dimly lit area. Buddy was curled up on a dark grey rug in the corner of his kennel. His water dish was empty, and his head rested on his paws.

Taking off his brace, Ronnie lowered himself onto the ground. "Hey, Buddy. It's me. Ronnie."

Buddy lifted his heavy eyes but didn't move.

Ronnie set his hand on the bars. "I'm sorry I haven't come to see you, but that doesn't mean I wasn't thinking of you."

Buddy was unresponsive, so Ronnie began to chitter. Buddy lifted his head, and Ronnie pulled a cracker from his pocket. "I've been carrying this cracker, just in case I got to see you again."

Slowly, Buddy got up, came over to the bars, and took the cracker from Ronnie. "There's a good boy."

Buddy licked Ronnie's fingers, and Ronnie laughed for the first time in days. "I know you're alone and scared, but don't you worry. I said a prayer, and I'm gonna get you out of here. I promise."

Buddy wagged his tail and leaned into Ronnie's caressing fingers.

Tammy opened the door and observed Ronnie rubbing Buddy's chin, and tears stung at her eyes. Ronnie shifted his gaze to Tammy then whispering something to Buddy, he pulled himself off the floor with a grimace.

"Do you need help putting your brace on?" Tammy asked, taking a step forward.

"Don't come any closer," Ronnie snapped.

"Now is not the time to be prideful. You're obviously in pain," Tammy said, picking up the brace and handing it to Ronnie. "I'll wait for you in the hall."

A few moments later, Ronnie joined Tammy in the hall and she silently walked him to the front door. Setting her hand on the latch, Tammy paused and met Ronnie's eyes with her damp ones. Reaching out she took a firm hold of Ronnie's hand. He studied her serious features for a few moments, and then, with a slight nod, Ronnie left the shelter.

91

BRONSON SAT WITH HIS FEET propped up on his desk, enjoying a cup of coffee and reading the morning newspaper. The front-page story highlighted the fire department's victory over a fire that burned down a barn off County Road 56. Rescuing four horses, two cows, three pigs, and four chickens, the fire department managed to put out the blaze without further damage to the property. Flipping through the pages, Bronson found only a small article about how the Christian Ladies Club was up in arms over the incident on Saturday. Things were returning to normal, and Bronson couldn't be more pleased. Taking a drink of coffee, he resumed reading about the Cubs game when a knock came on his door.

"Come in."

The door opened, and Murphy poked his head in. "Sorry to bother you, Chief, but Mrs. Taylor called again to complain about the crowd that has gathered in front of The Beat."

"Are they causing a disturbance?" Bronson asked.

"No, they are just waiting for Chandler to show up."

"Has Bruer called to complain?"

"No, but the group does practice above the record shop."

Bronson sighed.

"You want me to go over there and see what's happening?"
"No, send Murdock so Mrs. Taylor can see we are following up."
"Sure thing, Chief," Murphy said, shutting the door.
Bronson shook his head and resumed his reading.

92

Sitting cross-legged on the porch with her head in her hand, Carly watched an ambling pill bug cross the porch. Tormenting the tiny grey bug with a stick was one of Carly's favorite past times. Flipping the bug on its back, its flaying legs would turn in and transform the bug into a ball. Then, with glee, Carly would flick her finger and send the tiny sphere flying across the yard, but today Carly didn't feel like smiling about anything. Her mother was going on another date with a man Carly didn't like, and to make matters worse, she was leaving her with a babysitter because Stu was going out.

The latch on the front gate opened, and Carly looked up to see James, but his arrival brought no joy to her gloomy face.

"Hey Carly," James said, walking up to the porch. "How are you?"

"Rotten," Carly said, returning to her slouched position.

James sat on the step. "What's going on? You look like you lost your best friend."

Carly shrugged.

"Ah, come on, it must be something."

"My mom has a date," Carly mumbled.

"She does?"

Carly nodded. "And I don't like him."

"Why is that?"

"Because we have to clean the house every time he comes over, and I have to wear a dress."

James smiled. "Oh."

"It's horrible. I have to mind my manners and be quiet. I hate it."

"Well, your mother deserves some happiness, doesn't she?"

Carly looked up at James with her cheeks puffed out. "Not without my daddy!"

"Yeah, well, your daddy has been gone a long time."

"And it's all her fault! If she hadn't been so mean to him, he would still be here!" Carly said standing.

"I didn't mean to upset you," James clarified.

Scrunching up her face to keep from crying, Carly turned and ran inside, slamming the screen door after her.

James sighed.

"Carly? What's going on?" Helen said, opening the screen door to see James. Her hair was rolled up in large curlers, and her toes were separated by cotton balls.

James stood up. "Afternoon, Mrs. Williams."

"Oh James, what a pleasant surprise. I must look a fright!" Helen said, touching her curlers.

"You look fine."

"Well, that's sweet of you, but I know I look ghastly without my makeup."

"I didn't notice," James said.

Helen smiled and opened the door, letting James step inside.

"Thank you," James said.

Carly was right. James had never seen the house so clean. The clutter and misplaced items were all cleared away. The floors were vacuumed, the shelves dusted, and even the curtains hung straight. The smell of greasy food and stale smoke no longer hung in the air.

"The house looks wonderful," James said.

Helen beamed. "Thank you. I've decided to spruce things up a bit. You know, start fresh."

"Carly says you're seeing someone."

"Yes, his name is Thomas. He's an insurance agent."

"Oh?"

Helen folded her hands. "A nice, quiet, respectable, stable job. That's important."

"It is."

Helen folded her arms. "I wish Stu would get into a job like that, but he gets angry if I even mention stability. Sometimes he reminds me too much of his father."

"Maybe he will grow out of it," James offered.

"I wish he was more like you."

James rocked back on his heels. "I'm not so great."

"You know you are. Why, just think, one more year and you will be graduating."

"That is the plan."

"So, I suppose you're here to see Stu," Helen sighed.

"I am."

"He's downstairs, doing what I don't know, but you're welcome to find out."

James smiled. "Thanks, Mrs. Williams. It was good to see you."

"You as well, James."

Stu was lying on the couch reading a magazine when James descended the stairs. The upstairs was immaculate, but the basement was still the same old chaotic mess.

"Hey, buddy," James said.

Stu looked around the edge of his magazine to see James. "Oh, hey. I wondered who Mom was talking to. I did think it was too early to be Thomas."

James sat on the stool. "That's pretty terrific about your mom findin' someone, isn't it?"

Stu disappeared behind his magazine. "Yeah, sure."

"You don't like him?"

Stu shrugged. "He's none of my concern."

"Carly doesn't seem to like him."

"Carly's just upset because she has to behave herself, and Mom's attention is divided."

James leaned forward. "Does Carly know why your dad left?"

"So, what did you come by for?" Stu asked, avoiding the question.

"Do I need a reason?"

"You stopped dropping by a long time ago, James."

James stared at the back of Stu's magazine. "Would you mind putting that down so we can talk?"

Stu lowered the magazine, a blank look on his face.

"I wondered what happened to you after the show on Saturday night?" James asked.

"I got the hell out of there. Which is what anyone in their right mind should have done."

"I guess you know John went to jail."

Stu sat up. "Who doesn't know that? Heck, it's all anyone is talking about."

"I was headed to the rehearsal space to find out what is happening. You want to come with me?"

Stu crossed his legs. "Not particularly. I got plans for later this afternoon."

"Oh, you have to go to work?"

"No."

James expected Stu to elaborate on his plans, but his face was like a stone statue. "You still sore about what happened with John?"

Stu threw his magazine onto the coffee table. "Why would I be sore about that?"

"I know it didn't seem fair."

Stu began to laugh. "Fair? Nothing about that group is fair."

"You must have known when you came in that night John was going to be mad."

"Yeah, well, maybe I did, but I didn't think he would want me to be his lackey!" Stu got up from the couch and turned his back to James.

"I know he was a bit harsh."

Stu spun around. "I've never been so humiliated in my life! Cleaning up a mess that I didn't even make! Carrying out the trash and beating a rug that wasn't clean in the first place. Listening to him throw his weight around like he is some kind of dictator! Well, guess what? I'm done, finished, gone!"

"Oh, come on, Stu."

"Don't come on, Stu me! I don't want to be a part of it anymore," Stu said, slashing the air with his hand.

"I can't believe you're giving up. I thought you wanted to be in a band."

Stu chucked. "I do. As a matter of fact, I'm joining a new group."

"You are?"

"I am, and they're buying me an electric guitar," Stu said, folding his arms.

James widened his eyes. "Really?"

"Yep, a brand-new Stratocaster."

"Well, congratulations. I guess this means you made it."

Stu stuck his chin out. "I think it does."

James stood up. "So, when are you going to tell John that you quit?"

"Like he cares."

James rumpled his brow. "You have to tell him."

"I don't have to do anything anymore. I'm *done*," Stu retorted.

James put his hands in his pockets. "So, I guess there is nothing more to talk about."

"I guess so," Stu said, sitting on the couch.

"I hope this doesn't mean we're not friends anymore."

Stu sat back and put his feet up. "I guess that's up to you now, isn't it?"

"Me? You know it doesn't matter to me what group you're in. You'll always be my friend, right?"

Stu's shoulders relaxed. "Well, yeah."

"Why don't we go out to Be-Bops, huh? My treat."

"Thanks, but I already have plans."

James nodded. "Oh, okay. I guess I will talk to you soon, then?"

"Yeah, sure," Stu said, picking up his magazine.

"I can't wait to hear about the new group. When do you start?"

"Oh, soon. We're still working out the details."

"What's the name of the group?" James asked.

"They don't have one yet."

"Oh, so it's a new group?"

Stu opened the magazine. "Yeah."

"Cool. Well, I guess I can show myself out."

"You do that," Stu said not looking up from his magazine.

James slowly climbed the stairs, wondering what Stu was thinking. He could understand Stu being upset, but he wasn't acting like himself. He was angry and quarrelsome, and James was worried about him. Stepping outside the house, James walked to the end of the driveway when a shiny new teal Chevrolet Impala convertible pulled up to the curb. James thought it might be Helen's date, but when Patrick stepped out of the car, he couldn't believe his eyes. Wearing a sharp dark green suit, tan loafers, and sunglasses, Patrick stepped up onto the curb.

A smooth, cool smile spread his lips as he sized up James. "Hello, loser."

James's jaw immediately tightened. "What are you doing here?"

"I could ask you the same question."

"I came by to see my friend."

Patrick slid his sunglasses into his pocket. "What a coincidence, so did I."

"I didn't think you liked Stu."

"I never said that."

"Well, you sure didn't act like you did."

Patrick chuckled. "Is that right?"

"Yeah. You pretty much treated him like a dog."

"I think that's what John did, but then again, he treats everyone like a dog. Maybe that's why the group name is so appropriate."

James stepped up to Patrick. "What do you want with Stu?"

"What are you? His daddy?" Patrick scoffed.

"Let's just say that I have known Stu for a long time and look out for him."

"Ah, how noble of you, but you see, Stu's a grown man and can make his own decisions."

James flexed his fingers. "That may be, but I care about him."

"That's not how I heard it," Patrick said, shifting his weight. "The way I understood it, you pretty much stood by and let John berate Stu in front of the entire group."

James lowered his eyes. "That's not true."

"Isn't it?"

"Stu kind of asked for it because he was disrespectful to Danny."

Patrick snapped his fingers. "Ah, now everything makes perfect sense. Of course, this was all about Prince Danny. No one dares stand against him."

James shook his head. "You've got it all wrong."

"No, I don't think I do. Too bad the prince fell off his pedestal on Saturday night and ruined the show. Now everyone knows what a phony he truly is."

James' brow furrowed. "Danny didn't ruin the show! It was those thugs in the audience that stirred up all the trouble and ruined it for everybody."

"Well, maybe they wouldn't have gotten upset if the group was competent."

James narrowed his eyes and clenched his jaw.

"Don't take it too hard. Sooner or later, people would have figured out that you're all a bunch of bumbling chumps."

"I would rather be a chump than a deceitful, rotten cheat like you." James spat.

Patrick laughed. "Was that meant to hurt my feelings?"

"Nah. Obviously, you don't have any," James said pushing his way past Patrick.

"Oh, there is one other thing," Patrick said, stopping James midstride.

James turned.

"You can tell John that I will be taking my song back now."

James shook his head. "Nah, I'm not stickin' my foot in that bear trap. You can tell him yourself."

The smirk on Patrick's face became a flat line, and James walked away smiling to himself.

93

THE CROWD OUTSIDE THE RECORD shop had shrunk from the day before, but the diligent supporters remained vigilant, hoping to glimpse what they believed to be a genuine rock 'n' roll rebel.

Murdock turned up Mulberry Street and turned on the car's lights and siren. Three geese crossing the street took their sweet time as they waddled in front of the vehicle.

Annoyed that the geese had disrupted his grand entrance, Murdock pulled up next to the kids on the sidewalk. Stepping out of the car with a stern look, Murdock hitched up his pants and walked over to the group, who gave him a disinterested look.

"All right, you kids, you need to break this up and move along," Murdock said, waving his hands.

"We're not doin' anything wrong, Murdock," a young boy said.

"Yeah, we're just waitin' to see Chandler, is all," another boy chimed.

"Yeah, well, you're loitering is what you're doing," Murdock said, placing his hands on his hips.

The kids frowned at each other. "What is loitering?"

"You know, hanging around, looking for trouble."

"We're not looking for no trouble," a young woman said. "We just want to see him."

"And give him our phone number," another girl said, while the other girls giggled.

"You're all making the business owners in the area nervous," Murdock said.

"We ain't givin' um no grief," the first boy said.

"Yeah, Mr. Evans has no problem selling us as many sodas as we want," the first young woman commented.

"It's probably old Mrs. Taylor who keeps peeking out her window at us," another young woman said.

"She's an ol' busybody," the first young woman said.

Murdock opened his mouth to say something when one of the girls yelled, "There he is! I see him!"

Spotting John coming up the street, the crowd ran screaming down the block, leaving Murdock with his mouth open.

94

Fatigued and aching, John approached the record store. He had spent yesterday alone, resting, and even though he felt better, his heart didn't. John convinced himself that Anne was just another girl and he truly had no feelings for her. He had never needed any relationship or girl before, so why should this one be any different? Let her return home and resume her conventional life with her square, boring boyfriend. What did he care? He had plenty of girls willing to offer him the comfort he needed. All he had to do was move forward with his life and never fall into such a foolish trap again.

Turning up Mulberry Street, John was surprised when he saw a group of screaming teenagers running toward him. He thought by now everyone had forgotten Saturday night because he wanted to.

The kids rushed up to John and all started to talk at once.

"Hey, you all need to calm down!" John shouted. "I can't understand what anyone of you is asking."

"We just wanted to see you," a girl with wide brown eyes said, gazing at him.

"Yeah, what was it like being locked up?" one of the boys asked.

"It stunk," John said.

"Were they mean to you?"

"Yeah, was it a dark hole with no light?"

"We're you on the edge of starvation?"

John blinked at all the rapid-fire questions.

"Were there rats?" a girl with a ponytail asked.

"No, to all those questions," John said. "Now, if you will excuse me, I need to get to the record store."

"What are you going to do when you get there?" the girl with brown eyes asked, latching herself to John's arm as he walked forward.

"He's gonna play rock 'n' roll, dummy," the first boy said.

"Oh, John, can we listen?" the girl with the ponytail asked as she grabbed John's other arm.

"Yeah!" they all chimed.

"All right, that's enough. Break it up," Murdock said, catching up to the group.

"John is going to play for us," the first boy said, making all the girls scream and jump up and down.

"I am not going to play for anyone," John said over the screaming.

"Awww," they all moaned.

"When's your next show?" brown eyes asked.

"I have no idea. I don't think the people want to hear about another rock 'n' roll show right now."

"That's cause they're all a bunch of old party poopers who don't want us kids to have any fun," the oldest boy groused.

"You all need to scram," Murdock said.

"Don't forget we're all behind you," the girl with the ponytail said.

"Yeah, we all want to come to another show!" one of the boys exclaimed, while the rest cheered.

"Thanks, guys," John said.

The crowd started to move away when a young woman with black hair and dark, accented eyes stepped forward. Bold and confident, she stepped up to John and kissed him thoroughly. Everyone, including Murdock, looked on in shock. Pulling away, John glanced into her seductive cat eyes.

"Call me," she said smoothly, sticking a note into his jacket pocket.

Holding his eyes, she sauntered away, swinging her hips.

"Wow," Murdock said, pushing his hat back. "Maybe I should play in a rock 'n' roll band."

"I don't know, Murdock, what would we do without you protecting the peace?" John asked.

Murdock sniffed. "Well, bein' in law enforcement is a dangerous job."

"I can see that."

Murdock swung his arms forward and clapped his hands. "Looks like my job here is done. The crowd is dee-spurced, gone, outta here."

John laughed.

"Guess I'll go back to the office."

"Good plan," John said, walking up the block with Murdock.

"See ya around?" Murdock said.

"See ya around."

Murdock got in his car, turned off the lights, and pulled away. John stepped into the store. Eddie was sorting records at the counter.

"Hey, stranger," Eddie said.

"Hey, Eds."

"Looks like your fan club finally caught up with you."

John set his hands on the counter. "How long have they been hangin' around?"

"All day yesterday and this morning."

John raised his eyebrows. "Really?"

"Yup. Ol' Mrs. Taylor was about to have an aneurysm."

John chuckled. "Danny upstairs?"

"Not yet."

"Oh, well, I can wait," John said.

"Hey, what happened to your lips?" Eddie asked.

"My lips?"

"Yeah, they're really red."

"Oh," John said, wiping his thumb over the red smudge on his mouth.

"You must have made up with your girlfriend," Eddie said with a wink.

John frowned. "My girlfriend?"

"Yeah, she was real broken up yesterday, cryin' and carryin' on."

John's eyes narrowed. "You mean you saw her?"

"Yeah, she came in here. Talked to Danny for a while."

John took a step back from the counter. "How long was she here?"

Eddie shook his head. "I dunno, a half hour maybe."

John drummed his fingers on the countertop.

"You did see her, didn't you?"

John didn't say another word to Eddie. He turned and went upstairs. Eddie watched after him, then, shrugging, he went back to work.

95

DANNY STEPPED THROUGH THE DOOR of the rehearsal space, relieved to see John sitting cross-legged on the floor, tuning his guitar.

Danny sat his guitar down. "Hey."

"Hey," John said, not looking up.

"Missed you yesterday."

"Yeah, sorry about that, my head ached."

"I bet it did. Are you going to have it checked out?" Danny said, sitting across from him.

John shrugged. "Nah, I've taken worse blows, believe me."

"Okay. You know best," Danny said, setting his guitar on his lap.

"So, did anything, uh, interesting happen yesterday?" John asked.

Danny shook his head. "No, not really. I put my guitar back together."

"Did you figure out what went wrong?"

Danny bit his bottom lip. "I wasn't paying attention."

John glanced at Danny. "I find that hard to believe."

"I was nervous, and like a numbskull, I didn't check the tuning," Danny tittered.

John raised his eyebrow.

Danny cleared his throat and quickly changed the subject. "I went by the college yesterday and picked up my paperwork to start classes. Uncle Bob was happy about that."

"I'm sure he was."

"So, I know you were resting, but did you have a chance to think about what we should do about our situation?"

John plucked his G string and then turned its tuning peg. "Which part?"

"To be honest, I don't know. Everything seems upside down somehow."

"That's because it is."

Danny's gaze fell on the destroyed bass drum. "I guess a good place to start would be Ronnie."

John lifted an eyebrow. "How's that a good start?"

"Because we need to figure out how to repair his drum."

John shrugged. "I don't think there is any big hurry. I doubt he will be able to come to practice."

"Why not?"

"The headmistress pretty much blames us for all of Ronnie's problems. She forbids me from having any contact with him."

Danny blinked. "Are you serious?"

John paused. "Yeah. She was furious. Ronnie said he would be on punishment."

"What does that mean?"

John shook his head. "I don't know. He didn't say much, and I didn't push."

Danny tilted his head, his cheeks pulled up. "But isn't Ronnie a grown man?"

John sat his hand on his knee. "In some ways yes, but not so much in others."

Danny sighed, rubbing his forehead.

"I figured I would give it some time for things to calm down. Then I'll try and get in touch with him."

Danny leaned back against the couch. "I can't believe this. Everyone is against us."

"Maybe, but I agree with Bob. I think what we all need is a break," John said.

"You mean like break up the band?" Danny with a slight waiver in his voice.

"No. I just mean, take some time to relax. Catch our breath. Get a job."

Danny groaned.

"When do your classes start?"

Danny cast his eyes upward. "Next week."

"See, there you go. You need to focus on your studies."

"I hate studying," Danny groused.

"Oh, it won't be so bad. Maybe you'll meet some cute girls."

Danny scoffed. "I doubt it."

"So, did you see anyone yesterday?" John asked.

"No, it was quiet."

John crossed his arms on top of his guitar. "Eddie told me she was here."

"Eddie," Danny murmured.

"What did she tell you?"

"Nothing much really, just that she made a mistake."

"A mistake?" John hissed.

"Well, she didn't go into a lot of details."

John pursed his lips.

"Really, Barnaby. She didn't want to talk about it."

"Eddie says she was here for a half hour."

"A half-hour? It wasn't that long."

John's scowl unsettled Danny. "What do you want me to say? She was beside herself with grief."

"Grief, my foot!" John said, setting his guitar aside.

"Barnaby, if you could have seen her . . ."

"She ought to thank her lucky stars I didn't see her!" John said, rising to his feet.

Danny sat back, watching John pace in front of him.

"Grief, grief indeed!" John put his hands on his hips as he continued to pace. "I suppose she didn't mention how she *lied* to me!

How she manipulated and used me! I suppose those little facts didn't manage to come out, did they?"

Danny blinked. "Well . . ."

"She played me for a fool!" John turned, bending forward at the waist. "Well, let me tell you something—it's never going to happen again. *Ever!*"

Danny gulped and didn't move.

John slowly stood up like a tall, dark giant. His rage filled the room as deep, ragged breaths escaped his mouth. Danny let John have his moment, and when his hands finally fell to his side, John sat down on the edge of the couch and covered his mouth with his hand.

Danny propped his guitar against the couch and inched closer to John. "John, whatever happened between you and Anne is none of my business. All I can tell you is what I know. And I know I have never seen anyone so distraught and heartbroken in my life."

John's nostrils flared, and he didn't move.

"Say what you want, but you can't fake grief like that. She blames herself and knows what she did was wrong, but she's scared."

John's eyes shifted to Danny. "Of what?"

"Her parents. This is what they want for her. Not what she wants, and maybe while she was with you, she had a small taste of happiness."

John's dark eyes stared forward.

Danny reached into his pocket and pulled out the letter. "Here, she wanted you to have this."

John glared at the envelope. "What's that?"

"A letter she wrote for you."

"Yeah, well, I don't want it," John said. Leaning back, he let the cushion absorb his hostility.

Danny paused. "Let me say my piece, and then I promise not to say another word. But know this, that girl is about to throw her life away on a circumstance she feels is out of her control. She feels alone and scared. She believes no one gives a damn about her or what she wants. Now tell me you've never been there."

The tension left John's body, but his glare was steadfast.

Danny set the letter on the coffee table, then leaning back, he began to play a comforting tune. Propping his feet up, John closed his eyes, and five minutes later, he was asleep. A wave of relief washed over Danny. Rising to his feet, he went downstairs.

Eddie looked up from his comic. "Hey Dan, everything all right up there?"

"Yeah, the lion finally sleeps—no thanks to you," Danny growled.

"Why? What did I do?"

"You told him Anne was here yesterday."

"Was it some kind of a secret?"

Danny leaned on the counter. "No, I guess not, but gee, I wasn't ready to tell him."

Eddie set his comic down. "I'm sorry, but when I saw him with lipstick on his mouth, I figured they made up."

"Lipstick on his mouth?"

"Yeah, I guess one of his fans kissed him."

Danny chuckled. "I wouldn't doubt it."

"Thank goodness they're all gone now. Maybe we can get some peace around here."

Danny stepped over to the new release record bin. "Any new good releases come in this week?"

"A few, but nothing exciting."

Danny picked out a few records and moved to the turntable.

"Be careful with the tonearm. The counterweight is being fussy again," Eddie warned.

"I know it."

"I keep tellin' Dad we need to replace it, but it's low on his priority list."

Danny put a record on, and his foot started tapping.

"I'm goin' in the backroom to balance the register. You okay watching things for a while?"

"Yeah, sure."

"Holler if you need me," Eddie said, disappearing in the back.

Danny sat on the stool behind the counter and picked up Eddie's comic.

"Workin' hard, I see."

Danny looked up to see James. "Hey, Professor. What brings you down to this part of town?"

James shrugged. "I've been looking for a job and thought I would take a break."

"Any luck?"

"Honestly, I could get my old job back at Carter's, but I'm not excited about the prospect."

"I'm not excited about getting my GED, but I'm doin' it."

"It will be good for you," James said, taking the lid off the candy jar. "So how is John doin'?"

"He's all right. He's upstairs taking a nap," Danny said. "The last few days have been hard on him."

James put the jaw breaker in his mouth. "Did he say anything about Ronnie?"

Danny sighed. "Yeah, we're minus a drummer. At least for a while."

"Why? What happened?"

"The headmistress has forbidden him to have any contact with us."

James closed his eyes. "Great."

"John said he would wait a few days and then try and check on him."

James tapped his finger on the counter. "You know, I bet Marcy could visit him, especially if she took fresh muffins."

Danny perked up. "You think so?"

James shrugged. "It's worth a shot."

"That would be terrific. He needs to know we still need him."

"I'll talk to her."

"Cool."

James opened a magazine. "I saw Stu this morning."

"Oh?" Danny said, focusing on his fingertips.

"Yeah, apparently, he joined another group."

"Really? Which one?"

James turned the page. "He said they don't have a name yet."

"Well, good for Stu. I wish him all the best."

James felt the edge of the magazine. "There's one more thing. Patrick showed up when I was leaving."

"What was he doing there?"

"He was hanging out with Stu, I guess."

Danny rubbed his chin.

"Patrick sounded like they won."

Danny's head snapped up. "They didn't win anything. We were ambushed."

James crossed his feet. "I know it. Patrick told me to tell John he was taking his song back."

Danny scoffed. "Good luck with that."

James shook his head. "I don't understand why Stu is suddenly friends with Patrick."

"What makes you think it's sudden? Maybe they've been hanging out for a while."

James reflected, "You don't think . . ."

"What?"

James's nose and forehead scrunched up, and then, meeting Danny's eyes, he slowly closed his. The pieces of the last few weeks clicked into place. How could he have been so stupid? No wonder Stu hadn't been himself. No wonder he had been so flippant, so distant. Patrick was probably feeding Stu all kinds of lies, and being so desperate for acceptance, Stu fell for them.

"Professor?"

"I'm sorry, Danny, but I need to go," James said heading for the door.

"Wait, what's the matter?"

James raised his hand. "I'll talk to you later."

"Okay."

James left the store and Danny shook his head.

96

THE SOUND OF THE KEY turning in the lock caused the dogs to start barking. Humming to herself, Carrie hung up her coat and put on her panel apron before heading toward the food prep room. Flipping on the lights, she turned on the radio and Little Richard's raspy voice helped to drown out the sound of excited dogs. Shaking her hips and bouncing on her toes, Carrie lined the various-sized bowls on the counter. Then, doing a few quick skips, she picked up the dog food and began to fill the bowls. A few pieces fell onto the floor, but she would clean those up later.

Juggling six bowls, she walked over to the row of what she considered to be the good dogs.

"Morning, fellas!" she chimed. "Which one of you handsome devils wants to dance, huh?"

The dogs barked, and Carrie giggled. Saving the last bowl for her favorite dog, Max, she entered his cage and kissed him on the head. Max was an older border collie and had been with the shelter for a while. Carrie wanted to adopt him but would have to wait for the fall to get a dog.

Carrie set down his bowl and hugged him. "You know you're my prince, Max, and someday, I will take you away from here."

Max licked Carrie's cheek, and she gave him one last squeeze before leaving his cage.

Carrie fed the smaller dogs next because they were manageable. Then came the big dogs, who were a little more challenging, but she learned the process was easier if she could distract them long enough to set their bowl down.

Luck was on her side that morning, and fifteen minutes later, the shelter was quiet while the dogs ate. Wiping her hands on her apron, Carrie returned to the prep area. She only had one dog left to feed, and she was dreading it. Tammy assured her that she had nothing to worry about, but she could feel the dog's yellow eyes glaring at her every time she entered the back room.

Pulling on thick safety gloves, Carrie headed toward his cage. She wished the dogs were still barking because she wouldn't be apprehensive of every little sound.

Carrie stood outside the door, taking deep breaths before entering the room. Flipping on the light, she stepped toward the cage before she realized the kennel door was ajar. Sharp shots of panic coursed through Carrie's veins. Was the dog loose in the room somewhere?

Scared to move, Carrie's eyes darted around. If the dog was loose, there was no place he could hide without her spotting him. Obviously, someone was careless, and he was still in his cage. Maybe if she took a broom, she could close the door before he jumped out and attacked her, but then again, maybe having a broom poked at the cage might startle him, and he would attack anyway.

Carrie's heartbeat quickened as she took the last few cautious steps before peeking through the bars of the kennel door. Her eyes widened, and her mouth opened.

The dog was gone.

Sign up for Rebecca Hendricks' Newsletter
And receive and exclusive short origin story
Hound Dogged Beginnings for FREE

at

rebeccahendricksauthor.com